Treasure Me
Trust Me

One Night with Sole Regret Anthology
Volume 5

Olivia Cunning

ISBN-10: 1-939276-31-4
ISBN-13: 978-1-939276-31-5

CONTENTS

ALSO BY OLIVIA CUNNING

Sinner on Tour Series
Backstage Pass
Rock Hard
Hot Ticket
Wicked Beat
Double Time
Sinners at the Altar
Coming Soon:
Sinners in Paradise

One Night with

Series
Try Me Tempt Me Take Me
Share Me Touch Me Tie Me
Tease Me Tell Me
Treat Me Thrill Me
Treasure Me Trust Me
Coming Soon:
Love Me Tame Me

Exodus End

World Tour Series
Insider
Outsider
Coming Soon:
Staged

TREASURE
ME
More than
^One Night with Sole Regret 10
OLIVIA
CUNNING
NY Times Best-Selling Author

Treasure Me
One Night with Sole Regret #10

PROLOGUE

KELLEN WATCHED the heart monitor, his own heart skipping a beat when Sara's pulse rate unexpectedly jumped dozens of points at once.

He turned his head to look at her and found her brilliant blue eyes open and fixed on him for the first time in days. Her eyes were the only part of her recognizable. Her face had hollowed, lips gone as pale as the sallow skin surrounding them. Her long blond hair had fallen out months ago. But her eyes, her eyes were always the same, even though the morphine keeping her comfortable made them glassy.

"Sara." Her name erupted as a broken whisper.

"How long have you been sitting there?" she asked. Even her voice was foreign—tired and weak and hoarse—when it had once been so vibrant and passionate, especially when she shared her ardent opinions.

Kellen had been sitting at her bedside for days. Maybe a full week by now—he couldn't be sure. "It doesn't matter. How are you feeling?"

"Tired," she whispered, and her eyelids fluttered. Her wince of pain had his gaze darting to her IV bags to make sure her morphine drip hadn't gone empty. "It's almost time for me to go."

He chuckled and squeezed her frail hand. "You still have a lot more healing to do before they let you out of this place."

"That's not what I meant." Her eyes opened once more and

fixed on his. "I'm not getting better."

He knew that. The doctors knew that. All their friends and family knew she would never leave the sterile hospital alive, but no one ever said it aloud because reality was too fucking depressing to comprehend, much less put into words.

Kellen leaned in to kiss her cheek, the salt of her tears teasing his tongue. It took him a moment to realize that he was the one crying, not her. She'd always been stronger than him.

Her hand moved as if she wanted to touch him, but she gave up the effort after a few seconds. "After I'm gone—"

"No." If they admitted she was going to die, if they said the words, he'd lose his grip on the thin threads of hope he so desperately clung to. Hope was the only thing he had left. He couldn't lose that as well.

"Kelly, please listen. I don't have the strength to argue. I barely have enough to speak."

"Then stop," he said. "Save your strength for living."

"After I'm gone . . ."

He tried to cut her off again, but his throat had closed with anguish, and he couldn't get another word out.

". . . I want you to find someone to love you as much as I do."

He shook his head. "I promised you I'd love you forever, Sara." He gathered her hand between his, mindful of the IVs pumping fluids and pain relievers and who the hell knew what else into her wasted body. He kissed her knuckles and pressed them to his forehead, squeezing his eyes shut. "I'll never break my promises to you. Never."

He'd made many promises to her, and each was deeply carved into his aching heart. Her life might lack permanence, but those promises could be eternal.

"You have to." He shook his head, but she continued. "I'll haunt you if you don't."

Her soft laugh fluttered through his chest and stole his breath. Oh, how she used to laugh. He should have cherished every one of them when he'd had the opportunity.

"Then you'll just have to haunt me," he said, lifting his head to stare into her eyes. "When I said forever, I meant forever. I'll love you forever, Sara, whether you're here with me or not."

"You're too young to not love again. Too passionate not to

share that with another. Promise me you'll find someone."

He swallowed and shook his head again. He'd made a lot of promises to Sara in the few short years they'd had together, but replacing her was one he couldn't make.

"Stubborn," she said, closing her eyes with a shallow sigh.

It was the last word she ever said to him.

CHAPTER ONE

KELLEN RUBBED at the borrowed watch around his wrist, watching the motion so he'd keep his eyes off the pretty blonde near the back of the bus.

Sara had been haunting Kellen for five years now. Apparently she was better at keeping her promises than he was at keeping his. Even now, when he'd found a woman who might be worth the torment of his soul, Sara watched him. Well, Lindsey—not Sara, he reminded himself for the umpteenth time—was actually watching Owen at the moment, but Kellen could feel Sara's disdain chewing at his insides.

You broke your promise to me, Kellen. You did it with another woman.

It. Oh, he'd done *it* all right, and he'd like to do *it* again, but he wasn't sure he was capable. Not with her voice flitting through his conscience.

His conscience wasn't giving him grief about Lindsey. The down-on-her-luck groupie wasn't carrying Kellen's child. That was one benefit of being abstinent all those years; no surprise babies showing up on his tour-bus step. His conscience was talking about someone else. Someone spectacular and exciting and . . . well, perfect. He'd done *it* with a woman he'd just met. A woman who was sitting right beside him. A woman who should have heeded his warning and run far, far away from his messed-up emotional ties. A woman, unlike Sara, who wouldn't be embarrassed to call *it* sex or making love or maybe even fucking.

And he was convinced that his broken promise to Sara was why Lindsey was there. He knew in his soul that Sara was there to torment him through Lindsey. Lindsey, so obviously pregnant and resembling Sara so closely . . . He couldn't even look at her without guilt tearing into his gut.

Any rational man would know that the beautiful young woman couldn't be a reincarnation of his lost love. Lindsey couldn't have been born more than a few years after Sara. So even if he had

believed in reincarnation, Lindsey couldn't possibly be his Sara reborn. But Kellen wasn't feeling rational at the moment. What man could be rational when trapped on a tour bus with the ghost he'd slighted?

Lindsey coughed, and his eyes automatically sought her. A mistake.

God, they looked so much alike. The same angelic blue eyes. The exact same shade of golden-blond hair, long and with just enough waviness to make the bottom edge curl outward. The same heart-shaped face. Same wide mouth. Same skin tone. Same soft jawline. Lindsey's uncanny resemblance to Sara had Kellen uptight, holding his body so stiff that he ached. And why else would Lindsey-not-Sara show up *now*, when Kellen had brought a woman on tour with him for the first time? When he'd stuck his dick inside another woman after five years of abstinence? He couldn't even deny he felt something for Dawn, something deeper than lust. And he'd even come inside her. He hadn't looked at Dawn when he'd blown his load, and his promises to Sara had echoed through his thoughts the entire time he'd betrayed her, but that didn't matter. Why else would Lindsey turn up pregnant now—not six months ago? Why now? He knew exactly why.

Sara was there to haunt him and not just in his thoughts this time, but in a physical form. Kellen didn't believe in coincidence. He believed in fate, in destiny. Lindsey turning up now was not a coincidence. She was a flesh-and-blood reminder of his promises to Sara. Just looking at her ate him alive. And the way she was looking at Owen—the worshipful way Sara had once looked at him—made Kellen want to vomit.

At his side, Dawn lifted Kellen's hand and kissed his bare wrist. The pulse beneath her soft lips leaped and raced. He forced himself not to pull away, but he watched for Lindsey's reaction to Dawn's show of affection. Sara would have been spitting mad and jealous if a woman as beautiful, talented, and accomplished as Dawn O'Reilly had dared to touch him, but Lindsey was too busy trying to catch Owen's attention to pay Kellen any mind. Owen was the one staring at him with narrowed eyes. Kellen couldn't blame him for being pissed off. Kellen had been purposely avoiding him for hours. But his avoidance had very little to do with Owen and even less to do with Dawn. In truth, he was avoiding Lindsey so that he didn't have to feel so guilty about Sara. For the entire bus ride from Beaumont to New Orleans, Lindsey had been Owen's shadow. Maybe once they reached their destination, they could get away from the woman for a few minutes. He'd like Dawn to get to know his best friend a little better and for Owen to say more than hello to her, but as long as Lindsey was hanging around the guy, Kellen would maintain his distance.

He gave himself a hard mental shake and turned to Dawn.

"You seem distracted," she said. She lifted a lock of hair from his bare shoulder and ran it between her thumb and index finger.

"Who, me?" He grinned at her. "Must be your beauty. Totally distracting."

She rolled her eyes at him. "You seem distracted by *Lindsey*. Do you have a thing for her in particular or pregnant women in general?"

Gabe, who was sitting across the aisle and reading, snorted. "Jacob is the one with the pregnant-woman fetish."

Jacob backhanded Gabe, but since Gabe was quick, Jacob caught only Gabe's arm with his fingertips.

"I don't have a thing for her," Kellen said. "She just reminds me of someone."

"And who would that be?" Dawn asked.

"Sara," Gabe said, making it impossible for Kellen to avoid addressing her question.

Dawn's shoulders sagged, and Kellen scooped her into his arms, kissing her passionately. That way everyone—especially Kellen himself—would know that Dawn had his full attention.

"It's nothing," he assured her quietly when they drew apart. "I don't want to talk about Sara." Or look at her pregnant ghost. But the pregnant ghost waddled by and without an invitation plopped down next to them on the sofa.

"Is your father really Theodore O'Reilly?" Lindsey asked Dawn. "The guy who owns all those tropical resorts?"

Dawn groaned. "And don't forget his seventeen five-star hotels along both the Atlantic and Pacific coasts." She sounded like a perky salesgirl even when she added, "Because he won't let you."

Kellen blinked at her. How had he not made the connection between Dawn and infamous billionaire Theodore O'Reilly? Even Lindsey had figured it out. Dawn had told him that her parents were wealthy, but she was an heiress to a hotel and resort dynasty? No way! She was much too down to earth to be related to *that* pompous guy.

"When you hinted that you were rich," Kellen said, "I didn't realize you were set to inherit millions."

"Billions," she corrected with a shrug.

"Billions," he said flatly.

"Don't worry yourself about the inheritance tax too much. I'm bound to get myself disowned before he dies," Dawn said. "He'll probably leave it all to his beloved wolfhound, T-Rex." She pursed her lips and rolled her eyes. "Because plain ol' Rex isn't a big enough name for *his* dog."

Lindsey laughed. "I can't believe I'm talking to Theodore O'Reilly's daughter."

Dawn's muscles tensed beneath Kellen's palm.

"You must get to meet lots of famous people!"

"On occasion," Dawn said vaguely.

"Who is the most famous person you've met?" Lindsey asked, looking almost as star struck as she'd looked the night she'd followed Sole Regret's tour bus up a mountain pass and kept them all warm and entertained throughout the night.

Dawn linked her fingers with Kellen's and smiled at him. "Mr. Kellen Jamison, guitarist for . . ." She bit her lip, her cheeks flushing. "What was the name of your band again?"

Kellen snorted and couldn't resist kissing Dawn's pretty lips. "Sole Regret."

"Oh, that's right."

She winked at him, and he realized she was teasing. She knew exactly what the band was called. She'd scored VIP tickets for their show in Beaumont specifically to confront him for leaving her behind in Galveston with nothing but a stupid Dear Dawn letter to explain his absence.

"So how does a woman like you end up in a shithole like Galveston, Texas?" Jacob asked.

Kellen scowled. He liked Galveston. It wasn't a tropical paradise or anything, but it was an island and it was Texan, so that made it all right by him.

"I like the ocean," Dawn said. "It helps me concentrate on composing. The cadence of the waves in Galveston speaks to me for some reason."

"The rhythm is too slow," Adam said quietly as he leaned against the sofa arm.

Kellen hadn't realized he was listening. The guy had been on his phone with his girl, Madison, most of the morning. Kellen suspected they were meeting up in New Orleans for the weekend.

"I don't compose hard rock." Dawn squeezed Kellen's hand. "So the rhythm is perfect for me."

Kellen's body flushed when memories of the rhythm they'd found together flooded his thoughts. He'd much rather be in Galveston alone with Dawn, rediscovering their rhythm, than stuck on the tour bus with Sara's ghost giving poor her the third degree.

"So your father owns a resort in Galveston too?" Lindsey asked.

Dawn snorted so loud, she choked. "Uh, no. The water isn't pristine enough for one of his resorts."

Gulf water was gray and murky most days, but Kellen had never minded. The rhythm of the waves there connected with his soul. He was pretty sure that Dawn felt that same connection. But he was also pretty sure that wasn't why she'd chosen Galveston over the Bahamas, Hawaii, or Tahiti.

"You chose Galveston specifically because he *doesn't* own a resort there." Kellen was already starting to understand how Dawn ticked.

"Exactly. I moved to L.A. for two reasons: to start my career as a Hollywood composer and because my dad didn't have a hotel there."

"He doesn't?" Kellen found that hard to believe. Maybe, like Galveston, the beaches in southern California weren't exclusive enough for one of his resorts, but that seemed unlikely.

"He didn't have one there until this January. He even made me attend the ribbon cutting ceremony." She stuck her tongue out as if she'd just eaten something truly vile.

"I'd be proud of my dad if he was that successful," Lindsey said.

"He's proud enough of himself for the both of us," Dawn muttered.

Kellen and Dawn definitely came from two entirely different worlds—*ribbon cutting ceremony*. He didn't have a dad to be proud of, and the one who'd knocked up his mother wasn't worth his weight in mud, much less gold. But he and Dawn had far more important experiences in common. Music filled his soul and hers, so material differences didn't matter. Did they? They didn't matter to him, and it seemed they didn't matter to her either.

Owen laughed unexpectedly, and Kellen glanced his way to discover that he was on his cellphone again. The obnoxiousness of his laughter meant that he was talking to Caitlyn for the eleventh time that day. Yes, Kellen had counted. He wondered how Caitlyn was dealing with the knowledge that Owen had been volunteered to be a baby daddy, because Kellen wasn't dealing very well with Owen's predicament at all. And not only because Lindsey looked so much like Sara. He knew what kind of man his best friend was: too trusting, too giving, too easy to take advantage of. And while Kellen admired Owen's open mind and gentle spirit, he knew Owen could fall prey to someone with an agenda—like a woman with a baby on the way and apparently no one to help her out.

Then again, if Owen took Lindsey home over the weekend and left her there, Kellen wouldn't have to spend the rest of the tour watching his every move because he couldn't shake the feeling that Lindsey and Sara were cosmically linked *and* that Lindsey had been sent to spy on him and make him feel guilty for liking Dawn so much. For lusting after her.

Kellen's fingers returned to the silver band of Jacob's watch, rubbing it absently, as if Sara could hear the apology behind that repetitive motion.

The bus shuddered and the pitch of the engine lowered as the lumbering vehicle slowed to pull off the road.

"Finally," Adam said. "Is it just me or do these bus rides get longer and longer?"

"It's just you," Gabe said. "They just seem longer because you can't wait to see Madison."

Adam flushed, but he didn't refute Gabe's claim.

"I wonder if I have enough time to rent a bike before I pick her up at the airport," Adam mused.

Kellen chuckled to himself but didn't point out the folly of picking up someone at the airport on a motorcycle. Let the dumbass figure out where to store her luggage on his own.

"So do you think you can introduce me to Taylor Swift?" Lindsey asked. She'd been doing some online searching and had found a picture of Dawn with Taylor Swift posted somewhere.

Dawn shifted on Kellen's lap, straining her neck to peer out the window across the aisle as if she hadn't heard her.

"You two are friends, right?" Lindsey pressed.

"I've met her. That doesn't make us friends," Dawn said.

"How about Jennifer Lawrence, then?" she asked, lifting her phone to display a picture of Dawn with the beautiful starlet. "Are you two close?"

Dawn patted Lindsey on the shoulder. "You're barking up the wrong socialite tree, hon. It's really not my scene."

"But it could be if you wanted it to be," Lindsey said, reaching over to squeeze Dawn's hand. "Come on. Let me go with you to just one Hollywood party. I'll love you forever."

"I get flustered in the company of stars," Dawn said. "I don't belong among them."

"Sara, quit pestering her," Kellen said with a weary sigh. "Dawn is not going to introduce you to the rich and famous."

Dawn's head whipped around, her eyes wide as she gawked at him. He supposed she didn't appreciate him fighting her battles.

"My name is *Lindsey*," Lindsey said, covering her chest with one hand. "Jeez," she said under her breath, climbing to her feet. "At least Owen remembers my name."

Kellen stared after Lindsey as she headed toward Owen to bug the shit out of him some more.

"You called her Sara," Dawn whispered.

"I did?"

Dawn nodded, and Kellen's stomach twisted into a sick knot. Lindsey did look like Sara, but they weren't much alike in personality. How could he have made such a mistake?

"I think I need a drink," he said, even though alcohol had never been his go-to crutch.

"It's a little early for that, even in New Orleans," Dawn said. She shifted off his lap and took his hand, urging him to stand. "I'm sure there's something we can do to keep your mind off your worries."

Her voice had taken on a sultry timbre that claimed his full attention, and the suggestion in her eyes made his cock stir with interest. Oh yes, he was sure they could find something to occupy his mind, his hands, and especially his stupid mouth. And if Lindsey was out of sight, surely Sara would be out of mind.

CHAPTER TWO

DAWN CRANED her neck to peer out the side window of the tour bus. As they passed familiar sights of New Orleans, she was struck with nostalgia. If her career path had gone the way she'd originally intended, she would have become a jazz pianist instead of a classical one. For that reason alone, New Orleans was one of her favorite cities. Right after she'd graduated and her ex had gone to China to find himself—without her, thank God—she'd spent a year in NOLA trying to make it as a jazz performer. A fun year, but ultimately, just as Daddy had predicted, a failure.

When the bus pulled to a halt behind the venue where the band would play that night, Kellen couldn't get off fast enough. Maybe it was because she'd suggested they could get intimate, but more than likely it was because Lindsey was near. He took Dawn by the wrist and they were halfway to the backstage entrance when she realized she'd left her bag behind.

"Forgot my purse," she said, drawing to a halt so abruptly that Kellen stumbled.

"I thought you wanted to take my mind off my worries," he said.

"I do. But if I don't get my purse, I'll be the one with my mind riddled with worries." She already had that familiar panicky feeling she got whenever her purse wasn't within reach. She'd never understand the trend of carrying nothing but a cellphone.

"I'll grab it for you," he said, brushing a kiss against her cheek before dashing toward the bus.

He nearly tripped over his feet when Lindsey emerged from the stairwell. She smiled brightly at him, and he wrapped a hand around his silver wristwatch before diverting his gaze to the ground. Dawn knew that Lindsey reminded him of Sara, but Dawn wouldn't have ever guessed that Kellen could be so blatantly rude to anyone. Was there some deeper reason he couldn't stand the woman? She vowed to get him talking about what was really bothering him. She already knew him well enough to realize that he kept his emotions tightly bottled and that he fixated on certain issues, especially if they pertained to his Sara. Dawn sighed, wondering if he'd ever let himself be free of his first love.

Owen hopped off the bus after Lindsey, and Kellen at least smiled at his supposed best friend before hurrying up the now empty bus steps. The way Kellen had talked of Owen with admiration and obvious affection had made Dawn believe the two were close, but they sure didn't act close. In fact, Kellen had barely spoken to Owen all morning.

Owen watched Kellen disappear inside the bus, and Dawn recognized the hurt in his expression even from a distance. So she wasn't the only one confused by Kellen's behavior.

Dawn approached the sweet-faced bassist. "Do you think Kelly is acting a little off?" she asked.

"Yeah," he said, sparing her a glance laced with surprising dislike. "Ever since *you* showed up."

He turned without another word and hurried toward the building with Lindsey waddling after him.

Was it possible that Owen was jealous of Dawn? She wasn't sure she'd ever figure out the dynamics of this little group of men. Especially not the one between Kellen and Owen.

Kellen returned with her purse and nodded at her thank-you, but his gaze was on Owen's retreating back. He didn't turn his attention to her until Owen had entered the back of the arena and disappeared from sight.

"I thought you and Owen were best friends," Dawn said, as always, unable to keep her curiosity in check or her mouth shut.

"We are."

She shrugged. "You sure don't act like it. I don't think you've said more than two words to each other all day."

"Well, you're here," Kellen said, taking her hand and coaxing her to follow him toward the door Owen had just entered.

"Can you only talk to one person at a time?"

He grinned, and if she wasn't mistaken, a blush reddened the bronzed skin across his high cheekbones. "Uh, yeah, pretty much," he murmured.

"I wouldn't want to come between you and Owen," she said, though being the center of this man's attention was a rather heady experience. Everything about the man had her out of her head. Especially all that exposed taut skin on his arms, back, chest and abdomen and the delicious tattoos that decorated it all.

"He's got bigger problems to worry about at the moment," Kellen said.

Lindsey, she presumed. "Has Lindsey been following the tour for long?" She'd had tons of questions about the young woman since they'd boarded the bus in Beaumont, but they'd been in tight quarters so there'd been no way to ask without being rude.

"Since Houston. But I didn't ride with the guys that night. I went to Galveston instead and caught up with them in Beaumont for last night's show." He opened the door for her, but before she could enter, he drew her aside instead.

"That was a great show," she said. "I really enjoyed myself, and you have amazing fans."

"When I first saw Lindsey come down the bus steps in Beaumont, I literally thought she was Sara."

Dawn blinked at him. "Why would you think that? Didn't she pass away years ago?" Yet imagining he'd actually seen Sara would explain why he'd called Lindsey by the wrong name earlier.

"She did, so imagine my surprise when she turns up on the tour bus looking alive and healthy and pregnant."

"So that's what's been bothering you this entire trip. Not me. Not Owen or some natural on-the-road moodiness, but because Lindsey reminds you of Sara."

"Right before Sara passed away, she told me she'd haunt me if I didn't find someone to love. I must admit I'm feeling thoroughly haunted at the moment."

Dawn grinned at him. "That's an easy problem to solve. Just fall in love with me and she'll leave you in peace."

When he gawked at her, she hoped he didn't take her jest seriously. She held in a relieved sigh when he replaced his open-mouthed stare with an easy smile, looped an arm around her back, and opened the door again. "Well, that shouldn't be too challenging."

He said that, but the second they entered the building, to find the ghost of Sara standing just outside the dressing room door, he stopped short. He wasn't merely saying that Lindsey's presence bothered him; it was quite obvious that he struggled every time he saw her. Dawn wasn't sure if she should be relieved that his problem wasn't with her or perturbed that Sara still had such a hold on him. She'd wrongly assumed that when he'd made love to her, the shackles linking him to Sara had shattered.

"I'm hungry," Dawn said, trying to come up with an excuse to leave the premises, because this freaking-out-over-Lindsey version of Kellen wasn't very fun to be around.

"I'm sure there are sandwiches and snacks in the dressing room."

"Do you need to wait around here for sound check or a meet and greet or some other rock star shenanigans?"

"I won't be needed for any shenanigans until later this evening," he said with a soft laugh.

"Would you think me high maintenance if I insist on you taking me to one of my favorite restaurants for lunch?"

"I might. How five-star is the place?"

"Baby," she said, speaking in a faux haughty tone, "McDonald's is five-star when you're with me."

He laughed. "I believe that." He yelled at some member of the road crew, "We'll be back before sound check!"

Soon they were on their way to New Orleans's French Quarter by cab, and the farther they journeyed from the venue, the looser Kellen held his body, until they were practically snuggling in the back seat. Here was the guy she'd chased after. Here was the guy who made her body burn and her thoughts scatter. Here was the guy who didn't mind when she traced the contours of his muscular chest with one very happy finger. She'd been worried that she'd invented him, making him into something he wasn't.

"Maybe we should have asked Owen to join us," Dawn said. "I'd like to get to know him better."

"And he'd probably like a break from Lindsey as much as I needed one."

"I feel bad for her. It's like she has extrastrength cooties. It's not her fault she looks like Sara."

"She wouldn't have been invited on the bus that night if she hadn't looked like Sara. Owen always seems to think he could help me move on by trying to hook me up with women who resemble her."

Kellen might be haunted by Sara's ghost, but Dawn was left

shivering in the darkness of her shadow. Dawn was suddenly grateful that she looked nothing like his first love. "Twisted."

He grinned and wrapped an arm around her shoulders to give her a squeeze. "I tried to warn you, but you didn't run when you had the chance."

"Still not running," she whispered, lost in his heated gaze. The man wore his virility like a fine suit. She was suddenly thinking less of lunch and more about his devastatingly skilled mouth between her legs. She settled for a thought-stealing kiss instead, her fingers curling into the bare skin of his back.

When the cab drew to a halt in front of the restaurant she'd chosen, she had half a mind to tell the driver to circle the block until she'd had her fill of kissing Kellen, but they'd probably run out of gas before that happened.

When they stood on the sidewalk surrounded by the lunch crowd, she realized they wouldn't be seated with Kellen being shirtless. She'd become so accustomed to him walking around half naked that it hadn't occurred to her until she noticed all the female eyes glued to her companion's hard-muscled chest and gorgeous tattoos.

"Um," she said. "You need a shirt to get lunch."

"Not if we grab something from that street vendor," he said, his gaze focused on a food truck parked in a lot almost a block away.

"Good plan," she said with a laugh. She didn't want him covered up any more than he wanted to be.

"You seem familiar with the city," he said. "You didn't even have to ask for a restaurant recommendation."

She flushed, diverting her gaze and taking his hand as they headed toward the food truck.

"Have you spent a lot of time here in the past?"

She didn't like to talk about her failures and while she wouldn't want to forget the fun-yet-financially-strained year, she wasn't sure she wanted to tell him about it. And then her gums started flapping on their own accord.

"I lived here for a year. Right after I graduated from Curtis."

"You went to Curtis? Isn't that some fancy music school like Julliard?"

"Curtis is way better than Julliard." She grinned and leaned into his arm, squeezing his hand. "But I might be a tad partial toward my alma mater."

"Does New Orleans have a good symphony?" His brow furrowed. "Did you play with one while you lived here?"

"A symphony is a piece of music. An orchestra would be what *my* kind of band is called." She winked at him.

He laughed and slapped his forehead. "Okay, I obviously have no clue what I'm talking about. I definitely need to learn more about what you do. Our careers are far more different than they are similar. I'd probably know more about being a civil engineer than a classical pianist."

"And I know more about being a pastry chef than being a rock star."

"Considering how well you bake, you must be an expert rock musician."

She flushed with pleasure. He really was an expert rock musician, as well as an expert at delighting her.

"Flattery will get you everywhere."

They got in line behind the others waiting for their chance at a po'boy. She wasn't familiar with this particular food truck, but judging by the length of the line, Kellen had made an excellent choice.

"So you joined the orchestra in New Orleans? Why for only a year? Not a good fit?"

"New Orleans isn't really known for its orchestra," she said, still on the fence about spilling a secret she held close to her heart. "They have one, of course, but I could have had a spot in the Philadelphia Orchestra or the New York Philharmonic."

"Impressive," he said, and then lifted his brows. "Right?"

She laughed. "Yes. That's typically impressive." In her circle, when she threw that bit of information around, people were definitely impressed. It was kind of refreshing that he didn't look at her as some sort of prodigy.

"So not the orchestra." His eyes popped wide. "You didn't play jazz, did you?"

When she nodded slightly, he grimaced. It was the exact same reaction her father had had when she'd informed him she wasn't accepting the position with Philadelphia. She was going to follow a different dream to New Orleans. It wasn't as if the man had paid for her illustrious education. All students who managed to get into Curtis had full scholarships. He sure hadn't held back his disappointment about her choices—all of her choices. Dad had warned her that she'd fail, that she couldn't possibly make it as a jazz pianist, and his correct prediction had made her failure sting all the more.

"I played in a piano bar for a while, but I never had the right brand of funk. Patrons would request 'Flight of the Bumblebee' instead of 'Take the A Train.'"

"I'd love to hear you play 'Take the A Train,'" he said. "What's 'Take the A Train'?"

She shook her head. "Duke Ellington?" She could tell by his blank expression that he didn't know the song or the legend.

"You'll have to give me a private concert," he said. "Show me how jazz piano is supposed to be played."

"You're bound to be disappointed." She'd been disappointed in herself. She supposed classical music had been drummed into her at such an early age that she couldn't break free of its hold on her soul. She hadn't been good enough to be taken seriously as a jazz pianist. And as someone who was used to being the best, that revelation had crushed her.

"You are the least disappointing person I've ever met." Kellen nudged her arm with his elbow.

"You haven't known me long enough to make that claim."

"I knew that the moment I heard you banging out your composition at the beach. It isn't possible for the woman who'd created something that stirred me so completely to ever be a disappointment."

She tried not to smile at how good he made her feel about herself. She'd become accustomed to living up to her own exalted expectations early in life and not caring what others thought—or so she told herself—but she kept her agent around because he encouraged her, and she definitely wanted to keep Kellen around, so maybe she needed outside approval more than she thought. Maybe her father's continual disappointment—and his expression of his resentment at her choices—did bother her. She told herself she didn't care that the only kind of child he'd ever wanted was one willing to take over his financial legacy, but she craved approval from those who cared about her. Even those she'd known for only a few days.

Kellen placed a hand in the center of her back and urged her forward. The line was moving, but she'd been so wrapped up in him and her own thoughts, she hadn't noticed.

"Maybe tonight after your concert we can check out one of my old haunts," she said. "If you're not too tired, that is." He'd been too tired the night before to do anything besides sleep. Since she also zonked out after performances, she'd tried not to take his disinterest in sex personally.

When she looked up at him, he was smiling at her. His happiness even touched his dark eyes, and she couldn't help but smile back.

"I'd really like that," he said.

"I think my old roommates still live in town. Maybe I'll give them a call and see if they'd like to meet us."

"I'd like that too." The line moved forward another customer, and Kellen stepped closer to her. "You know what else I'd like?" His whispered words tickled her ear, shattering her concentration and making her shiver.

Before she could gather her thoughts, he murmured, "A taste of that honey between your legs."

At his suggestive teasing, her honey began to flow for him. She'd been starting to think she wasn't sexy enough to keep his attention, so she was gratified by his words.

"Before we head back to the venue," he said, "we should stop by the hotel to make sure our bags have been delivered to our suite."

"Is it possible they haven't?" She glanced up at him, worried. There were valuable clothes in her suitcase. She hadn't had time to pack her less formal attire before following Kellen to Beaumont, so she was stuck with the formal belongings in the suitcase she'd left in the car when she'd arrived at the beach house in Galveston. At the time, she didn't think she'd need her gowns and dressy clothes, so hadn't bothered lugging the extra baggage upstairs, but now she was just glad she had clean underwear and a couple of changes of clothes with her, no matter how rock-concert inappropriate they happened to be.

"I'm sure it's all there," he said. "It's just that the dessert I crave requires a location more private than a street corner."

"Oh." Her face went hot. "Yes, we should definitely stop by the hotel. What hotel are we staying at?"

"I think it's the Courtyard."

"That's only a few blocks in that direction." She pointed

toward the northwest. "After lunch, we can walk there."

They were third in line now after having waited for twenty minutes.

"I'd really like to start with dessert," he murmured, his dark eyes glassy with desire. For her.

"It'll be better if you wait. The more you want it, the better it tastes when you finally earn your sweet reward."

She got lost in his eyes and wasn't sure if she was suddenly so hot because the muggy New Orleans air had become even more oppressive or because he was looking at her like she was the dessert of a lifetime.

"Can I help you?" the woman at the counter called out to them. A large gap had cleared out between them and the food truck.

"Change of plans," Dawn said. She grabbed Kellen's hand and hurried up the street in the direction of their hotel, tugging a laughing Kellen behind her.

By the time they entered their room, lunch and suitcases were completely forgotten. He practically tossed her onto the bed. Her skirt went up, panties went down. He spread her legs wide and stared down at the hot, achy flesh between her legs. She gasped when he bent over her, his breath tickling her pussy. He hesitated just before his mouth claimed the dessert he'd wanted, and yet before she could relax enough to enjoy his warm mouth, he stood.

"I have a better idea," he said.

Better than his mouth on her? Impossible. Unless he was planning to put his cock inside her. He hadn't done that since before they'd parted in Galveston. She lifted her head and watched him hurry to his suitcase.

"My suitcase is there, isn't it?" she asked, feeling more than a little perturbed that he'd stop to check his bag now.

When he pulled out a length of soft pink rope, she understood his unexpected interest in his luggage. He wanted to tie her. She wasn't sure she had the patience for that right now. As much as she loved the slow and careful attention he showed her when he turned her body into a work of art with nothing but lengths of rope, sometimes a woman just needed a tongue on her clit followed by a quick and hard fuck.

"Kellen, it's not necessary. I'm already beyond turned on."

"I need it."

At least he was quick about it. Standing over her at the edge of the bed, he tied each wrist to a thigh, still fumbling with the final knot when his mouth latched on to her clit. He sucked and nibbled, licked and kissed, until her back arched and her feet curled and her center pulsed with release. He straightened and entered her, filling her with deep, hard strokes until her orgasm subsided, and then he pulled out. He bent over her to eat her pussy again, quickly bringing her to a second peak. Apparently her shuddering cry of release was his cue to fuck her again. She wanted to watch his face as they came together, but it felt so good to have her clenching pussy filled while she came that she couldn't open her eyes. And when the ripples of pleasure finally stilled enough for her to pry her eyes open, he was back to sucking and licking and biting and oh, God, what was he doing now?

She lost track of how many times he brought her to orgasm with his mouth, how often he rewarded her release with fast, hard strokes with his hard-as-stone cock.

"I thought I could do one more," he said brokenly.

He pulled out before she'd settled from her most recent orgasm. A slick pounding sound that unfortunately did not involve her body gave her the strength to open her eyes. Transfixed, her heart hammering in her chest, she watched him stroke his cock with one hand. She yanked at her bonds, wanting that beautiful cock between her palms, and then gasped aloud when he came on her mound. Eyes squeezed shut, he swayed on his feet, rubbing his tip into the cum he'd left on her skin.

"That was perfect," he said.

Dawn agreed and watched as he pulled his pants up, tucking his spent cock into his jeans and fastening them. She had to admit that her body was completely satisfied, but her heart and soul cried out for him as he turned and disappeared into the bathroom.

She guessed he wasn't the type to cuddle.

Dawn realized how uncomfortable her body was positioned after she'd been lying there a couple of minutes. He usually took such care when he tied her, and she wondered why he'd bother tying her at all if he wasn't going to do it right. Water ran in the bathroom sink, and a moment later he emerged, looking so devastatingly gorgeous and apologetic that she couldn't stay perturbed at him. He carried a towel and several wash cloths. As he slowly approached the bed, his gaze caressed every inch of her exposed body. Though his knotting technique didn't live up to his usual care and imagination, it did effectively hold her legs wide open. She let him look at her—not that she had much of a choice—but even if she hadn't been bound, she wouldn't have tried to block his view. That sensual stare of his made her feel beautiful and desired, treasured even.

He didn't speak as he leaned over her and very slowly, very gently, began to clean his cum from her skin. His free hand caressed her thigh, her hip, and the curve of her waist as he tenderly washed her highly satisfied pussy. As she lay watching him, feeling him, she wondered why her pussy was the only part of her that felt satisfied. She wanted more of him. Not his cock. Not even that talented mouth of his. She wanted to feel him against her.

"Kelly," she whispered, her voice scratchy from all the moaning she'd done.

He lifted his chin and met her eyes.

"Will you ever be able to make love to me without tying me?"

"I hope so," he said, his hand moving to the ropes that bound her forearms to her calves. "I'm not quite there yet."

She tried to be understanding—even nodded—but wasn't sure why this particular vice of his and his inability to get past it hurt her heart.

"I still feel guilty for wanting you. For acting on it." His smile became wicked. "Just not guilty enough to stop."

"Do you tie me so you feel like all the blame for our coming together rests on you? Because I'm definitely half of this equation." And while she enjoyed when he took control and made her come over and over again while she was forced to accept whatever he did to her, she would also like to be more than a recipient. She'd like to give him as much pleasure as he gave her.

After a moment, during which he watched the action of his hands as he continued to wash her skin, he again lifted his head. "That's part of it," he said. "I guess I like to feel miserable about my choices."

How could anyone *like* to feel miserable?

"But the bigger part is even more selfish. I love the way you look when you're all helpless and at my mercy. If you weren't tied right now, I doubt you'd be holding still while I clean you."

"I'd be plastered to your body so I could feel every inch of you against every inch of me. I want that."

"I'd be happy to make all your wants a reality," he said, working at one of the knots that kept her immobilized.

"You would?"

"All you have to do is ask."

Her leg came free, and he massaged her hip to help her extend it. Her shoulder ached a bit as she straightened her arm and before she could complain, he massaged that joint as well. He untied her other leg and repeated the gentle massages on that side. She shifted to a seated position, wrapped her arms around him and pulled until he tumbled onto the bed on top of her. She pressed her chest and belly up against him, disappointed that they were both still partially clothed.

"Take your pants off," she said, putting a hand on his chest and squirming for a bit of space so she could shed her shirt and bra.

His body stiffened, and his heart thudded faster beneath her palm. "I'm not ready for this."

His eyes were wide as a spooked horse's.

"I don't want more sex," she said. "Just some skin on skin cuddling."

When her words didn't relax him, she stroked his back with slow, gentle caresses. She figured she was stuck with above the waist petting for now. She was okay with that.

"Leave them on then," she said. "It's okay."

"I'm already getting excited again," he said with a breathless chuckle. "And we both know where that will lead if I take my pants off."

She didn't want to pressure him—much—but she was more than ready to go exactly where that would lead. He wasn't, though. "Just relax," she said, her voice low and hopefully soothing. "I won't make you do anything you don't want to do."

"But I want to do it all. With you."

He released a long breath and allowed the stiffness to flow out of his muscles, so that his weight was on her. She couldn't stop herself from sighing in contentment. Yes, she needed this. To feel his body against hers. To be surrounded by his scent and his warmth. To delight in the tickle of his long hair brushing her neck. To hear his breath close to her ear. After a moment of lying in her arms, he shifted onto his side, drawing her against him. That was when her hands began to wander and her lips began to caress his neck, his jaw, his chin. She couldn't be expected to just lie there when she had this much man in her arms. To her surprise, he didn't stop her. His hands and lips began to wander as well. He left no inch of her unexplored, unkissed, and yet just when she was certain he was at a point of excitement where sex sans ropes was inevitable, he pulled away from her and climbed from the bed.

"We'd better head back to the venue," he said, retrieving her panties from the floor and slipping them over her feet. "It's getting late."

She figured it was bad form to complain that she was excited and aroused when it had been her idea to cuddle, but they'd done so much more than cuddle. Eventually they'd make love together rather than him making love to her while she had no choice but to take and take and take some more, but apparently that wouldn't be happening just now. She'd wait, wait for however long it took for him to allow himself pleasure without guilt. He was worth the wait. So she found her discarded clothing and made herself decent, noting that he was facing the wall with his hands on his hips as he waited for her.

"You don't want to watch me dress?" she asked.

He shook his head, and she grinned. He was turned on too, she knew he was. It was his stupid little rule to keep promises that should have long ago been broken that prevented them both from being fully satisfied, but she'd wait. He was worth the wait.

When she finished dressing, she went to him, resting a hand on his back and dropping a kiss between his shoulder blades, where the gorgeous gray-scale rendering of a life-like stallion decorated his skin.

"The naughty naked lady is all covered now," she said.

"You'd think years of celibacy would make this easier," he said with a pained chuckle. "I think it actually makes it more difficult. I wish I could take everything you're offering me, Dawn."

"You can." One arm wrapped around his waist, and she splayed her hand over the center of his chest. He covered her hand and held it there against his pounding heart. "The only thing stopping you is you."

"I know. I make myself sick!"

She laughed. He was worth the wait. He had to be.

He'd better be.

A LIMO WAS WAITING to take them back to the venue, and Dawn didn't complain as they slid into the cavernous back seat. She wouldn't have minded a bit more snuggling while they rode, but Kellen whipped out his phone and checked his messages. He immediately burst out laughing. When Dawn nudged him and lifted her brows, he passed her the phone.

"Is that Owen?" she asked, squinting at the screen and the rather white ass filling it. "What is he doing?"

"Mooning cows."

Dawn cocked one brow at him. "Why?"

"Letting off a little steam. I'm glad Jacob got him away from Lindsey for a couple of hours. They're bringing back crawdads and jambalaya for dinner."

Dawn's stomach growled, and she covered it with one hand. "Good. I'm starved. Not naming any names, but *someone* distracted me from getting lunch."

"That's unfortunate. I enjoyed the most delicious honeyed dessert."

Dawn crossed her legs and squeezed them together as her body very clearly remembered his sweet feasting.

When the limo pulled to a halt, the door immediately opened, and Gabe—looking very stern—practically yanked Dawn out.

"If you let me stay, I'll talk Mel into a threesome," said a pretty, young brunette to the crimson-Mohawked drummer. Gabe firmly shook his head. "Come on, Force," the woman said. "We'd rock your world."

"I don't want to have a threesome with you, or anyone else for that matter. I'd just like a little time alone with Melanie, if you don't mind."

As soon as Kellen emerged from the car, Gabe began to stuff the good-time woman inside. "Parker, take her back to the hotel. Don't let her talk you into any side adventures, be they threesomes or anything else."

"Uh," the limo driver muttered, his eyes wide and mouth agape.

"I'm sure Parker knows how to have more fun than you do," the woman sputtered. "What kind of rock star doesn't want to bang two gorgeous chicks at the same time?"

"The kind trying to make a serious connection with the friend you claim to care about," he said, slamming the door before she could reply.

Dawn exchanged a confused look with Kellen, who shrugged. The limo window hummed as it rolled down.

"I do care about her."

"Then give her a fucking break, Nikki."

Nikki scowled at Gabe before she slumped back into the seat, crossing her arms over her chest and setting her beautiful face into an unbecoming pout.

"I just want to have a good time," she said. "I'm sure you could easily talk Melanie into a threesome with us."

"I will not now, nor will I ever, pressure Melanie into spreading her legs for you, Nikki."

"You're so mean," she said, tears falling in torrents from her blue eyes.

Dawn might have felt sorry for the obviously distraught woman if Nikki's reason for crying hadn't been so absurd.

The limo eased forward.

"And stay out of trouble!" Gabe called after the retreating car. Nikki gave him the finger and rolled up the window.

"Do I want to ask?" Kellen asked Gabe.

"Melanie's baggage is driving me insane." Gabe offered Dawn a nod of greeting, which she returned, before he stalked off toward the arena's door.

"Are threesomes common among rock stars?" Dawn asked, hiding a teasing smile behind a fake cough.

"Depends on the rock star." Kellen wrapped an arm around her lower back and directed her toward the backstage entrance.

Owen practically pounced on Kellen the moment he entered the dressing room, launching into a spiel about being chased down by an angry bull and Jacob being more concerned about preserving the moment in pictures than saving his life.

"We can always find another bassist," Kellen teased.

"Hey," Owen said, slapping his friend on the arm. "Don't forget you wouldn't even be in this band if it wasn't for me."

"How could I forget something you remind me of at every opportunity?"

Dawn felt incredibly third-wheelish standing there next to them, but was glad to finally see evidence of the friendship between the two men. They both lit up with delight, clicking together so perfectly that she had a hard time following some of their conversation. Or they were that way until Lindsey headed their way. The instant Kellen saw her, he shifted his hand to cover his wristwatch and went all quiet and stiff. Owen actually flinched when he caught sight of the woman.

"There you are," Lindsey said, covering her belly with one hand.

Dawn wasn't sure if her action was a protective reflex or if she was intentionally drawing attention to her condition.

"I was getting so lonely here with no one but Jordan to keep me company."

Dawn did a quick check of the room and spotted a young man watching Lindsey with an intensity that reminded her of a junior high boy with his first crush—Jordan, she presumed. Lindsey didn't notice Jordan's stare of longing; she was too busy looping her arm through Owen's and sniffing the air with a deep inhale.

"That Cajun food you brought smells absolutely delicious. Is it time to eat? You're always so thoughtful and thinking of others. I've never met anyone as considerate as you are."

Owen actually smiled at her compliment and allowed her to direct him toward the rapidly forming buffet line.

Kellen didn't follow. Instead he turned to Dawn. "Are you ready to eat?"

She lifted a brow at him. "Does Lindsey stick to Owen like industrial strength glue?"

He glanced after his stuck friend. "Uh, *yeah?*"

"There's your answer."

Dawn tried to keep Kellen talking, but they ended up a couple of people in line behind the pregnant ghost of Sara, and he couldn't seem to focus on anything but misery.

"She's not Sara," Dawn said quietly when the line moved but he hadn't.

"I know," he said, scooping jambalaya onto his paper plate.

Maybe he did know Lindsey wasn't Sara's ghost, but Dawn could tell he was struggling.

Spicy and savory, the food was excellent, though it had gotten a little cold in transport. Yet not nearly as cold as Kellen had become as he sat beside her in sullen silence. Every time she tried to strike up conversation, he gave her a one-word answer if he even bothered answering. She had to help him free himself from his past love once and for all so that he didn't sport that guilty, crippled-soul look on his face every time he was around someone or something that reminded him of Sara. Had he really been living like this for five years? How miserable for him. Dawn searched for his hand beneath the table and found it wrapped around his wrist again. She covered it and squeezed. If he couldn't get past this on his own, then they'd get past it together. Avoiding Lindsey wasn't the answer. He needed to move on so that the mere presence of the woman didn't tie him in knots. Especially if she became a fixture in his best friend's life.

After dinner Dawn had the privilege of hanging around in the green room with the band and a couple of their girlfriends. Sweet, seemingly shy Madison was focused on Adam with a worshipful stare that left no doubt that she was completely besotted with the lead guitarist. She could scarcely get out two words without flushing. Melanie, in contrast, had more than a few words for Gabe. The strikingly lovely and leggy brunette seemed upset about the argument that had resulted in threesome-desiring Nikki leaving the premises. Gabe was doing his best to distract Melanie by introducing her to everyone in the room. When the couple reached Dawn and Kellen, the first thing out of Kellen's mouth was, "This is Dawn O'Reilly. Not only is she beautiful, smart, and talented, but she won a Grammy earlier this year."

Dawn flushed and elbowed him in the ribs. Not that she didn't like his compliments, but it was hard to be considered normal and approachable after an introduction like that.

"You're a musician?" Melanie sputtered, giving her the twice-over. Maybe she assumed Dawn was a rock musician or a pop star. Admittedly, she looked neither part.

"The Grammy was for one of my compositions," Dawn said, hoping her smile looked friendly. Dear lord, what was she supposed to say to Melanie now? Dawn couldn't stand a braggart. Her father was the biggest braggart she'd ever encountered. Had her statement about her Grammy sounded like bragging? God, she hoped not.

"She does play the piano," Kellen added. "Her fingers are magical."

"Oh, I bet," Gabe said with a smirk. "It isn't every gorgeous redhead who can get this tough crack to nut."

Dawn puzzled over Gabe's idiom. "Isn't the saying 'tough nut to crack'?"

"Oh, I know the saying," Gabe said, his smirk widening. "I said exactly what I meant."

It took Kellen slugging Gabe in the arm for her to realize that Gabe was making a joke, and a few times of running Gabe's muddled saying through her head to figure out he was razzing them about sex. Her inability to blend in might not be Kellen's fault after all, but rather her own. Dawn wasn't sure if she should be more embarrassed by Kellen bringing up her Grammy or her apparent lack of a sense of humor.

"When she plays that piano," Kellen said, "it makes my soul shudder as if in orgasm. Is a soulgasm a thing? Because she gives them to me."

Unable to believe he'd said that in polite company—if Gabe and Melanie could be considered polite company—Dawn blinked and then said, "Will you quit?"

"And you should hear the song she composed the other night," Kellen said, his low voice dancing along her spine. If he kept talking like that, she'd insist they spend the time before the show alone together so she could make good on the promise in his tone.

The suggestiveness of his comment did not go unnoticed by Gabe, who bit his bottom lip and lifted his brows. Dawn licked her lips and turned to Kellen, figuring the best way to stop the teasing was to play along. She pinned Kellen with her most sultry gaze, hoping she looked more like Marilyn Monroe and less like Debbie doing-all-of-Dallas, and said, "Maybe I'll write another tonight."

His hand resting on her lower back tightened into a fist, tugging her top against her skin and instantly enslaving her to his mercy. He didn't need ropes to do that. He just had to look at her as if he intended to devour her whole.

Someone cleared his throat. "Would you two like to be alone?" Gabe asked, breaking the spell Kellen had cast over her.

Kellen turned to Gabe and drew back, as if startled. "Gabe! When did you get here?"

"I was here before you arrived."

"Didn't notice."

Gabe nodded in Dawn's direction and grinned. "With Dawn beside you, I doubt you'd notice if the room was on fire."

But judging by his cringe, he had noticed that Lindsey had just come out of the bathroom and was searching the room for signs of poor Owen again. Dawn wondered what Owen's new woman was like. Was Caitlyn truly as fabulous as Owen claimed, or was he just acting infatuated to throw Lindsey off his scent? A new girlfriend would have to be infinitely patient to deal with his current situation.

Someone called Kellen to the stage, and Dawn tagged along, interested in anything related to music, even all the massive technologically enhanced equipment that went with putting on a huge rock concert. Kellen was amused by her questions and had returned to his normal easy-going self within moments of leaving his band behind in the dressing room.

"So are you always tense around the guys in your band?" she asked as they made their way back to the dressing room, where he'd likely become that closeted stranger again. "It must make touring difficult."

"What do you mean? I'm not tense around the guys."

"You sure seem tense to me. Every time we're with them, you get all quiet and closed off." Well, that wasn't exactly true. He'd been fine talking to Owen and Gabe when they'd interacted one-on-one. Maybe he just couldn't deal with more than one person at a time.

"You're imagining things," he said.

He opened the dressing room door and peeked inside. He released a relieved breath and entered the room, heading directly for the unoccupied sofa. In fact, the entire room was currently unoccupied. And Kellen was once again perfectly at ease.

"See," Dawn said, following him. "They're not here and you're all relaxed and calm."

"*She's* not here," he corrected.

"Who?" But the moment she asked, she knew who he was referring to. "Lindsey."

He nodded and slumped onto the sofa. She sat beside him.

"I wish she didn't make me feel this way," he said, "but I can't help it. Every time I see her, I feel so fucking guilty for being with you. And you're the one I want to be with. The only one."

She wanted to be with him too, even if their relationship took a bit of effort.

"It's okay. We'll figure out a way to get you through this. If making this work requires throwing her off a bridge, I'll throw her off a damned bridge."

He laughed, but shook his head. "That won't be necessary. I just have to put up with her for a couple more hours and then hopefully I never have to see her again."

"Even if she marries your best friend?"

Kellen covered his belly with one hand and pressed his lips together. Dawn was pretty sure he was going to throw up.

"Over my dead body," he muttered.

"You realize that as Owen's best man, you'll be the one to raise a toast in their honor at their wedding reception."

"Stop," he said, grabbing her and tickling her until she was bucking around on the sofa. "That's not even remotely funny."

The dressing room door opened, and they separated like a pair of teenagers who'd been caught making out on her parents' sofa.

Owen poked his head in, and Kellen loosed a relieved sigh.

"There you are," Owen said, entering the room.

When Lindsey waddled in after him, Kellen groaned aloud. Dawn was becoming very fond of her throwing-Lindsey-off-a-bridge idea.

"It's like you're intentionally avoiding me or something."

"I'm not," Kellen said.

Owen narrowed his eyes and twisted his mouth to one side, but Kellen *wasn't* avoiding Owen, just the young blonde attached to his hip. He wouldn't even look at her, and Dawn understood why. Maybe she should hand Owen a clue. He was obviously sporting hurt feelings over Kellen's reaction to him.

"Every time you get a girlfriend, it's as if I don't exist," Owen said, tossing an undeserved glare of malice in Dawn's direction.

He stalked off, Lindsey in his wake, and headed for the bar in the back of the room. Kellen squeezed his eyes shut.

"You should explain that it's not him you're avoiding," Dawn whispered to him.

"I will," Kellen said, "after she's gone."

Someone sat beside her on the sofa, and Dawn was surprised to find Adam looking at her expectantly. He seemed to think she could read his mind.

"How did you get past your writer's block?" Adam asked when she just stared at him.

Other than Gabe, with his bright red Mohawk and dragon tattoos, Adam looked more like a rock star than the rest of the band. His shoulder-length ebony hair—a shade too dark to be natural—was purposely sticking up in all directions, and he wore chains and leather as if he'd emerged from the womb ready to ride a Harley.

Dawn's face went hot as memories of how Kellen had gotten her over her writing hump—erm, slump—by engaging her in a rather vigorous, uh, hump. "Um, well, I uh . . ."

Adam lifted an eyebrow at Kellen, who was smiling rather self-indulgently.

"She was inspired," Kellen said.

Adam snorted on a laugh. "By your dick?"

"Uh . . ." Dawn reminded herself that she didn't have to censor herself around these guys, which was actually a welcome change from her usual crowd. "No, his dick came later."

Kellen laughed and wrapped an arm around her shoulders. "Not that much later."

"Stop," she said, slapping his thigh. "You make it sound so tawdry, and it was beautiful."

She turned her attention to Adam, finding him as intense as usual. "I was inspired by his passion."

Adam actually took a moment to give Kellen the twice-over, as if he were considering being inspired by his bandmate's passion. "Whelp," he said, pushing off his thighs to stand. "That's out."

Chuckling, Dawn grabbed Adam's wrist and tugged him back down beside her. Knowing how hard it was to deal with being stuck, she wanted to help him overcome his block. "Your inspiration doesn't have to be a gorgeous, soaking wet warrior of a man rising from the sea in a storm."

"Say what?" Owen said from near the bar.

Jacob, who was apparently also listening, laughed.

"I think inspiration can be found in anything that shakes you up." Dawn took a deep shuddering breath, thoughts of that night—deliciously dirty thoughts—circulating through her head. She touched her hot cheeks, willing herself to calm down, but it was no use. "I don't know, maybe it *was* his dick that I found so inspiring."

"Care for a bit more inspiration?" Kellen whispered.

"You don't have enough time before the show to give me the care and attention I deserve." If they started something now, she would need it to continue for hours. Dawn kissed his nose and melded into his side.

When Madison entered the room, Adam completely lost interest in their conversation and rose from the sofa. "Uh, later."

He was gone before Dawn could even say goodbye. "He really has a thing for her," Dawn said, watching him cross to the bar. Even as he was ordering, his attention was on Madison.

"Well, she did save his life."

Dawn's curiosity was stirred. "In what way?"

"She was his addiction counselor. He stays clean for her."

"Sounds complicated."

"Everything about this band is complicated," Kellen said. That was no lie.

CHAPTER THREE

AFTER THE CONCERT, KELLEN REMOVED the wide silver watch from his wrist and set it on Jacob's bunk. Before Dawn had arrived to inform him it wasn't his place to tell her he wasn't good for her, he'd needed something to replace the cuff he usually wore—the one Owen had confiscated and buried somewhere—but now that she was here and Lindsey was on her way to Austin, he felt he could take the steps he needed to finally move on. And the first step was ridding himself of the ridiculous need to cover his wrist. Maybe with it gone, he could stop fixating on an object that served to remind him of his commitment to Sara. Correction, his broken commitment. He picked up the watch again—examining it, considering it—and then shoved it under Jacob's pillow so that it was completely out of sight. He didn't want it fucking with his head for another second.

Dawn's hand pressed against the base of Kellen's spine, and she leaned against his bare back. He'd known her two days, yet he already knew her touch and even her presence without having to look at her.

"Are you sure you want to spend the weekend in Galveston?" she asked. "We could stay here in New Orleans or go someplace else. Someplace where you don't have memories of Sara to haunt you."

He turned and folded her in his arms. "I'm sure you hate feeling like you're in her shadow." Especially since he'd been acting like an ass every time Lindsey made an appearance that day. But he didn't have to see Sara's ghost anymore. Owen had taken her back to Austin, so along with the watch that had served as a reminder, the bigger reminder was now gone. He could breathe freely again.

"I don't mind," Dawn said.

"Liar."

She laughed. "She's part of you. I know she comes as part of the package."

But that wasn't fair to Dawn.

"I need to release myself from her hold once and for all, do what I'd planned to do the night we met. But I can put that off if you don't want to be there for me."

He cringed; his words hadn't come out right. He'd meant that it was something he could do alone, not that he thought she couldn't support him.

Dawn shifted away and gazed up at him with those green-flecked hazel eyes that he loved staring into. Long strands of her hair tickled his arm when the glorious red waves brushed against his skin. She was gorgeous.

"Of course I want to be there for you."

"That's not what I meant," he said, but of course she thought that with the stupid way he'd worded his statement. He didn't usually have a problem expressing himself, but this woman had him uncharacteristically out of his head. The last woman who'd made him all topsy-turvy was Sara, and though he was ready to leave her in the past, he wasn't sure if he was ready to give himself over to the same set of emotions again. Was it wise to free himself only to tie himself to another?

He rephrased his attempt to let Dawn off the hook. "I wouldn't mind your support, but I can do this on my own if you have better things to do." Definitely better.

She lifted her eyebrows at him. Okay, so not better.

"What I'm trying to say—"

She silenced him by covering his mouth with her fingertips. "I get it. You'd like my support, but don't want to actually ask for it."

That was closer to what he'd been trying to say, but still not exactly right. He didn't want his time with Dawn to be intruded upon by memories of Sara, but until he truly laid his departed fiancée to rest, she'd always be there just beneath the surface, waiting to twist him into knots.

He took Dawn's hand from his mouth and pressed it against his chest over his heart. "I can put Sara's memories in the mental box I normally keep them in and try to ignore them like usual. If I do that, I swear we can have an enjoyable weekend together. Or I can include you in the mess of trying to sort us out—me and Sara. I've tried so many times to do this in the past—alone—and thus far I've always failed, but you've given me a great reason to move forward. Maybe this time will be different. Either way—"

"We're going to Galveston," Dawn said.

"And stay at Sara's house?" Kellen asked, thinking he might actually be able to stand being in that sunny, yellow beach house with Dawn beside him.

Dawn shook her head. "It's not Sara's house, it's *your* house."

"But I bought it for her."

"And maybe you should sell it for you."

She was probably right, but he couldn't do that. Not when a big part of him still wanted to hold on to Sara. That house and its contents were all he had left of her, of them. And he didn't want to forget her or the time they'd spent together. But maybe if he dealt with his sorrow and the guilt that ate him alive, he could figure out how to move on. Something had to change; he was miserable. He'd been miserable for a long time. He just hadn't realized it until Dawn played her way under his skin and into his heart.

"Do you want to stay here in New Orleans tonight or leave for Galveston right away?" he asked.

With the exception of Adam, the rest of the band had cleared out of New Orleans so they could catch a plane back to Austin for their weekend off. Kellen was admittedly tired after the performance, and it was at least a six-hour drive to the island, but they could get a head start if they left right away.

"Don't you still have that lovely suite in the hotel that's going to waste?" she asked.

"Yeah. The band rented that whole block of rooms for the weekend, and Adam is the only one putting his to good use." And Kellen was sure that with Madison there for the weekend, Adam was putting that room to *very* good use.

"So let's stay here tonight and leave in the morning. We can grab a late dinner and have some fun on Bourbon Street. I never managed to reach my friends, but we can venture out on our own."

That sounded like a frivolous start to what was sure to be an emotionally trying weekend. Maybe they'd decide to play in New Orleans the entire time. That option would keep things light and entertaining, the way a budding relationship should be.

"Great plan," Kellen said.

He called for a cab since neither of them wanted the attention that came with taking the limo. He wasn't sure it had returned from dropping the guys—and Lindsey—at the airstrip anyway.

"Any idea where you want to go?" Kellen asked, checking an app on his phone for suggestions as they waited for their ride. "There's never a lack of activities in New Orleans. And you did promise to play me that jazz song." Though he couldn't for the life of him remember the title of it. Something about a train.

"I'm surprised you remembered, but yeah, I'll play you a tune. Have you ever been to the Carousel Bar?"

"Never heard of it," he admitted. Owen usually picked the spots to visit when they were on tour, and he always chose sex clubs, so those were the only places Kellen knew about in the cities he'd visited. Kellen didn't even want to suggest something like an evening at a sex club to a sophisticated woman like Dawn.

"It's in the Monteleone Hotel on Bourbon Street in the French Quarter. You'll love it."

He had heard of Bourbon Street and the French Quarter—they'd been in that general area earlier that day—but he wasn't familiar with the Mont-whatever Hotel. "I'm game," he said. "Do I have to wear a shirt?"

She laughed and placed a kiss on his chest, her fingers tracing the outlines of the many tattoos that decorated his skin. "I prefer you like this, but if we want service, you'll have to hide this man candy from view."

"Man candy?" Kellen was used to Owen being the man candy when he went out. Kellen served as his wing man, and he wasn't sure he wanted Owen's role. He'd much rather be admired for his ideals, interests, and talents than for his body. But maybe Dawn could appreciate him for all those qualities and his body too.

"Candy delicious enough to lick," Dawn said, her tongue sliding over one pec, which flexed involuntarily beneath her exploration.

He enjoyed her touching him—he couldn't deny that—but he still didn't feel comfortable under her attention. Especially when he didn't have ropes binding her gorgeous body. He had no problem doting on her; admittedly, he'd been doing that all day.

But when they were alone together and their making out progressed to making love, he had to tie her up before he could fuck her properly. He needed time to reflect on that need, and he sure couldn't do that with her beguiling mouth on his flesh.

He took her by the shoulders, not to push her away or to draw her closer, but to encourage her to stay right where she was—neither too far, nor too close. He wondered if she really understood what she'd gotten herself into when she'd sought him out and pledged to give their relationship a try. He already knew opening his heart to a new woman would not be easy for him, and by extension, it would be challenging for Dawn as well.

"We'll have to stop by the hotel before we go out," he said. "All of my clothes are there."

"Perhaps," she said, her lips sucking kisses along his chest, "we should just stay in."

"Or we could savor each other's company outside the bedroom." Where ropes weren't required.

Her head tilted, her pretty eyes searching his face. "If you were any other man, I'd take that as a stinging rejection."

He'd done the same to her the night before. He hoped he didn't make her feel unwanted. She was definitely wanted. He was the problem, not her.

"I'm not rejecting you. I'd very much like to tie you into little knots both inside and out and then deep, deep inside."

She shivered beneath his fingertips, and he felt the pull of her body on his in the primal place he'd kept locked tight until she'd smashed it open the night they'd met.

"But . . ." She encouraged him to continue.

"But if we start with outside knots and move to those deep inside knots, which is what will happen if we're alone together in my hotel room, we'll be skipping that first step."

"And how does that first step work?"

He lifted his brows at her. "Tying you in knots on the inside?"

She nodded, a smile on her lush lips.

"I guess you'll have to wait and see."

He held her hand in the cab to the hotel, his thumb rubbing the pulse point in her wrist.

"I enjoyed the concert," Dawn said. "Even though I saw your show just last night, it still feels new and exciting."

"Do you often go to the orchestra?"

She smiled and ducked her head. "I often *am* the orchestra. I do quite a few solo concerts."

"So you don't just compose, you perform? Professionally?" He realized he knew very little about her day-to-day activities. He'd met her when she'd been hiding from the world in a beach house and searching for her muse. He was glad she'd found inspiration in him, but he had no idea what her real life was like.

"I go back and forth," she said. "Sometimes the music comes pouring out of my soul—that's when I compose—and sometimes it pours from my heart—that's when I perform."

"I'd like to watch you perform sometime."

"I was able to drool over you onstage last night and tonight, so I suppose it's only fair that you get to do the same. I'll check my calendar and see what I have coming up. I think I have an event next week in Prague." She scrunched her brows together and tilted her head slightly. "Or maybe it's Rome next week and Prague the following week. Or is it Warsaw?" She chewed on her lip, her features tense with concentration.

Kellen tried not to look too astonished, but he was most likely failing at that. "You perform overseas?"

Dawn shrugged. "Quite a bit, actually. At least when I'm not on a deadline for some composition. There's a different appreciation for classical music in Europe. Its roots are there, if that makes sense. It's like how Nashville is immersed in country music and New Orleans in jazz; Prague is all about classical. You'll have to come with me sometime when you're not on tour and experience it for yourself."

"Now, that would be cool." And not something he'd ever thought to do on his own. This woman could broaden his horizons far more than he could broaden hers.

"We're here." She leaned close to the window and peered up at the tall hotel.

Already? Kellen hadn't even noticed the taxi had stopped. The door was opened by a helpful valet, and the tidy older gentleman offered a hand to Dawn. She thanked him graciously, and Kellen scrambled out after her. She linked her arm through Kellen's and placed a hand on his bare belly, which instantly began to quiver beneath her light touch.

Maybe they should stay in after all. He did have more rope

in his luggage—a soft and supple length in a muted sage green and a coarser coil of red that would likely leave marks on her pale, freckled skin. He'd take his time with each knot this time. He could already picture her as a bound work of art, so beautiful he'd have no choice to but to eat her sweet pussy until she came and came and he unleashed his cock and plunged—

"I don't think Owen likes me much," Dawn said, drawing Kellen out of his fantasy so quickly that he groaned aloud.

"What makes you say that?"

Kellen had noticed Owen trying to draw his attention from Dawn most of the day. Like Kellen would want to experience Owen's ordinary when he had the extraordinary at his side. He could see Owen any time. Owen *without* Lindsey in tow. Dawn would be going back to L.A. soon, or to Rome or Prague or someplace equally less Texas. She'd said so herself.

"Just a vibe he was giving off," she said.

"It's Lindsey. He'll be less weird once he rids himself of her."

"Isn't he kind of stuck with her for life? Or at least the next twenty years or so?"

Kellen's stomach plummeted. "Don't say that." They ventured toward the elevator since he still had his keycard from earlier.

"Do you always have such a hard time accepting reality?" she asked and then bit her lip. "I'm sorry. Sometimes my tongue gets away from me. I didn't mean to just blurt that out."

"No, you're right. Sara is gone and will never be replaced. Owen's gotten a girl in trouble"—*maybe*—"which comes with lifelong responsibility. I'm with a beautiful, intelligent woman who will soon discover I'm not worth the headaches I cause her."

"That last part is definitely not reality," she said.

He grinned. "Hey, I'm trying here."

In their suite, he found a plain white V-necked T-shirt in his luggage and pulled it on. The fabric felt stifling and restrictive against his chest and back. He immediately wanted to take the shirt off again. He'd just opened his mouth to tell Dawn that they should stay in after all when she stepped out of the bathroom in an elegant black dress. He blinked at her, trying to remember how to make his mouth function as his gaze journeyed from her simple up-do that showed off the length of her slender neck down the curve of cleavage hinted at by the low-cut bodice of her gown and along the narrowing of her trim waist, the slight flare of her hips, the long length of her shapely leg, and to the slender ankle and spike-heeled shoes that made his toes curl in appreciation. And then his lucky eyes took the reverse journey back to her face.

"You just happened to have that dress in your luggage," Kellen said when he found his tongue.

She ran her hands over the silky fabric that clung to her devastatingly gorgeous body. "All the clothes I have with me are like this. You don't like it? Should I change?"

"What? Hell no. You're the most stunning woman I've ever laid eyes on." He frowned down at his jeans and T-shirt before meeting her gaze again. "I just feel a bit underdressed."

She grinned. "You look overdressed to me. I've become accustomed to ogling your shirtless chest, belly, back, shoulders, arms." Each word came out a bit slower than the last as she eyed each part she listed.

She licked her lips, and his gaze was drawn to the small bumps at the tips of her breasts. He had a sudden, powerful urge to draw those hardened nipples into his mouth and slide his hands up the backs of her thighs. But that would be entirely inappropriate. Unrestrained.

"Maybe we should stop at a hardware store on the way back," he murmured. "Pick up some rope."

"Only if I get to tie you up this time," she said.

He grinned. He liked the sound of that.

As she stood on the elevator clutching her small purse, he couldn't help but stare at the lovely length of bare leg showing along the slit up her thigh. She looked far too classy and sophisticated in her form-hugging black dress to be hanging out with the likes of him.

It turned out that the Carousel Bar was built on an actual carousel. It even spun slowly in a circle. Kellen had to wonder if the bartender at the center suffered from vertigo. Every chair along the rotating bar was occupied, so Kellen stretched to look over the crowd for a table on the unmoving part of the floor.

"Dawn O'Reilly?" a woman's voice carried over the crowd. "Shut the fuck up! Why didn't you tell me you were in town?"

Beside him, Dawn sucked in a breath. Before Kellen could

even blink, Dawn was being drawn into an exuberant hug by a young woman and then being shaken back and forth to make sure the hug stuck. Or broke Dawn's back; Kellen couldn't tell which.

"Come sit with us," the excited stranger said. "We have a great table by the piano."

"Great. Is there a performance tonight?" Dawn asked.

"There's a performance every night. You know that." The woman finally focused her gaze on Kellen. "Is this guy with you? I thought you swore off dating."

"I swore back on the moment I laid eyes on him."

The still-unnamed woman laughed. Her enormous Afro of loose curls made her pretty features look uncommonly petite. "Can't blame you there. But Jimmy will be heartbroken. You told him you were gay."

"So he'd leave me alone." Dawn cringed. "He's not here, is he?"

"Nope. He wanted to be a homebody tonight. If I text him and let him know you're here, I'm sure he'll put on pants to come see you."

"I'd rather you didn't. I'm sure Kellen is already uncomfortable enough without Jimmy wishing him dead."

"Forgive me," Kellen said, "but I'm a little lost here."

"You didn't tell him about me and Jimmy?" Dawn's friend asked, a dark scowl on her face.

"I don't like to dwell on my failures."

The woman rolled her eyes. "Since Dawn has forgotten her manners, I'll introduce myself," she said. "I'm Chantel. We were roommates for a year. We had a little jazz band together with Jimmy Zeta for a while. We lived on macaroni and cheese and cheap wine." She lifted a hand to her temple and sighed. "Yet she never calls anymore."

"I called you this afternoon. Your number was disconnected."

Chantel waved a hand. "I didn't have phone service for a while. Too broke to pay for it. I've got a prepaid el cheapo phone now. Doesn't break the bank."

"I'm Kellen." He introduced himself when he found a narrow opening.

Chantel looped her arm through his and began directing him

toward the area near a large grand piano. "You're a musician, aren't you?"

"Why do you say that?" Not that he was denying it. He just wondered how she could know.

"Kindred spirit. Dawn and I are about as different as we can be," Chantel said. She paused to twist toward Dawn, who'd fallen in step behind them. "I mean, will you look at her? She looks like a movie star."

Oh yeah, he couldn't help but notice all the heads turning to check Dawn out.

"You look like a dead hooker on CSI," Dawn said with an ornery grin Kellen had never seen before.

Chantel gave her the finger before pushing him toward a table and stuffing him into a chair. "Even so, we're kindred spirits."

She introduced him to her motley group of friends. All musicians, coincidentally. Dawn needed no introduction; they even razzed her about her rich girl dress.

"So you have a Grammy," Chantel said, "yet you're still hanging out with the riffraff."

"Kellen's not riffraff," Dawn said.

Compared to Dawn, he was definitely riffraff, but she never went out of her way to make him feel that way.

"I was referring to us," Chantel said, waving a hand at her three companions.

"Is this your new band?" Dawn asked.

Chantel shook her head. "Naw, we never joined a new band after you left. Jimmy and I have expanded our horizons."

"Does that mean you're smoking more pot?" Dawn asked.

Kellen laughed, liking this side of Dawn he never knew existed.

"Maybe a little, but that's not the horizon I'm referring to. I'll text Jimmy now. He'll want to tell you himself."

Dawn smiled and seated herself on Kellen's knee since there weren't any free chairs. She ordered a martini and he a beer. The noise in the place was deafening, every person trying to talk louder than the next so they could be heard. When the din suddenly faded, Kellen glanced around for the reason.

An older black gentleman climbed up on the stage to sit at the piano. He fingered a few keys, and Chantel yelled, "Hey,

Bobbie, look who's back in town."

The pianist glanced at their table and was immediately on his feet. "Oh my Dawn," he said. He hobbled off the stage to pull her off Kellen's lap and into a sturdy hug. "It's so good to see you again. You have to play for us tonight."

"You're the star of this show," Dawn said, drawing away and holding him at arm's length. Her fondness for the man was written all over her face. Kindred spirits, Kellen supposed.

"Just one song," Bobbie said, giving her slender bare arms a squeeze for emphasis. "For me?"

"Well, I did promise Kellen I'd play 'Take the A Train' for him." She offered Kellen a smile. "Can you believe he's never heard it?"

Bobbie laughed. "That definitely needs remedied."

"Play a song," Chantel chanted. "Play a song. Play a song."

The entire table began to imitate her, and the chorus soon spread throughout the bar.

"One song," Dawn said, lifting a finger.

"As many as you'd like," Bobbie said, nudging her toward the stage. "I can take the night off."

Kellen sat up straighter as Dawn approached the piano. She ran a finger over the keys, so lightly that they made no sound. A lover's caress. Every eye in the room was turned in her direction. He wasn't sure if it was his association of Dawn plus piano equaling sex, or the way she so easily commanded the massive instrument with a mix of confidence, genuine love for music, and talent, or the way she looked in that dress that had him instantly aroused, but he was suddenly glad he had a sturdy table to hide his lap from view.

"Jimmy better hurry," Chantel said. "He'll kill me if he misses this, and maybe if he sees her with a hot guy, he'll finally get over her."

Kellen couldn't take his eyes off Dawn to spare Chantel a glance. He murmured, "Mmm hmm," which seemed to appease her enough to silence her chatter.

Dawn slid onto the piano bench and adjusted the microphone. "I won't damage your hearing with my singing," she said, and several quiet laughs circulated around the room, "but if you know the words, feel free to sing along."

Kellen's heart raced as she began the song, and the melody

did seem familiar, so he must have heard the tune at some point. Maybe Adam had played it. He'd played jazz guitar in the past. Bopping around in her chair like she had restless butt syndrome, Chantel sang the chorus, and though she had a phenomenal voice, Kellen wished she'd shut the fuck up so he could focus on Dawn's playing. During the piano solo, the entire bar fell silent— even Chantel. Perhaps the other patrons were also holding their breaths as Dawn played a series of notes so quick and clear and perfect, he never wanted her to stop. But she did stop eventually, to segue back into the chorus.

"And that's why I told her she had to leave," Chantel said with a sad sigh.

Kellen blinked to reset his brain and gave her a look that should have sent her diving under the table for cover, but she had her elbow on the table and her chin in her hand as she watched Dawn play, her body rocking with the beat. How could anyone ask Dawn to leave? Couldn't this idiot hear how perfectly Dawn played?

"She didn't miss a note," Kellen said. "She never misses a note. That was spectacular."

Chantel's light brown eyes shifted to him. "Actually, she missed *every* note, because she makes every song her own. If you knew the original, you'd realize that."

"She makes every note better," Bobbie said, a wide smile on his face. "But she doesn't belong here. Her talent is wasted on the likes of us."

"You told her to leave because she was wasting her talent?" Kellen knew he'd never have the strength to do that for her. He too much wanted to be with her. He was already dreading the idea of her returning to Los Angeles. But he could deal with a long distance relationship if he had to. That was what planes were for.

"Sometimes she needs nudging," Chantel said. "Doesn't know what's best for her. Lets her emotional attachments to people get in the way of her dreams."

And maybe that was why he'd found her alone in that beach house. He'd thought it unusual that some lucky man hadn't already made her his.

"So don't you get in her way, mister." Chantel poked him in the arm. "She needs support behind her, not in front of her barring her path to greatness."

"How about beside her?" Kellen asked, thinking there was no way he'd ever stand in her way.

"Maybe," she said as the song ended and she jumped to her feet to applaud.

Kellen clapped along with the rest of the bar and winked at Dawn when she turned his way. It was almost as if she was looking for his approval, but she sure didn't need it. The woman was spectacular in every sense of the word. And she didn't need to perform for him to recognize it.

"Play 'Flight of the Bumblebee'!" someone yelled from across the bar.

She turned on the bench, and Kellen thought she might tell off the requester—as she'd mentioned how much it bothered her to have to play that song in jazz clubs—but she squinted into the gloom near the bar entrance and asked, "Jimmy?"

"Dawn!" The man yelled again and shoved through the crowd, jostling people unnecessarily as he headed for the stage.

"Jimmy?" she repeated.

"Dawn!"

Kellen laughed as he was reminded of the scene from *Rocky* when Adrian and Rocky continued to call for each other. His laughter died when Jimmy reached the stage and scooped a laughing Dawn into his arms. Kellen didn't know what he'd expected—some unattractive slob, apparently—so when he recognized Jimmy as the prime specimen he was, Kellen rose to his feet. The dude had the body of a boxer, the face of a male model, and the messy hair of someone who didn't own a comb.

Chantel grabbed Kellen's wrist. "They're just friends," she said.

"I put pants on for you," Jimmy told Dawn loud enough for everyone to hear. "And ran three blocks."

"But didn't bother combing your hair." Dawn tried flattening it with one hand, and Kellen recognized affection between them, but no attraction. At least not on her end.

"She treats him like a little brother," Chantel added. "He's got girls tripping over each other to be with him, yet he talks about her all the time. All. The. Time. He's so pathetic."

"Some guys are like that. They only want what they can't have." As soon as he said it, he thought of Sara. Was that why he was still hanging on to her, because he couldn't have her? He dismissed the thought and reclaimed his seat, watching Dawn avoid a misguided kiss from Jimmy.

"I brought my trumpet," Jimmy said, lifting the case he held in one hand. "Thought we could have a band reunion." He searched the crowd, and Chantel waved a hand to gain his attention. "There's my little Chanty. Got your sticks?"

Chantel slid out from behind the table and pulled a pair of drumsticks from the back pocket of her faded jeans. "Never leave home without them."

It turned out that Chantel also sang. The little trio was quite good. Even a rocker who didn't typically listen to jazz recognized that. Bobbie especially seemed to enjoy his unexpected night off as he bobbed and swayed to the music. Kellen liked watching Dawn play, but he missed her proximity. He wondered if she'd felt that way while watching his performance earlier that night. Knowing her, she'd probably been so busy rewriting all their songs for them that she hadn't paid him much mind.

After half a dozen songs, the trio let Bobbie reclaim his stage, but Jimmy wouldn't let Dawn get off the piano bench until she agreed to play "Flight of the Bumblebee." Kellen was up and ready to rescue her, but she conceded to play and even sent Kellen a little smile, rolling her eyes, before she turned back to the keyboard. Still on his feet, Kellen felt his jaw drop when her fingers flew over the keys. And while she'd started off playing the fast, familiar melody, once again she made it her own, making the piece even more complex than the original.

When she finished, the bar erupted into cheers, and Kellen simply gawked. He knew she was good—great—spectacular. But she continued to surprise him by how good, great, and spectacular she truly was.

"Too talented for the likes of us," Bobbie said, clapping Kellen on the back. "Take good care of our pretty little prodigy."

Kellen smiled. "I will."

Slightly breathless, Dawn approached the table and hugged Bobbie before shooing him back toward the stage. Kellen wasn't sure why he pulled her into his arms and claimed her mouth in a deep, satisfying kiss; he wasn't usually big on public displays. Maybe it was because Jimmy was hanging awfully close to her. When they drew apart, Kellen lifted his gaze to meet Jimmy's eyes. He expected Jimmy to be angry or at the very least jealous, but the guy just grinned.

"Did Dawn finally get laid?" He turned to the table and said, "Dawn got laid." Dawn elbowed him in the ribs, which made him shout to the entire bar, "Did everyone hear? Dawn finally got laid!"

"And that is why I never dated him," Dawn said, shaking her head. "He's incorrigible."

"I don't even know what that means," Jimmy said with a grin. "But I choose to take it as a compliment."

"That was amazing," Kellen said. "Not sure why Dawn keeps her jazz-playing days a secret."

"She's embarrassed by us," Chantel said, plopping into an empty chair and gulping the remains of the beer she'd abandoned nearly an hour before.

"I am not." Dawn patted Jimmy on the arm. "I just don't understand the point of dwelling on the past."

"You've always been annoyingly forward thinking," Chantel said. "Now sit and tell us what it's like to walk the red carpet."

"I'd rather know what you two have been up to," Dawn said, waiting for Kellen to find his seat so she could sit on his knee again.

He wrapped one arm around her. Yes, he wanted her close, not up on that stage. On his lap, in his arms. Now if only they were alone . . . But she obviously wanted to catch up with her friends, so he'd just breathe her in and think about everything he planned to do to her graceful body later.

"Chantel said you were broadening your horizons."

Jimmy shrugged. "I'm still writing music for video games."

Kellen straightened and turned toward Jimmy. "She did tell me about that."

"She's the one who got me started," Jimmy said. "She doesn't stick to one thing for long. She gets bored and moves on."

Kellen assumed that was a dig on him. That Dawn would soon get bored with him and move on.

"I guess I'll just have to be the most interesting man in the world."

"Stop," Dawn said, resting a hand on his chest. "I don't need some beer commercial hero. I just hadn't found what I was looking for. Until now."

The weight of her claim lay heavily on him, but he shook the stupid feeling aside and smiled, running a finger down her bare back until she shivered.

"For now," Jimmy said. "Chantel is thinking about giving up the drums and pursuing singing."

If his tactic was to drive Dawn's attention away from Kellen, he succeeded.

"But you love the drums!" Dawn said.

"A front man—or woman—needs to be out front," Chantel said. "Drummers shouldn't sing."

"Phil Collins probably wouldn't agree with that," Kellen said.

"That's one success story." Chantel lifted one finger in the air. "One!"

"There are others. Don Henley. Uh . . . David Grohl." Kellen struggled for more names. There really weren't many successful drummer singers.

"David Grohl doesn't play drums anymore," Chantel said.

"I don't even know who David Grohl is." Dawn cringed when Chantel gasped.

"Heads the Foo Fighters?"

Dawn shook her head.

"Originally the drummer for Nirvana?"

Dawn brightened. "I've heard of Nirvana. They did 'Smells Like Teen Spearmint,' right?"

Kellen snorted on a laugh but didn't correct her.

"We tried to get her to live in the twenty-first century," Jimmy said, shaking his head, "but she insists on staying in the sixteenth."

"Sheesh. I'm not *that* old-fashioned." Dawn slugged Jimmy in the arm. "There were some greats in the Baroque period—like Bach and Vivaldi—but I'm much more into the late eighteenth or early nineteenth centuries."

Kellen snorted on another laugh and hugged her tight. Nope, the eighteenth century wasn't old school at all.

"So you forget what's usual and become the next Phil Collins," Dawn said to Chantel. "Sing from behind your drums."

"But jazz," Jimmy added.

"It will have to be pop." Chantel released a deep sigh. "No

one listens to jazz anymore. Like I said, I have to broaden my horizons. Or narrow them."

"No one listens to classical either," Dawn said. "You have to make your own niche, girl. Get out there. Let your soul shine."

Chantel squeezed Dawn's hand. "I've missed this. Missed you. You always did make me believe I was capable of anything."

"Because you are."

Apparently his Dawn wasn't just the beacon in *his* darkness. Her light shone brightly on all those she touched.

CHAPTER FOUR

"ROAD TRIP!" DAWN SHOUTED as she climbed into the car beside Kellen the next morning. She'd been in a great mood since she'd woken to find Kellen watching her sleep as if she were the world's greatest treasure. And then it occurred to her that they got to spend the entire day alone together, and she doubted anything could knock her out of the clouds and back to earth.

Stifling his yawn with a laugh—Chantel and Jimmy had kept them out late even by rock star standards—he started the car. "We need snacks," he said.

"And good tunes."

"I'm not sure our ideas of good tunes are the same."

So the stuff she listened to wasn't last decade or even last century. As far as she was concerned, excellent music was timeless.

"What kind of music do you listen to in the car?" she asked.

"Classic rock mostly. And you?"

She lifted an eyebrow at him. "You have to ask?"

"A different type of classic," he guessed.

"We should share our favorite playlists," she said. "I can listen to some of your favorites and you can do the same with mine. It'll be fun."

"Fun? I'm pretty sure classical music will put me to sleep while I'm driving."

She slapped at his arm playfully. "It will not. It will stir your soul."

"And classic rock will stir . . ." He grinned. "Something else."

"I'm game for all sorts of stirring."

He laughed and pulled into a gas station that had a convenience store. "Snacks first. Get all your favorites and we'll share."

This was fun, she decided as she hunted for pizza-flavored Combos, a corn dog that had been rolling on a heating plate for at least seven or eight days, and her favorite Starbursts. Few knew of her addiction to any of those things. She also got a bottle of cranberry juice and a second of orange juice, and then picked out a travel mug in which to mix the two.

Kellen had already checked out, his food treasures hidden in a concealing bag. She tried blocking her own purchases from his sight so she could surprise him with her finds as well.

When they reached the car, she mixed her orange and cranberry juices and offered him a sip.

"That's actually really good," he said.

"And healthier than whatever soda you pulled off the shelf. Wait, let me guess . . ." She closed one eye and assessed him as if reading his mind. "Mountain Dew?"

He pulled out a bottle of peach-flavored sparkling water. "Do not tell the guys I drink this stuff," he said. "They'll take my man card."

She laughed and took a taste. "Not bad," she said. Not good either, but if she were stranded in a desert, she'd drink it. After she ran out of her own urine maybe.

They laughed when they discovered they'd both bought Starbursts, though he'd gotten original flavors and she favored the tropical ones. He was aghast to find she actually liked the lemon chews.

"Gross. I usually throw the yellows away."

"Save those for me, then."

She was nibbling on her corn dog after chomping down half of his taquito as she began to compile her playlist on her phone. She really needed to put some lesser-known compositions on the device. Her digital collection couldn't compare to her at-home collection in either size or diversity. And as a purist, she preferred vinyl, but she had yet to ride in a car that boasted a turntable.

"So the trip will take, what, six hours?" she asked, offering him a bite of her dried-out corn dog—just the way she liked them.

"About that long," he said, making a face of disgust and spitting the corn dog into his hand. He dropped it out the window for crows or seagulls or whatever kind of birds scavenged convenience store parking lots in these parts.

She flicked through her list of songs, the title of each composition making her fingers long for a keyboard as each played through her thoughts. "Some of these symphonies are over an hour long."

"An hour? For one song?"

When she glanced at Kellen, his mouth was turned down and his nose was crinkled up. Okay, so maybe she should stick to shorter pieces for now. She didn't want to turn him off her genre by overplaying one composer. When he stuck his tongue out and shuddered, she said, "An hour isn't *that* bad."

"Give me another drink of your juice."

She handed over her travel mug grudgingly. She didn't usually have to share. Especially not with someone who drank in enormous gulps. When he handed the mug back, her drink was nearly gone. She scowled at the too-light mug.

"Had to wash the taste of ass out of my mouth," he said.

"Corn dogs do not taste like ass."

"You sure about that? I'll run in and get you another drink," he said.

"It's okay."

He grinned. "But I want more. I'm officially changing my favorite beverage to yours."

"Glad I have a good influence on you. That sparkling water is nasty."

"Not as nasty as that dried-out dick on a stick," he said, opening the door again.

So far, their road trip hadn't put many miles behind them. Not any.

"Get your playlist ready while I'm inside. I already have a list on my phone that has all of my musical influences."

"Get me another taquito while you're in there," she called after him as he shut the door. He gave her a thumbs-up and hurried inside.

She put a lot of thought into assembling her playlist, selecting pieces that weren't too long or too slow. Ones she hoped he'd like. It would be nice if more people appreciated classical music. Sometimes she felt that she'd been born about three hundred years too late. But women hadn't really been big in the music business back then. She'd probably have been burned as a witch or something equally horrific for having fast fingers.

"Did you get it figured out?" Kellen asked when he returned to the car.

"I think so," she said.

Chopin, Mozart, Beethoven—the usual stuff. She loved them all, but there were lesser-known compositions that really made her soul sing, ones that couldn't be readily downloaded. She'd just have to share those treasures with him when—*if*—he visited her in Los Angeles, where her massive classical music collection was housed. She did have a few of her favorites on CD at the beach house, but they wouldn't do her any good on their road trip.

After mixing them both a cranberry/orange juice blend in their matching travel mugs, he tossed a PayDay candy bar into her lap.

"Another favorite of mine," he said.

She picked it up by one end as if it had been floating in a toilet.

"What's the point of these things?" she asked. "There's no chocolate on them."

"I don't really like chocolate."

"Blasphemy!"

He jumped at her sudden outburst, and then laughed at his startle. "Just eat your PayDay and be happy I was thinking of you."

"I will not." She dropped it in his lap. "I'm not wasting calories on anything not dipped in chocolate."

"That's too bad," he said, reaching into the brown paper sack and pulling out a greasy, meaty, spicy-smelling taquito. "They were fresh out of chocolate-dipped taquitos."

"Give me that." She snatched it from his hand and scrunched the paper covering down so she could take a bite.

Grinning, he connected his phone to the car's Bluetooth system, while she munched on her chocolate-free taquito.

"I'm not sure getting to know each other is a good idea," she teased as she popped the last bite into her mouth. "Now that I know you don't like chocolate, I'm not sure we can be friends."

"And now that I know you actually eat yellow Starbursts, I'm sure you're a space alien."

She stuck out her tongue at him, and he flicked her nose with one finger.

"I guess I can overlook the small stuff," she said with a shrug. "No one is perfect."

"I like our differences," he said. "All of them. If I didn't, I'd date a mirror."

"I tried that once," she said. "I'm not a very good kisser. My lips are all hard and cold. It was like kissing a pane of glass."

Kellen laughed. "I don't recall kissing you being like that at all." He leaned in to prove himself correct.

When he drew away, she was craving something a bit more satisfying than junk food.

"Are we ready?" he asked.

"I think so. We can stop halfway and get some more of those taquitos, right?" Because she'd already finished the one he'd just given her.

"Right." He grinned. "They're so much better than dried-out corn dogs."

They were, but she wasn't prepared to admit that to him.

When they entered the highway a few minutes later, she flicked through the playlist Kellen indicated on his phone. Black Sabbath, Queen, Deep Purple, Aerosmith. At least she'd heard of those bands. She still wasn't sure what a Foo Fighter was. Or what exactly they were fighting. "Who goes first?" she asked. "Me or you?"

"Flip a coin."

She won the coin toss and selected Chopin. "I'm playing this song at a recital next week. I think it's next week." She scowled as she tried to remember what day it was. She'd lost track while she'd been holed up in the beach rental with nothing but writer's block to keep her company. Until Kellen showed up.

"It's lovely. A bit slower than the jazz you played for me."

"If you weren't driving, I'd tell you to close your eyes and listen closely. Chopin is best enjoyed without any outside distractions."

"So I'd have to close my eyes and also toss you out on the side of the road to truly appreciate this piece? Because you are my greatest distraction."

She shook her head, her face aching from all the smiling. Apparently those smile muscles of hers didn't typically get enough of a workout. Kellen was definitely putting them through their paces.

They fell silent for a long moment, listening to the build of the song. In her head, she was hearing different notes, though.

Her own twist on the music—the way she would have changed the composition to her personal taste. She felt guilty when her thoughts warped the perfections of the classics, but it wasn't anything she could help. She supposed it was the composer in her that made that happen. Listening to music without rewriting it into her own creation was hard for her.

"Do you like performing?" Kellen asked, drawing her from her mental composing.

"I do," she said. "It makes me feel connected to people. Composing is a lonely venture."

"Unless I'm there." He leaned over and squeezed her knee.

She couldn't argue since he happened to be right.

"One reason I think I'll keep you despite your dislike of chocolate."

"And do you like composing? Actually *like* it?"

"That's a tough question," she said. "It's more a compulsion, I guess. I can't *not* do it. In fact, I'm doing it in my head right now."

"In what way?"

"When I hear a piece of music, sometimes I reinvent it in my own style. I'd really like to compose symphonies, music that will still be played hundreds of years in the future."

She'd only ever mentioned that overreaching dream to one person—the piano teacher she'd once idolized—and he'd laughed at her. So she'd molded her dream into something more attainable—composing for Hollywood movies. She was relieved when Kellen didn't laugh at her.

"That sounds like a fine aspiration to me."

"It does?"

"I'd pay to hear them."

She snorted. "You would not."

"If you wrote a symphony, I'm sure it would give me a major boner."

She gaped at him. He said the most guy-like things sometimes. She wasn't sure why she found it so shocking. He was a rock star; he even looked like one. But his soul was so deep and his words often so poetic, that it was hard for her to think of him as a regular guy.

"I've only ever told one other person about that dream," she said. "And he made fun of it too."

"I wasn't making fun," he said, taking his eyes off the road just long enough to meet her eyes. "I really think you should go for it."

"But the time I devote to composing has to pay my bills."

"Like Hollywood."

She nodded. "It's worked so far."

After a moment, he asked, "So who made fun of your dream? 'Cause I'd like to knock his teeth out."

She wouldn't want that. Pierre had just been keeping her head out of the clouds. As a teen, she'd been so idealistic, she'd never bothered to tread with her feet on the ground.

"Old boyfriend?" he pressed.

"I told you about Pierre."

"The gay French piano teacher you were infatuated with?"

"He's not gay." She pressed cool fingertips into her suddenly flushed cheeks. "He was lovely. And talented. He pushed me to do better. Try harder. Reach farther."

"But he laughed at your dream."

"He redirected it," she said. "To make it something attainable." And then he'd up and left one day without any explanation or even a good-bye. She'd floundered without direction for years before she'd gone to Curtis and found a new mentor. One she didn't let herself love quite as much as she'd loved Pierre. She doubted it was possible to connect to any other musician the way she'd connected with him.

Kellen's voice pulled her out of her thoughts. "So write full-blown classical compositions on the side. For fun."

"For fun?"

He nodded. "Nothing takes the fun out of creativity faster than having to do it to make a living."

There was some truth to that.

"I guess it wouldn't hurt." She shrugged. "Unless it interfered with my deadlines."

"Can we listen to some Queen now? This Chopin stuff really does put me to sleep. Not like your music. Your music . . ."

"Gives you a boner?"

He laughed. "Yeah, it does."

"And you'd really pay for that experience?"

"Every day. Even Sunday."

She supposed there was something inspiring about that

knowledge. She could make it her life's work to compose classical symphonies that gave Kellen Jamison wood.

CHAPTER FIVE

THE SUN SHONE off the Gulf's water, giving it an illusion of deep blue clarity. A line of pelicans raced over the surface, the lead bird dipping under the water and emerging with a fish in its beak. Kellen stood on the front deck of Sara's house and watched the birds swoop and glide for several minutes, trying to find the courage to go inside. He'd had a fantastic time with Dawn during their road trip—living in the now, considering the direction of his future—but the time had come for him to confront his past. Dawn had volunteered to join him, but he wanted to enter the house alone the first time since he'd broken his promise to Sara.

The pelicans flew out into the Gulf until they shrank into nothingness. He supposed he had nothing left to use as an excuse to procrastinate. Taking a deep breath and putting the Gulf to his back, he inserted his key into the lock and opened the hurricane door. As usual, it stuck, and he was swamped with a memory of him and Sara trying to figure out how to get the blasted thing open when they'd first vacationed there.

The living room was dusty, but nothing else was different or out of place. The sofa he'd brought from Sara's apartment still looked small in the cavernous room. The shelf that contained all of her dolphin figurines took up one corner. Her books on animals and environmental science and fictional vampires crowded another shelf along the far wall, and then there were the pictures—pictures of her, of the two of them, of her with her family, and a few with Owen. There was even one with him, Sara, and both Mitchell brothers. Kellen smiled at the four of them holding up Solo cups, looking like they were drinking themselves into a stupor, but there'd been no alcohol in those cups. He fondly remembered the day they'd spent with Chad right before he headed off to boot camp. They'd gone fishing but ended up rescuing tadpoles from an evaporating puddle because Sara just couldn't stand the thought of the slimy things dying. Frogs. She'd saved frogs in cups brought for partying.

There wasn't a single reminder of her illness in the beach house. This was his shrine to her life, not to her pain or her death. He closed the door behind him and sat on the sofa. They'd spent a lot of time kissing on this sofa. They'd even made love on it a time a two. He wondered if she'd lived if she'd have grown more sexually bold with experience. Most likely he never would have discovered Shibari if she hadn't died, but they would have had a lifetime to discover what sexual acts thrilled them. He also wondered if he'd have a lifetime to discover such things with Dawn, or if she'd eventually figure out that he wasn't worth the headache and split.

He sat in the silence, listening for sounds of Sara's laughter, but heard only the repetitive call of a distant gull.

Maybe she wasn't here for him anymore. Maybe she was really gone.

Deciding that the room wasn't going to dust itself, he went to the utility closet for cleaning supplies.

A knock on the door drew Kellen from the closet. It had to be Dawn, and he should probably be angry with her for meddling in his private time with memories of Sara, but he felt oddly relieved. He could spend the day at her rental instead of his place. Being anywhere else might just lift the oppressive burden that had settled in his chest. He opened the door, and Dawn's sunny smile lifted the storm clouds from his thoughts.

"Well, hello, handsome. I'm staying in the house next door and thought I should come over and introduce myself. See if there's anything you might need."

He lifted a puzzled eyebrow, but played along. "Very neighborly of you. I'm Kellen," he said, "and you would be?"

She pressed her beautiful hand to her equally beguiling chest. "I'm Dawn." She peeked around his shoulder. "I was hoping you'd introduce me to the lady of the house."

His heart produced an irregular thud. "I'm sorry, but she passed away many years ago."

"Are you sure? I think I see her in every nook and cranny."

Dawn, smart woman that she was, was entirely correct. Sara was there. She was everywhere.

"Come in," he said, stepping aside.

Dawn entered Sara's house and immediately moved to the photographs that had been arranged in brightly colored frames along one wall. Kellen followed her, his chest tight and his lips pressed together. He imagined that this was what it felt like to introduce the woman you loved to your family. He wouldn't know, as his grandfather and estranged father had died before he'd met Sara and he didn't speak to his mom, but the feeling had to be similar. He so wanted Dawn to like Sara—weird as that sounded—and he wanted Sara to accept Dawn.

I'm all sorts of fucked up in the head.

"So *this* is Sara," Dawn said. "She's very pretty. And you're right, she does look like Lindsey."

She slipped her hand into his and squeezed. Was her palm the sweaty one or did that dampness belong to him?

"It's uncanny, isn't it?"

"I totally get why being around Lindsey was freaking you out. So tell me about the days captured in these photographs."

At her invitation, he went on a long and probably boring spiel about their various adventures: kayaking the Rio Grande in Big Bend, picnicking at Mount Bonnell overlooking the Colorado River, hiking through Arbor Hills, swimming through the waterfall in Hamilton Pool, and their road trip through the desert when Sara got it into her head to take a picture of every species of cactus in Texas—all one hundred of them. He'd always loved the outdoors, and he and Sara had spent countless hours exploring the great state of Texas. Dawn laughed at his funny stories, smiled when he was nostalgic, and encouraged him to share details that were becoming embarrassingly fuzzy in his memory.

"I've never spent much time outdoors, but it looks fun. Maybe we could do things like this together." She glanced at him. "Or would that make you uncomfortable?"

"Why would it make me uncomfortable? I love the outdoors."

"Well, those are activities you shared with Sara, so I thought maybe I'd be trespassing or something."

"I did this kind of thing before I met her. And I still do this kind of thing with Owen. So, no, you wouldn't be trespassing. I'd like to show you the world—the natural part of it."

"And I'd like to show you the world—the historical cities, the rich cultures."

He grinned. "Sounds like we'll be busy."

She stared at him for an extended moment, as if she were seeing their future together. When she smiled, he figured she liked what she saw.

She turned to the next picture on the wall—him and Sara on one jet ski and Owen on another, riding solo. "Where's this?"

"Uh, that's Lake Travis in Austin."

"Did you two hang out with Owen often?" She angled her face toward him, and he rubbed the back of his neck.

"Actually, no. I'm singularly focused when I'm involved with a woman. I'm kind of a dick to him, to tell the truth."

"I noticed that," Dawn said. "I thought maybe you were always a dick to him and just didn't realize it."

"I have this very strange inability to focus my attention on more than one person at a time."

"I'm a bit like that myself. But it is possible to date one person and have a brilliant friendship with another."

He grinned. "I'll have to try that sometime."

"And who is this handsome guy?" Dawn said, her attention on the fishing trip photo.

Sara was plastered to Kellen's side, a net in one hand and a Solo cup holding tadpoles in the other. The two of them were smiling like idiots. Chad had an arm around Owen's shoulders as they posed for Jodie, who'd been volunteered to take a group picture of them. They probably should have found a stranger to take the shot so Chad's girlfriend could have been included in the picture.

"You don't see the resemblance?"

"He looks a lot like Owen," Dawn said. "A bit less pretty boy, but they definitely have the same eyes."

Kellen chuckled. Owen was somewhat of a pretty boy.

"That's Chad, Owen's older brother. He'd just joined the army and left us right after that was taken."

"Is he still serving?"

"Yeah, he's in Afghanistan. Cleaning up IEDs or something. We don't really talk about that stuff when we hear from him. He just wants to know what's going on back home."

"That makes total sense to me."

"He's supposed to be coming home soon. Owen is stoked." Kellen was pretty stoked too, but he was a little better at hiding it.

"Maybe I'll get to meet him." She glanced up at him,

expectation in her eyes. She wanted to be a deeper part of his life; he recognized that. He just hoped he could allow it before he did something totally idiotic and pushed her away.

Kellen pulled his gaze from hers and focused on the picture again. "Well, if you're not into saving tadpoles when you're supposed to be tossing back beers and landing a huge fish, I'm sure he'd be happy to have you along."

Kellen soon had her laughing about the slipperiness of tadpoles and Sara's insistence that none of them be squashed by their man-hands and using all their beer cups for her rescue mission.

"You don't have to worry about me trying to save slimy creatures," Dawn said. "I nearly catapulted myself into the Gulf when I stepped on a jellyfish."

"Sorry I missed that," he said, chuckling as he imagined her leaping into the air. "You didn't get stung, did you?"

"No, but I was traumatized just the same."

"So what do you like besides pianos and baking and being a general pain in your father's ass?"

She laughed, the corners of her eyes crinkling. "There's more to life than that?"

"Just a bit."

"I like you," she said.

He had the sudden urge to kiss her, but couldn't bring himself to do it with dozens of pictures of Sara all staring at him. "And what else?" he asked, standing up straight when he realized he'd been leaning in to steal the kiss.

"Being tied with my legs wide open and your mouth reminding my pussy what it was made for."

He felt a flush creep up his cheeks, but wasn't sure if it was due to embarrassment or undeniable arousal. Why had he insisted on coming here first? If they'd started at Dawn's place, he could already be giving her pussy another reminder. Maybe even two by now.

"What else?" he asked, hoping she'd change the subject and at the same time wishing she'd demand he take her home and then directly to her bed.

"I also like the scent of lilacs. Exploring foreign villages. The sound of rain against the roof. The tastes of cinnamon and vanilla. What do you like, Kelly?"

"The taste of you."

She bit her lip, her gaze heated as it searched his bare chest before settling on his eyes. "I'm willing when you're able."

Was he able? He caught sight of Sara's bright blue eyes in a nearby photo and decided not quite yet. The true test of letting her go would be fucking Dawn in the bed he'd once shared with Sara, and he wasn't sure if he'd take that step this weekend or in the future or ever. But he could fuck Dawn in her own bed, and he would even allow himself to enjoy it.

"We'll go back to your place soon." He nodded toward Sara's collection of figurines. "Sara also had a thing for dolphins."

Dawn's sigh made him squeeze his eyes shut. He sorely hated to disappoint her and wondered how many times she'd put up with disappointment before she told him to get lost.

"Did you buy all of these dolphins for her?" There were at least fifty of them in the collection, ranging from a tiny silver earring to a large crystal sculpture.

"Just a few."

Dawn listened carefully as he told her about each piece he'd bought, where he'd gotten it, how Sara had reacted to it. He had no idea how the poor woman could stomach his dull, one-sided conversation, but she took it in like an eager student trying to memorize information for a midterm. Dawn couldn't possibly give a fig about how happy Sara had been on their first Christmas together when she'd opened the jewelry box shaped like a dolphin and found an engagement ring inside. In fact, he was pretty sure Dawn wanted to fling the pretty box with the mother of pearl inlay out the nearest window. That was what he would want to do if he were in her position, but she merely smiled at him.

"Very romantic of you," she said. "I figured you were more the grand gesture type."

"Is that what you're expecting when a man proposes to you?" Not that he was planning on proposing any time soon, but her answer would reveal a lot about her, and he might need that information at a much later date.

"I'll probably be the one to do the proposing," she said. "I'm not a patient woman."

He snorted. "You're infinitely patient, Dawn. I don't know how you can stomach listening to all my stories about Sara."

"I want to understand her so I can understand you better."

"Why?"

"Because you're worth getting to know, and that makes her worth getting to know."

She pointed at the wooden sculpture of a dolphin in the center of the top shelf. The teak had gathered dust, so it lacked the usual shine that accented the dark and light grain of the wood to perfection.

"What's the story behind that one?"

"Her father gave her that when she graduated from high school." He grinned. "Well, that and a car."

"My father bought me a car when I graduated as well."

"Was it a Prius?"

She flushed from the roots of her lovely red hair to the hint of cleavage at the open neck of her button-down shirt. He wondered if she also flushed in the places he couldn't see.

"Uh, no. A Mercedes."

He laughed. "I should have known."

"I shouldn't have accepted it, but it was so lovely." She sighed as if enraptured.

"Why shouldn't you accept his gifts? Your father has the means to give you nice things. You shouldn't feel guilty about taking them."

"I suppose not, but he isn't the type who gives gifts without expectations. He uses them to pressure me into doing his bidding. He said that if I didn't go to the University of Pennsylvania and major in business, he wasn't going to pay my tuition and would take the car away."

"So how did you end up at Curtis?"

She laughed. "That's simple. I was good enough and it was free. Everyone who gets in automatically gets a full scholarship, so it didn't matter that Daddy wasn't paying my tuition. I earned it myself."

"And the car?"

"He let me keep it when I wiped out on some girl's bike and he got a call from the hospital."

"Did you wipe out on purpose?"

She laughed and shook her head. "Now wouldn't that have been fabulous if I had? But no. I'm sort of all legs, and my brain can't seem to keep them coordinated."

He had noticed how long and sexy her legs were, but had witnessed no signs of clumsiness. "I would never have guessed. When you walked in those heels of yours at the bar in New Orleans, I was the one tripping over myself."

"Walking in heels took years of practice to perfect. I'm still working on the riding a bike thing."

As far as he was concerned, walking in heels suited her far better than riding a bike, but then he was partial to those long legs of hers. Dawn held his gaze for a moment and then turned toward the case overflowing with Sara's books. Damn if the back of her looked as spectacular as the front.

"Are these all hers?"

Kellen pulled his appreciative gaze from the curve of Dawn's ass and turned it to the batch of books that had never interested him in the slightest. "Yes. She insisted on keeping up with her major even after she graduated."

"So what did she do? As a career? Something with animals?" Dawn scanned the titles on multicolored book spines. "Or the environment?"

"She'd just started working for some PhD at UT doing research on the long-term effects of the Gulf oil spill on crabs or oysters or something when I found that lump in her breast."

Dawn's head swiveled in his direction. Her eyes were wide with surprise. "*You* found the lump?"

"We used to joke around that if I'd been less of a gentleman and felt her up sooner, I might have saved her life."

Dawn's brow crumpled. "That's an awful responsibility to place on yourself."

It was. He hadn't really ever thought of it that way. And Sara had been so distraught about her diagnosis that she probably hadn't considered how it had made Kellen feel to think he might have saved her if he'd been more diligent.

"Do you mind if I ask about her illness?" Dawn asked. "I know you don't like to dwell on it, and I won't blame you if you don't want to discuss it, but I'm curious."

"You can ask," he said. "I don't have to answer."

"How long did she suffer?"

He bit his lip, a huge lump forming in his throat. That had been the worst of it. Sara *had* suffered, and though she'd fought to live, she'd lost her battle, so the suffering had been for nothing.

"I . . ." He swallowed. He'd lost his ability to speak.

"Forget I asked," Dawn said, squeezing his hand. "What else happy can you tell me about her?"

Kellen was already getting tired of talking about Sara. He turned and bumped his shin on a chair next to the bookshelf, trying not to dwell on the memory of pulling the thing out of someone's roadside trash heap at Sara's insistence, stuffing it into the trunk of his Firebird, and later helping her reupholster the hideous burnt-orange monstrosity. It wasn't even a comfortable chair, but it was a recycled chair, so Sara had loved it.

"Let's go for a walk on the beach before it gets dark," he said as he stepped around the chair.

"It won't get dark for hours," Dawn said with a smile.

"I'm expecting I'll need an exceptionally long walk to clear my head. Don't you like to walk on the beach?"

"I love to, but I want to ask something of you first, and I won't take no for answer."

He loved the spark of mischief in her eyes almost as much as the challenge she presented.

"What?"

"Kiss me."

"Every five steps up the beach," he promised, walking backward toward the door and urging her forward by the hand he still held. "And every three steps back."

"Okay, but that's not my request."

She was so wonderful to him, so caring and understanding and patient—how could he refuse her anything?

"Kiss me right here. In Sara's living room."

He could refuse her after all. "No."

She tugged her hand free of his and turned back to the room. He'd almost had her to the door. Almost.

"Then tell me more about her," she said. "Is this her furniture? I wouldn't think it was your taste, but maybe I'm wrong."

"It's hers," he said.

"Did you get rid of anything that belonged to her? If I go upstairs will her clothes be in the closet? Her slippers by the bed? Her toothbrush near the sink?"

How could Dawn know that? Did she know he still had a

coffee cup—Sara's lipstick on the edge—that he refused to wash?

He rested his hands on his hips and stared her down. "What's your point?"

"You aren't ever going to move on at this rate," she said. "Let's go get some boxes, clear out all her stuff, and donate it to a charity. I think she'd like that idea."

"You don't know her." Kellen crossed his arms over his chest and set his jaw in a harsh line. "I'm not getting rid of her belongings. They're all I have left of her."

"You're wrong. You have memories of her. Lots of good memories. You just shared many of them with me."

"They're fading already," he said. "Seeing her things reminds me of them."

Dawn lifted a hand to touch him, but he stepped back. She closed her hand into a fist and pressed it over her heart.

"She wouldn't want this for you, Kelly. Not if she truly loved you. She would want you to be happy. She would want you to kiss a sexy redhead when she asks you to."

Dawn struck what he assumed she thought was a sexy pose and gave him a heated look. He snorted on a laugh.

"Sara was the most jealous woman I've ever met. The truth is, I never found it difficult to maintain friendships while dating women before her, but she insisted I spend all my free time with her and if I didn't, she'd call to check up on me. She was convinced that I'd find someone new."

"So not all of your memories with Sara are happy," Dawn said.

"Of course not, but the happy ones are the only ones I want to remember."

Dawn shook her head. "There is no way I can ever measure up to her, to all happiness all the time. Don't you get that?"

"This isn't about you."

"It *is* about me. Not all of it, clearly, but part of it is about me. I really want to be with you, Kelly, but damned if you aren't making it impossible for me."

"Then maybe this isn't going to work out."

"Do you even want it to work out?"

"I do, Dawn. More than anything."

"Prove it."

"How the hell am I supposed to do that?"

"Kiss me."

It was a simple request, really, though it felt like a monumental task. But maybe, just maybe . . .

He crushed her against him, a hand fisting in her hair—for what, to punish her for pushing him where he knew he needed to go?—and ground his mouth against hers. The lust that slammed into his groin and heated his blood was no surprise, but the emotion that clogged his throat and tried to choke him caught him off guard. Pressure built behind his eyes, forcing up tears so rapidly that they fell before he could shove them back behind the wall he'd built as their dam long ago.

A sob ripped from him, breaking against Dawn's soft lips, pulling her under with him as her tears mingled with his.

"It's okay," she whispered between tender kisses. "It's okay, Kelly."

It didn't feel okay; for chrissakes, he was shaking all over and showing his weakness to the one person he wanted to see him as strong. Dawn had broken him. Was she happy now? He'd been holding it together for so long—*so long*—and with one stupid kiss, she'd completely shattered him. But she felt so good—*so good*—in his arms, her softness against his chest, her encouraging whispers in his ear, her sweet scent surrounding him. She was his strength, his salvation. And he feared he was still in love with another woman when the one he wanted to love, the one he needed to love, was right there in his arms.

CHAPTER SIX

DAWN HATED that Kelly looked so embarrassed as he pulled away and wiped away his tears with both hands. He couldn't even bring himself to look at her as he pulled in a deep breath and then tore open the front door and rushed out to stand on the deck. Eyes closed, he tilted his face toward the sun and basked in its warm, golden rays.

She wondered if they could recover from this—this line they'd crossed. That *she'd* crossed. She hadn't expected him to actually break down, but was glad he had. Not because she enjoyed watching him suffer, but because he needed to fall apart—really fall apart—before he could start to put himself back together. And if her persistence to push him forward ultimately tore them apart, she knew she'd mourn what could have been, but maybe he'd finally be able to move on with some other lucky woman. Not that she was giving up on him. She'd never met a man who could love as deeply as this man loved, be as committed as this man committed himself, and she'd be a fool to let him get away. She just hoped that he could love her and be as committed to her as he had been—still was—to Sara.

Dawn followed him outside. The wind caught the door and its slam made his body stiffen, but he turned. Maybe to see if she was still there. She was and always would be, if he'd let her.

"Sorry about that," he said, the breathless hitch in his voice twisting the ache in her chest. "I usually suffer my emotional breakdowns in private."

"You've cried over losing her before, haven't you?" If he'd kept that all bottled up inside him for five years, it was a wonder he was still standing.

His nod was barely perceptible. "Not while anyone was watching."

She grinned crookedly, hoping to loosen the tension between them, because it was unbearable after the fun, carefree day they'd spent together in the car. "I felt it more than watched it."

"Oh." He raked a hand through his long hair, the shiny ebony strands catching the sunshine. "I didn't squeeze you too tight, did I?"

She shook her head. "You could never squeeze me too tight."

"Can we go?" He nodded toward the beach. "I could really use that walk."

"You want me to come with you?" Maybe that shouldn't surprise her, but after witnessing his reaction to her pushing, she'd been certain he'd be shoving her away.

"Only if you'll hold my hand."

She bit her lip at the sudden rush of emotion that caught her off guard and left her breathless. "I'll hold on tight," she promised.

His smile suggested he understood the subtext behind her promise. And again he didn't shove her away. In fact, when he reached for her hand and took it in his, he tugged her to stand so close beside him that her bare arm touched his and that now familiar flutter of excitement set her trembling.

"Thanks for being a pain in my ass," he said.

Her mouth dropped open in surprise, and then she laughed. "Any time."

The wooden steps from the deck to the ground were wide enough for two, but they had to separate as they scrambled over a weedy sand dune to get to the beach on the other side. A balmy breeze tossed her hair into a tangled mass and coated her bare skin with a light mist of briny water. The beach was mostly empty along this particular stretch of high-end homes, but in the distance people were flying colorful kites and relaxing in the sand. Kellen lifted Dawn over the icky row of black seaweed on the edge of the surf and set her down in ankle-deep waves. She found the action incredibly gallant.

When she smiled up at him, he said, "I guess I should have asked if you like to walk the beach with the waves washing over your feet or—"

She touched his lips with her fingertips to cut him off. "I like to walk the beach with *you*."

The where, the when, even the why didn't matter. Just the who.

This time when his mouth claimed hers, there was no turmoil behind the brush of his lips, only passion. He drew away much too quickly, took her hand, and started up the beach, the bath-warm waves lapping against their ankles and calves.

They'd gone all of five steps when he turned to her, cupped her face in both hands, and kissed her. Her eyes drifted shut as his lips lingered, and then he drew away, tugging her into motion again. She'd scarcely gotten her legs to move properly when he stopped once more and kissed her again. Thinking this was the best beach walk she'd ever been on, she allowed her hands to drift to his bare back, curling into the hard muscle she found there to draw him closer. Before she'd had her fill, he drew away and resumed strolling. She opened her mouth to question what he was doing, but he kissed her again, and she decided they weren't going to get much talking done on their walk and that was fine by her.

"Every five steps," he whispered against her lips before starting up the beach again. True to his word, after five steps she was in his arms again, being kissed into a mindless oblivion of sensation and connection.

"At this rate, this is going to be a very long walk," she said when he tugged her forward another five paces and kissed her again.

She deepened this kiss, her tongue caressing his lip, and he groaned. His hand slid down to cup her ass and drew her against him. The unmistakable hard ridge in his shorts sent curls of desire twisting inside her.

"Or a very short one," he said, nipping her lip, her jaw, the tender spot beneath her ear.

He squeezed her ass, and she whimpered, so glad that he'd slipped out of his earlier funk over Sara. She wasn't going to ask what had changed. She sure as hell didn't want to bring up the subject again and ruin their enchanting moments in the surf.

"Let's go back to your place," he said, "before we scandalize that group of elderly ladies."

Dawn shifted her gaze to the beach walkers passing them as they followed the curving ridge of collected seaweed. The women didn't look scandalized at all. Every one shared a knowing smile with her when their eyes briefly met. Dawn was more concerned about their influence on the preteen boys gawking at them from beneath a shady fabric gazebo near the dunes. Had it been a weekday, they'd have likely had the beach all to themselves and been able to make out without an audience. Perhaps tonight, after the sun set, they would do just that.

"Let's walk a bit farther," she said. "It's such a nice day." And she was enjoying the foreplay.

"If we continue, I'm not sure I'll make it back."

He shifted his hips slightly, rubbing his arousal against her. She was equally aroused, but she had the advantage of being able to hide that fact.

"You don't have to kiss me every five steps," she said, doubling down on this little stop by stealing another kiss from his gorgeous lips. When she drew away, she opened her eyes and met his stare.

Those dark eyes of his made her heart thud with excitement. He was looking at her now the way he looked at her when she was naked and bound and begging him to take her.

"Yes, I do," he said, his voice low and husky. It caressed her deep inside where she ached for his hardness.

"I know you have an issue with breaking promises—"

"That's not why I have to kiss you," he interrupted. "I thought you couldn't be any more gorgeous than you are by candlelight, but the sunshine makes your hair glow like fire, the green in your eyes brighten, and those sexy as fuck freckles of yours pepper your skin."

Damn, she hated her freckles, but she liked that he referred to them as sexy as fuck.

He leaned close to her ear and whispered, "I can't wait to get you naked, to rediscover every freckle on your body."

Yes, please. She'd like some of that.

"Every wave that washes over my feet reminds me of the slow, sensual rhythm that drives us both and demands I take you to its steady cadence."

And she'd really like some of that.

"Oh wow." She blew out a weary sigh and reached her arms high over her head in an exaggerated stretch. "I'm beat from all this walking. I should probably head home for an afternoon nap."

He chuckled. "You read my mind."

"Darn." She pouted at him. "I hoped you had something a

bit more invigorating on your mind than a nap."

He laughed again. "You have no idea how invigorating my naptime can be."

"Please tell me I'm about to find out."

She squealed in surprise when he scooped her up into his arms and headed back the short distance to the beach house. As promised, he paused every three steps on the return trip to kiss her, but these weren't the toe-curling, leisurely smooches of before. These were hurried pecks so that his kisses wouldn't hinder their progress.

She couldn't wait to be alone, without beach-goers or even the ghost of Sara between them.

He didn't glance at Sara's house as they passed the large, sunny yellow structure. His attention was on Dawn and getting to the blue rental next door as quickly as he could traverse the powdery sand of the dune. It tugged mercilessly at his bare feet, slowing him down.

"Damned sand."

"I can walk," she said, drawing her fingers through the long silky strands of his hair, though she rather enjoyed how feminine he made her feel. She was tall for a woman and had never been as light as air. Not many men could lift her, much less carry her.

He didn't set her down until he reached the steps, and when her feet touched the ground, she turned and bolted up the stairs as fast as she could move. She wouldn't be stopping every three steps for a little kiss; she wanted so much more of him than that. He was laughing as he chased her. The rich happy sound spread through her, reminding her how joyful he could be when his mind was free of troubles. The man was an expert at compartmentalizing.

Glad she hadn't bothered to lock the door when she'd gone next door earlier, she bolted inside the house and was surprised to find herself caught in Kellen's arms as he bumped into her from behind. He was faster than she'd estimated. She hadn't even had time to shed her clothes in the hopes of tempting him to get right down to business.

He seemed to be of the same mind as he kicked the door shut. His mouth was on her neck, one hand on her breast, the other hiking up her skirt until he found . . . yes.

"I want you," he said near her ear. "I know I shouldn't, but

I can't help myself."

She stifled her words, knowing that if she said what was on her mind—why shouldn't you want me?—that they'd end up talking, most likely about Sara, and she did not want to squelch the passion that burned so brightly between them when they allowed it.

"Then take me." She reached behind her, her hand easily finding his hard length. He gasped, and when she wasted no time freeing him from his shorts, her name shuddered out from between his lips. "Take me right here."

His groan of torment made her core pulse with need, and yet as turned on as she was, she was after something much deeper than his cock inside her. She stifled a moan of disappointment when he didn't yank her panties off and bury himself deep. Control. The man had way too much control. He walked farther into the house, his arms tight around her, carrying most of her weight since her feet were barely on the floor. He headed for her piano. God, she hoped he didn't request that she play right now. Was it too damned much to ask that he give up a shred of that control and fuck her when she needed to be fucked?

He flattened her palms on the closed lid of the piano and leaned over her, his weight bending her over the smooth surface. "Don't move," he said, his voice a low, tortured growl rising from deep in his chest.

Her breath caught when his hands moved under her skirt and tugged her panties down her thighs. His fingers brushed the wetness between her swollen lips. She lifted a hand from the piano to reach behind her—wanting to touch him as much as she wanted him to continue touching her.

"You can't move, Dawn, or I'll need to tie you."

She returned her palm to the lid of the piano, and before she could ponder the meaning behind his words, he was inside her. His deep thrusts were oh so slow. Oh so exquisite. Perfectly in sync with the lapping waves outside. His hands moved from her hips to rest on the piano on either side of her. Their only connections were where their bodies were joined and in the sensual rhythm that drove them both.

"Why do you torment me?" His breath ticked the back of her shoulder, and she wasn't sure if he was referring to her or to

Sara. "Why does everything you do turn me on? Why do I resent my feelings for her so much when I'm with you?"

She didn't dare answer his questions. He was lost in her and in himself. And was finally, *finally*, making love to her without having to tie her. This was an important step. She wasn't sure if it was a huge step for him or a tiny one, but they were moving in the right direction. Maybe someday he'd let her make love to him or better yet, they'd make love together, but this time she let him have his way and held still because, frankly, he was good at this and if she shut off her thoughts and just let herself feel him, he awakened her body and heightened her senses to a pinnacle she'd never reached with any other man.

"You feel so good," he whispered.

She nodded, concentrating hard on not rocking back to drive him deeper. She wanted him to feel comfortable—safe about taking her without ropes forcing her cooperation—but damn it was a challenge to hold still when every instinct told her to meet his strokes.

His steady, deep thrusts took her up, up, up. She bit her lip, trying to hold back moans of pleasure, but it was futile. The rhythm was driving her closer to the edge. If he would just . . . oh . . .

She was so far beyond her usual point of release that she was afraid to let go. If he'd give her clit the attention he usually showed it, she could come and be done with it. Hell, if he squeezed her nipple at this point, she'd likely explode. But no. The same deep and slow rhythm continued to drag her higher and higher. She needed release so bad that her pussy ached from being so swollen, so thoroughly fucked.

"I can't take much more," she said.

"You will."

She would, because his possession felt fucking amazing, but she really couldn't take more. *Oh God, please, just let me come.* She hadn't realized she'd begged out loud until he chuckled. Her whole body was so sensitive, his laughter sounded cruel.

"I could let you come. Your clit must be driving you insane, because your pussy is unbelievably swollen and tight right now. You have no idea how good it feels to fuck you when you're this turned on."

She had some idea. She squirmed, and even that slight

change in contact had her gasping for air. Her hips began to rock on their own. She dug her fingers into the lid of the piano, trying to halt her mindless need to urge him into a faster pace, but once she started moving, she couldn't stop. He met her strokes— faster, faster—and each time they came together, his cock bumped into her cervix, sending waves of pleasure deeper than he'd ever reached. A scream tore from her as everything inside her tightened to an unbearable degree and then exploded in mind-blowing waves of pleasure, ripping through her entire body. Hell, she felt her orgasm in her hair follicles and the soles of her feet. Every muscle was quivering, every pleasure sensor ignited. She was scarcely aware of Kellen's encouraging words as he continued to pound into her, drawing her orgasm out as long as possible.

"That's it, baby, come. Give me all of it." His breath caught, and he grabbed her hips to still her motion, but her mindless rocking couldn't be stopped. "Shit," he groaned, his fingers digging hard into her flesh. "Don't move or I'm going to—"

She smiled in satisfaction when he gave up a piece of his control and came inside her. The insides of her thighs were drenched with his cum and hers when he finally collapsed onto her back, breathing so hard she feared his lungs might explode.

"I meant to stop," he said breathlessly.

She knew it was one of his promises to Sara—to never come inside a woman—and Dawn was sure he'd become all moody and morose over what he'd think was a betrayal and a mistake, but for Dawn, the cum trickling down her thigh was a victory and she savored it.

"I'm glad you didn't," she said.

He laughed and snuggled his face into her back. "Me too. That was amazing."

Happiness bubbled through her, and her smile spread so wide, her eyes watered. She blinked back tears, figuring he'd mistake her crying after sex as something negative.

"I just wanted to tide you over until I could tie you properly."

Being slowly tied up—with all the treasuring intention she knew he'd show—was precisely what she needed at the moment.

"Mmm," she murmured. "I'd say you did a great job of tiding us both over."

"I've never licked my own cum out of a pussy before."

Her eyes widened, and she twisted to look over her shoulder. His face wore an odd look of contemplation.

"I wonder how that tastes."

"Only one way to find out," she said breathlessly.

He grinned. "Let's go upstairs."

"Yes, sir."

Dawn no longer resented the man's unbreakable vows. As promised, he'd tied her in emotional knots on the inside and spent the next hours constructing a beautiful web of red, blue, and yellow knots on the outside. As she lay trembling in the aftermath of his sweet, satisfying torture, she could feel his knots so deep inside her that she knew she'd never be free of him.

And she was perfectly okay with that.

CHAPTER SEVEN

KELLEN LAY beside Dawn, tossing stray bits of rope lying in disarray around her off the bed. He'd managed to maintain control for quite some time, but after touching her and tasting her for hours, he'd finally allowed himself to fuck her, and the ropes he'd so carefully secured around her long beautiful legs had gotten in his way, so he'd had to cut them. A shame really—after all that work—but he thought he might die if he didn't get his dick into her at one point, so the scissors had made short work of his living sculpture, and her tight, molten pussy had been worth every snip of the rope.

After he'd exploded inside her—filled her with more of his broken promises—he'd given himself a moment to catch his breath before starting the slow, attentive process of untying each remaining knot and working the blood flow back through her muscles and joints. She was completely sated.

"Show me how to tie you now," Dawn said, reaching for a long length of red rope that had bound her arms together from wrists to shoulder not long before.

Okay, apparently she wasn't *completely* sated.

Kellen's heart rate accelerated because, yes, he wanted her to tie him. Wanted to give her control as she had gifted him with hers. But wanting something and making that desire a reality were two very different things. Once he was at her mercy, he wouldn't be able to escape even if he wanted to. He had no way of predicting how he'd react once he was bound and helpless. "It's easier if I show you how on someone else first," he said. "Maybe Owen will volunteer."

He was positive Owen would volunteer. Thinking about showing Dawn how to tie knots on Owen's hard body had parts of Kellen growing hard again.

"I can follow instructions," she said. "Show me a few knots."

He sat beside her on the bed, took a black rope in his hands, and showed her how to tie several knots. She was a fast learner, much faster than he'd been. Her fingers worked the rope like magic, and watching her manipulate the knots on her thigh, which she was using for practice, was giving him far more than the courage to try being tied. It made him want it implicitly.

"So maybe I should start with your legs," she said. "That way if I do something wrong, your hands will be free and you can correct me."

His heart was thudding so hard, he thought it might burst in his chest, and even though he'd just come inside her, his cock was rigid with anticipation. "Good idea."

"Or I could tie your wrists and ankles to the bedposts and have my way with you."

He found that idea less than inspiring. "Would you prefer I do that to you rather than take my time tying each knot in a way that treasures each inch of your body?"

"Hell no, but I'm not sure I'm patient enough to give you the full experience before I get my own relief."

"It will be worth the wait."

She smiled and rolled her eyes to the heavens. "It always is."

He allowed her to position his body as she wanted it—flat on his back with his legs slightly splayed. He already felt vulnerable. Wasn't sure why that feeling turned him on so much.

"I definitely want to feature that glorious erection you got going on there," she said. When he laughed, she added, "But the rest of you deserves attention as well. Your thighs and hips and chest and arms. Your throat and ass and back."

"You have to pick a side. You won't be able to reach it all unless I'm standing, and I don't think that's wise since I'll likely fall when I zone out."

"That zoning out is almost my favorite part."

"Almost?"

"The orgasm tops it," she said. She pinched her thumb and forefinger together. "But just barely."

"I've never had an orgasm while tied. Toshi just left me there when he tied me up. But I remember dwelling on how much I needed to come until I was able to find that zone. Then the orgasm didn't matter."

"Trust me," she said, "it matters."

She settled on focusing her creative knots on his front side.

"I'll do your back next time."

He liked the sound of that. How amazing was it that she enjoyed the art of Shibari as much as he did. If they both became masters, there was no limit to the amount of pleasure they could share.

"Now relax," she murmured, settling into a kneeling position between his feet. "It's my first time. It might take me a while."

He wriggled his toes as she settled the first knot at the sole of one foot. He directed her—*a little to the right, down*—until the knot hit his sweet spot. His toes curled under, and a sigh of pleasure erupted from him.

"Right there," she murmured, looping the end of the rope around his ankle to hold the knot in place.

Her manipulation moved the knot slightly, so it was no longer centered over a pleasure point, but she patiently redid her work until it was perfect. She bent his knee into position and formed a crisscrossing suspension pattern between his shin and thigh. Her hands were like soft magic against his skin; the rope gave more solid, focused sensations wherever it tightened. He was painfully aware of how hard he was and how neglected his cock felt as she centered all her attention on his left leg. When she was satisfied with her work, she looked to him for approval.

"Does that feel okay?"

"Feels great." His hand moved to his cock of its own accord. "Everything about you turns me on. Did you know that?"

She lifted a brow at him. "*Everything* about me?"

"At the moment? Yes, everything."

"I was going to do your other leg next, but if you're going to cheat and touch yourself, I should probably work on your arms."

"Are you sure this is cheating?" He pulled his hand up and down his length slowly, shuddering as the intensity of his pleasure overwhelmed him.

"Definitely cheating." She leaned over his lap to draw the tip of his cock into her hot, wet mouth.

His back arched in bliss as she sucked him gently, and he stroked his shaft in rapid strokes. He'd be coming in seconds at this rate, and so far all she'd done was tie one leg. She released her suction with a little popping sound and covered his hand with hers to still its motion.

"That's enough cheating."

She reached for the black rope he'd been using to teach her and looped it around his wrist. With a bit of careful manipulation and his complete cooperation, she tied his hand—palm flat against his hip—so that the V formed between his thumb and forefinger was inches from his now-throbbing cock.

"This really makes me want to touch myself," he murmured, taking his cock in his unbound hand.

She pinched his nipple, which sent a jolt of unexpected pleasure through his chest. "You're cheating again."

"If you'd stop being so fucking sexy, I might be able to control myself."

"Well, *that* isn't happening," she said with a grin, "so I guess the ropes will have to keep you in line."

She tied his free hand down on the other side of his cock. The tips of his thumbs were just touching above it, but no amount of stretching would allow him to grasp his dick in his fist. She stared down at her first work of bondage.

"That's probably the sexiest thing I've ever seen in my life," she murmured, circling his cock with one hand. She lifted her chin and stared into his eyes as she stroked his length. His hands twitched, fingers curling as best they could in their helpless positions on either side of his arousal. He wanted nothing more than to cover her hands and make her jerk him off with the same firm tug that Owen used. Yeah, that was what he wanted right now, a strong grip yanking him quickly to orgasm. Dawn's slow, gentle touch was driving him insane.

"Harder," he said, his voice harsh and strained as he tried to twist his body with one leg tied, and attempted rather gracelessly to thrust into her hand.

"You need to give yourself over to me," she said. "Allow me and the ropes to provide all of your pleasure."

She was right, but he struggled with the idea of relinquishing control and wasn't sure why. He'd struggled with giving up control the first several times Toshi had tied him, and those experiences hadn't had the added sexual component. All the arousal Kellen had felt with the Shibari master had been in his head. Kellen's homoerotic fantasies of Toshi tying him and making him entirely helpless so he could fuck him had never come to fruition because the Shibari master had never wanted him in a sexual capacity. Toshi would never have used bondage to force anyone into doing something they didn't want. But if Kellen had been fantasizing about being forced, it wasn't truly rape. Or was it? There was a fuzzy gray line there, but it didn't matter because his teacher had never crossed it.

Kellen, however, had come dangerously close to crossing that line when he had Owen tied and at his mercy.

Kellen shook his head, rejecting mental images of his friend tied and helpless, reminding himself that he was now the one in that position. He needed to calm the fire within himself quickly and focus on the moment, not on past experiences left unfulfilled. A woman had never tied him before, and he planned to enjoy every minute of her experimentation.

If he could just manage to get out of his own head and his own way, he was sure the experience would be far more enjoyable and exciting than being dominated by a man. He wasn't even attracted to men. Not usually.

Kellen closed his eyes and shut off his mind, concentrating on sensation instead of unattainable fantasies. Dawn's gentle touch was beguilingly pleasurable. The ropes around his wrists and waist, shin and thigh, and especially the knot against his instep delighted his nerve endings. A moan escaped his throat as he stopped fighting and started feeling.

"That's better," Dawn murmured. Her breath warmed the head of his cock just before she took it into the satiny recesses of her mouth.

He couldn't help but rub the foot of his unbound leg against the tangled sheets as she stroked and sucked him. It was the one appendage not at her mercy, the one part of him that he had some control over, that and his neck he realized as he tossed his head back and forth, some stupid part of him still fighting for control.

Without a word, Dawn released his cock, giving the opening at its tip a gentle probe with her tongue before reaching for another rope. She shifted position to work on his free leg, tying it the same way she'd tied the other one. He found his ankles tied together and his knees slightly bent, the angle supported by the suspending lengths of rope. If he pushed his knees closer together, he did have quite a bit of give in the ropes, but doing so tugged at his ankles painfully, so he went still and allowed the ropes to support him. He felt almost weightless. If not for the bed at his back, he could have been floating.

"Not bad at all for your first piece of work," he said to Dawn.

She ignored his compliment and took a thin length of plastic twine into her hands. "I hope you're feeling kinky," she said with what he could only take as an evil grin.

For a moment, his trust faltered. He was helpless; she could do anything to him. But then he decided he was willing to take whatever she dished out, so he said, "Do your worst, baby."

She tied several small knots in one end of the stretchy twine, each about an inch apart. When she finished, she pressed the end-most knot into the underside of the base of his cock. Stretching the knotted twine up the bottom of his shaft, she positioned each knot along the ridge there until she reached the rim of his head, and then she began to wrap his cock with twine to hold those devastating knots in place. Fascinated, he watched as his entire cock was encased within the stretchy black cord until nothing but the head was visible. The tightness of her handiwork had him gasping for air. And those knots? They felt so good, they almost hurt. When she reached the base of his cock with the coiling twine and secured it in place, she met his eyes.

"I hope you're feeling *exceptionally* kinky," she said.

Kinkier than having his cock encased in twine?

When she threaded three large beads onto the free end of her cord, he bit his lip. He'd bought those beads and the twine for her, but hadn't gotten around to using them because he wanted his cock, rather than any object, inside her. He had a suspicion about where she was going to put those beads, but maybe he was giving her kink too much credit.

The cord tightened against his balls, separating them to either side of the soft and pliable twine. He gasped at the added sensation, paralyzed with pleasure; his thoughts scattered and were no longer coherent. He then felt something hard and smooth against his ass, and if he hadn't been tied, he'd likely have sprung off the bed.

"Easy," she said. "We haven't gotten to the kinky part yet."

What?

A bead pressed against his never-before-penetrated asshole, and with a little manipulation and persistence, she used two fingertips to work it inside him.

It was official. Dawn O'Reilly was far kinkier than he had ever aspired to be.

"Wait." He gasped brokenly as she pushed a second bead inside him.

"One more," she whispered, rubbing the third bead around his hole.

God, he wanted it.

"Okay," he said.

When she popped it into his ass, his entire body jolted and began to quiver uncontrollably. He could feel the beads inside him, foreign and invasive. Dawn pressed a hand against the underside of his cock, which tightened the rope to rub against the seam of his balls and simultaneously tug at the beads in his ass. One almost popped free—almost—but she shifted his cock down and his body tugged it right back inside.

"Fuck me," he swore as pleasure sensors he never knew existed ignited. He was pretty sure he was coming, but the binding wrapped around his overstimulated cock wouldn't allow him to erupt.

"I'm not sure this next part will work," she said, "but I'm going to try."

There was more? How could there possibly be more?

Gasping and caught in an endless orgasm, Kellen tried to puzzle through Dawn's drenching his encased cock with lube. Then she straddled him, taking a moment to find places for her legs among his bound appendages and the ropes. With a hand between their bodies, she took his now slippery, still-tied cock into her hand and pressed it into her hot pussy. If he hadn't been coming before, he was definitely coming now. Due to the ropes, she was forced to lean forward until their bellies touched as she rode him. That position happened to stretch taut the rope tying his cock to his ass. Each motion of her body threatened to pop a bead free, but it held and held and held. Fuck. Fuck. Fuck! Was it possible to die from pleasure?

"Oh. Oh yes," Dawn cried, riding him faster, harder. "This feels amazing."

He'd have agreed if he could remember how to speak.

He wasn't even sure what she was doing any longer. He could only concentrate on physical sensation. Most of it was pleasure, but some pain, a bit of friction and tugging and release and being held back from that same release. And God he was hot and shaking and had the shivers and goosebumps. Every muscle in his body was tight. His mind was free of all thought. And . . . fuck, he was surely dying.

He wasn't sure when she finished, but suddenly she wasn't on top of him any longer. The beads in his ass were yanked free, each releasing a burst of ecstasy. Kellen cried out as he came again, or had he ever stopped coming? The tightness around his cock loosened, and then a firm hand circled his bare cock and tugged and tugged and tugged, pulling every drop of cum from his body. Finally, relief. Blessed release. And it had never felt so good in his life.

He didn't even realize words were erupting from his mouth until the hand went still and Dawn said, "*Owen?*" She slapped him hard on his belly. "Did you *really* just call his name?"

What?

CHAPTER EIGHT

WHILE DAWN HAD BEEN orchestrating one of the most exhilarating and liberating sexual experiences of her rather sheltered life, her partner had been fantasizing about another person. A man! Now wasn't that just perfect? She should have known things were going too well between her and Kellen. She was pretty sure he was on the right track with moving past Sara, but instead of focusing his newly freed devotion on Dawn, he'd instead diverted it to Owen.

"I didn't really call Owen's name, did I?" Kellen said in a voice so low and quiet, she scarcely heard him over the roar of the blood rushing through her head.

"Yeah. Several times." She repeated his words, now likely scored into her memory for the rest of her life. "Oh yes, Owen. Make me come. Owen. Owen!"

He burst out laughing, and she wasn't sure if it was a nervous reaction or if he actually thought it was funny to call his best friend's name while she'd been stroking his cock. Hell, she'd been concerned that his angry-looking dick wouldn't survive the force of his ejaculation, and he hadn't even been thinking about the person actually responsible for that orgasm.

"That's just perfect," he muttered when his laughter died down.

"Is there something you want to tell me?" she said, sinking down beside him on the bed. She considered running off and leaving him to waste away tied up on her bed, but she liked this guy. Really liked him. And if he was secretly having an affair with a man, she'd be devastated. She silently prayed that there was another reason behind his slipup. In the throes of ecstasy she'd once called her lover by her long-time crush's name, not because she'd actually wanted to be with Pierre but because she'd been fantasizing about him while her bore-in-the-sack boyfriend was making love to her.

Oh shit.

"Are you and Owen lovers?"

"Of course not," he said.

"Of course not? That's your response?"

He released a forlorn sigh. "Untie me, and I'll explain."

"Explain and then I'll untie you." She figured if she untied him, he'd rush off and she'd never get a decent answer out of him.

"I think I'm mixed up because I've only ever been tied up by one person. And it happened to be a man."

"Owen tied you up?" He'd already told her about Toshi, the man who'd taught him Shibari, but then that would mean two different men had tied him, so that didn't make sense. But he'd clearly been thinking of Owen, not Toshi.

"No. Owen's never tied me, but I have tied him."

"Did you take advantage of him when he was defenseless?"

"No." He squeezed his eyes shut. "Maybe. I don't know. I just touched him. But we've been jacking each other off for years, so it doesn't mean anything."

Of course that meant something. Was he really that dumb or just in denial?

Dawn's tongue felt thick in her mouth. She couldn't even close her jaw. "What?"

"After Sara died, I needed relief, and sometimes Owen helped me out with a little handy. It was only fair that I helped him out too, right?"

Dawn's head was shaking, but she wasn't doing it consciously. She was so shocked by what he was saying— shocked that he didn't see the deeper issue—that her body was on autopilot. And her thoughts were in hyperdrive.

"That's not something friends do," she said.

"I know that. I've always struggled mentally with the physical part of our relationship, but it feels so good. It's the only real form of sexual release I've had until just recently." His fingers twitched, and had he been untied, she was certain he'd be reaching for her. "Please don't let this come between us. I'm not sure I can take another heartbreak."

"*I'm* not letting anything come between us," she said, her disbelief rapidly turning to rage. Was he really trying to place blame on *her* for the sudden and unexpected differences between them? She would not put up with that sort of bullshit. "You're the one fantasizing about your best friend while you're coming."

"Your grip was so solid, so firm, I guess I lost track of who was touching me."

"You are not putting any blame on me for this, Kellen Jamison. I won't let you."

He sighed but didn't drop his gaze. His eyes bored into hers until she had no choice but to believe him. To trust him.

"I don't blame you, sunshine. And I don't want to hurt you. I never want to hurt you."

"But if you want him, that will hurt me, if not now, then at some point in the future."

"I don't want him."

She could see the sincerity in his dark eyes. His honesty and frankness were two of his most appealing traits. But some part of her couldn't believe him. She didn't doubt that Kellen believed that he didn't want Owen, but greater convictions than sexual fantasies had been built upon false theories.

"Then what is it?" She rubbed a hand up her chilled arm. "I still don't understand."

He took a deep breath, his gaze shifting to the ceiling. "It's being tied. It makes me crave the touch of a man." His intense gaze met hers again, and his passion for life, for her, blazed fiercely in his eyes. "Do you think I *want* to feel that way when the most gorgeous woman in existence is giving me more pleasure than I can handle? You are amazing, Dawn. Everything about you is amazing. And I'm sorry. For everything I've ever done that has hurt you, I'm sorry."

He was sorry? What good did that do? Frustrated and more hurt than she cared to admit, she climbed from the bed and slipped her free-flowing sundress over her head. She then cut the ropes off his right wrist with the scissors and left him there to free himself. She wasn't disgusted by his fantasies; she thought they were downright sexy. But if Kellen was actually in love with Owen and simply didn't realize it, she didn't stand a chance at holding Kellen's attention. The two men had a long history of friendship and support. Hell, they basically shared a life. Being on the road together for their careers, spending all their at-home free time together, being cared for by the same family made them more like a couple than most couples in her book. The only parts of couplehood they didn't share were sex and romantic love. Or so she'd thought. They had apparently shared some sex—maybe not full out dick-in-ass gay sex, but still . . . It seemed likely that their next step was romantic love.

Not knowing how she'd even gotten outside, Dawn stirred up sand as she scrambled over the dunes to the beach. Maybe she should just drown herself; then she wouldn't have to sort through the jumble of her thoughts and emotions.

Why did the most alluring man she'd ever met have to be so fucking complicated? She kicked at the sand in her path, hoping her feet knew where to take her, because her head and her heart were obviously leading her in the wrong direction.

"Dawn!" Kellen's voice carried across the dunes. "Please. I really need to talk about this."

He needed to talk about this? Just like he needed help getting over Sara. Just like he needed to tie her up in order to fuck her. Yeah? Well, what about what *she* needed?

"Don't follow me!" she yelled, not knowing if he were even attempting to do so. She couldn't see where she was going through the unwanted tears blurring her vision. She didn't realize how close she was to the water until a warm wave washed over her bare feet.

Something squished beneath her toes, and stinging pain wrapped around her ankle and shot up her leg. She cried out and tumbled onto the beach, ripping the offensive jellyfish tentacle from her smarting flesh and tossing the vile creature back into the water. Tears of anguish mingled with those of emotional turmoil, and she wrapped her arms around her shin, wanting to coddle her wound but afraid to actually touch it.

Kellen's bare feet appeared in her line of sight. Yeah, she was so infatuated with the man that she recognized his goddamned feet.

He squatted in front of her and captured her upper arms between his hands, but she refused to look at him.

"Are you okay? Did it sting you?"

"Yeah, it stung me." Stupid jellyfish. But the squishy creature's tentacles stung a lot less than playing second fiddle to Owen for Kellen's affection. Make that third fiddle. Freaking Sara had claimed first chair.

"Hold still," he said. "I'll pee on it."

She blinked up at him. "What?"

"It'll take the sting out. I read it online."

"You are not pissing on my leg!"

"I'm just trying to help you."

His gorgeous brown eyes were filled with concern, but his expression didn't weaken her resolve.

"By peeing on me? Are you crazy?"

The corner of his mouth twitched, and within seconds they were laughing. It felt so much better to laugh with him—even if it was at her expense—than to cry over him.

"I think that's an old wives' tale anyway," he said. "Do you have any vinegar at your house?"

"I might. I'm not sure."

"Baking soda, then?"

She smiled. "You're asking me, the stress baker, if I have baking soda?"

"Good point. Can you stand?"

"It's a jellyfish sting," she said, still feeling testy, "not a broken ankle."

She pushed him aside and got to her feet, taking what she intended to be a confident step. The pain in her skin where the tentacle had wrapped around her ankle made her calf muscle seize up, so she stumbled despite her valiant effort not to look like a total wimp.

"I'll carry you."

"I don't need you to carry me," she insisted, limping several paces before she stepped on a very sharp seashell. "Ow!"

"Don't you get that this isn't about what you need, but rather what I want?"

She turned to look at him, not sure if he was referring to her proclivity for injury or if there was a deeper meaning behind his words.

"Don't look at me like that," he said, settling his hands on his hips and looking—with the sun kissing his bronze skin and the waves churning behind him—very much like the god of the ocean she'd taken him for at their first meeting

"Like what?"

"Like I can't take the criticism I have coming."

Had she been looking at him like that?

"I do get how selfish I've been acting, concentrating on what I want at the expense of your needs."

It was a rare man who would recognize such behavior in himself. In her mind, that made him worth the hassle and heartache she experienced along the way. "You have a reason to be selfish. This is hard for you."

"Dawn, stop making excuses for me. I make enough of them for myself." He rubbed a hand over his face and murmured under his breath, "I've told her to run from me how many times? And the first time she does, I immediately chase after her."

"Are you talking to yourself?"

His eyes flicked upward to meet hers. "Did I say that aloud?"

She nodded, a little smile curving her lips. "I'm glad you chased after me."

"Would you have stopped running? If the jellyfish hadn't stung you?"

Her ankle throbbed at the mention of her injury. Only a few of the jellyfish's tentacles had wrapped around her ankle. It could have been far worse.

"Did you command that creature of the deep to attack me, Neptune, so that I'd stop?"

"I'd never command one of my charges to harm you, sunshine," he said, running a knuckle down the bridge of her nose and gently flicking its tip. "Let's get you home so I can concentrate on fixing your hurts."

She smiled weakly, knowing her little physical ailments didn't cut nearly as deep as his emotional wounds. But with the right care, she believed they could heal each other.

CHAPTER NINE

KELLEN COULD NOT BELIEVE that he'd called Owen's name while he'd been coming. It was one thing to fantasize while you were getting off, quite another to blurt out your fantasy to your partner. He'd hurt Dawn. He knew he had. He could see it in the way her pretty hazel eyes never quite met his as he consulted the Internet with his phone for the proper treatment of a jellyfish sting. Several red stripes marred her trim ankle. If she hadn't already tossed that gross sea creature back into the ocean, he would have pulverized it for causing her pain. Just as he was mentally pulverizing himself for the same reason.

He flushed the reddened area of her sting with salt water— which he could have done on the beach had he known what he was doing—and then used the edge of her driver's license to scrape out stingers the jellyfish had left behind. The harsh lines on her skin were becoming welts, and though she only occasionally sucked breath through her teeth as he worked at his internet-directed first aid, they had to hurt far more than she was letting on.

"I didn't know you wore glasses," he said, grinning at how cute she looked in them in her driver's license photo.

"I don't anymore," she said. "I had Lasik done a couple of years ago. That picture is old."

"That would explain why you look about twelve years old in it." The braids on either side of her freckled face didn't make her look any more mature.

She stuck her tongue out at him, and he chuckled.

"You still look twelve when you do that."

"I feel twelve sitting up here on the counter while you put Band-Aids on my booboos."

"It says not to bandage it," he said as he slopped on the baking soda paste he'd mixed.

A relieved sigh escaped her.

"That feels much better," she said. "I don't think he got me very good."

"If I hadn't upset you, he wouldn't have gotten you at all." He looked up from the white, goopy mess on her ankle and held her gaze. "If you don't want to talk about what happened earlier, we can ignore it. I'm really good at ignoring things that bother me." At least outwardly. Inwardly, his little slip would continue to eat at him for as long as the situation remained unresolved. He had hoped not to continue to make the mistake of internalizing his troubles while he was with Dawn. He wanted an open, honest relationship with her. He longed for the feelings developing between them to flourish and to last, but he did find it easier not to put all of his thoughts out in the open. "But I don't think we want this to stand between us."

"Are . . ." She pulled her gaze from his and stared over his head. "Are you going to do anything about your attraction to him?"

His attraction to Owen was one of those things Kellen had been ignoring—and denying—for a couple of years now. He was certain that Owen was just being Owen and trying to help out his mixed-up, celibate friend with the occasional hand job, and Kellen didn't want to upset their friendship by putting his attraction—an attraction Owen did not share—out in the open. Kellen thought plenty of women were sexy, but that didn't mean he had to act on those attractions. So he didn't have to act on the strange desire he had for Owen either. Wanting someone was not the same as actively pursuing that want.

"No," he said. "You're the only person I'm going to do. I'm the most faithful man you'll ever know." He'd been faithful to Sara even years after she'd passed. Being faithful to the beautiful, delightful, sexy, and very much alive Dawn O'Reilly would be easy in comparison.

"But you'll tell him about your feelings, right?" she said. "What if he's attracted to you too?"

"It doesn't matter. Nothing of a serious romantic nature will ever progress between Owen and me. Not ever. You have my word."

She didn't look convinced.

"But if you're hung up on him, like you've been hung up on Sara, you won't be able to concentrate your full attention on me. On us. There is an us, isn't there?"

Her hopeful expression made his throat tighten. He rose from his crouched position at her feet and shifted between her splayed legs, wanting to be closer to her. He couldn't stand that there was any distance between them, physical or emotional.

"There's an us," he said. "There's definitely an us. And it's wonderful."

Her smile was a little hesitant, but she didn't resist when he leaned in and stole a passionate kiss from her soft lips.

"It's getting late," she said. "Do you want to go out for dinner or stay in?"

"Will you make me French toast?"

"I think I can handle that."

"Then I definitely want to stay in."

"I figured you'd want a corn dog from the gas station."

He curled his lip in disgust. "I'd rather eat sand."

He helped her off the counter, stealing another kiss before he let her go, and then joined her in the kitchen. He secretly wanted her recipe just in case she decided he wasn't worth the trouble and he was forced to live without her. He imagined he'd spend the rest of his life putting on the pounds as he ate her French toast and reminisced about their time together.

"What are you thinking about?" she asked as she searched her collection of homemade bread for a mold-free loaf. "I'm going to have to make some bread," she said as she discovered all loaves but one were inedible. "Unless you're taking me out for breakfast in the morning."

"I'd like to watch you bake," he said. That was his stomach talking.

"And I'd like to watch you grill. Do you barbeque?"

"I do at home."

"Which is next door," she said. "You have a grill under the deck. I saw it."

Next door. He'd almost forgotten it existed.

"We can go grocery shopping tomorrow morning. I'll grill steaks. Do you like steak?"

"I love steak."

This felt like making future plans, and he had to admit looking forward instead of backward felt good. And maybe they'd dine at Sara's house—*his* house—and he wouldn't feel like he was desecrating a shrine.

CHAPTER TEN

PULLED FROM a wonderful dream by the ring of her phone, Dawn lifted the annoying device and scowled at her caller ID. It was barely Sunday—wasn't she allowed an entire weekend off? She'd met her deadline, what more did Wes want from her? She considered not answering, but couldn't help but wonder what the movie studio thought of the song. It was probably too soon for them to have an opinion about "Blue," she told herself, still not sure if she was answering on the third ring. Maybe the fax of the music scores hadn't gone through or . . . .

"Hello," she answered.

"Hey, kiddo. Sorry to bother you at this hour, but I need you to come back to L.A. before you head to Prague on Wednesday."

"I leave for Prague on Wednesday?" That was too soon. She'd been so busy enjoying Kellen that she hadn't even practiced her program. Shit!

"Actually, you leave Tuesday night. Your performance is Wednesday."

Double shit!

"My flight is out of Houston, isn't it?" She wasn't even sure. She really needed to hire a good personal assistant. Especially now that her thoughts were muddled with great sex and magnificent company. Kellen stirred beside her, his hand reaching across the bed to rest on her bare thigh, but he didn't open his eyes. After they'd finished their French toast, he'd seemed determined to demonstrate that he'd only be calling *her* name in ecstasy from that night forward.

"Why do you need me in L.A.?"

"The movie executives listened to your song and want to meet you in person as soon as possible."

"Oh," she said flatly. They must have thousands of ideas on how to improve the score and as she was under contract, she was obligated to alter the song to suit their needs. It was the worst part about getting paid for her music, second only to those dreaded deadlines.

"They loved it, by the way. Don't sound so discouraged."

"If they loved it, why do they want to meet in person?" A movie executive had never asked to meet her in person. She'd never even met the producer or director of *Ashen Falls* until after she'd won the Grammy for the closing credits song.

"Because you're a star, sweetheart. Everyone wants to meet stars."

Dawn snorted. "Me? A star? I might be sleeping with one, but—"

Wes's bark of laughter cut her off. "When are you going to figure this out, kid? You are a star. You might not be in the spotlight, but your music is known. People will hear it and think of you and not even know who they're thinking of."

"Right. So I'm not a star."

Wes sighed so loud, she couldn't help but chuckle.

"Will you just get your ass to L.A.? I'll have Glenda rearrange your travel plans so you can make your flight to Prague on time."

"Fine," she said. "I suppose I won't be able to catch the Sole Regret show on Monday night, then."

Now it was Wes's turn to chuckle. "You really are a band groupie, aren't you?"

She stroked a long lock of silky black hair from Kellen's bronze shoulder. "Just for their guitarist."

Wes laughed again. "Good for you."

"And, Wes?"

"Yeah, kiddo?"

"You wouldn't happen to have my program for the Prague show, would you?"

"You haven't been rehearsing?"

Her face went hot. She should have been practicing for the past few weeks, but first her writer's block had interrupted her schedule and now she had much better prospects taking over her time. "Of course I have," she lied. "I just want to make sure I've been practicing the right pieces."

"I'll have Glenda email it to you in the morning."

"Probably best if I get that email tonight."

"You haven't been practicing at all, have you?"

"I'd planned to rehearse this weekend, but I've been preoccupied."

"With that guitarist."

Dawn ran a finger along Kellen's shoulder. He was definitely a preoccupation.

"Yeah."

"Is he what got you over your writer's block?"

"Yep."

"Then I won't scold you, but you'd better start practicing."

"I know every note," she said. Chopin was her favorite composer. She'd played every piece of piano music he'd ever written hundreds of times. But she could definitely use a refresher. She loved Prague and wouldn't want to disappoint her *fans*. She laughed at herself for even thinking of them that way.

"Do you still want your career divided into performances and composing? Because if you want to give up performing to concentrate on—"

"No," she blurted. She needed to perform. She needed the attentive audience and the applause. She didn't get that from composing. "Performances pay my bills." They did, but that wasn't really why she needed to perform. "I can't say the same for my composing."

"You might think differently come Monday evening. You know I'm here to guide you, whatever you decide."

Her heart thudded and began to race. "What are you saying, Wes? What's this meeting about?"

"Your future. If you so choose." Wes chuckled. "I promised not to spill the beans—what few they gave me—so I'm hanging up now."

"Wes?"

"I'll email the set list to you."

"Wes! What's the meeting about?"

"Get your fill of that guitarist," he said. "You might be too busy to see him for a while."

The phone went silent as Wes disconnected.

Thousands of thoughts swirled through her head as she waited for Wes's email. Maybe he'd offer her further clues about the upcoming meeting with the movie executives.

Movie executives? She couldn't begin to fathom why they'd want to meet with her in the first place. And what had Wes meant about her being able to choose between performances and composing? Composing took forever and the payoff was small in comparison to her performances, which took little time and had a huge payoff. If she could make a living at composing would she want to stop performing? Not entirely, but maybe she'd accept fewer invitations. And, and how could Kellen sleep at a time like this?

She grabbed a pillow and hit him in the back. He squeezed his eyelids tighter and rolled from his stomach to his side.

"Hey, sleepyhead, my agent just called. The movie executives liked the song."

"Of course they did," he mumbled. "It's a masterpiece."

"But they want to meet with me tomorrow. Why do they want to meet with me?"

"Because you're a star. Everyone wants to meet stars."

Dawn rolled her eyes. "You sound like Wes. I'm not a star. You're a star."

"I'm a flicker to your supernova."

She squeaked in surprise when his arm looped around her belly and he pulled her down onto the mattress beside him. "Come here, supernova. I've got the sudden need to be caught in your explosion."

She laughed. "Sometimes you say the corniest things."

CHAPTER ELEVEN

KELLEN WOKE to the beautiful sound of stirring piano music. He rolled onto his back and stared up at the ceiling, his gaze unfocused as he let the sound wash over him. It wasn't an original Dawn O'Reilly composition—the sequence of notes wasn't arousing enough to be hers—but she was the one playing the piano piece that filled the house with music. He'd know that tone, that skill, anywhere, even if he'd had to pick her playing out of a thousand virtuosos. He could tell it was her by the aggression of her playing, the way one note blended seamlessly into the next, and the way shivers raced down his spine each time she transitioned into a new stanza. She was a rare artist. He could have listened to her play all day or all night. The inky darkness outside gave no hint to the time, but it had to be either very late or incredibly early.

When the music ended, he took a deep breath and held it, anticipating more. Longing for more. When the first note of the next song greeted his ears, a spasm clenched his abdomen and he released a tortured gasp. Lord, what her playing did to him. He'd never been a huge fan of classical piano until Dawn.

At the end of the next song, the piano fell silent and he waited in breathless anticipation for the next to begin. When it didn't start at once, he sat up in the bed. When minutes passed and he heard nothing but the muted sounds of the crashing waves outside, he climbed from the mattress and padded to the upper landing, straining for sounds of her. He took the steps slowly, one at a time, listening. When an almost imperceptible tinkling of the piano keys greeted his ears, he paused about halfway down the stairs. He stood there for a long moment, letting the slowly building music wash over him, and when the bones went out of his legs, he sat right there on the stairs, closed his eyes, and relaxed into her sound. Rock music invigorated him, and he'd always be a fan, but this . . . this music, this sound, made him feel something deeper, something magical, some connection outside of himself.

He almost wished he wasn't currently on tour so he could follow her to Prague and watch her perform. Would it be difficult to sit among an audience who would be as enraptured by her as he was? Or would it make him proud that she'd chosen him? That he knew her. That he'd touched her, kissed her, made love to her.

When that piece ended, he heard her sigh.

"Again, Dawn," she said, as if coaching herself. She played the same piece over from the start, and if it was any different from her first run-through, his ear wasn't trained well enough to pick up any variances. She paused about halfway through a particularly rapid series of notes and played the same measures again and again before finally moving on. She was trying to improve upon perfection, he realized, when as far as he was concerned, no improvements were possible.

At the end of the piece, Dawn grumbled, "Stop thinking about him and focus, Dawn."

Kellen grinned—hoping the distraction she referred to was himself—and rose from the steps, hurrying to make it to the piano before she started playing her next piece and made him weak in the knees once more.

He paused behind her bench, and her body stiffened. He knew he hadn't made a sound as he'd crossed the tile floor barefoot, but she obviously sensed his presence since she turned.

"Did I wake you?" she asked, the low light of a nearby lamp casting gold over the deep red waves of her hair. "What am I saying? Of course I woke you, banging on the piano at four a.m. I'm sorry. Maybe you should go to your place to sleep. I really need to practice."

"I'd rather stay," he said. "If it won't disturb you."

"Disturb me? I'm the one doing the disturbing here."

He smiled. "That's not the word I'd use for what you were doing. Entertaining. Enchanting. Enrapturing. But not disturbing."

"Wes sent me my set list for Prague. I allowed them to choose which songs they wanted me to play, and of course they chose the one most challenging for me. I figured they'd just want the nocturnes and ballades. Those were written for solo piano, and I know them all by heart, but they've chosen several piano excerpts from his concertos. Not unheard of, but definitely not the norm. Apparently I approved the set list weeks ago without looking at it closely. I was in writer's-block deadline hell at the time."

"You could always tell them to change the set list."

"They've already printed the programs. I'll get it. I just need to practice. So if you want to sleep—"

He shook his head before she finished the thought. "I want to watch. Will it make you nervous?"

She grinned. "I'm the odd sort who performs better under pressure."

"Just tell me where to apply my pressure, and I'm on it."

"Pierre used to stand right behind me and stare at my hands." She produced an adorable little snort. "God, how that used to turn me on."

"This sounds like a win-win to me." He shifted to stand directly behind her, and a shudder moved through her lithe figure. If all it took to turn her on was for him to stand behind her while she played, he'd be wearing a spot through the tile behind her bench.

She stretched her fingers, scrunched them into little fists, shook out her hands, and then set her fingers on the keys. He watched her hands as she played, imagining them on his body, remembering her sure, firm grip. The music poured from her, flowed into him, and bound them together.

"There it is," she murmured, apparently pleased by whatever nuance she'd now perfected. "When I'd finally get something perfect, Pierre would touch my shoulder to let me know I'd pleased him," she said.

Kellen supposed that was his cue. He wasn't sure he liked following in her music teacher's footsteps, but she seemed to need reassurance. He lifted a hand and gently touched her shoulder. She missed a note. He actually heard that mistake.

"And when I'd make a mistake like that, he'd drag me off the piano bench and kiss me breathless."

Kellen's eyes widened. "What?"

She laughed. "If he'd really done that, I'd have been messing up on purpose."

"Were you really that into him? I mean his name was *Pierre*, for fuck's sake."

"He's a brilliant teacher, an amazing pianist, and has the sexiest French accent I've ever heard in my life." She produced an appreciate purr and returned her hands to her keyboard.

"So it was him you were thinking of earlier when you couldn't focus."

"Huh?" She peered at him over her shoulder, her fingers hovering over the keys.

"I heard you say to stop thinking about him and focus. I thought it was me—"

"It was definitely you stealing my focus. I was remembering our first time on the lid of this piano."

"Ah, so this Pierre talk is just to make me jealous?"

She lifted a brow at him. "Is it working?"

"You were a girl when you wanted him," he said, lowering his hand to cup one of her small, firm breasts. "You're very much a woman now. So, no, I'm not jealous of Pierre." Much.

Her fingers began to move on the keys again. He caught the rhythm—a stranger's rhythm—and gently massaged her nipple to keep time. After a moment she jerked her hands from the keyboard and released a shuddering sigh. "You shouldn't do that while I play my set list," she said. "If I start to equate Chopin with your touch, I'll end up embarrassing myself with a rather large puddle on my bench."

He chuckled softly, still tormenting the hardened peak at the tip of her breast. "Then maybe you should play something sexier. Something of yours."

"I need to practice," she said, but he didn't think she was saying it to him.

Her hands shifted down the keyboard to a lower register. From the first note of "Blue." he felt her. Not only the soft breast in his hand or her back brushing against his rapidly rising cock when she moved, but the embodiment of her soul rising up and reaching out from her composition. It tangled around him like an invisible rope, binding him to her in a connection he knew he'd never escape. He never wanted to escape. His hand circled her long throat, fingertips finding the rapid pulse. Could this song possibly affect her as intensely as it affected him? He was torn between the unmistakable need to possess her body, to forge a deep physical connection between them, and his unquenchable thirst to hear this melody.

Maybe there was a way he could have both.

Tugging upward on her throat and breast, he urged her to stand. He shoved the bench aside with his leg and shifted his hand from her breast to her skirt. The song sounded different without her feet operating the pedals, but it was close enough. He could still hear its usual perfection in his head. When he sank into her hot, soft center, they both gasped. She fumbled over a few notes, but soon found enough focus to continue playing.

He was lost in her—her body, her music, her heat. Still holding her neck with one hand, his other found her clit and he played her just as fiercely as she pounded out the rising crescendo of "Blue." Higher they moved together. Higher and higher. Until the final note rang out and they touched the stars.

CHAPTER TWELVE

DAWN SQUEEZED her eyes shut against the glare of the intrusive sun. Tucked along Kellen's side, her back squished into the back of the sofa, she was too comfortable, too content, too fulfilled to want her day to begin just yet. Even her sudden urge to work on the new melody tugging at her subconscious wasn't enough motivation to move from her current perfect, close-to-Kellen position.

Kellen's deep and even breathing grew slightly more rapid and shallow. He covered his eyes with one hand and turned his face toward her.

"Don't move," she murmured. "I just want to lie here like this all day."

"Can I move enough to kiss you good morning?"

The sleepy rasp of his voice played along her spine, making her shiver with delight.

"Maybe in an hour or two," she whispered.

Her time with him was magic. She wasn't ready for his spell to be broken just yet. Yet when his toe brushed the instep of her foot, she started to think maybe a little movement would be even more delightful.

"Did you know you hum in your sleep?" Kellen asked.

She'd been told that a time or two. "Only when I'm particularly inspired," she said.

"Is my dick inspiring you again?"

She laughed, enjoying the new happiness spell he cast over her almost as much as she'd loved his previous contentment spell. "Your dick is *incredibly* inspirational."

He took her hand and wrapped her fingers around her rapidly hardening muse. "How about a little morning inspiration?" he murmured before nibbling on a sensitive spot just beneath her ear.

Her toes curled, sending a spark of pain up her ankle and calf where the jellyfish had stung her, but that was easy enough to ignore.

"Not sure if I'm ready for inspiration quite yet," she said, shifting so she could press her mouth—her hidden grin—into his throat.

"That's unfortunate. I'm really in the mood to inspire this morning."

"Perhaps that talented mouth of yours could put me in the mood."

"It's worth a shot," he said, slipping from the sofa and spreading her thighs. She slid her fingers into his long, silky hair and held on tight as he licked and sucked her pussy until she was begging for her muse.

By the time they headed up for a shower, she'd been so thoroughly inspired that she had trouble climbing the stairs on her wobbly legs. She soon learned that while she hummed in her sleep, Kellen sang in the shower. He even pulled her back against his front and used her arm as a fret board and strummed her belly like a guitar until she was laughing so hard from his ticklish serenade, she had to cling to his thigh to remain standing.

"I can't remember the last time I was this happy," he said as he dried himself. She stood there in her towel, watching, her mouth hanging open. The only finer eye candy than wet, shirtless Kellen Jamison was wet, entirely naked Kellen Jamison. No sea god could be any more enticing than he was.

She sucked the drool back into her mouth and said, "Me neither." And she meant that. Being with him had her giddy with happiness.

"How about you practice your set list while I make breakfast?" he offered.

That sounded spectacular, but she said, "I figured you'd want French toast."

"I've watched you make it enough times now. I think I've got the gist of it."

"You realize that's my grandmother's secret recipe and you can't be allowed to escape with that knowledge."

His smile made her heart flutter. "I'm not planning to escape. Not ever."

Her breath caught, and she struggled to find words, to tell him that she wanted to be with him too, but he dropped his towel on the edge of the tub, leaving every inch of himself as a feast for her eyes, and she forgot how to speak. She remembered how to walk, though, and she followed his perfect naked ass into the bedroom.

He lifted a pair of boxers out of his open overnight bag and caught her gaping. "You, Miss O'Reilly, have a staring problem."

"No problem from my perspective," she said, waggling her brows and grinning.

She somehow found clothes and allowed him to get dressed as well. Downstairs, she righted her piano bench, thoughts of their pre-dawn romp making her crave more inspiration. Dear lord, how could she be horny again? Oh yes, naked Kellen would cause that condition. Newly inspired, she sat down to play through her set list again.

"I think you're going to have to settle for eggs, no toast," he called to her from the kitchen area of the large open room. "Every bit of this bread is culturing an antibiotic."

She'd forgotten she was going to make fresh bread, probably because she wasn't stressed enough to have the urge to bake.

"That's fine."

"There's a bit of bacon left too, but not much else."

"I knew I'd be leaving soon, so I've been trying to finish off my supplies."

"Oh . . ." His voice was so low and flat that she scarcely heard him. When the only noises coming from the kitchen were the banging of pans and the rush of water, she started through her playlist. Soon the delicious smell of bacon had her belly rumbling. She didn't need to practice, she decided. She knew every note already. What she needed was to spend every second left of this weekend with that wonderful man in her kitchen.

She headed for the coffee pot and found coffee already brewing. She could definitely get used to this. She sent a grateful smile in Kellen's direction, but he was so singularly focused on not burning the bacon and avoiding grease popping on his bare belly that he didn't see. She poured herself a cup of coffee and sat at the breakfast bar to watch him. He didn't glance up at her once, and she wasn't sure if he was really focused on cooking or if something was bothering him.

"What are we going to do with our last day together?" she asked.

He went entirely still, a piece of bacon dangling from the tongs in his hand, and lifted his gaze to hers. "Last day?"

"Not our last day ever. I meant of our weekend."

"This is going to be hard, isn't it?" He dropped the bacon into the sizzling pan and clamped on to a different slice. "Finding time to be together."

"Yeah," she admitted, taking a tentative sip of scalding coffee. "But being together will be worth a little effort. We just have to make the most of the time we do have."

Kellen began removing the bacon from the pan, laying the strips side by side on a paper towel.

"I thought we could explore the island a bit when we go out to buy steaks for dinner, but maybe we should spend the entire day in bed. We can open the doors to the upstairs deck and let the sound of the waves drive our rhythm. Let the ocean breezes caress our skin. Let the brine in the air enrich your taste, your scent."

Dawn sighed aloud and rested her chin in her hand. The man was a romantic through and through, and she loved his plan. But she didn't want their relationship to be built only on great sex. She wanted this to last and knew they'd have to have a deeper-than-physical connection to get them through the lengthy separations they faced.

"Can we do a little of both?" she asked. "Well, more bed time than island time, but we do need to pick up something for dinner. Man cannot live on pussy alone."

He laughed and used one hand to crack eggs into the hot bacon grease. "I'm not so sure about that."

"Well, I sure can't." Her heart thundered as she considered confessing something that no one but the party involved knew about her. And then her big blurty mouth opened up and said, "I tried it once, you know? Eating pussy."

Kellen dropped his spatula. "I guess I shouldn't be surprised after you let that hidden kinky vixen out the other night when you tied me up. So who was it?"

Her face was flaming, but she didn't waver. "You've met her."

"Chantel?"

Dawn nodded and waited for his reaction.

"Did you enjoy it?"

"The during? Very much. The after was incredibly awkward. We tried it only that once."

"And did your other roommate—*Jimmy*—did he get to watch?" His quirked eyebrow was a tad infuriating.

"Of course not! It was a private . . . experiment."

Her face was now hotter than the coffee in her cup. Why had she brought that incident up? She and Chantel had sworn to never speak of it, and here she was blabbing her dirty little secrets to Kellen while he cooked her breakfast.

"For future reference, if you ever want to eat pussy, I'm fine with it, but only if I get to watch." He shut off the burner and scooped eggs onto their plates.

"You can't be serious," she blurted.

He held her gaze when he said, "You should know me well enough by now to realize how seriously I take eating pussy."

"I know you excel at doing it, I just didn't realize . . ." She couldn't bring herself to finish that thought.

"I like watching almost as much as I like delivering."

And boy did the man deliver.

She released a nervous chuckle. "Well, the next time I go down on a woman, I'll be sure to call you as a witness." Not!

"That's all I ask." His tone was so serious that she couldn't tell if he was joking. Surely he was joking!

He set her plate in front of her, which finally let her off the hook. She was kicking herself for bringing that up, but then . . .

"Have you ever performed oral on a guy?" She bit her lip, cursing her blurty mouth for giving that question wind.

He slid onto the stool beside her. "No," he said. "Hand jobs are as far as I've ever gone with Owen."

Owen. Right. She'd been thinking with any other guy ever, but of course Kellen would equate her question with Owen. "And is Owen the only one you've . . ."

"Jerked off?" He munched his bacon as if they were discussing the weather. "Yep. I don't find men attractive."

"Just Owen."

"Do you really want to talk about this right now?" he asked.

No. "Yes," she said.

"I'm not attracted to Owen. He's just been there when I needed someone to touch me. Someone who could make me come but wouldn't have me breaking my oaths to Sara. Because I never promised her that I wouldn't let another guy choke my chicken. Pretty fucked up, huh?"

She wasn't sure if she should laugh or cry. "Are you still fixating on breaking promises to her when you're with me?"

"Not unless you bring it up."

She cringed and turned her attention to her plate. She would not be bringing up Sara or Owen again, even if that meant she had to duct tape her blurty lips together.

"This looks and smells phenomenal," she said, wanting very much to change the subject, knowing damned well she'd been the one to divert their conversation down the path it had taken.

"And tastes even better," he said, munching another piece of bacon.

His smile was reassuring. The gentle hand he rested on her back doubly so. She felt like she could tell him anything. She'd never experienced that kind of openness with anyone before. This man could be her best friend and confidant, her lover, her muse. This man could be her everything. She reached for the orange and cranberry juice he'd mixed for her without even asking and took a huge gulp. The boundless ocean that was Kellen Jamison had swept her up into its current, and she was drowning in him. Blissfully drowning. And she wasn't even going to try to fight it.

After breakfast Kellen helped her slather on some SPF2000—she loved the sun, but her ultra-fair skin did not—and then drove them from the more desolate end of the island where they were staying toward the small city of Galveston. Their beachy retreat was surrounded by residential homes and vacation rentals, but there wasn't a real grocery store for miles.

"I got a speeding ticket here the day I ran away from you," he said as they stopped at the single traffic light in the tiny town of Jamaica Beach.

"You just couldn't get away from me fast enough," she said, a teasing smile on her lips.

"You terrified me. Still do to an extent."

"What? Why?"

"Because you make me reevaluate my entire perception of what it means to love. I have always believed that there is only one true love for each person. I'd already found mine in Sara. I still believe that. But I lost her, so I was prepared to live out the rest of my life alone to be true to her. You, Miss O'Reilly, made me question that belief, made me wonder if a man could find a second true love."

There was no way she could feel defensive when someone was as utterly romantic as this man. She struggled not to sigh like a fangirl, even though she was his biggest fan.

"Have you come to a conclusion yet?" she asked, not sure she was ready to hear if he thought what was building between them was true love, but dying to know his deepest feelings anyway.

He chuckled. "Wouldn't you like to know?"

She stuck her tongue out at him because yes, *dammit*, she would. "I'm going to pretend you're being mysterious, but I think you haven't decided yet."

Once the highway turned into Seawall Boulevard, the buildings all ran along one side of the road, giving Dawn an unobstructed view of the ocean as they entered the outskirts of town. The weather was warm and sunny, making the typically murky water sparkle a deep blue. The sidewalk along the seawall and the beaches below it were packed with the usual mix of locals, day visitors from the Houston area, and vacationers from home and abroad. She much preferred the less populated beaches of the east end of the island, but it was fun to people-watch here. A glare on her left side drew her attention from the ocean to the buildings they passed. Just visible near the bay side of the island stood three enormous silver and glass pyramids.

"Have you been to Moody Gardens?" Dawn asked. "I've been meaning to check it out."

He chuckled. "They have a rainforest with live animals and birds roaming free inside one of those pyramids. Do you really think I could visit Galveston with Sara and not go half a dozen times? I thought she was going to rent space and pitch her tent there at one point."

"Oh . . ."

He switched on his blinker and got behind a long line of cars turning left. "I think you'll love it. They have an aquarium too. And beautiful gardens to walk through if you're into that kind of thing."

She was sure she'd love the place if it didn't remind him of Sara the entire time, and she knew it would. "Maybe we need to find our own haunts."

"Ones not haunted by Sara," he added quietly.

"I don't mean to be selfish. I just—"

"Want something special. I get it."

She reached over and squeezed his hand, glad he understood.

"Then we'll haunt the Strand. It's kind of like New Orleans with an island flair."

"I love the Strand," she said. "I've shopped there a few times." When she'd been looking for a little retail inspiration to overcome her writer's block. She'd left with her wallet lighter, but not so much as a note had been sparked by her excursions.

"Sara wasn't a fan—too much civilization for her tastes—but I'd love to explore the downtown area." He took his eyes off the road long enough to smile at her. "With you."

Once they found a place to park, they browsed through touristy T-shirt shops, art galleries, a truly wild women's clothing store—she fast-talked Kellen out of buying her a corset—and a cluttered but fun to explore antique store. Kellen loved the architecture of the pre-1900 hurricane buildings. Dawn was far more interested in Kellen.

At a confectionery they watched a live taffy pull, and she learned of Kellen's weakness for licorice-flavored salt water taffy—*yuck*. He was equally disturbed by her love of all things chocolate. As they were strolling along Post Office Street to check out a boutique that a local recommended for its merchandise and its *micheladas*—some fruity drink she'd never heard of—Kellen stopped short when a young couple pedaled past them on a tandem bike.

"We're doing that next," he said, pointing at the license plate on the back that displayed a bike rental shop's name.

Dawn's eyes widened. It did look sort of fun and wildly romantic, but . . . "Remember when I said I wiped out on a bike in college?"

"You'll be fine," he said. "It's not that hard."

"It is for me. I wiped out because . . ." She closed one eye to avoid seeing his reaction. "I don't know how to ride a bike."

"What?"

"No one ever taught me."

"You were too rich to learn to ride a bike?"

"My parents were too busy to teach me."

And thus teaching Dawn to ride a bike became Kellen's newest mission. After dropping off their purchases in the car—her chocolate was sure to become one big sloppy mess in the heat, but he was so insistent that she couldn't refuse to join his adventure over a bit of melted candy—they strolled toward the seawall where several bike rental shops could be found. She felt like a fool—all knees and elbows—as he started her off on a big-girl bike without any training wheels. He didn't let her crash, but nearly did in his own shin a few times when he had to catch her until she found her balance. It wasn't nearly as difficult as she'd thought it would be. Elation made her breathless when she finally took off without him holding on. She let out a whoop of triumph, the sea breeze blowing through her hair as she circled the parking lot.

A large curb raced toward her.

"How do I stop this thing?" she yelled.

"Use your hands. Squeeze the brakes!"

She pulled one of the levers and felt the front of the bike—but not the back—pull to a sudden halt. The rear tire left the ground as she skidded. Having long legs was an advantage. She stood and caught herself with several running steps, before letting go of the bike. The bike wasn't so lucky. Its momentum carried it to the curb and beyond. Flipping forward, it clattered to the ground right next to a parked car. Dawn squeezed her eyes shut, praying it wasn't too badly damaged.

"You did great," he said—such a liar—and hugged her against him. She wasn't sure whose heart was thudding harder, hers or his.

"That was fun," she said, laughing, "until that dumb curb jumped out in front of me."

"Maybe we should hold off on the tandem bike. I've only ridden one a few times, and being the stoker can be a bit unnerving. You have to have complete faith in your captain to not steer you both into the Gulf."

"Did you ride one with Sara?"

"No, with Owen. Sara was too chicken to try it."

There was no way in hell Dawn would miss an opportunity to be braver than Sara. She squeezed him tightly. "I want to do it. I have complete faith in you." She hoped he couldn't feel how hard her heart was thudding and wondered if that big medical school hospital on the island was any good at setting broken bones and applying sidewalk-burn skin grafts.

The owner of the bike shop gave them both a helmet and plenty of tips, and since Dawn didn't have any bad habits of riding solo to unlearn, they didn't do too badly on their first few takeoffs.

"You two ride well together and have a natural rhythm," their instructor said. "I can tell you've been together a long time."

Kellen chuckled. "You can tell that, can you?"

Their short-term instructor nodded. "Totally obvious. Have fun."

Dawn sat poised with both feet on the pedals, gripping handlebars that did not steer, no matter how much she tried to backseat drive. Kellen had been right to say she had to have complete faith in him. She could help pedal and balance, but basically she was a passenger on his long-ass bike.

He kicked off and got the bike going. They lucked out by hitting a green crossing light and crossed over Seawall Boulevard to the wide sidewalk shared by pedestrians, bikes, and surreys. They could continue along the path for miles in either direction. Once she got used to being out of control, Dawn decided she liked riding in the back. When she got tired of staring at Kellen's gorgeous back and ass—which honestly took quite a while—she was free to take in the sights as they pedaled along the shore while he was forced to pay attention to their trajectory and speed, as well as avoid any large bumps that might unseat her.

"Ever been to the Pleasure Pier?" she asked Kellen as they slowly made their way through the crowd near the small amusement park built on a pier.

"It hadn't opened yet when Sara was alive. We can go there if you want."

"Do you like roller coasters?" She craned her neck to watch the small coaster on the pier zip around its track. At one point it looked as if it hurdled beyond the pier and over the water.

"They're okay. Owen loves them."

"What do you love?"

"Being with you."

She traced a hoof of the rearing stallion tattoo on his back and felt his muscles tense beneath her light touch. She loved being with him too. And she was having a great time, but . . .

"I can't stay out in the sun much longer," she said. "Even with all that sunscreen, I'll still burn to a crisp."

"Are you ready to head indoors?"

"I'm ready to head for bed. Assuming you'll be in it."

He chuckled and looked over his shoulder to meet her eyes. "That's a fair assumption."

"I do want to get the most out of this bike ride, though," she said. "The view is spectacular." She gave his tanned, muscular back an appreciative twice-over, his perfect ass a four-times-over. He laughed again and swerved around a jogger pushing a three-wheeled baby stroller.

The breeze felt nice against her heated face and throat on their trip back up the sidewalk. The rental shop employee was proud to see them return without any broken bones or scrapes and with the tandem bike in one piece. Dawn's legs were wobbly from using muscles she didn't often use, but her aches would be worth it. She just hoped they didn't make playing on Wednesday too difficult. She held Kellen's hand on the way back to the car, and they stopped at a huge grocery store to pick up steaks, fresh-caught jumbo shrimp, and other necessities for their evening meal.

Turned out, Kellen grilled a delicious steak and even more delicious shrimp. He had insisted on dragging the grill over to her place, and her spirits were too high to push him into confronting his issues about Sara's house. They didn't have to tackle those problems all at once. They had plenty of time to take baby steps if he needed to do that.

Full to the gills, Dawn settled into an Adirondack chair on the deck and watched the birds skitter through the surf as they scrounged up their own meal. Kellen brought her a bowl of vanilla ice cream covered in the remnants of her melted chocolate.

"I couldn't possibly eat another bite," she said, but she took the bowl and couldn't resist a small taste.

He grinned at her when less than ten minutes later she was scraping the bottom of her bowl with her spoon. Her stomach had protested every bite, but her tongue had insisted she continue to stuff her face.

They sat on the deck and talked until the sun sank below the bay behind them. She couldn't remember ever having a more perfect day. The thought that she had to leave him tomorrow to meet with a bunch of self-important Hollywood executives was too depressing to bear, so she didn't dwell on that painful truth when he talked her into sitting at her piano bench and playing some of her classics with a twist and even a few compositions of her own that she'd deemed not good enough for human ears.

"Every song you've written turns me on," he murmured as they came together on the lid of her piano. "Why is that?"

Her toes curled as he thrust into her. Deeper. Deeper. Yes, please, deeper. "You're a horny bastard?"

He shrugged. "Can't deny either of those labels."

She bit her lip, wishing she'd chosen gentler words. He never spoke of his parents, and maybe he'd be annoyed that she'd brought up more of his past, but she wanted to know about his family. She wanted to learn everything about him—how to please his body and make him laugh. The way his mind worked. What his soul yearned for. How to claim his heart as her own. Because that was what she truly wanted. All of him. And for the first time in her life she was ready to give someone all of herself in return.

CHAPTER THIRTEEN

KELLEN WATCHED Dawn exit the realtor's office with a lump in his throat. So that was it, then. The rental house—where they'd met, where they'd first made love, where he'd developed such strong feelings for her, where she'd composed their song—was now back in the hands of strangers. Maybe he should buy that house and make sure the piano was part of the deal.

She climbed into the car beside him and after she'd buckled herself in, he took her hand and kissed her knuckles.

"Are you sure you have time to take me to the airport?" she asked. "It's over an hour out of your way."

"I'm sure." He wanted to spend every possible second with her, knowing she'd soon be in L.A. and then in Prague. He'd be back on tour, pretending his life hadn't been completely turned around in the course of days by this perfect, perfect woman.

"Not if we sit here for eons with you staring at me like that."

She grinned at him, but he feigned ignorance. "Look at you like what?"

"Like we're never going to see each other again."

Didn't she understand that it was a concern? "I was thinking," he said, still looking at her with his heart in his throat. "Maybe I should sell Sara's house—"

"I think you'd be much happier if you did."

"—and buy the one next door. I hear it has a beautiful grand piano that an inspiring and famous song was composed on."

Her eyes narrowed, and the happy smile he was expecting ended up a harsh frown. "Don't you dare do that to yourself. To us."

Puzzled, he squeezed her hand. "We have so many memories there."

Her sigh of frustration was even more baffling than her scowl. She tugged her hand free of his and sat straighter in her seat. "I'm going to miss my plane."

He backed out of the parking spot and once they were in the flow of traffic, he asked, "You don't like that house?"

"I do," she said, "but I already have a house. You already have a house."

"But *we* don't have a house."

"And maybe someday we will, but it won't be that one."

Maybe he did understand where she was coming from. "Because it's next door to Sara's."

"No, because I don't want you to link me to a place. I don't want to think that sometime in the future you might erect a shrine to me in some beach house and not let yourself move on. *For years.* I won't have that hanging over me. Over us."

"So I should start preparing myself to get over you?"

She covered her forehead with both hands, curling forward, her shoulder straining against her seatbelt, and shook her head. "No, I hope you never have to get over me. I hope we live a healthy, happy life together until we're both in our nineties and die in each other's arms at the exact same moment. That's what I hope."

The hard knot in his throat loosened slightly. "I knew you were a romantic."

"Kellen, don't buy that house. Please don't tie me to a place."

"How about a bed? Can I tie you to a bed?"

She laughed, and the horrible tension that had built between them the second he'd mentioned buying the beach house lessened.

"You can tie me to all sorts of beds. Don't limit me to just one."

And then he truly understood where she was coming from. Maybe. "I guess we can make memories together in a lot of beds and on various pianos."

"I sure hope so." She shifted and laced her fingers through his. "When Sole Regret's tour is over, I want you to come see me in L.A. and maybe come with me to Europe."

"I'm sure I'll see you before the tour is over, Dawn. We'll find a way." He took his eyes off the road long enough to glance at her. Her lips were pressed together, and her eyes were glassy. "Hey," he said, elbowing her gently, "we'll find a way."

Her smile was a bit wobbly, but genuine. "I have the feeling this meeting tomorrow is going to change my life and make it harder to be with you, not easier. And then . . . and then I don't know what I'll do."

"Don't worry about that until you know for sure." He shook his head. "Actually, don't worry about that at all. If opportunity is knocking on your door, you'd better fucking open it."

Her smile brightened. "We'll find a way," she said.

Traffic into Houston crawled—nothing unusual about that—but he was now worried that she'd miss her plane and opportunity would miss the opportunity to knock.

"When is your meeting?"

She glanced at the clock. "In about eight hours."

"So if you miss your flight?" He squirmed in his seat, wishing the rental car had wings so he could soar over stalled traffic.

"I'll miss the meeting and maybe my flight to Prague. My life will be over."

His eyes widened, and he whipped his head around to stare at her. She winked at him and leaned over to rub his thigh. "It will be fine. If I miss the flight to L.A., I'll just hang out at the Houston airport until my flight to Prague leaves tomorrow."

"They must really need to see you to put such a burden on you. You're going to be exhausted for your performance." Momentarily glad they were sitting on a freeway-turned-parking-lot, he brushed her hair from her face and kissed her cheek.

"I'll be okay, and I'm sure they didn't do this to me because they need to see me *immediately*. They're in a rush because it serves their Hollywood agenda. I've no doubt that my hectic schedule didn't even come into consideration when they made their plans."

Traffic inched forward and after they'd creeped through a relatively mild accident scene, the interstate opened up and the rest of their journey was swift. A bit too swift. Kellen had been planning to drop her off at the door and make his way to New Orleans, but needed more time with her. He pulled into the parking garage, and Dawn shook her head at him.

"I'm not the only one with a tight schedule here. You have a concert to get to."

"I have plenty of time," he assured her. He unfastened her

seat belt, needing to touch her as much as he could.

Once he started kissing her, he didn't want to stop. He almost had her convinced to venture to the back seat when she pulled away.

"I have to go now," she said, succumbing to one more kiss before she opened the door. "You sure don't make this easy on a girl."

He grinned. "I don't want you to forget me while you're away."

"As if I could."

He climbed out after her and opened the trunk, lugging her bags out. She had four, and it hit him again that they wouldn't be returning to the beach house.

"You should have just dropped me off at the curb. Let someone else handle my bags."

"They wouldn't have let me linger."

She shook her head, but her soft smile told him that she was pleased and that maybe she didn't want to part from him any more than he wanted to part from her.

Glad her expensive-looking luggage set—he was pretty sure it was genuine leather—at least had wheels, he grabbed her two large suitcases and slung her carry-on over one handle while she carried her smaller suitcase and her purse.

"When you get back from Prague—"

"I'll catch up with you as soon as I can," she promised. "I hope to see you by Friday."

Less than a week, and yet it stretched out before him like a desolate eternity. "We'll figure it out," he said. "How to be together."

"We have to," she said as they exited the parking garage and headed for the terminal.

They found her airline and got in line to check her luggage.

"What's your house like?" he asked, realizing they hadn't discussed things like that over their weekend. He needed more time. He wasn't sure why he felt that way. This wasn't a forever goodbye—not like the one he'd had to suffer through with Sara—but that knowledge didn't make separating any easier.

"It's a condo, actually. Ground floor because my piano wouldn't fit on the elevator." She grinned. "Another reason why I decided to rent a place to compose. My neighbors were starting to complain about the three a.m. writing sessions."

"If you ever need a quiet place to work, my cabin doesn't have neighbors. At least, not any you can see."

They moved forward a spot in line, which got her closer to leaving. He placed a hand on her back and shifted into her warmth. He didn't want her to go. How would he get through the next five days without seeing her, touching her, tasting her? He hoped she liked talking on the phone, because at the very least he'd need to hear her voice.

"You live in the wilderness?" she asked.

"Surprised?"

She laughed. "Not one bit."

"It was my grandfather's property. He left it to my mom when he passed, but she'd always hated it out there in the sticks, so she sold it to me. She's down in Florida with her new husband. Well, not so new. They've been married almost ten years."

"You never talk about your family," she said.

"Nothing to tell."

"I'm sure there's plenty to tell, so I want to hear about them the next time we're together. It will give us something to talk about."

He wrapped a wavy strand of hair around one finger and leaned closer. "The last thing I'll want to do when we see each other again is talk."

He kissed her to give her a small sample of what he had in mind.

When they separated, she said, "You really don't make this easy on a girl."

Once her bags were checked, he followed her to the security checkpoint, knowing they wouldn't let him through without a ticket. He considered buying one just so he could sit beside her until she boarded.

"As much as I want you to stay here with me, I know you have a long drive ahead of you. You need to go."

"I know." He pressed his forehead against hers, one hand resting on her cheek to commit the texture of her skin to memory, his other hand clinging to her fingers. "I've never been good at goodbyes."

"This isn't goodbye. This is until next time."

She kissed him, soft lips lingering on his for a long moment that felt much too short, and then she slowly pulled away. He held onto her hand as she backed up, forcing his feet to stay rooted to the spot. When their fingertips separated, a lump settled in his belly, but he let her go. He did watch until she made her way through the X-ray machine and disappeared from sight.

Yep, he sucked at goodbyes. "Until next time," he whispered under his breath as he turned away.

THE DRIVE to New Orleans was unbearably long. Kellen reminisced about the amazing weekend he'd shared with Dawn and tried not to worry that she'd be too busy to see him again anytime soon. He had every other weekend off—thanks to Jacob's visitations with Julie—and there were these inventions called airplanes. He'd be sure to make good use of them. The two of them just had to coordinate schedules, that was all. And once the summer was over, he'd be off tour and in the studio recording Sole Regret's next album—assuming that Adam starting writing songs soon. But his time would be much less restricted than it was for the next several months. He hoped Dawn was okay with him following her around, because he planned to make a genuine nuisance of himself.

The sun was already setting when he reached the Louisiana border. The guys were going to be beyond pissed with him if he was late. Hell, he'd be pissed with himself. He'd needed just one more kiss before he let Dawn go through airport security. He'd needed something to keep her with him for as long as possible.

An incoming call made his heart leap. Had Dawn landed already? He smiled when he saw it was Owen calling. He suddenly missed the guy terribly. They hadn't spoken much that weekend. A brief call or text seeking advice about Caitlyn and their apparent breakup—temporary, Kellen was sure—but otherwise, silence.

"Glad you called. I was getting really bored," Kellen said.

"How far out are you?"

Owen sounded as desperate for company as Kellen felt. The drive from New Orleans to Galveston with Dawn beside him had flown by. The return trip to New Orleans *alone* seemed to be taking eons. And as much as he enjoyed listening to his personal virtuoso play the piano, listening to the classical music on the radio was a total snorefest. He was surprised he hadn't yet nodded off and driven into a ditch.

"I got a late start this morning," he said. "If traffic cooperates, I should get there about an hour before we go onstage."

"Oh."

Yeah, the guy definitely needed a sounding board. Maybe Caitlyn's dumping Owen had been more hurtful and permanent than Kellen had suspected.

"How are you holding up?" he asked. "I know what you're like after a chick dumps you."

"She didn't dump me. At least I don't think she did. I'm not sure. She's none too happy about Lindsey living with me."

Wait, what? When had that happened? Kellen really was out of Owen's loop.

"Lindsey is living with you? I thought Mom was going to take her in." At least that had been the last plan he'd heard.

"She tried. My parents were going to rent the apartment to her."

The one over their garage. "That's a nice place." He'd have suggested it if he'd thought of it. It hadn't occurred to him until that moment that it might be vacant since its usual renters were college students who took off for the summer months.

"*Was* a nice place. Lindsey had a huge asthma attack. Apparently there's mold in the bathroom, so everything has to be ripped out and redone."

"That sucks. So she's just staying with you until the bathroom is finished."

"God, I hope so. It's nice to have someone to cook me breakfast, but Caitlyn was none too pleased when she overheard Lindsey calling me to eat this morning."

Kellen shook his head. "You didn't tell her about Lindsey? So she caught you."

"I didn't have the chance to tell her. She wasn't talking to me, and then when she finally answered my eight millionth call, Lindsey had completely slipped my mind."

Typical Owen. Kellen couldn't help but laugh at him. "Well, you know how you could have avoided the entire situation,"

Kellen said, surprised Owen hadn't mucked up things even worse without Kellen there to interject his advice any time his friend needed it, which happened to be quite often.

"How?"

"Told her up front that Lindsey was living with you and not tried to hide it."

"I wasn't trying to hide it. Lindsey wasn't staying at my place when I'd last spoken with Caitlyn. Circumstances changed."

"So you really want to make this thing with Caitlyn work?"

Kellen liked Caitlyn, so he wasn't sure why the idea of Owen committing himself to her settled oddly on his stomach. Maybe he just needed a taquito and some cranberry orange juice.

"I do."

Kellen spotted a sign for a gas station. Perfect timing. Apparently he was starving. "Whatever makes you happy. I'm stopping for gas now. I'll see you when I get into New Orleans."

"Okay," Owen said.

Several hours later, Owen called back. And thank heavens. Kellen had been sitting on the freeway, inching his way through some accident scene for well over an hour now.

"Hey," Owen said. "Are you okay? I have this weird feeling that something is wrong."

For some reason hearing Owen's voice made Kellen's thoughts drift to the night Dawn had tied him. His cock twitched at how amazing it had felt to have that twine wrapped around his dick, those beads up his ass, and when he'd come, it hadn't been Dawn's name that had spilled from his lips. Heat flooded Kellen's face as the image of Owen tied over a pommel entered his thoughts. What the fuck was wrong with him? He must be fucking bored. And horny. Why was he horny? He missed Dawn. It was the only explanation.

"I'm fine," Kellen said. Well, mostly. "I'm stuck in traffic. Some accident has the entire highway closed. I hope I can get to the show in time."

"You're okay, though?" Owen asked.

"Of course. Other than being highly annoyed. Sorry to worry you."

"Like I'd ever worry about you."

Kellen knew he was lying, but he didn't embarrass Owen about his concern. That big heart of his was what allowed their friendship to develop and stay strong through the years.

"I'll let the guys know you might be late."

"I refuse to be late, even if I have to hydroplane this rental car through the bayou."

Owen's laugh made Kellen smile. He missed the guy and couldn't remember the last time they'd been separated for longer than a day. He wondered if now that they both had girlfriends, if they'd see each other less. Kellen guessed it was inevitable. While he was excited to build a future with Dawn, he'd likely never get over Owen. But maybe he didn't have to. They could be couple-friends with Owen and Caitlyn; that was a thing. And he was sure Dawn would love Owen as much as he did once she got the chance to know him. Kellen had enjoyed what little time he'd spent with Caitlyn, and he could see the two women becoming friends just as he and Owen were friends. Caitlyn was busy with her company, but surely they could make this work.

Kellen was thinking about the future and all the fun times in store for the four of them long after Owen disconnected. The next time his phone rang, it was Dawn. And immediately the semi he'd been sporting became a raging hard-on. He glared at his crotch, wondering what was so stimulating about talking on the phone while stuck in traffic.

"I'm safe in L.A.," she said. "And so nervous, I think I'm going to be sick."

"You'll be great. They'll love you."

"I'm not even sure why I want them to love me. I can't believe Wes is being so tightlipped. He's usually the type to brag about how awesome his plans for my future are."

She laughed, and he had to admit that she sounded nervous. Or maybe he heard nerves in her voice just because they were speaking on the phone for the first time. She might always have that high-pitched edge to her voice on the phone.

"So do you think that means this potential deal is huge or embarrassingly small?"

"Oh," she said. "You know, maybe that's it. I never even considered that it's something so small that he was too embarrassed to tell me about it." She laughed—almost hysterically. "That must be it. And I worried over it the entire flight."

Kellen didn't have the heart to point out that they probably wouldn't have flown her to L.A. in such a rush if it wasn't a big deal.

"So how is New Orleans? We really need to spend more time there. I had so much fun."

"I'm not quite there yet," he said. "I ran into more traffic."

"Oh no, will you make it to your show in time?"

He glanced at the clock, and his belly fluttered. "I'll be cutting it close, but I'll make it." He hoped.

"I'd say you should have just dumped me off at the terminal, but I'd be lying if I said I didn't like your many marvelous goodbyes."

He loved the way she made him feel. Not just in the bedroom—though that was pretty spectacular—but every single time she opened that gorgeous mouth of hers.

"If I'm late, I'm late," he said. "The guys will get over it. I've never been late in my life. Adam's the one that usually has us waiting." Making people wait never gave Adam pause, but being late would bother Kellen.

"I hope you make it on time, but don't be reckless. Get there safe."

Not many people cared about Kellen enough to tell him to be safe, so her words hit him hard. Hell, everything about Dawn O'Reilly hit him hard. He was lucky to have found her. Lucky to have bought that stupid house on the Galveston shore. Lucky that she'd been playing that song—their song—that night when he'd been mourning on the beach. Their stars were aligned, perfectly aligned. His only fear was that something would fuck it all up.

"I'll be safe," he promised. "You be safe too. And promise you'll let me know how your dinner meeting goes."

She laughed. "I'm sure it will be lame."

And he was sure someone in Hollywood had figured out that his girlfriend was amazing. "Have fun."

"I'll try. But I'd be having more fun there with you."

KELLEN ARRIVED at the stadium just minutes before they were scheduled to take the stage.

He hurried through the backstage area, glad the roadies

cleared a path for him, and found Owen standing near the stage entrance with his bass strapped on and hooked up to the sound equipment. Kellen had cut it really close.

"You made it," Owen said, slapping him on the arm.

"Remind me never to drive from Galveston to New Orleans again." At least not alone. Lord, he'd been ready to drive into the nearest moss-draped bald cypress by the end of it.

The technician handed Kellen his guitar, and he flipped the strap over his head, glad he didn't have to worry about makeup and a costume change.

"Dawn didn't come back with you?" Owen asked.

Kellen shook his head. "We're trying to sort out where we go next." Well, she was going places. He was mostly just worried he'd be left behind.

Owen scratched at a bit of beard growth. "Yeah, Caitlyn and I hit that point as well. Fortunately, we talked it out and are moving forward."

Kellen smiled, the adrenaline rush of his near lateness waning and sapping his energy. "That's great."

Owen frowned and gnawed on his lip. "You ever get the feeling that something is wrong? Or that something bad is about to happen?"

"Sometimes," Kellen said. Owen did look worried. Antsy even.

"I've been feeling like that for about an hour. I called a bunch of people, and everyone assures me they're okay, but this feeling of dread won't go away."

Kellen opened his mouth to assure Owen that he was sure everyone was fine, but was interrupted by Jacob asking, "Where's Adam?"

Owen glanced around, and then shrugged. "No idea."

Jacob pointed out Adam's guitar sitting untouched in its stand. "He left his guitar."

"Maybe he had to go to the bathroom," Kellen said. "Ever try to take a piss with a guitar strapped on?" He'd once had to throw away a perfectly good guitar because his aim had been off.

"Can't say that I have," Jacob said. He stared at the door as if Adam coming through it depended solely on his focus.

A few minutes later, Gabe hopped down from the stage, his drumsticks in one hand. "What's the holdup?"

"Adam's missing," Jacob said.

"Missing?"

"Yeah, he was just here."

And Kellen had been worried that people would be waiting on *him* for a change.

Owen grabbed Kellen's arm and attention. "Should we go look for him?"

"Let the road crew handle it." Kellen doubted they'd have to wait much longer. "We wouldn't want them to have to round us all up again when they find him."

Kellen was rethinking his doubt when the road crew turned up and claimed there were no signs of Adam, not even the motorcycle he'd rented. Apparently he'd taken off without letting anyone know where he was going.

"Fuck!" Jacob yelled, turning accusative eyes in his bandmates' direction as if they'd given Adam the okay to blow off the show. "Did he say anything to any of you?"

Owen cringed beneath Jacob's anger and shook his head. Kellen mimicked Owen's motion. Why would they stand there for ten minutes waiting for Adam to show up and then suddenly remember they knew exactly where he was? Sometimes Jacob made no sense.

"Fuck!" Jacob shouted again. "What in the hell is he thinking?"

"Maybe there's an emergency," Owen said exactly what Kellen was thinking.

"Even if there is, he could have taken a few seconds to tell someone," Jacob said.

True, but if the emergency involved Adam, maybe he was physically incapable of telling someone.

"Fuck!" Jacob yelled. "I'm going after him."

"Do you know where he went?" Gabe asked.

Jacob checked the Adam-tracking app on his phone, but all he could tell was that Adam was headed west.

"What's west?" Kellen asked. Besides Dawn.

"Texas. Madison. His fucking heroin dealer. How the hell should I know?"

"Calm down," Owen said. "We'll figure something out."

"I'll try calling him," Kellen said. "Maybe he'll answer." He hoped that by presenting a calm front, the rest of them would follow his lead. Because they were all freaking out. He listened to Adam's phone ring and ring, but he got no answer. While he was leaving a message, Sally joined them.

"What's going on?" she asked. "Why aren't you on stage?"

"Adam isn't here," Jacob said. "We can't perform without our lead guitarist, can we?"

"I'm worried." Owen looked at Kellen and lifted his brows in an unspoken question.

Kellen shook his head—he hadn't been able to reach Adam. He tucked his phone back into his pocket.

"He wouldn't just run off like that unless it was a life or death situation."

"Yes, he would," Jacob said.

Kellen could see both their points. It was very possible that Adam was in trouble, but it was equally likely that Adam was just being irresponsible Adam. It wouldn't be the first time. Why would anyone think it would be his last?

Jacob took a moment to remind them of Adam's addiction problems and how Jacob himself had always been the one who'd scraped the guy off rock bottom.

"He's changed, Jacob," Gabe said, though he was looking at the floor, so Kellen didn't think he was convinced that Adam had changed.

"He has?" Jacob shook his head. "Sorry, but I don't see it."

While the rest of them looked on, wondering what the hell he was doing, Jacob jogged out onto the stage.

"Good evening, New Orleans," he called out to the audience. "You look ready to rock!"

They cheered, and Kellen cringed. Why was Jacob getting them amped up when there was no way for them to perform?

"Unfortunately, our performance is not going to happen tonight. Our lead guitarist, Adam Taylor, was called away on an emergency. So we have to cancel the show."

The crowd roared in angry disappointment, and Jacob promised to square them away, but even if they refunded the tickets or rescheduled, the fans would never get back the time they'd wasted coming to the arena only to be turned away.

"This is a fucking nightmare," Gabe said.

"Understatement of the century," Owen said. "The fans are pissed."

Kellen was starting to get that way himself, and it took a lot to piss him off.

Jacob returned a few minutes later with some teenager wearing a beanie hat, and asked Kellen if he'd reached Adam. Kellen shook his head. Obviously not.

"Okay."

Jacob explained his plan B: having a young guitarist, who they didn't know from Adam—actually, they *did* know he wasn't Adam—take their wildly talented and popular lead guitarist's place that night.

Desperate much, Jacob?

"So I say we give him a chance to prove himself," Jacob was saying. "What's your name?"

He didn't even know the guy's name?

"Wes."

The same name as Dawn's agent—what were the odds? Maybe it was a sign. Maybe the kid knew the ins and outs of the music business just as Dawn's agent did. Or maybe the guy couldn't tell a fretboard from a tuning peg.

Kellen's jaw dropped when Wes played every requested Sole Regret riff and solo with surprising skill. He was no Adam Taylor. Hell, Kellen was no Adam Taylor and he'd played with the guy for a decade. But the kid could play. So they held the concert without Adam and let young Wes be a rock star for an evening.

Perhaps someone—Jacob—should have asked Kellen to fill in for Adam. He could have handled it. He didn't want the job full-time or anything, but fuck, no one—certainly not Jacob—had even asked Kellen if he wanted to play lead in Adam's place. One of the technicians could have probably played Kellen's part on rhythm guitar. Maybe Kellen should have said something instead of assuming one of the guys would read his mind. But he didn't hold any of that against young Wes.

Kellen actually had a good time with Owen onstage. They played off one another, leaving Wes alone so that he could concentrate. Playing with Owen took the edge off, even though Kellen was already missing Dawn and still worried about Adam.

Once the concert ended, he followed Owen back to the tour bus, checking his phone for messages. One from his cellular carrier, but nothing he wanted to hear or read. Nothing from

Adam. Nothing from Dawn.

Kellen sighed and plopped down on the sofa next to Owen. "I actually think Jacob was okay with that little scenario."

"More than okay with it," Gabe said. "I think he preferred it. He had Sally get that kid's information."

"He's a nice kid and all," Owen said, "but . . ."

". . . he's no Adam Taylor," the three said in unison.

Jacob had reached the bus before them all, heading straight for the back to be alone or avoid them or who knew what. Kellen was having a hard time reading Jacob tonight. Something was bothering him. Maybe it was just the situation with Adam, but Kellen got the feeling there was more to it than another disappointment. This wasn't the first show that Adam had derailed. He'd once passed out in the middle of a performance from an overdose of whatever junk he'd shot into his veins. At least Adam was clean now. Or was he?

Jacob sauntered in their direction. "Anyone hear from Adam yet?" Jacob asked.

That strange vibe Kellen had been getting from Jacob all night intensified as soon as he and the others admitted they still hadn't heard from Adam.

"I've had it with his bullshit," Jacob said. Without taking a breath, he blurted, "Adam's out of the band."

Owen stiffened beside Kellen. "What?"

Kellen was too shocked to even get a word out. They couldn't do that to Adam. They couldn't do that to Sole Regret. Neither would survive.

"He's toxic," Jacob said. "We need to get rid of him. Replace him with someone who takes our success seriously."

There was more than one problem with getting rid of Adam.

"Adam writes all of our music," Kellen reminded them. Maybe Jacob didn't realize how important a composer was to the success of a band, but he sure as hell did. "We can't just kick him out."

Jacob shrugged. "We'll write the music ourselves and if necessary, hire songwriters."

Uh, no. That wasn't going to happen.

"This is bullshit," Kellen said. Jacob was the self-proclaimed leader of the band, but he did not get to make all the decisions without input from the rest of them. "Adam is one of us. He's always been one of us. We can't do this to him."

"We don't even know why he took off," Owen said, obviously still focused on the idea that Adam was hurt or in danger. "I'm sure he had a good reason."

"More than two hours later, and he still hasn't checked in to let us know what the fuck is going on!" Jacob yelled. "He obviously doesn't give a shit about any of us or the fans or the music. All he cares about is himself. It's time to cut him loose. If he wants to destroy himself, fine, but I'm not letting him take the rest of us down with him."

"I want to hear what he has to say before I weigh in." Gabe finally broke his silence. "For all we know, he's dead in a ditch somewhere."

Owen flinched and leaned closer to Kellen, as if he could guard him from that possibility. "Don't even say that."

"It would save me the trouble of telling him to fuck off," Jacob said in a growl.

This wasn't the Jacob they knew. There was a line a man should never cross and then there was a line past that one. Jacob had leapt over all the lines and was so far beyond acceptable behavior that Kellen had a mind to punch him.

"You're such an asshole," Owen said.

Exactly.

Jacob further demonstrated his assholery by getting right into Owen's face. "I'd rather be an asshole than a spineless wuss," he growled at him.

Kellen bristled, fighting the urge to wallop Jacob. He knew if he fought Owen's battles, he'd be giving credibility to Jacob's insults, but fuck, Jacob was pushing all of Kellen's anger buttons at once. He couldn't remember ever being this pissed at anyone, much less someone he considered one of his best friends.

"What's that supposed to mean?" Owen shoved Jacob away.

"You're a pushover, Owen," Jacob said. "You always have been."

"Don't take your frustration with Adam out on Owen," Kellen said. He squeezed Owen's leg to keep himself from punching Jacob. He refused to stoop to that level just yet. Jacob was under a lot of pressure. And though it might make Kellen feel better, beating the crap out of Jacob would only make things worse in the long run. "You're the one who never bends. You're the mighty oak, standing tall and rigid against any force that threatens your position."

"Someone has to be strong."

"Listen to what Kellen is trying to warn you about," Gabe said. "If you never bend, you will break, Jacob. Don't you see that? We'll figure out what to do after we talk to Adam."

"Kellen could play lead," Jacob said.

So *now* that was his solution? Not when they performed, but afterwards? Kellen couldn't believe Jacob had the nerve to suggest it.

"And Adam play rhythm?" Owen asked. "He'd never agree to that."

Jacob gaped at Owen as if he couldn't figure out how someone so clueless could find the mental capacity to breathe. "No. We'd get a new rhythm guitarist."

"I prefer rhythm guitar," Kellen said. It linked him with Owen in a way he wasn't willing to give up. And he knew Adam would be back soon. Adam always came back. *And* Kellen refused to give Jacob what he thought was an easy solution. It wasn't a solution at all, just a different set of problems.

"Then we get a new lead guitarist," Jacob said, tossing his hands in the air and shaking his head. "I don't care either way, I just want Adam gone. And not temporarily. For good."

"What's wrong with you?" Owen said, again mirroring Kellen's thoughts. "I'm sure he'll explain everything when he gets back. He deserves a second chance."

"A second chance?" Jacob sucked in a harsh breath.

Kellen nodded. Yes, Adam deserved a second chance.

"He's already had a hundred second chances," Jacob said. "Or more! He's gone too far this time. I'm not putting up with his shit anymore. So if you won't get rid of him, then I'm out of here."

Did he really mean that? Or was he drawing a line he thought they wouldn't cross?

Gabe's breathless *what* actually forced Jacob to turn away.

"There's the door," Owen said, pointing in case Jacob had forgotten where it was.

Jacob stared at Owen for a long moment as if measuring the weight of his words. He bit his lip and nodded slightly before he said, "So Owen chooses Adam over me." He turned his attention to Kellen. "What about you, Kellen? I'm sure you'll go along with whatever Owen says since you can't live without each other."

Of course he'd think that was why he sided with Owen. Not because Owen was right—in Kellen's opinion Owen was right to show Jacob the door if he wanted to leave so bad—but because he thought Kellen was incapable of forming an opinion of his own.

"Fuck you, Jacob," Kellen said.

Jacob turned to Gabe, who was still trying to reason with the bastard.

"Don't do this, Jacob. It isn't worth it," Gabe said.

Jacob crumpled, defeated by the one he likely considered a guaranteed ally. "I guess this is goodbye, then. Good luck with Adam. He's only going to drag you down with him. I guess you'll just have to see it for yourself. I'm through being his buffer. None of you have any idea how bad he can get—you have absolutely no clue. But you'll figure it out soon enough, and I might have already moved on."

Jacob took his bag to the front of the bus and talked the driver into pulling over onto the shoulder of the road.

"What do you think you're doing?" Gabe asked.

Kellen cringed. He wouldn't really take it this far would he? Based on Owen's concerned grimace, he decided they were still thinking alike. They wanted Jacob to back down, not hitchhike himself into a grave.

"I'm leaving," Jacob said.

"Be reasonable, Jacob." Gabe went after him, grasping his shoulder, but Jacob shrugged away. "We can work through this. Stay. Let's talk about it."

"Open the door," Jacob demanded.

Owen started to rise, but Kellen figured if the guy was going to go, the guy was going to go. No one would be able to change his mind. Jacob would have to come to the conclusion that he was a fucking rash idiot on his own.

"Great fucking plan, Jacob," Gabe called after him. "This doesn't solve a goddamned thing. Jacob!"

"Let him go if that's what he wants," Kellen said. "God knows he's a stubborn son of a bitch." The understatement of the evening.

"He might get hit by a car," Owen said.

Kellen snorted. Leave it to Owen to be worried for someone who had called him a wuss and then destroyed their livelihood in the space of twenty minutes. The bus rolled forward and returned to the traffic lane, leaving Jacob behind on the side of the road.

"What the fuck just happened?" Gabe stared at him and Owen as if he didn't recognize them. "What the *fuck* just happened?"

"Jacob just screwed us all, that's what happened," Kellen said. And Jacob thought Adam was the irresponsible, selfish jackhole of the band? The man needed to take a look in the mirror.

"Did Sole Regret just break up?" Owen grabbed Kellen's arm. "Did he actually leave? He's coming back, though, right? After we find Adam and Jacob clears his head, he'll be back."

"I'm not so sure," Kellen said. "I think we're through."

Now what the fuck was he supposed to do?

CHAPTER FOURTEEN

DAWN SMOOTHED her hands over her clingy sage-green evening gown. She hoped it appeared to be a movement of elegance rather than what it actually was—a way to wipe off her sweaty palms. She wasn't sure why she was so nervous. Perhaps because this meeting was being held at Spago Beverly Hills and there were several highly recognizable A-list actors seated at nearby tables. A few of them had even glanced her way. Probably wondering what a nobody like her was doing sitting at a large table by herself. Or maybe they'd seen the ugly red jellyfish sting welts on her ankle as she'd crossed the floor. There'd been no way to hid them in this dress.

Wes had already texted that they were on their way. They would have picked her up from home, but she had been coming from the opposite side of town and didn't want to put anyone out. But that meant she'd arrived alone, and despite policy, they'd seated her before her party arrived. Two buckets holding chilled champagne sat near the table.

A group of laughing men and women entered the restaurant, and Dawn was equal parts relieved and terrified to see Wes heading the large party. She tore her eyes away from the one familiar face in the crowd, only to realize she recognized at least half of the other faces. Two major directors, a well-known producer who also happened to be a famous actress, a world-renowned composer of blockbuster films—a job she currently wanted—and to her utter astonishment, her former music teacher, Pierre.

"I hope you haven't been waiting long," Wes said, rushing past the maître d' to kiss Dawn's suddenly clammy cheek.

What the hell was Pierre doing there?

Into Dawn's ear, Wes whispered, "You look gorgeous, so save the deer-in-the-headlight look. Take a deep breath, kiddo."

Dawn did what she was told, sucking in an enormous breath, and then she commenced to gush.

"Oh, Mr. Steinberg, I'm such a fan of all your movies. Oh, Dr. Everlong, the compositions in *Space Trek* were so moving." She was sure she said equally stupid shit to the rest of the group, and then she was being hugged by Pierre and the entire world stood still. She was back to being that fifteen-year-old girl who trembled when he sat beside her on the piano bench.

"I'm so proud of you. I knew you'd be great. From the moment I first saw your fingers strike the ivories, I knew."

He said that now. When he'd been instructing her, she'd felt she'd never live up to his expectations of perfection. But maybe that was why she'd tried so hard to please him. Maybe that was why she'd been so head over heels in love with the man.

A hand on her elbow drew Dawn back to the present, and she felt her face smiling as Wes encouraged her to take a seat between Mr. Steinberg and Dr. Everlong. Pierre was seated on the other side of Dr. Everlong, so unless she leaned forward or back, he was out of sight. Which was good. Not because she didn't like to look at Pierre—he was still as devastatingly gorgeous as she remembered—but because she couldn't spark a single thought beyond *What the hell is Pierre doing here*, as long as he was in view.

"Terribly sorry to make you come all this way to meet with us, Ms. O'Reilly," Mr. Steinberg said, "but I'm off to shoot a film in Ireland tomorrow, and Drew and Pierre are off to Venice. Jill leaves for Toronto, but we were all here in L.A. this weekend. Except you. I hear you're leaving for Prague soon."

"Uh." She was having a hard time following him, because he'd called Dr. Andrew Everlong, Drew, and Jillian Calipso, Jill, and was she really sitting at a table with these powerhouses?

"She has a performance," Wes said. "Chopin."

"I adore Chopin," Dr. Everlong said.

"I hear him in your compositions," Dawn said.

"And I, yours," Dr. Everlong said. Which meant he'd listened to her compositions. The idea blew her mind.

"I've always thought his sound is timeless," she said, her brain finally kicking on. She always got all-star struck and stupid—not usually to this degree—but . . . *What the hell is Pierre doing here?* She leaned forward and found him toying with the napkin on his plate. "You're going to Venice with Dr. Everlong?"

Dr. Everlong elbowed Pierre in the side and offered Dawn a

kind smile. His blue eyes twinkled with mischief. "He's the one who brought you to our attention."

Wes cleared his throat. "I was the one who suggested Dawn for the project when you called my agency."

Dawn didn't bother hiding her smile. Wes never shirked on taking credit when due.

"But why do you think we called your agency?" Dr. Everlong asked.

"I'm still confused as to what this meeting is about," Dawn said.

"We'll explain," Jillian Calipso said. "But let's order first. I'm starved."

The award-winning actress was so strikingly beautiful that Dawn couldn't help but stare. She'd seen Jillian Calipso on the big screen countless times, but it was hard to believe she was as achingly gorgeous in real life as she was in the movies. Was she even wearing makeup? Lord.

When it was Dawn's turn to order, she realized she hadn't even glanced at the menu. She was surprised to find it open in front her. "Uh." She pointed at some random entree. "I'll have this."

The waiter was kind enough to walk her through the rest of the ordering process. She hoped she hadn't accidentally ordered something gross. She'd been to enough fancy restaurants to know they sometimes disguised disgusting food with a fancy name. She'd once consumed ox balls and hadn't realized it until she'd posted about her meal online and some follower had taken it upon herself to point out Dawn's folly. They hadn't actually tasted bad, but Dawn would rather not have a repeat performance.

While they waited for their meal, Dr. Everlong said, "So tell everyone how you know Pierre."

She'd rather Pierre tell her what he was doing at a business meeting with Hollywood heavyweights, but she nodded. "He taught me to play piano."

"Non, ma petite cherie. You taught me how to teach piano."

She craned her neck to look around Dr. Everlong and lifted a brow at Pierre, but he merely smiled at her.

"Sometimes the student teaches us more than we could ever teach them."

That sexy French accent of his did strange twisty things to her insides, but she had to wonder at his sudden sappiness.

Wes cleared his throat. "This is all very charming and nostalgic," he said. "Teacher loves student, student loves teacher. But I for one can't take the suspense any longer. Why are we here?"

Dawn whirled around to gape at her agent. He didn't know why they were there? And he'd called her all the way from Houston, cutting into her time with Kellen and making her trip to Prague an exhausting marathon of airplane rides, knowing only as much as she did, which was essentially nothing?

Mr. Steinberg leaned closer to the table. "We're collaborating on a new project, a trilogy of fantasy films. Very hush-hush, so the details will be forthcoming, but we already have an exalted vision for the musical scores. Think *Star Wars* in scope. It needs to be that grand. And memorable. And the score must be as amazing as the script and the cinematography."

"It must be *more* amazing than the script," Dr. Everlong said. "Pierre and I have been knocking our heads together over this for a month."

"Six weeks," Pierre said, his fingers tangling in his napkin.

"And what we have is good, but not great. We need fresh talent. Inspirational talent. A talent like yours, Ms. O'Reilly."

Dawn had to admit she was flattered. Perhaps that was why she laughed. But more likely it was because they had no idea how hard it was for her to find inspiration. Talent alone did not magically produce her compositions. It took a lot of hard work and failure to find a single note of success. Everyone at the table stared at her sudden bout of inappropriate hilarity.

She lifted her napkin to dab tears out of her eyes and took a deep gasping breath before releasing a few more nervous giggles. "I fear you're wasting your time," she eventually said. "I have to wring every note out of my pathetically uninspired brain when I compose. There is no magic happening at my piano bench, trust me on that."

For a moment she could feel Kellen standing at her shoulder, then sitting beside her, offering her support and the passion she'd needed to break free of her damned writer's block. And as handsome as Pierre was—or maybe because of it—he'd never inspired a creative spark within her. He'd pushed her performance, not her creativity. And trying to compose at the elbow of a modern legend like Dr. Everlong? Dear lord, she'd likely forget how to play scales with him looming over her.

"We heard your new song," Mr. Steinberg said. "Giovani was bragging about the closing credit song he'd just received."

"Galahan just loved rubbing that song in my face," Dr. Everlong said.

Wait? Giovanni Galahan—*the* Giovanni Galahan—had been bragging about "Blue"? She'd barely turned the score over to Wes. How was he bragging about it already? And why was he bragging to Mr. Steinberg? And he was seriously bragging about her little song? Dawn giggled at how surreal all of this was. The giants of Hollywood were talking about her music. She couldn't even comprehend that reality.

"She giggles when she's nervous," Wes commented, and Dawn bit her lip. She did giggle when she was nervous and didn't even realize she was doing it, but she was actually laughing at how unbelievable this entire conversation had become.

"Composing is damned near impossible on your own," Dr. Everlong said, laying an encouraging hand on her back. "I've spent many an hour staring at a piano keyboard or holding a violin at the ready and not a single note is produced. I've learned over the years that when you're stuck, brainstorming with other creative minds is the solution."

"That's where I was supposed to come in," Pierre said.

"You've done a wonderful job," Dr. Everlong said, his other hand resting on Pierre's back, and then Dawn got what was really going on. Maybe.

Everlong wrung the talent and hard work out of less experienced and far less famous musicians and stamped his name all over the compositions.

"So who gets credit for the compositions? Royalties? That sort of thing?" she asked. Someone kicked her under the table, and she turned her head toward Wes, who was glaring at her in warning. Yes, she understood. The business part of these deals was Wes's responsibility. She was just supposed to do all the creative work.

"Drew will get first billing, naturally, but if you agree, you'll get second credit and a fair share of royalties."

"And Pierre?" she asked, wishing her mouth would stop

running away with her.

"I am well compensated," Pierre said, offering her a lopsided grin.

Dawn gnawed on her lip. This was a life-changing opportunity. She knew that. If Dr. Everlong took her under his wing this early in her career, there was no telling how far she might go. But his glory might also mask hers. It might be best to create her own coattails instead of clinging to his. This was a big decision, and she refused to take it lightly or make up her mind without consulting those she trusted to set her straight.

Wes would have her back when it came to money and legalities, but who could she seek for advice? Pierre was obviously already snuggly in Dr. Everlong's pocket, though he might have some helpful insight, assuming he was honest with her. And Kellen knew the ins and outs of the rock and roll business, but this was far out of his scope of knowledge. Still, she'd ask his opinion. Maybe her professors at Curtis would have useful advice. Or maybe she should just go for it. It wasn't every day that opportunity as grand as this knocked on her door. Maybe she should just answer without asking who was there and what they wanted, and without peeking at them through the peephole. *Just go for it, Dawn.*

She glanced up to find everyone staring at her hopefully, as if they couldn't find some other more experienced, more talented composer to jump on this opportunity. And maybe they couldn't. What did she know?

"I need some time to consider this," she said. "I want to fully understand all the details before I commit."

Wes's shoulders sagged, and she heard Pierre release a sigh, but otherwise no one seemed overly upset about her indecision.

"We'll need an answer within the next few days," Mr. Steinberg said. "We wanted to approach you first, because we think you're the best, but we can't wait for long. We're already behind schedule."

Dawn snorted on another laugh and covered her mouth with one hand. The *best*. Really? These folks really didn't know a thing about her. Wes must have really talked her up.

"We all have deadlines to meet," Mr. Steinberg added.

Her belly did a backflip at that dreaded word: deadline. But maybe it wouldn't be so bad when she had others to rely on and help her meet those deadlines. Maybe team composing was the way to go. She couldn't know if she didn't try.

Their meal arrived, and Dawn was relieved that she'd ordered some sort of chicken. She wasn't sure what the green and purple leaves on her plate were, but everything else was not only beautiful to look at, but also pleasing to her taste buds. She wondered if Kellen would like to eat here sometime. Assuming she became famous enough to get a reservation. She was glad when conversation turned to politics, because it was easy to pretend that she didn't have an opinion and let her thoughts wander to her own situation. She wasn't sure she could handle making conversation at the moment. As her entree had been about the size of a naked chicken nugget, it didn't take long to finish her meal. She found herself trapped between the heated debate of Everlong and Steinberg—one a centrist, the other very liberal. She waited for an opening in their incessant arguing about their not-really-so-opposing views on how to handle illegal immigration before she excused herself to go to the ladies room.

She was surprised when the only other woman at the table—the legendary actress turned producer Jillian Calipso—joined her. Dawn had a sudden and strange longing for Lindsey's presence. Lindsey could have distracted Jillian with excited fangirling while Dawn did her business. She was surprised the actress needed to pee at all. Jillian Calipso was on par with a goddess, and Dawn was certain that goddesses didn't answer the call of nature.

"Too much testosterone at that table for my liking," Jillian said as they entered the bathroom in single file.

Dawn laughed like a preteen talking to her crush for the first time. She was starting to think she had some sort of laughing Tourette's. They all must think she was a blubbering idiot. "You must deal with that a lot."

Jillian smiled and caught Dawn's arm before she disappeared into a stall. "I don't actually have to use the facilities," Jillian said.

Hah! Dawn had been right. The woman didn't lower herself to perform natural bodily functions.

"I want to encourage you to sign with us."

"Oh," Dawn said flatly. She couldn't seem to stop herself from frowning any more than she could stop giggling. Coincidentally, she sucked at poker.

"There aren't nearly enough women in your profession."

"Which is one reason I hesitate," Dawn said. "If I become an extension of Dr. Everlong instead of rising to the top alone, I might never find my own footing."

"You will," Jillian said with a smile. "It's hard to rise in this business, especially for women and minorities—don't let anyone convince you otherwise—but instead of fighting the establishment, use it. Use it for *your* gain, not theirs."

Dawn wasn't sure she was capable of using people to climb her ladder of success. She'd rather create her own ladder than patch together the ladders of others, but she had to admit Jillian's advice was sound, and she was speaking from experience. She wasn't a composer, but she was part of the Hollywood elite.

"You might think you want to reinvent the wheel here, hon, but take this opportunity. If it doesn't work out the way you hope, you can always find a different path to the top." Jillian touched Dawn's bare arm, and the small action made her seem far more human and far less godlike. "You do want to rise to the top, don't you?"

Dawn smiled. "Somehow."

Jillian returned her smile. "Good. Now go out there and tell those men you'll do what they want, when in reality they'll be doing what you want."

Was that how women became successful? Not all, Dawn realized, but utilizing other's might make obtaining success easier, assuming she could hold her own with the men who were already at the top. She doubted she'd get far if she kept breaking into fits of giggles for no justifiable reason.

"Thanks for the advice, Jillian. I appreciate your guidance. I have to admit I was flipping out a bit."

"That's what they want. That's why they didn't tell Wes what to expect, why they scheduled this meeting when you didn't have time to meet with us. Why they invited several people who don't have anything to do with the movie's score, myself included. I'd better head back, or they'll be on to me." Jillian squeezed her arm and offered her the signature wink that she'd likely trademarked. "You look out for yourself, hon."

Jillian left, and Dawn stared at the back of the closed door until another woman entered the restroom and startled her out of her thoughts. She went into the stall and sat there long after she'd finished tinkling, wondering if she should follow Jillian's advice and use this opportunity as a shortcut to her future or if she was even strong and smart enough to do so. When she finally left the restroom—the entire table must be wondering what she was giving birth to in there that would take so long—Pierre was milling about just outside the door.

"I was about to enter and see if you'd drowned yourself."

She chuckled. "I needed a moment to collect my thoughts. Long time, no see, Teach." She lifted her arms to hug him, thought better of it and started to lower them again, but he closed the gap between them, drawing her against him for a tight squeeze.

"You've grown into such a lovely woman, precious one."

"Having second thoughts about turning me down now that I've grown into my awkwardly long limbs?"

He caught her face between his palms and kissed the tip of her nose. "You do know I'm gay, right?"

Dawn's face fell. Pierre was gay? No, she hadn't realized that, but then her gaydar was perpetually broken.

"Your song, ma petite, is miraculous."

"Miraculous?" She laughed. "You mean 'Ashes'?"

"That piece was stirring. It deserved the Grammy. This new song, what is it called?"

"'Blue'?"

"Ah, perfect. Yes, 'Blue.' It grabbed me from the first note, ripped my soul from my body, stirred it into a frenzy, smoothed it like warm butter, and put it back inside me at a higher level."

She laughed. "You always did exaggerate."

"Non, this is no exaggeration, ma petite. This music you created, it is a gift from God."

Dawn rolled her eyes and shook her head. Yes, it was her best work, and she knew it was good, but it wasn't that big of a deal. She hadn't even polished it yet.

"Are you really gay?" she blurted. "I had such a crush on you as a teen."

"And it never made sense to me, because I'm as queer as they come."

"Kellen will be glad to hear that," she said.

"Please, please, join us to create the scores for this project."

"Maybe I want to create my own score on another project."

"Plenty of time for that, ma cherie. You're young. Everlong and I? Not so much."

Everlong was pushing eighty, but Pierre was not yet fifty. He had plenty of time to compose. Which reminded her . . .

"When did you start composing? Have you given up on teaching?"

"You, cherie. You inspired me to follow my true dream. You were so young yet so certain of your path. So driven despite your father's wishes. So passionate and talented. And when you told me you didn't really want to perform despite how much effort and love you put into every performance, that you actually wanted to write because writing was a true expression of the soul—performing but an expression of the heart, the mind and body—I couldn't stop thinking about your words, and I followed the path you directed me toward."

"Me? I was fifteen when I said that." She laughed and hugged him again. "Who takes a fifteen year old seriously?"

"A man smart enough to recognize true genius."

"I thought you'd drowned," Wes said from several steps away.

What exactly did these guys think she did with toilets that would lead to her drowning?

"I almost did, but Pierre rescued me."

Wes chuckled. "I actually thought you were freaking out in the bathroom. I'm glad I don't have to go in there after you."

"I was freaking out in the bathroom."

"Understandable. They're sending the contracts to my office tomorrow morning. You should have time to sign them before you catch your flight."

Dawn took Pierre's hand and squeezed. "I'm not yet sure I'm signing."

Wes blinked at her. "What? You're kidding, right? This isn't the kind of opportunity you consider, it's the kind you jump on."

"Let her follow her heart," Pierre said, lifting her hand and kissing her knuckles. He was so dreamy. He was going to make some lucky guy very happy one day. "Her heart has never steered her wrong."

An image of Kellen flitted through her thoughts, and she smiled. She was certain that Pierre was right; her heart never steered her wrong. And while her head was ready to accept whatever crappy deal these people sent her way, her heart wanted a little longer to consider where this future might lead her.

"I'll read them tomorrow," Dawn promised. "I just don't want you to promise anyone I'll sign them."

"You want to negotiate." Wes's eyes lit with excitement, and Dawn grinned at him. Nothing excited Wes more than a brutal round of contract negotiations.

"I might. Let's see what the deal is before we make a move."

Wes grabbed her head between his palms, dropping a kiss on her forehead. "This one," he said. "She's going places."

Pierre smiled. "Hopefully at my piano bench once more. I have so missed the way she plays. I've been to several of her performances, but they're never as amazing as her private recitals for one."

And the only recitals for one in her future would be with an audience of Kellen Jamison. Those special sessions always ended with hot and heavy sex and an earth-shattering orgasm. She flushed at the direction of her thoughts. They'd been apart mere hours and already she missed him. Craved him. She wondered how his concert for thousands was going.

"I didn't know you attended my performances," Dawn said. "I wish you'd let me know; we could have met after the show." God, she was lonely after shows. Her reality wasn't anything like Kellen's where each show was bookended with fun and shenanigans. A certain level of propriety was expected of her. She might have wine or champagne, but had never had a crowd of fans try to do something outlandish like sneak into her dressing room and wait for her naked, lubed up, and ready to roll. She'd have called the cops if one had.

"I didn't think you'd want to see me after the way you had me fired," Pierre said.

Dawn scrunched her eyebrows together. "The way I had you fired? What do you mean? You quit. Never even said goodbye to me. I thought it was because I tried to seduce you."

"I had no choice but to leave after you told your father I had behaved most ungentlemanly."

Dawn shook her head. "Of course I wouldn't tell my father that. Especially since it wasn't true."

"He showed me your torn dress and told me if he ever saw my face again, he'd have me tossed in prison."

Dawn couldn't believe what she was hearing. She'd been devastated when Pierre had quit offering her private lessons right after she'd thrown himself at him. There'd been no torn dress. And though he'd turned her down, he hadn't been cruel about it. He hadn't laughed at her for trying to be an adult when she'd been a child.

So her *father* had chased Pierre away. She should have guessed as much.

"I cannot believe that man!" And yet, she could. She knew how tirelessly her father worked to rule her life. She was sure there were many more instances of him trying to set her on the path he'd chosen for her even as she'd wandered as far from it as possible.

She grabbed Pierre's arm, and stared up into his kind eyes. "I hope you believe I never accused you of any wrongdoing— and my father should be the one apologizing—but I'm sorry you got caught between us. I'm sorry he threatened you. I'm sor—"

Pierre covered her lips with two fingers. "Non." He shook his head. "I'm sorry for believing you capable of such lies."

"Dawn," Wes interrupted, "we'd better get back to the table. They'll think we're conspiring."

She wasn't conspiring, she was fuming. She'd never connected with another musician the way she'd connected with Pierre. He'd understood exactly how to get the best sound from her and made her dream of creating her own music. Her own songs. He was the one who'd given her the confidence to pursue music as a career, not just as a hobby that won her pretty ribbons and trophies.

"Pierre, if I sign this deal, will we be working together or will I be with Everlong?"

"He's fantastic, cherie. You will learn so much from him. It is he you should be excited to work with, not I."

"I feel comfortable with you. Perhaps that's why I thought I was in love with you. I think he'll just make me nervous."

"I have no doubt that he will at first. He is not easy to know, but don't let that stop you from learning from him."

"And how did you meet him?"

Pierre flushed and pressed a hand against her back to urge her back to the dining area. "Perhaps I'll explain another time."

She beamed at him. "Thank you for thinking of me for this

opportunity, Pierre. Your faith in my ability took me much farther than you can imagine."

"This is what I mean about her teaching me to be a teacher," he said to Wes, who was following close behind them. "She says what's on her mind. In her heart."

"It's called being a blabber mouth," Dawn said, sliding into her seat. She'd missed dessert and coffee, but everyone just seemed happy to see her. I can do this, she told herself. I can make this work. I can work beside these masters and learn and grow, and it doesn't matter if I have to share the credit for the work we create. The journey is more important.

She couldn't wait to tell Kellen.

"We'll need your answer by Friday," Dr. Everlong said. "That's when we go to Venice and get to work."

Hold up. "Venice?"

"Wait until you hear the scope of this project, cherie. We'll be busy for years."

Years? "But what about Kellen?" she blurted.

"Who?"

"My boyfriend." The man her heart told her to follow while at the same time telling her to follow Pierre to Venice. Maybe her heart wasn't so wise after all.

CHAPTER FIFTEEN

KELLEN HELD his phone in his hand, staring at the screen, waiting for Dawn's call. It was after midnight in Mississippi, but just after ten on the West Coast. He wasn't sure how long meetings with Hollywood producers took, but he'd promised himself he wouldn't interrupt Dawn's important dinner, no matter how much his life had turned upside down in the hours since they'd parted.

When his phone dinged with a text message, his breath caught. It was her.

When is rockstar bedtime? Are you still up?

He didn't bother texting her back, just called. He needed to hear her reassuring voice, because no matter how cool he was playing to the guys, on the inside he was freaking out and he couldn't even share that with Owen, because Owen had locked himself in the bathroom of their hotel room and was in there talking to Caitlyn or jacking off or slitting his wrists. Who knew?

"You will not believe the night I had," Dawn said, her excitement and glee tangible even over the phone.

"I had quite the night myself."

"They want me to co-write the scores for an upcoming fantasy trilogy with Dr. Andrew Everlong."

Andrew Everlong? Even Kellen knew who he was. Dr. Everlong had come up with the mood-evoking theme music from the Space Trek movies—all nine of them. "Wow," he said. "That's huge! Congratulations."

"I'm not sure I should take the job, though. I won't be able to see you much if I do."

There was no way in hell he was standing in the way of that kind of opportunity. "Don't worry about that. We'll figure out a way to make us work."

Especially now that he was probably out of a job.

"And I'm worried that I'll end up as a ghostwriter of sorts. I do all the work, Everlong takes all the credit."

"So you didn't jump on it?"

"No. I want to at least sleep on it. If I take the job, I'll have to go to Venice next week."

"Prague, Venice. What's next, Rome?" He chuckled, his chest swelling with pride. She was so accomplished, yet so down to earth about it. A rare woman. He'd be an idiot to let her go, but an even bigger idiot to stand in her way.

"Maybe. Everlong wants to draw inspiration from centers of renaissance art and culture. I'd rather be inspired by you."

Yep, a rare woman. She filled him with such hope and longing.

"So how was your show?" she asked.

"We'll get to that in a minute," he said. "I want you tell me everything great about this contract they're offering you. Just the great stuff."

She shared her list—a long list—of how working with Everlong would be a learning experience. How she'd see a side of composing she wouldn't get to see any other way. The money was good apparently. Their writing team was all but guaranteed to win awards. She'd meet great, talented stars and see amazing sights and . . . Kellen knew he couldn't compete with that. And he didn't want to. He wanted her to reach for her stars.

"Oh," she said after several minutes of fanning her own flames of excitement. "Pierre will be there too."

"Pierre?" Why did that name sound familiar? And then he remembered making fun of the name when Dawn had told him about her unhealthy obsession with her music teacher and how he'd rejected her attempts to seduce him. "The Pierre you were in love with as a teenager?"

"Yeah. He's actually the one who encouraged them to contact me."

"So you saw him?" Kellen's hands were sweating. Between this new job opportunity and the potential for her to rekindle an old flame, he was starting to feel that he should discourage her. For his sake. But even the thought was disgustingly selfish of him.

"He was at the dinner, and he encouraged me to sign the contract. He's started composing too. Actually, he said I was the one who gave him that dream. I didn't even know he was considering it. And he's been working with Everlong for a few months now. I think they're lovers."

Kellen choked. "What?"

"Yeah, apparently my gaydar is broken. I had no idea Pierre was into men." She laughed. "Maybe that's why I never felt threatened by him."

So Kellen didn't have to worry about Pierre stealing his girl. At least not romantically.

"And now that you've weighed all the positives, what are the negatives?"

He could hear the smile in her voice when she said, "This is why I didn't want to sign that contract until I spoke to you. I knew you'd help me approach it logically."

"You should probably just follow your heart," he said, suddenly feeling like an ass for forcing her to see the opportunity as anything less than perfect.

"That's what Pierre told me, but if I followed my heart, I'd turn this down. My heart wants to follow you."

A mix of joy and terror swirled through Kellen's chest. "Would you be okay with me following you instead?"

"I'm not sure if I can wait until your tour is over, Kellen. I miss you so much already."

"The tour is already over," he said. "My band broke up."

Saying the words made it more real, and that panicky feeling he'd been trying to quash before he heard Dawn's voice began rising again, making it difficult to draw air.

"Wait. I think I heard you wrong," Dawn said. "Did you just say your band broke up?"

"Yeah. We can't find Adam. He took off right before we were set to go onstage and didn't let anyone know where he was going. It was the final straw for Jacob. The rest of us were pretty much in shock when he made us choose between kicking Adam out of the band or him leaving. So he left."

"I— I don't know what to say. I'm sorry. Do you think you guys can work things out?"

Kellen bit his lip. "I keep saying that, keep telling myself that we can. But deep down I'm not sure. I'm not sure about anything right now." He took a deep breath. "Except you. I'm sure about you, Dawn."

"I'll cancel this week's performance and meet you in . . . Where are you?"

"No. Don't do that. Go to Prague. Make grown men weep with the beauty of your music. By the time you get back, I'm sure I'll have myself sorted out."

"I feel terrible," she said. "Everything is going so well for me, and your band is falling apart. I know how important they are to you. Do you want to come to Prague?"

He did want to go to her. Go to Prague. Hold her as tightly as he needed to be held, but . . .

"We might get this mess sorted out, and I'll need to be here for the next tour date. I'm sort of stuck at the moment."

"I wish I could be there with you," she said.

He wished that too, but didn't want to make her feel any worse. "I'll be okay."

Owen came out of the bathroom, which he'd been using as his personal sanctuary, and Kellen offered him a comforting smile. "I'm going to let you go," he told Dawn. "You have to be up early for your flight. I'll talk to you soon."

"If you need me for anything, call. I might not be able to be there in person, but I'm there in spirit."

"I know you are. I can feel you."

After they said their goodbyes, he tucked his phone into his pocket. He patted the sofa beside him, and Owen collapsed into the spot. Owen tilted his head back and rubbed his eyes with one hand as he let loose a lion-size yawn.

"Did you talk to Caitlyn?" Kellen asked, figuring that was what he'd been doing in the bathroom for over an hour.

"Yeah, she's going to visit soon. Either here or in Austin, depending on what Sally decides to do in the morning. What about Dawn?"

Kellen shrugged. "She's busy." And he left it at that. He'd never been one to discuss his girl troubles—or perfection, in Dawn's case—with anyone. Not even Owen.

"I should probably hit the sheets."

"It has been a long day."

"Do you think we're over?" Owen asked. "The band, I mean. Not us. We'll always be best friends."

Kellen wasn't sure why those words closed around his throat like a fist. For the past few days, he'd felt that Owen was drifting away. That feeling was probably due to their brief separation over the weekend, but something felt different between them, and Kellen couldn't put his finger on what.

"I don't know. Jacob was monumentally pissed. I think that anger has been building inside him for a long time. To us, his breaking off from the band might have felt like a sudden, rash decision, but I don't think that's the case with him. He's probably been considering this for a while now."

"I have a sick feeling in the pit of my stomach," Owen said. "I told you earlier that something was wrong, but the feeling hasn't gone away, even with Jacob taking off. I'm starting to think something truly terrible has happened to Adam."

Adam being in real trouble would explain why no one had heard from him for hours, but Kellen slapped Owen on the arm and said, "He's fine. He's been to hell and back how many times? He can survive anything."

"He's always survived because Jacob comes to his rescue."

That sick feeling Owen described settled in Kellen's gut as he realized Owen was right.

"Adam has Madison now," Kellen said, trying to make himself feel better as much as he was hoping to placate Owen's fears.

CHAPTER SIXTEEN

THE NEXT EVENING KELLEN SAT in his Firebird in front of Owen's house, staring at the familiar and welcoming blue cottage. He hesitated to go inside, even though he felt drawn to Owen in this time of uncertainty and Owen was expecting his visit. Sally had let Kellen know that Jacob would be on the local evening news—hopefully to explain why he'd said the band was over, why he'd taken off in the middle of the tour, and generally why he wasn't making a lick of sense.

Jacob had to know that he wasn't the only one affected by his rash decision. If the band didn't get back together, there was no reserve plan ready to sweep in and rescue them all. Kellen had focused his life on perfecting the guitar—it was all he had going for him—and yet by remaining a rhythm guitarist instead of ever taking lead, he was essentially unknown. Adam was Sole Regret's guitarist. Adam was the one the fans cheered for. Adam was the one they knew by name. Adam was the one who could leave right before a New Orleans concert to check on his injured girlfriend in Dallas-fucking-Texas and still have everyone scrambling to kiss his ass. Kellen wasn't sure if the guy was an asshole or a hero.

Kellen climbed the front step and stood in the cool shade of the porch.

He might get a gig with another band—most likely an obscure band—but would Owen be a part of that? He wasn't sure if he could play with another bassist. And the thought of not being able to play with Owen was far more frightening to him than splitting off from the rest of the band. He considered all the guys close friends, but Owen was an integral part of his life. He wouldn't know how to get by without him.

Maybe the two of them could form their own band. But neither of them had Jacob's drive , Gabe's energy, or the dark, demonic muse that possessed Adam, so the two of them would never replicate the magic of Sole Regret, and Kellen wasn't ready to give up on that magic yet. So it was best that he and Owen help Jacob remove his head from his ass, calm Gabe enough for him to think rationally, and get Adam to talk to them about what was going on in his twisted mind, because they obviously weren't relating to each other the way they should.

And though all of these worries were weighing heavily on Kellen's heart, he wasn't still sitting in his car staring at Owen's house for that reason. No, he was roasting alive in his Firebird's stifling interior solely because he wasn't sure how he would react to seeing Lindsey again. Since she was staying with Owen temporarily, he was bound to run into her. What if the mere sight of her reversed all the soul-healing progress he'd made with Dawn's help last weekend? He guessed he'd just have to hole up somewhere with Dawn for another private weekend and set himself straight again. Not exactly a burden.

He stared at the house. He could do it. He could handle seeing the pretty pregnant ghost again. Besides, Sara—damn—*Lindsey* was a minor concern compared to getting the band together. He climbed out of his car and hurried up the front walk, playing different conversations through his head. He needed a different approach for each guy. Gabe was driven by his head, Adam by his gut, Jacob by his heart, and Owen . . . Kellen didn't actually need an approach for Owen. They were always on the same wavelength.

When Kellen reached the front door, he hesitated for just a second before he tried the knob and found it unlocked. Owen's home had always been like his own, just as Kellen's door was always open for Owen. Even though he had guests, Owen would expect him to come inside. And based on the enormous black pickup parked out front, not every guest was a woman.

"Is Gabe here too?" Kellen called to announce his arrival. "Isn't that his truck taking up half the street?"

"Hey." Gabe nodded at Kellen when he entered the living room. His green eyes were troubled, and he looked about as well-rested as Kellen felt, which wasn't well at all considering he hadn't slept in over twenty-four hours.

Caitlyn was sitting beside Owen, holding his hand, offering the support that Kellen usually gave him. Kellen didn't feel jealous, not exactly. He felt lost. Where was his place if it wasn't beside Owen? Maybe if Dawn was there to hold his hand, he'd feel a bit more grounded, but she was en route to Prague. As much as he missed her, he was proud that she was so worldly. He'd sort all the crap out somehow, but doing so would have to wait until he was alone and he could reflect. At the moment, there was too much turmoil in the band for him to reflect on anything but their pile of rubble.

He doubted any of them would be able to sort themselves out if the band didn't get back together. Jacob was obviously even more lost than Kellen—his actions were a cry for help. And as Jacob was the one who understood Adam best, without Jacob, Adam would be lost as well. The two needed each other, just as he and Owen needed one another. He wondered what it felt like to be Gabe, who didn't need any of them to feel grounded and who never felt lost. Or did he? Based on his expression, perhaps Gabe was feeling lost as well.

Kellen played it cool as he flopped down on the sofa next to Owen. He knew they expected him to be the even-tempered one and was committed to doing his best to be the guy they needed. Kellen glanced at the television, surprised they were watching a baseball game instead of Jacob's news segment. He'd called Owen ahead of time with a heads-up.

"Turn the channel," Kellen said, extending a hand toward the television. "It should be starting."

"Already?" Owen scrambled for the remote. "I thought you said tonight."

"At five."

Owen cringed and flipped through the channels until Jacob's face filled the screen. And then the camera panned out to show a woman sitting beside him.

Tina? Kellen exchanged a flabbergasted look with Owen before searching the television screen for clues to the reason their obviously insane lead singer was holding hands with his ex-wife on live television. Last Kellen had heard, Jacob despised Tina and was getting pretty serious about her sister, Amanda.

Owen couldn't even get a full sentence out of his gaping mouth. "What the . . . ?"

"That settles it," Gabe said. "He's completely lost his shit. We're having him committed."

Owen cranked up the volume so they could hear better. Jacob's words scarcely registered with Kellen—something about family being more important than success. Kellen was more interested in body language. Jacob sat as rigid as the oak tree Kellen often likened him to, while Tina leaned into him with a satisfied smile on her pretty face. She was holding Jacob's hand, not the other way around, and there was something in her eyes. Something triumphant. There was something in Jacob's too. His expression was closer to defeat. Despair? It was hard to read him clearly on television.

"So the rest of Sole Regret's summer tour is canceled," Jacob announced in a flat tone. "I'll personally repay the fans for any nonrefundable tickets."

"What?" Tina's triumph faltered just a bit as she turned her astonished gaze on Jacob before fixing her stare back on the camera.

"What?" Gabe shouted at the television.

"Are you back together with your ex-wife?" a reporter asked. "If I recall correctly, your divorce was rather messy."

"And final!" Gabe leaned closer to the TV as if he wanted to climb inside and strangle Jacob.

"We're going to live together as a family," Jacob said. For a second, a small smile turned up the corner of his mouth.

Kellen recognized the smile Jacob reserved for his little girl. He could very easily see Jacob giving up everything for Julie. But not for Tina. Never for Tina. Kellen searched his memory for some clue as to why Jacob's world had apparently tilted on its side, but came up lacking. He'd been so concerned with his own drama that he hadn't been paying attention to anyone else's.

"I won't be able to afford two homes once all the lawsuits start being filed," Jacob continued, "so I've moved back in with my w-*wife* and daughter."

And there would be lawsuits. Lots and lots of lawsuits. Kellen wasn't even sure how many contracts they were breaking here.

"Lawsuits?" Tina asked. Her confident smile was gone now. She gawked at Jacob, but it was the way she suddenly released his hand that made Kellen wonder if the band breakup was a front for something that had nothing to do with Sole Regret. But Jacob wouldn't use them for selfish gain, would he?

"I'm breaking all sorts of contracts to be with you," Jacob said, his gaze turning soft, almost loving, as he looked at her. Kellen shook his head at the TV. Jacob's mixed signals were impossible to read, but Tina seemed to be as stunned by his claims as the rest of them. "But none of that's important. My career is over. I'll be utterly broke, but none of that matters. All that matters is that you get what you want, Tina. You want me, right?"

Tina blinked at him. Her gaze shifted to her lap where her hands were now folded. "Of course I do."

But there was an unspoken stipulation there, Kellen mused. He could practically see it on her forehead. She wanted Shade Silverton, the rock star, not Jacob Silverton, the regular guy, and Jacob seemed to realize that that was the only card he had left to play in their troubling game.

"Does he really not care that he's going to lose everything?" Gabe fumed, barely staying in his chair. "He doesn't even *like* her!"

"All we need is love," Jacob said, his gaze solidly locked with Tina's.

Maybe she would settle for Jacob the gifted actor, because wow, Kellen could almost buy his sincerity. If he hadn't known Jacob better, hadn't lived with him through the hell of his divorce, hadn't witnessed how hard it had been for Jacob to straighten out his life after Tina had insisted they split, Kellen would have though Jacob was in love with the gold-digger.

"Isn't that right, sweetheart?" Jacob kissed Tina's hand. Her lips were pursed too rigidly to actually smile.

"That's right," she managed to say.

A vicious game was being played out right before them. Tina held all the aces, or made Jacob think she did, but Jacob wasn't as stupid as she thought he was. He knew what she was really after and knew how to take it away. Kellen didn't like that he'd tangled Sole Regret up in his scheme, but they couldn't accept the situation at face value. Deeper issues were churning beneath the surface.

"We're missing something," Owen said. "Something monumental."

Exactly. Kellen snorted because Owen's thoughts mirrored his. "Don't you see what he's doing?" Kellen asked.

"Being the biggest fucking idiot who ever lived?" Gabe yelled.

"He's calling her bluff."

Tina didn't have as many aces as she thought she did.

"What bluff?" Owen asked.

"I don't know," Kellen said, "but look at her face. She started off smug—like she had him by the balls, like she was in charge and held all the aces. And now she looks like she's ready to fold." Or puke.

"You don't honestly think he's willing to give up everything just to get back at her?" Gabe said. "And he's not the only one he's screwing here. What about us? We have a stake in this too. Did he ever consider how this would affect anyone but himself?"

"It has to have something to do with Julie," Owen said.

Kellen's heart skipped a beat. Owen was probably right. Jacob's seemingly irrational behavior likely involved Julie. She was the only person on the planet that Jacob would sacrifice everything to protect.

"I'm going to kill him," Gabe said. "If Adam doesn't get to him before I do, I'm going to reach into his gut and yank out his balls from the inside."

"Give him a little time to sort himself out," Kellen said. Jacob wouldn't betray them for the hell of it. Kellen hadn't been sure of that before, but now, seeing him with Tina, he had no doubt that she'd somehow forced his hand, and he'd called her on it.

"He's getting back together with Tina." Owen pointed at the television where Jacob was discussing plans for his less than spectacular future.

"I might paint houses," Jacob said. "Or sell tires. I do want to finish my education—get my GED and set the right example for my daughter."

"I don't think he is." Kellen tilted his head slightly, looking for more clues in the couple's body language. All was not easy and happy in the Silverton household, that much was clear.

"You're going to let him get away with this bullshit?" Gabe said. "He walked out on us, Kellen. And without him fronting the band, Sole Regret will never be the same."

Lead singers almost always made the band. Kellen couldn't deny how much easier it was to find a replacement for a rhythm guitarist, a bassist, even a drummer. But a singer? Or their lead guitarist and songwriter? The two of them really made the band. None of them could deny that reality.

"Maybe he'll change his mind," Owen said.

"And maybe we'll tell him to fuck off," Gabe said.

"He's obviously struggling. Look at him." Kellen rose to his feet and pointed at the screen. Couldn't they see the tension right before them? Or maybe he was the odd one for recognizing it so easily. "Look at his posture."

When Owen and Gabe looked at him as if he were discussing an imaginary friend, Kellen sighed. They really didn't see it. Did either of them ever pay attention to how Jacob normally behaved?

"He was acting off before Adam left, you morons. I'm telling you, something is going on with him that he didn't share with us."

"Obviously," Gabe said. "But that's no excuse to stab your friends in the back. He just up and left."

"Adam also *fucking* left," Kellen shouted, since calm discussions didn't get through to Gabe.

Gabe punched the sofa's arm and growled, "And the three of us are left here holding our dicks."

Kellen couldn't argue that fact. The three of them were totally screwed if Jacob and Adam never reconciled. And Jacob was the key to settling their differences. Adam was too self-centered to put anyone before his own agenda.

"Jacob has only fucked us over this once; Adam has left us high and dry dozens of times," Owen said.

Kellen smiled at his friend—who always sided with him, always had his back—but Owen's attention was fixed on Gabe, so he offered no return smile. Jacob had left, but only because Adam had added the final straw. Jacob needed their backing right now, not their animosity. Adam needed support as well. Hell, Kellen could use a little reassurance himself, and he was sure he wasn't the only man in the room feeling that need. They had to come up with a way to get everyone back together and on speaking terms, or this band really would be over.

"I think we have to support him until he figures out what he wants," Kellen said, figuring Gabe wasn't ready to hear that. He'd never seen the guy so angry before.

"I'm not supporting his insanity." Gabe jerked to his feet and covered his head with his ball cap. "We put all our faith in him, and he left us. Without a word, he left."

Gabe's anger was a front for his hurt, Kellen realized. Jacob had hurt Gabe by leaving, by potentially breaking up the band, and Gabe didn't know how else to react.

"You need to think this through before you go off, Gabe," Kellen said. "You could make things worse."

"Stop being so goddamned even-tempered, Cuff! This doesn't piss you off? Not even a little?"

Kelly shook his head. "It makes me sad." Which hadn't been his first reaction. Like Gabe, he'd been pissed, but Kellen was past anger now and falling into despair.

Gabe glared at Owen, who grimaced. "And I suppose you're in agreement with your friend here. You two practically share a brain."

"Maybe Julie is sick," Owen said, and immediately Kellen's heart sank. Julie being sick would be terrible, but it would explain Jacob's rash behavior.

Gabe's rage finally ratcheted down a notch. "Why would you think that?"

"He's been adamant about spending time with Julie lately. Scheduled the entire tour around his visitation days. So maybe something is terribly wrong with her."

"It could be that," Kellen said. He hoped not from the depths of his soul and searched for any reason to discredit the idea, because thinking Julie was sick was too agonizing to face. "But I don't think he'd hide that from us."

Gabe was standing over them with his fists on his thighs—a divisive force in the room. Except nothing would ever divide Kellen and Owen. Not even Gabe's temper.

"Will you sit down?" Kellen said to him. "We need to figure this mess out."

"We need to get Shade back," Owen said.

Kellen loved that they were thinking the same way—not that it surprised him. He smiled and nodded at Owen, but noticed that Caitlyn was doing a good job of offering her silent support to Owen, so turned back to Gabe.

"Maybe I don't want him back," Gabe said, but he sat.

"Which of us do you think he'd be most likely to listen to?" Kellen asked.

"Gabe," Owen said. "But not if he goes there all pissed off like he is now."

"I'm not pissed off," Gabe said.

"Riiiight," Owen said, rolling his eyes, and Caitlyn giggled.

"Why shouldn't I be pissed off? The fucking dolt has destroyed my career just like that." Gabe snapped his fingers. "If Sole Regret is really over, what am I supposed to do with the rest of my life? I don't have a fucking plan B, okay? I don't know how to proceed."

Kellen caught movement out of the corner of his eye and for an instant, he thought Sara had risen from the grave to stand crying in the doorway, but it was Lindsey. He would likely never get used to how much she resembled Sara, but now when he looked at her, he didn't see Sara. He saw a pretty young blonde trying to sort out her life. To that he could relate.

"Are you okay?" Owen was instantly on his feet, squeezing Lindsey's slight shoulder and looking her over with concern. "Are you in pain? Is it the baby?"

Kellen didn't miss the way Caitlyn stiffened when Owen touched Lindsey, but Owen didn't see her reaction.

"Is Sole Regret really breaking up?" Lindsey asked.

She was crying over that? Now that Kellen thought about it, there would be a lot of upset fans when news of the band's demise spread.

"We hope not."

Lindsey hugged Owen, who cringed and tried patting her without actually touching her. He glanced at Caitlyn, but she just shrugged. She probably recognized that Lindsey wasn't a threat for Owen's affection. If that was his baby, though, Kellen hoped Caitlyn realized there would be no way that Owen could give up his child.

"It's all my fault." Lindsey sniffled. "I show up pregnant, and you all start arguing and then Adam leaves and now Shade is gone and . . . and . . ."

"This has nothing to do with you," Gabe said. "Adam has been unreliable and self-absorbed since the day I met him."

"But he left to be reliable for Madison," Kellen reminded him. "*Selfless* for Madison." Stepping up to help another person was a big step in Adam's personal growth, even if his action negatively impacted the band.

"How very nice for Madison," Gabe grumbled. "How utterly devastating for the rest of us. Did Adam even admit he was in the wrong when you talked to him?" he asked Owen. "Because when I talked to him, all he wanted to know was what *Jacob* had done."

Owen shrugged. "He admitted he should have told us where he was going. He seemed sorry."

"But he didn't say it."

Owen shook his head. No surprise there, but Kellen knew Adam felt deeply, no matter how much he tried to hide his emotions.

"Adam's always been unapologetic," Kellen said. "It doesn't mean he doesn't feel remorse. He just doesn't express it."

Owen looked down at Lindsey. "We're going to do whatever we can to keep Sole Regret together. No more crying over this."

Well, at least three of the band members wanted to fix this shitstorm. If it came to a majority vote, they'd win, but they couldn't force Shade to sing. Couldn't force Adam to play.

Lindsey wiped at her face with the back of her hand and nodded. "I came to tell you dinner is ready and overheard you talking about the band."

"I can't stay." Gabe stood and inched toward the door. "I'm going to see if I can find out some real information. Maybe I can corner Jacob outside the news studio if I hurry."

Owen bumped fists with Gabe. "Keep us posted."

"Once things settle down, I want a backgammon rematch," Caitlyn said.

Gabe stopped retreating and grinned over his shoulder. "Eager to lose again?"

"Oh, I'll be winning this time," she promised.

Kellen smiled to himself. He really did like Caitlyn. She was a good match for Owen. Kellen wondered if his own good match was having a nice time in Prague.

"We'll see about that."

After a quick wave, Gabe left. Should Kellen have tried to stop him? If Gabe confronted Jacob while he was angry, he would probably make Jacob defensive, and he'd be acting like that unbendable oak again. But at least Jacob would know that his bandmates weren't going to accept his decision without a fight. Kellen preferred to have a plan and a united front before confronting Jacob. He wanted to put more thought into what he'd do before he acted. He was sure he and Owen could come up with a strategy if left to their own devices.

"Are you staying?" Owen's question drew Kellen from his thoughts.

"Free home-cooked meal?" Kellen sniffed at the delicious aromas wafting through the house. "Fried chicken, if I'm not mistaken. Do you need to ask?"

Owen chuckled, and Kellen followed Lindsey back to the kitchen.

At the table, Kellen sat across from Owen. He was surprised that Caitlyn was capable of releasing Owen's hand long enough to pick up her fork. He had a hard time watching their tender affection. Kellen supposed it was because seeing the couple together made him miss Dawn. She should be landing across the globe within a few hours and could take her phone off airplane mode. Those long trans-Atlantic flights were going to put a damper on his communication with her. He knew she wanted to be with him—supporting him through this crisis—and he could feel her in spirit, but she still wasn't there in person the way Caitlyn was.

Kellen waited for Owen and Lindsey to say grace. He wasn't Christian and apparently neither was Caitlyn. Her eyes met his and then darted downward in respect as Owen thanked God for their meal and Lindsey gave off an aura of reverence. The rest of the meal was far less uncomfortable.

"I don't think I'll be able to touch raw chicken ever again," Lindsey said. "I never used to have a weak stomach. Or mood swings. Or stretch marks."

"Or such a swollen face, I'm sure," Caitlyn said, with a sweet-as-honey smile.

Kellen struggled not to laugh as Owen loaded up his plate with mashed potatoes. Did he really not see that Caitlyn was beside herself with jealousy?

Lindsey's eyes widened. "You can tell?"

"Of course not," Caitlyn said. "Well, maybe a little, but I'm sure you'll lose all that extra weight when the baby is born."

"I like curvy women," Owen said, offering Caitlyn an approving wink.

Based on her scowl, Caitlyn didn't seem to appreciate his compliment, but the woman did have amazing curves in all the right places. Personally, he preferred Dawn's tall, lean form, but he could clearly see why Owen was so turned on by his dark and sexy engineer.

"This is the best fried chicken I've ever had," Owen said, digging into his second piece. "Don't tell my mom I said that."

"That's quite a compliment," Kellen said to Lindsey. "As far as Owen is concerned, his mom is the only woman who knows how to cook properly."

Lindsey beamed, and Kellen was surprised her wide smile didn't make him long for Sara. In fact, he noticed he wasn't thinking about Sara much at all. Not the way he had been fixating on her every time Lindsey caught his eye in New Orleans. But that was before his wonderful weekend with Dawn. Before she'd helped him begin to move forward.

By the time everyone had finished, Kellen's sleepless night was catching up with him. He couldn't have stifled his yawn if he'd tried. "Good food leads to really good naps."

"You'll have to take the couch," Owen said. "Lindsey's got the guest room, and Caitlyn and I will be napping or not-so-napping in my bed."

"We can finish what we started before your mom showed up," Caitlyn said, her tanned face flushed.

Lindsey cringed. "I won't be able to hear you two going at it, will I?"

"That's a definite yes," Caitlyn said, and Kellen bit his lip to hold in a chuckle. He wasn't sure how vocal Caitlyn usually was, but with Lindsey within earshot, she'd likely scream Owen's name at top volume.

"Well, that's my cue to start the dishes," Owen said, rising from his chair.

He leaned over Lindsey as he reached for her plate. "Have you gotten any job interviews yet?" he asked her.

She released a morose sigh. "Not yet, but I've had a few good leads—most telling me to come back in six months. The problem is that no one is going to offer me a job when I'm going to need to be on maternity leave very soon."

Kellen knew it bothered her to be out of work. Or at least it seemed that way. The longer he was around her, the more he started to believe she hadn't shown up late in her pregnancy because she wanted a handout. She wanted a father for her baby.

Emotional support. And he knew from experience that when you were broke as fuck, it was hard to feel stable in any capacity. Not being able to offer your newborn baby stability had to be a frightening proposition.

"I don't have a problem with you waiting to find work until after the baby is born," Owen said.

Kellen grimaced and shook his head. That wasn't what she wanted. She wanted to be useful. Wasn't that obvious? Was he the only guy paying attention here?

"I have a problem with it," Lindsey said. "I'm not a mooch."

Caitlyn collected their drinking glasses and headed for the kitchen. "I might have some contacts in Austin that could help you out," she said over her shoulder. "I'll look into it when I return to the office."

"That's nice of you," Lindsey said with a smile.

"Have you thought about temp work for now?" Kellen suggested with an encouraging smile. "Maybe an agency has an assignment that will last a couple of months. And then you can find something permanent later."

"That's a great idea, Cuff!" Lindsey placed the dishes she carried into the sink and offered him a nice hug.

Something inside his brain clicked. He could take a bit of the burden off Owen and help him take care of Lindsey. Why not?

"Have you been to the doctor?" he asked, suddenly worried about her well-being. Before, all he could see was how much she looked like Sara. All he could dwell on was how guilty she made him feel. But he didn't feel that way at all now. And he was starting to see why Owen put up with her. She needed their help. And the Mitchells had instilled in him a response to her need as much as they had their biological sons.

"Joan took me to meet her ob/gyn yesterday. We scheduled a thorough appointment for Friday. I'm going to have an ultrasound and everything."

"And a paternity test?" Kellen asked. He figured Owen wouldn't pressure her about it, so it was his responsibility to remind her as often as necessary.

Lindsey glanced at Owen, and then Caitlyn. Her face turned red. "If I have to."

"If it's not Owen's baby, do you still plan on staying here?" Caitlyn asked.

"I suppose I'll have to leave."

Lindsey looked at Owen, her desperation tangible, and even before he spoke, Kellen knew what the big softy was going to say.

"She can stay here." Owen shrugged. "Even if it's not my kid."

A loud clang from the direction of the sink gave Kellen a start. Apparently Caitlyn didn't know Owen quite as well as he did. Or maybe she hoped Owen would abandon the young woman if Caitlyn was passive-aggressive enough.

"I'd accuse you of being an idiot," Kellen said, "but your family took me in and made me feel welcome, so I can't insist you offer Lindsey any less." He smiled at Lindsey, and said, "I can help you out too."

"But it's definitely not yours, Cuff." Lindsey rubbed her belly protectively.

"I don't have to be responsible to want to help you, do I?" Kellen asked, because in reality he wanted to help Owen—to relieve some of the burden troubling his friend. And if the baby was Owen's, Kellen hoped the child would be part of his life too. He always thought he'd make a good uncle.

Caitlyn's passive-aggressive loading of the dishwasher intensified as she jammed silverware into various slots with as much noise as possible.

Lindsey hugged Kellen again, this time nuzzling into his bare chest. "Thank you so much, Cuff. You're almost as nice as Owen is."

"Almost." Kellen winked at Owen, who seemed confused about Kellen's sudden change of heart. Kellen hadn't yet had time to talk to him about his weekend or how he was finally moving on after losing Sara. The part about Kellen being sexually attracted to his best friend? Well, he'd be keeping that little secret all to himself, even though he did finally recognize it for what it was.

The baby was something he could share with Owen beyond their music. He could be the child's godfather, if they'd allow it. And maybe Dawn would like to have a baby of her own. Their sons or daughters could grow up together. Kellen cringed inwardly. What was he thinking? The woman didn't have time to be a mother at this juncture in her career. Hell, she barely had time to be a girlfriend. And if she signed that contract with Everlong—he was pretty sure she wouldn't be able to refuse it once she had time to consider the opportunity—she would be traveling the world for her inspiration to write more songs. He doubted she'd need him at all. Pushing thoughts of future babies aside—he had no business considering children when his own career was so rocky at the moment—he couldn't help but grin as Owen completely missed Caitlyn's pissed-as-hell and jealous cues. Kellen might have come to terms with Owen becoming a father, but his new girlfriend was obviously still struggling with the idea.

"Excuse me," Caitlyn said, giving Owen a pointed look he didn't understand. "I need to use the bathroom." When he didn't respond, she added, "Upstairs."

Kellen feared his friend was in big trouble.

Owen blinked at Caitlyn like a clueless idiot. Kellen stifled a laugh as Caitlyn glared at Owen so hard, he was surprised the poor guy could remain standing. Apparently giving up on Owen reading her mind—or her very clear body language—Caitlyn dried her hands and stormed out of the room with a frustrated snarl.

"You're supposed to go after her," Kellen advised as she tromped up the stairs like she was performing the stomp dance his grandfather had taught him.

Owen crinkled his nose. "No thanks. What she does in that bathroom is her business."

Lord, was he clueless. "Trust me," Kellen said. "You need to go after her."

Owen didn't seem too keen on following her upstairs. Every interaction Kellen had had with Caitlyn, she'd come across as even-tempered and easy-going. He doubted she was planning to take off Owen's head at the neck, but she was pissed. She probably just wanted him to put up a few barriers around himself when it came to Lindsey. Lindsey was obviously trying to court his favor, and she did have the added pull of a baby on the way. And now that Kellen was onboard with helping, Owen would likely get behind the idea of becoming a father even more.

Owen shrugged, but before he could go upstairs to get his deserved tongue lashing from Caitlyn, his phone rang. He looked visibly relieved when he answered it.

"Hey, Mom, we just fin—" His body stilled as he listened to whatever his mother was saying on the other end of the line.

His lips trembled when he asked, "What's wrong?" Owen visibly paled. "I'll be right there."

Before Kellen could ask what had happened, Owen dashed out of the house at a full run, not even bothering to shut the front door.

Kellen took off after him, watching him race down the sidewalk toward his parents' house. "Owen, what is it?" he called, but Owen didn't miss a step.

A hand grabbed Kellen's arm. "Where's he going so fast?"

Kellen didn't even bother to look at Lindsey when he said, "Something's wrong."

"Do you think it's Joan?"

He didn't even want to consider the possibility. The woman was a mother to him. Owen's parents meant far more to Kellen than his own parents ever had. They'd given him the family he'd craved when his own had been worthless. As Kellen started up the sidewalk, his hurried steps hastened until he too was running. "Wait," Lindsey hollered. "I can't keep up with you."

He wanted to race after Owen, but slowed to give Lindsey time to catch up and then took her hand, urging her to waddle as fast as she could.

When Owen yanked open the gate of his parents' front yard, Kellen tried to get Lindsey to move faster. Owen didn't slow down as he bounded up the porch steps and tore into the house. Kellen left Lindsey at the gate and raced after him. He stopped short in the foyer. Joan's broken voice came from the living room, but he couldn't understand her words. Kellen hurried in that direction and paused in the doorway. The sight of Joan crumpled on the floor, tears streaming down her face as she told Owen things that Kellen couldn't comprehend, tore him to shreds. He didn't go to her to offer comfort, knowing she'd rather lean on her real son, not the wannabe watching her fall apart from the doorway. The numbness in Kellen's throat spread through his chest, down his arms, and all the way to his fingertips as what she was saying began to sink in.

Chad—Owen's older brother, the older brother of Kellen's heart—was finally coming back from war. He wasn't returning in a coffin—by some miracle—but he'd been injured. *Grievously* injured. A loud buzz filled Kellen's head. There was no air in the room. He couldn't breathe. Choking on emotion, he turned from the sight of Owen trying to comfort his distraught mother and stumbled to the front porch. He gasped for breath, surprised there was no air outside either. James's familiar car roared up the driveway and into the garage off the side of the house. Kellen closed his eyes, glad he wouldn't have to see James's face when he heard the news about his eldest son. Kellen bit his lip, fighting the pain that threatened to suffocate him.

He wasn't sure how long he'd been standing there when he heard footsteps stop behind him.

He turned to find Owen, face white with shock, standing on the porch. His stunned expression blurred as the tears Kellen had been fighting flooded his eyes. He grabbed onto Owen, not sure if he was trying to comfort or be comforted, but he needed something to keep him standing. Emotions warred within him as he pulled Owen closer. And Kellen had no idea what possessed him when Owen tilted his head back to look up at him. Kellen leaned closer—wanting Owen to stop looking so sad, wanting him to smile again, wanting something . . . something *more.*

Kellen kissed him, wishing Owen resisted, wishing Owen didn't feel so right against him, wishing—some part of him wishing—that Owen was his. The feelings Kellen felt as he deepened the kiss were even more confusing than the all-encompassing lust that slammed into his lower gut. Desire heated his blood, and the kiss, which had started as a way to comfort, burned through him so hot, he was completely out of his mind.

When he tugged away gently, the need to tell Owen what had been building inside him for years outweighed his need to continue kissing him. "I want you," Kellen said. He wanted him in every capacity of that word. Not just physically, but on every level.

Owen blinked—awakening from his stupor. "You want me?"

God, yes, why had he been denying it so long? "I want you."

Owen's face crumpled with anguish, and Kellen was so shocked by his reaction that Owen slipped from his grasp. And then Owen was running. Running away. Not returning Kellen's newly realized feelings. Running. Running so hard he crashed into the front gate and struggled to get it open before he stumbled onto the sidewalk and then jetted toward home.

"Owen," Kellen called after him, tripping down the porch steps. He covered his mouth with one hand, the feel of Owen's lips still on his own.

"What have I done?" he said into his hand.

That had actually happened. He hadn't imagined it while tied up and on the verge of orgasm. Kellen had kissed Owen, and while their mouths had been pressed together and Owen had gone submissive in his arms, Kellen had convinced himself that what he'd done had been natural. That it had been right.

But there was nothing right about that kiss except the way it had made him feel at the time. But not the way he felt now. He'd taken advantage of Owen's grief to take something from him.

"Owen," he called again, though Owen was much too far away to hear him now.

"He wants you too," Lindsey said from behind him. "I saw it in you both that night on the bus."

Lindsey was the absolute last person Kellen wanted validation from. He didn't say a word to her as he walked toward the gate. And then he was trotting, then jogging, then running as fast as his legs would carry him.

When he reached Owen's front door, he tried to open it, but found it locked. He rang the doorbell, knocked, banged on the polished mahogany surface until his entire arm ached, but no one answered his summons.

"Owen, please, we need to talk. I didn't mean—" He cut off his own lie. He had meant it. Maybe not at first, but once their lips had met, he'd meant every caress, every shred of lust swirling through his body. What he hadn't meant to do was hurt Owen, not in any way. "I'm sorry. Please, just . . . We need to talk."

The door opened, but it wasn't Owen who faced him. It was Caitlyn. He wasn't sure what to expect from Owen's new girlfriend. Would she be furious? Upset? Hurt? Strangely, she seemed sad. Was his ability to read people slipping?

"Bad timing, Kellen," she said. "He's devastated over his brother, and you pick that moment to finally be honest with him?" She shook her head. "I think you should leave. He might forgive you later, but right now? He feels betrayed."

"He told you?" And why wouldn't he? Owen hadn't done

anything but accept Kellen's advance until he'd come to his senses enough to push him away. "I want to talk to him. Apologize. I didn't mean for that to happen."

"I don't think he'll talk to you right now. He's got a whole lot of anger brewing inside him over Chad, and you gave him something to direct that anger at."

"That's fine. He can kick my ass if that's what he needs to do, but I couldn't stand it if we leave this as it is. If he shuts me out."

"I'll talk to him on your behalf," she said, but Kellen wasn't sure if she'd say the things that needed to be said. What if she made the situation worse? Right. How could anything she said be worse than what he'd done?

"I—" Kellen licked his lips, searching for words. He should apologize. Not just to Owen, but to Caitlyn. And to Dawn. Oh God . . . *Dawn.* What was he going to tell Dawn?

"Just so you know, I'm not letting you have him," Caitlyn said, and before her words had sunk in, she shut the door in his face.

CHAPTER SEVENTEEN

PRAGUE HAD ALWAYS BEEN one of Dawn's favorite cities. The red rooftops and countless spires puncturing the skyline were pleasing to the eye, and the Czech people were kind and patient—if not perpetually amused—as she struggled to communicate in their language. She'd always been better at understanding foreign languages than speaking them, so while she caught most of what was said to her, she was pretty sure she'd told the taxi driver that her cat liked yellow pillows. Dawn didn't even have a cat.

Though she adored the local beer—in her experience, the best pilsner on the planet—touring the mix of ancient attractions and the art nouveau buildings of downtown, and gawking at the amazing workings of the astronomical clock for an hour or two, what really cemented Dawn's link to the city was the music. String quartets accompanied by flutes often entertained passersby right on the street. Live classical music could be heard in ordinary bars as well as more formal venues. The entire area had a healthy obsession with Mozart. Every time she visited, she felt she'd found the city of her heart. Well, that title was a toss-up between Prague and Warsaw. She loved both cities dearly. She'd been in Prague just a month ago for the Spring International Music Festival, but had jumped at the chance at a repeat performance. She wished Kellen had come. Even though he was a rock musician, she felt that every music lover should experience Prague at least once in their life. If this had been a leisure trip, she'd have taken in several concerts, an opera or two, and maybe even a ballet, but she was short on time and still not sure if she was signing that contract to compose for Hollywood. If she was, she'd have to be in Venice by the end of the week. Would she even have time to sneak in a few days in Texas to comfort Kellen about his band breaking up?

She'd never meant for her stint in Hollywood to become permanent. Truthfully, she wanted to compose the type of symphonies that musicians would still be playing in Prague and around the world a hundred years in the future. But the money Hollywood offered was hard to pass up. No starving musician truly wanted to starve; she was proud to be able to wring out a living with her creative work. Then again, no musician wanted to be a sellout either. As she browsed a farmers' market for lunch, her mind churned her worries into a hot mess. How could she follow her head or her heart when neither part knew what it wanted, much less what *she* wanted?

Her walking and sightseeing did a lot to clear her head, easing her into the right frame of mind to perform that evening. If she'd cloistered herself in her hotel suite all day, she'd have become a pacing basket case; she'd learned that the hard way long ago. Dawn was accustomed to being alone before her shows, so it was probably a good thing that Kellen wasn't with her. He would have undoubtedly destroyed her focus, and focus was truly what she needed before a performance. She arrived at the concert hall a few hours early to give herself time to get to know the piano she'd be playing.

"Miss O'Reilly, we have refreshments for you in the green room," said a helpful staff member who spoke perfect English. "My name is Bridget. I am here to offer any assistance you require."

Refreshments would be nice, but Dawn wanted to get in a practice run of her set list before concertgoers arrived. Now that she was at the venue, her belly was aflutter with nerves. She doubted she could keep a cracker down.

"I'd like to check my instrument before the performance."

Bridget stiffened slightly, as if Dawn's comment was a personal affront to her ability to properly do her job. "The tuner just left and assured us that the piano is ready to go."

Dawn smiled, figuring her nervousness was coming across as haughtiness. She was sure it wasn't the easiest job in the world to deal with demanding virtuosos on a regular basis.

"I've no doubt of that," Dawn said. "I know it sounds odd, but I like to become acquainted with an instrument before I perform on it." She leaned in closer and whispered, "I also want to make sure I remember how to play."

Bridget laughed, her tense expression melting into a smile. "Of course, Miss O'Reilly. This way."

Dawn followed her to the backstage area and into the wings of the elaborate stage surrounded by gleaming wood carvings and lavish golden curtains. A magnificent mahogany grand piano set center stage, and Dawn felt an instant connection with the gorgeous instrument. She was pleased to recognize the same piano she'd played the month before. It had a beautiful, resonating sound. They played well together.

"I'll get someone to turn up the lights," Bridgett said.

"It's fine. I like to play in the dark."

The stage wasn't completely dark. The dim lighting added to the subdued mood she'd soon banish from the theater—from pit to rafters. She would bring the place alive with sound.

"Won't you need lights to see the scores?" Bridgett asked.

Dawn shook her head. "I don't need printed scores. I know my set list by heart." Including the less familiar concertos someone had selected for her to play.

Dawn crossed the stage, her worn tennis shoes silent on the floorboards, and took a seat on the bench. She put her feet on the pedals and squirmed around—a luxury she wouldn't have when the crowd had congregated—until she found a comfortable position. She scooted the bench over to the right and back a few inches and tested the comfort again. Satisfied with the position of the bench, she lifted the fallboard. She played a few scales, paying attention to the way her wrists, elbows, and shoulders felt. Her set list was long and the pieces challenging. She didn't want to wind up with kinks in her muscles halfway through her performance. She'd been in that position more than once and had ended her set list in agony. She repositioned the bench yet again, and took several deep breaths. Starting with her first piece for the evening—from Chopin's Piano Concerto no. 1—she played the stirring excerpt from beginning to end. She didn't miss a note, but didn't feel settled enough into her zone—damn her real-life issues, anyway—so she started over and played it again. About halfway through her second attempt, she found her stride. Every thought melted from her mind. She wasn't even thinking about the music anymore. It poured from her soul as if glad to finally be free from its cage inside her. Without more than a few seconds pause, she segued into her second piece of the evening—Chopin's Nocturne 20—one of her all-time favorites. By the time she concluded her entire set list an hour later, she felt rejuvenated, free, and grateful to Chopin for writing music that touched, inspired, and evoked so many moods.

No, she would not be giving up her performances to become a full-time composer. Composing was frustrating. It took long hours, and while the final product did give her that rush she craved, it might take months to get to that point. She needed to perform to get her musician's high. And while playing alone on a near-dark stage fulfilled a need within her, she knew it in no way compared to have an entire audience holding their breath, least the sound of their own airflow interfere with their enjoyment of her playing.

"Play 'Freebird'!" a familiar voice called from the dark stage-left wing.

"Wes?" She squinted toward the wings, and her agent emerged from the shadows, clapping as he approached her bench.

"Phenomenal as always," he said.

"What are you doing here?" Attending one of her overseas performances was not normal behavior for him.

"I'm supposed to put the squeeze on you. Steinberg and Everlong want an answer."

"I'm still not ready to give it," she said.

"Are you going to let this opportunity pass you by? Isn't it what you've always wanted? I don't understand your hesitation. Talk to me, kiddo."

Dawn pushed her fingers into her hair, shifting the heavy mass of curls from her shoulders, and sighed. "I still want to perform. I need it in my life."

"Okay. And that's fine. There is no conflict of interest in that. But that can't be the reason you're hesitating. We already know you can handle both."

She cringed. He'd never seen her try to write before. Never witnessed the turmoil. The anxiety. The frustration. He never had to sit on a hard piano bench for hours on end and hear nothing, feel nothing, but silence. Wes just got the end product as if it magically fell out of her ass or something.

"I don't want to go to Venice," she said, hoping that was enough of a reason to put them off.

"I thought you loved Venice."

"I do, but I'm not prepared to pack up my life and move to

a foreign city for months on end."

Wes cocked a brow at her. It was hard to read his expression in the dim light, but she read it as confused.

"What are you talking about? The trip to Venice is for a week. Then you'll spend a week in the studio in Los Angeles. Only if Pierre and Everlong are still blocked do they plan to go to Rome after that."

"So since I'm not blocked, I can skip Venice?" Though she could tolerate a week away from Kellen. Maybe. She knew he was struggling with the band breakup, no matter how calm he claimed to be about it.

"I don't think that's a good idea. Traveling with them will give you the chance to get to know your co-writers in a less formal setting. And come on, kiddo—it's freaking Venice. You *love* Venice."

But she loved Kellen more, and she was very concerned for him. She'd already arranged her flight out of Prague for a day earlier; she'd be leaving for Houston in the morning. She'd tried for a flight directly to Austin, but couldn't find an empty seat to any airport closer than Houston. Her crazy travel plans probably weren't the best for avoiding the jetlag that was sure to knock her on her ass, but even though Kellen had insisted he didn't need her and that he was fine, she wanted to be there for him. Needed to be there for him.

"Can I go to Venice for just the final three days of their trip? Do you think they'll compromise?"

"Kiddo, I'm sure they'll compromise. They're trying to play it cool, but it's not normal for them to hound a new star's poor agent ten times a day, and it's really not normal for them to send him to Prague to encourage her to sign their contract. You tell me what you want, and I'm sure I can get it. Dream big, kiddo. Let's make it happen."

She hugged him. He'd been her champion from the beginning, learning how to represent a classical artist because he'd always been more of an agent for popstars and rappers and the occasional rock band. She'd never understand how she got so lucky to have someone as keen as she was on making her dreams come true. Of course, the ten percent commission he earned from her had to be one of his motivations, but his dedication was more than that. Her success was his success.

"Okay," she said breathlessly. Just admitting that she wanted to go forward with the deal added a new twist to the knot that had been churning in her gut all day.

"I'm going to go make a call and tell them you're willing to negotiate but want some provisions. We'll work on the specifics after your performance."

He squeezed her hand and patted her back.

The nervousness that had vanished while she'd been practicing began to bubble up inside her again. Her hands were shaking. She couldn't perform with shaking hands.

Wes rubbed her back. "Why don't you go through your set list again? It'll calm you down."

"So I look as freaked out as I feel?" Perhaps her face wasn't obscured in shadows as his was.

"You're trembling." He squeezed her hand again. "You got this, kid."

Dawn smiled, not sure if he could see her gratitude. "Thanks. I do need to hear that on occasion."

"I'll try to remember that. It's hard when someone blows you away every time you see them work."

"Quit," she said, giving him a playful shove.

"See you later."

He climbed from the bench, and she played him off the stage with her classically inspired version of "Freebird."

HER PERFORMANCE EARNED her a standing ovation, and she treated the audience to Mozart's Piano Concerto no. 21 as an encore, which earned her an even longer ovation, which led to a second encore—her souped-up version of "Flight of the Bumblebee." And they loved it. By the time she was escorted to the green room, her initial exhilaration had waned, leaving her exhausted. She spoke to a few local fans—could she call them fans?—who showered her with compliments in a mix of English and Czech. Well, she assumed they were being complimentary by their grins and nervous twittering. They could have called her a twisted goat herder and she'd have smiled and thanked them anyway. She was given several bouquets of roses, champagne—which she planned to drink straight from the bottle—and even more compliments. Wes stood off to the side of the room, talking to a manager or agent or some other bigwig in the music industry. He's lovely wife, Corrine, stood at his side. Wes spared Dawn the occasional glance and proud smile. He was the type of man she'd wished for in her father, and maybe that was why she adored him so much. Wes was only fifteen years her senior, though, so while it was biologically possible for him to have a daughter her age, she didn't think he held a paternal affection for her. Not exactly.

When the dressing room finally cleared out, it was quite late. Only early evening, stateside, however. Dawn was wiped out, her fingers stiff, her back and shoulders achy.

Wes shared a few words with Corrine, and after she kissed her husband's cheek and gave Dawn's arm a squeeze punctuated with heartfelt congratulations, she left the green room and closed the door behind her.

"I wouldn't mind if she stayed," Dawn said, feeling bad for sending Corrine out on her own in a foreign place.

"She wanted to go stand on the stage. She misses it."

Dawn had forgotten that Corrine had once been a pop singer in a girl band. At least as a classical musician Dawn wouldn't be kicked to the curb for having the audacity to age.

"I spoke to Everlong. Steinberg was unreachable."

"And?"

"He wants you in Venice. So bad he can taste it."

Dawn laughed, wondering what that would taste like.

"He wants me to keep pressuring you to sign, and my every instinct wants to do exactly that. Dawn, you aren't going to get an opportunity like this ever again. I don't understand why you're even hesitating."

"Let's sit," she said, nodding toward a small plum-colored settee. She carefully laid her roses on a coffee table and set her bottle of champagne aside.

"Let me explain my hesitation. I know it's your job to help me make the best career decisions, but hear me out."

"You already explained this in L.A.," he said, sitting next to her. "I know you're afraid that you'll be trapped as a ghostwriter and never be able to succeed on your own, but I don't think that's going to happen, kiddo. I won't let that happen. This opportunity will be your step up."

His assertion made her feel marginally better, but she knew there were no guarantees in life. "That's some of my hesitation," she said. "There's more."

Wes sighed. "This is about your new guy, isn't it?"

Was she that transparent? She chuckled. "He is part of the puzzle, but not what I wanted to discuss. My ultimate goal— that's what I need to tell you about."

"Writing scores for Steinberg movies isn't your ultimate goal?"

"No."

Wes blinked at her. "You want to work for a different director, is that it? Do you have an ethical aversion to fantasy and science fiction or something?"

Now she was laughing; it was fun to listen to his guesses. It proved to her that he really didn't see past the Hollywood sign. "No."

"Well, don't keep me guessing. We'll be here all night."

"I want . . ." She licked her lips and folded her hands in her lap. She'd never told anyone—except Kellen and Pierre—about this dream of hers, and only Kellen had taken her seriously. She doubted Wes would be impressed. "I want to compose the kind of timeless symphonies that orchestras play."

Wes cringed. "There's no money in that."

"It's not about the money, it's about a legacy. My legacy." She flushed. Damn, that had sounded cheesy. She wasn't even thirty years old and she was talking about legacies. "I don't mind being known as a Hollywood composer, but it's not what I dream about."

Wes gnawed on his lip as he looked at her. "I don't know how to help you with that, kiddo. I wish I did."

"I know," she said. "I don't really expect you to, but I'm afraid if I take this wide open road set before me, I'll never try that scary, twisted path that probably leads to nowhere. But how can I know where it goes if I don't take a step in that direction? Maybe the scary, twisted path leads to the realization of my perfect dream."

"Sometimes," Wes said, holding up his hands—palms facing one another in front of him. "Sometimes the road and the path run alongside each other, so you can keep that path in sight as you confidently take the road." He curved his left hand back and forth, but shook the right—the straight and steady path—up and down for emphasis. "Take the road, Dawn."

She should take the road. Why was she so hesitant?

"Why don't you write the symphonics of your heart in your free time?"

Dawn hadn't realized that Corrine had returned until she asked her question.

"I won't have much free time," Dawn said.

"You will after the movies are finished."

"And when will that be?"

Wes smiled at his wife before turning back to Dawn. "We can limit the contract to a year with a chance at renewal. Will that make you feel less skittish?"

"A year?" That wasn't long. She could give her all to this project for a year and if it didn't work out, she could walk away. Reach for her next star, a star she was unlikely to ever hold in her hand. But she wanted to at least try to capture it. "I think I can handle a year."

She'd expected that making her decision would offer some relief, but she still felt off, felt unsure. Wes, who instantly crumpled into the sofa and covered his eyes with both hands, obviously didn't hold her reservations.

"Kid, you are going to be the death of me," he said. "I honestly thought you might turn this offer down flat out. I was prepared to forge your signature."

She knew he was joking, so she laughed.

"Thanks to my brilliant wife for her eavesdropping."

"They wouldn't let me on the stage," Corrine said. "They were cleaning it."

"It's not really your kind of stage anyway." Wes pulled a folded contract out of the inner pocket of his tux and smoothed it on his knee. "Let's hammer out your demands so I can negotiate for you," he said to Dawn. "Besides needing a few days to get your affairs in order before you start and limiting the term to a year, what else do you want?"

"Equal billing with Everlong. I want to be a co-writer, not a ghostwriter."

Wes beamed at her. "Now we're talking. What else?"

Contract negotiations were like a drug to him. She was happy to give him his next fix.

After Wes finally returned her to her hotel room, a face-splitting smile still in place as she closed her door, she pulled out her phone and collapsed on the bed. The first time Dawn tried calling Kellen to share her news—her scary decision, one that could affect their future together—he didn't answer. Perhaps he was asleep; it was after one in the morning. But then she remembered it was closer to six in the evening where he was, so unless he took evening naps, he wouldn't be sleeping. Maybe his band had reconciled, gotten back together, and he was rehearsing for that night's performance. That would be so awesome. Then she wouldn't have to feel the slightest bit of guilt for her career gains.

She had made the right decision, hadn't she?

It still didn't feel right, but maybe after she joined her co-writers and actually got to work, her heart would open to this idea as much as her head had.

She got ready for bed, wanting to steal a few hours of sleep or at least rest before catching her flight in about six hours. She could never sleep on a plane, no matter how long the flight or how tired she was. She'd have to be at the airport in four hours. Before she climbed between the sheets, she tried Kellen again. This time he answered.

"Dawn," he said, a breathless hitch in his voice. "I don't know what to say other than I'm sorry. I'm so sorry. I'm not the kind of guy who cheats. I should have never . . . I shouldn't have . . . I'm sorry."

Wait? Did he say he cheated? The man who had remained faithful to his deceased fiancée for five years couldn't keep it in his pants for one *day* for her?

"What?" she said, plopping down on the bed and drawing a pillow to her lap. She hugged it against her belly, which was suddenly heavy and achy. Or maybe that was her heart down there hurting so bad. It had definitely sunk at his confession.

"He looked so sad and he was so close and I still don't understand why I wanted him right then—I wasn't even tied up. But it was like I couldn't help myself, and once I got started, I couldn't stop."

Wait? Did Kellen say *he*?

"You slept with Owen?" It was even worse than she'd realized. She knew Kellen cared about Owen. This· wasn't just some random affair with someone he didn't have feelings for.

"Slept with?"

She actually heard him swallow over the phone.

"No. I *kissed* him."

Dawn covered her mouth with a trembling hand and tried to calm her breathing. Kellen kissing Owen was a betrayal, she couldn't deny that, but she could get over it. She could forgive him for that. But only if it never progressed. If it hadn't meant anything.

Of course it meant something.

"Was it like a little kiss?" she asked.

"I wish I could say it was. Maybe then he'd speak to me."

"So he wasn't pleased?" Her crumbling world stopped falling apart.

"Pleased?" Kellen's scoffing snort sounded desperate. "No, he wasn't pleased. He was upset over Chad, and I made it worse for him. God, what the fuck is wrong with me?"

"Start from the beginning." Maybe once he explained, she wouldn't be so confused.

He told her everything. The way watching Owen with Caitlyn had made him feel lost and almost jealous, how being around Lindsey no longer made him feel like Sara was watching him, how Jacob's strange interview on the evening news had made him doubt Sole Regret would survive their separation, and the devastating news concerning Chad. She tried to be supportive through it all. Parts of his long spiel gave her hope, other parts made her nervous, but most of it just broke her heart.

"You were upset too, Kelly," she said. "You were hurting too. And no one was there to comfort you, so you reached for Owen." Dawn wished she'd been there so she'd have been the one he reached for. And now that she'd agreed to sign that contract, she'd be there for him less, not more. She supposed there was no reason to hold back the truth from him. What had been her good news to share suddenly became more bad news for him. "I'm going to sign the contract to do the scores for the Steinberg movies."

"Oh," he said. "If that's what you want to do, then you should."

She wasn't sure it was what she wanted to do. Now more than ever she was filled with doubt. "I think it will be best."

"Don't sign just to get back at me for hurting you."

Kellen wasn't usually self-centered, so his words cut her. Did he really think she was stupid and emotional enough to make that kind of decision to get back at a man for hurting her?

"I decided before I knew you rammed your tongue down Owen's throat."

That was how she got back at a guy for hurting her, by cutting him to the quick. Not by signing a life-altering contract.

"Oh," he said flatly. "I really am trying to distance myself from everything and everyone important to me, aren't I?"

That sounded more like the Kelly she knew.

"I don't want you to distance yourself from me," Dawn said. "I'm taking an early flight in the morning. I should be in Houston around three in the afternoon."

"If you're signing the contract, won't you be going to Venice?"

"One of my conditions was that the contract doesn't start until Friday. I said I needed time to get my affairs in order, but I really just needed to see you again. And apparently get *your* affairs in order."

"I'm not having an affair, Dawn. I won't cheat again," he said. "I hate to do this over the phone. I want to look you in the eye when I pledge—"

"Don't," she said. "Don't put yourself in the same position you were in with Sara. Don't do that to yourself."

"You don't want me to promise?"

"I want you to follow your heart, and you can't do that if it's tied." And if she wasn't where his heart was leading, she'd suffer—God, how she'd suffer—but she didn't want to be the one he settled for. She wanted to be the one he loved above all others.

"Do you think my heart wants Owen?" Kellen asked. "It doesn't. It wants you."

That was his head talking, and she knew it. She bit her lip and blinked, trying to hold back the tears swimming in her eyes. "I'm not sure I can let myself believe that right now."

He was quiet for a long moment. "I understand."

"Do you want me to come see you tomorrow in Austin or—" Because she *would* see him. She had not given up. She just didn't want to hash this out over the goddamned phone while oceans separated them.

"Can I pick you up at the airport?"

"That's a bit out of your way, isn't it? I was going to rent a car."

"If you don't want to be trapped in a car with me, I understand, but I really need to be trapped in a car with you for a few hours."

She smiled, her heart lightening at memories of their road trip from New Orleans to Galveston. How well they'd clicked. How much better they'd gotten to know each other. They did need to be trapped in a car together for a few hours to sort their mess out.

"I'd like for you to pick me up. If it's not too much of an inconvenience."

"I miss you," he whispered. "So much it hurts."

That was a great sign that they could work things out.

"I've never felt as alone as I do right now," he continued. "Not even when Sara passed."

Dawn realized that by damaging his friendship with Owen, he'd lost more than a good friend. He'd lost a family he considered his own. He'd lost an important connection with his turbulent career. He'd lost so much and gained nothing. Over a kiss. Just a kiss. The kiss that shattered his entire world. She wouldn't let it destroy them as well.

"Things will work out with Owen," she said, not wanting Kellen to feel the pain that would come if the opposite proved true. Owen was important to him. He needed Owen, and she wasn't selfish enough to push a larger wedge between them even though she knew how easy it would be to take Kellen all for herself. All she had to do was make him feel guilty about cheating, and he'd be hers, but she refused to break him. He'd been broken too many times already.

"You're beyond terrific," he said. "I think I'm starting to have feelings for you."

The hint of laughter in his voice made her heavy heart lighten.

"Starting? You should be full out in love with me by now," she teased.

"Oh, I am. I'm just playing it cool. I'll see you tomorrow."

She was so stunned by his claim that she didn't answer

immediately. Was he in love with her or just teasing? Because she wanted that—his heart. She wanted it more than she was willing to admit.

"Dawn?" he said after an awkward silence.

"See you tomorrow." She hung up before she did something as stupid as confess her own strong feelings.

CHAPTER EIGHTEEN

KELLEN SPENT the day in his car. It was only a few hours to the Houston airport, but he needed the time to clear his head. He called Owen every hour or two, hoping he'd eventually wear the guy down or annoy him enough that he'd answer. So far, his plan wasn't working.

What Kellen wouldn't give for a time machine. For as magical as that kiss had been, no moment of bliss was worth losing their friendship. He felt like part of him was missing, and he didn't know how he'd go on with yet another piece of himself taken by someone he loved. He didn't have Sara's piece of him back; he's just finally found a way to live without it. And his grandfather's piece? Yeah, Dawn didn't know about that missing piece yet, but he planned to show her during her visit. He told himself that he wasn't attached enough to Dawn to lose more of himself if she left, but deep down, he knew that wasn't true. He'd already willingly handed over another piece of himself, and when she left him, there wouldn't be much left of Kellen at all.

Although Owen wasn't answering his calls, Kellen did manage to get a hold of Joan, who had moved beyond despair to a place of hope and gratitude that Chad was alive. Chad had made it through surgery, survived the most critical night, and was currently sedated in a hospital in Germany. His commanding officer had been kind enough to video chat with Joan and James while at Chad's bedside and show them that their son was breathing, that his heart was beating, and though he was unconscious and his body was scarcely recognizable from the damage he'd suffered, that he was likely to recover if no complications arose. When Joan asked why Kellen had called her instead of Owen, he hadn't told her the real reason. He wasn't sure how she'd take the news that Kellen had done something as foolish, impulsive, and hurtful as make a move on her younger son when he'd just been stricken with devastating news about her older one. Jane was a wonderful, loving woman, but she was fiercely protective of her sons, as she should be. And as much as Kellen longed to be hers, he would never be her son.

He reached the airport about an hour before Dawn was scheduled to land. Inside the parked Firebird, he pulled on the white T-shirt he'd tossed into the passenger seat over the gift-wrapped box that now seemed trivial, and then he hurried inside the busy terminal to wait. He wanted to make sure she knew he was sorry, sure she knew he'd never meant to hurt her, sure she knew he'd never cheat again. Not with Owen. Not with anyone.

He watched the departures/arrivals board, fixated on her flight data and its "on time" status. When her plane landed, he stood and stared at the spot where she was likely to emerge from the terminal. He knew it would be a while before she could make her way through customs, but he didn't want to miss his first possible glimpse of her. Had it only been days since they'd parted? It felt like an eternity. His entire life had changed since he'd kissed her goodbye in this very airport, and so had hers. She'd do great with Everlong and Pierre, and Kellen knew how lucky he was that she'd put her career off for even a few days to be with him.

When he spotted her, his breath caught. Her gorgeous, deep red hair was tied back at her nape, accentuating her graceful throat. He wanted to press his face into that neck—breathe her in, taste her skin, feel her pulse race beneath his lips—but he held back, even when her eyes found him and she smiled. He had no right to touch her, to take what he wanted. Not when he'd betrayed her.

She raced forward and dropped her bags at his feet before capturing him in her arms. The leash he'd used to tether himself snapped. His trembling hands rose to cup her lovely face, and he searched her green-flecked eyes for signs of hurt or mistrust. He found none. She looked damned happy to see him. Lucky, lucky man, he told himself as he bent to accept the kiss she offered and he did not deserve.

When he drew away, he held her gaze as he said, "I'm so—"

She shook her head. "Give me a minute to be happy to see you before you remind me of what an ass you were in my absence."

So she wasn't going to let him off the hook. He silently thanked her for knowing her worth, for not giving him an easy out. He was so much harder on himself than she could ever be on him. She probably didn't know she was doing him a favor by holding him accountable for his actions.

"Did you have a nice time in Prague?" he asked, kissing her again before she could answer, because she was beautiful and wonderful and caring and perfect and he just couldn't help himself.

"I did. Wes followed me there. Did I mention that?"

Wes? Her agent? That seemed odd. "Do I have a reason to be jealous?"

"Of Wes?" When he nodded, she smiled. "Not unless you really wanted to see me perform."

"Of course I did."

"He's happily married. And his wife was with him."

"Then why was he—"

"To pressure me into signing that contract. Do you think I did the right thing?"

He kissed her crumpled brow. He really was an ass. She'd called him from Prague for reassurance about her life-changing decision, and he'd been so focused on himself, he'd basically brushed off her concerns.

"What's done is done," he said, and she tilted her head to look up at him.

She lifted both eyebrows. "I'm still not letting you off the hook, Kellen Jamison."

"I wasn't referring to what I did. I expect to do a lot of groveling."

Her little smirk made his heart tremble. "Good. Grab my bags, will you? And point me in the direction of your car."

He slung her carry-on over one shoulder and grabbed the handle of her small suitcase. His free hand sought hers and when she looked at him, he said, "Groveling will include lots of hand-holding, stolen kisses, lovesick looks, and oral pleasure."

She bit her lip, the tiniest of moans escaping her, and allowed him to hold her hand as they made their way to his car.

"Do they even make these things anymore?" she asked as he opened the trunk of his perfectly restored '73 Pontiac Firebird Trans Am.

"No, ma'am. It was my grandfather's." Most of the material possessions he loved and held dear had once belonged to his grandfather.

"Should have known you'd drive a badass car." She grinned at him. "I didn't think that Toyota was you."

"That was a rental." He stowed her luggage in the trunk and opened the passenger door.

She pointed at the small box on her seat.

"That's for you," he said. "When you're ready to start hearing my apologies."

She lifted the box before settling into the leather bucket seat and setting her gift on her lap. He waited a breath to see if she'd open it and when she didn't, he carefully closed her door and ventured to the driver's side. He took a deep steadying breath before climbing in beside her. She still hadn't unwrapped the gift or even fingered the ribbon he'd tied in a complicated design around the box. She was staring straight ahead at the dashboard, as if opening the small token of his regret was her forgiveness and she wasn't quite ready to take that step yet. He wouldn't push her. He had no right to.

"Did you enjoy kissing Owen?" she asked quietly. The fist on her lap was clenched so tightly that her knuckles were white.

He could lie and lessen her pain, but she deserved to hear the truth. "Very much."

"And you want him, don't you?"

"Not as much as I want you."

"And he wants you?"

"Not at all."

Her tongue wet her lips. "He told you as much?"

"He hasn't spoken to me since it happened. I'd say there's my answer."

Her finger traced the black ribbon crisscrossing the shiny red box. "I don't think it's the answer you believe it to be," she said quietly, and then, as if she hadn't spoken the most confusing words he'd ever heard, she asked, "Can we stop somewhere for lunch?"

"Whatever your heart desires."

She reached over and covered his hand, which was gripping the steering wheel. "You. My heart desires you. That's why all of this is so damned hard."

Her lashes flicked upward, and all the hurt he'd expected to see in the terminal was now written in her troubled gaze.

"Your heart already has me," he said.

"Then I want a hamburger."

His snorted laugh was laced with agony. He hated that he'd caused her to doubt his feelings—his sincerity. Hated that he'd broken her trust.

"I love you." The words slipped out before he could consider what he was saying or how it would make her feel at that moment.

Her hand slid from the back of his, but he caught it before she could take her touch from him, and pressed her knuckles against his thudding heart.

"You're not allowed to say that to me right now," she whispered, a single tear streaking down her cheek.

"Then I'll just think it."

She swallowed and turned to look out her window. He'd yet to start the car, so her view was of the big white SUV parked beside them. "I want fries too."

He blew out a breath and released her hand so he could start the car. It roared to life, its familiar rumble steadying him as he shifted into reverse. They'd get through this. They had to. He couldn't take another heartbreak.

CHAPTER NINETEEN

AS HUNGRY AS SHE WAS, DAWN ONLY TOOK a few bites of the hamburger she'd claimed to want. She didn't even touch her fries. She'd thought being trapped in a car with Kellen for a few hours would allow them to talk and sort through their differences. Instead, the silence that spread between them seemed unbreakable. She pretended to nap, but her thoughts were too full to allow anything as restful as sleep.

"We're almost there," Kellen said when they were close to Austin. "Aren't you going to open your gift?"

The smallish red box sat on her lap, its ribbon laced in an intricate pattern that reminded her of a spider web. She found the end of the black satin tucked into the underside and began the long involved process of untying the binding. It was strangely cathartic, as if each released knot allowed her to let go of her pain one piece at a time.

She could still hear Kellen's whispered confession—*I love you*—echoing through her thoughts and squeezing at her heart. But could she bring herself to truly believe it when she knew he longed for another?

When the ribbon finally fell free as one long silky piece, she fingered the box lid with indecision before lifting it. Inside was a small wooden music box. Hadn't Kellen proposed to Sara by putting her engagement ring in a music box? A dolphin-shaped music box. Dawn clearly remembered him telling her that.

She glanced at him, looking for clues, but his eyes were on the road. She lifted the music box out of its container and the lid opened slightly, causing it to release the sound of a single tinkling note. Just one note, but she already knew what song it would play—her favorite of Chopin's nocturnes.

Her hands trembled as she opened the lid. Would there be a ring inside? What would she do if there was? They hadn't known each other long enough to consider such a hefty commitment. She had yet to tell him she loved him.

When the lid was fully lifted, she found she'd been right. The song was Nocturne 20. A folded note was nestled among the black velvet lining of the box. She looked at Kellen—still minding the road like a first-time driver—and then unfolded the paper.

Were you expecting a ring?

She laughed and tossed the paper at him. "That was mean."

"Did you want it to be a ring?" he asked.

She had, damn him, but bit her lip so she didn't let that desire slip from her blurty mouth. She'd already forgiven him, damn him even more, and wished they could just put this mess behind them, damn him again.

"You want the grand gesture," he said, looking at her at long last. "Remember?"

How could she forget?

She turned her attention to the now-empty box, listening to the soft tinkling it made. "I should make you squirm," she said. "Make you feel as terrible as I feel."

"I'm dying on the inside, if that knowledge is helpful."

The song played slower and slower until the pin drum got hung up on a note and fell silent.

"I love you," she said, not looking at him. She'd say it again later while staring into his dark eyes, but not this first time. This first time was much too terrifying.

"You're sure? I have issues, you know."

She laughed and closed the music box. "I'm sure. Take me to Owen's house. I need to talk to him."

"It wasn't his fault. Don't place the blame on him because you have feelings for me."

"Who said I had feelings for you?" she teased.

"I think it was you."

"It's going to take a lot of mind-blowing orgasms to get me to admit that again."

He laughed. "Challenge accepted."

OWEN'S LITTLE BLUE COTTAGE WAS EVEN MORE adorable than the man himself. They'd tried to call him, to warn him of their arrival, but he still wasn't answering Kellen's calls. The anguished look on Kellen's face as he shook his head and hung up for the third time tore at Dawn's chest.

"Maybe you should have one of your bandmates call him on your behalf," Dawn said.

"That might work," he said, "assuming they're speaking to me. I doubt Jacob and Adam will answer."

"What about Gabe?"

"He was supposed to keep us posted on the situation with Jacob, but I haven't heard from him. Maybe he called Owen, though."

Kellen dialed Gabe's number. No answer there either.

"I'm going to knock on the door," Dawn said, reaching over to touch his cheek. "You stay here. We don't want to spook him."

Kellen smiled slightly. "He's not a horse."

"He's acting like one's ass at the moment. At the very least he should hear you out. You two have been friends for a very long time." And Kellen was the type who could not easily let go of deep connections. As far as Dawn was concerned, these two had to settle their differences for her sanity, if not for their own.

He squeezed her hand as she opened the car door. She squeezed back before leaving him behind and walking up the path. She rang the doorbell and glanced back at the car. Kellen was watching her, both hands gripping the Trans Am's steering wheel.

The door creaked as it was slowly opened. Expecting Owen, or maybe even Lindsey, she was surprised to come face to face with a stunning woman—dark hair, dark eyes, gorgeous tanned skin. Dawn was at once reminded of a feminine version of Kellen. Her tongue forgot how to work as she gaped.

"Owen doesn't want to talk to him," the woman said, nodding toward the car.

So this *was* the right house.

"Not to either of you," she added, even as she started to close the door.

Recovering from her initial surprise, Dawn slammed her forearm into the wooden surface to hold the door slightly ajar.

"Will *you* talk to us?" Dawn asked. "It's Caitlyn, right?"

Caitlyn nodded, to which question, Dawn couldn't be sure.

"I already spoke to Kellen. Owen still isn't ready to face

him. He isn't handling this well." Caitlyn glanced away and released a heavy sigh. "Or at all. He'd take my speaking to you as fraternizing with the enemy." She rolled her eyes and whispered, "He tends to overreact."

Dawn chuckled. "Mine fixates. He doesn't know how to move on. And he's sorry, Caitlyn. He's really sorry for taking advantage of a terrible situation." She didn't say kissing Owen, because she wasn't convinced he was sorry for the kiss itself. She knew he was sorry about the timing and the feelings of betrayal that kiss had caused.

"Try convincing Owen of that." Caitlyn ran a hand over her face. She looked as tired as Dawn felt.

"I'd love to try. Will you ask him if he'll talk to me?"

"He's a cheater, Dawn!" Owen yelled from inside the house. Apparently, he'd been eavesdropping. "You should dump his ass."

"Still overreacting," Caitlyn said as she stepped onto the porch. She shut the door behind her and spoke in a hushed tone. "We have to do something to get these two back on speaking terms. I love the guy, but he is driving me nuts over one stupid kiss. He had absolutely no problem with Kellen jerking his dick at the sex club."

"You were there?" Of course she was.

"To be honest, it was sexy as hell. Owen even called Kellen's name when he came. I happened to be fucking him in the ass with a strap-on dildo at the time."

Dawn's jaw dropped, not at the kinky sex but at the déjà vu she was suddenly experiencing. "You're kidding."

Caitlyn shook her head. "It was a bit unsettling."

"Kellen called Owen's name when I had him tied up a couple of nights ago," Dawn said, still whispering.

Now Caitlyn's jaw was on the porch. "Get the fuck out of here."

"Do you think—do you think they're in love with each other and just won't admit it?" She'd suspected as much, but when they were together they didn't act like they were in love. They didn't exchange longing glances or find excuses to touch each other. They acted like straight-guy buddies. She hadn't even noticed any bromance between them, but then Kellen had been fixated on Lindsey, so maybe she'd missed something. Caitlyn had seen the pair interact much more often than Dawn had.

"I hope not," Caitlyn said. "I really thought I'd finally found a guy I could love forever."

Dawn squeezed her shoulder. "I'm in the exact same position."

"I think we're going to have to play dirty to get these two face-to-face."

Dawn grinned. She adored the woman already. "What did you have in mind?"

A few minutes later, Dawn returned to the car. Caitlyn had her number. They'd brainstorm and conspire when Owen wasn't peering out at them through a window and Kellen wasn't watching them from his souped-up Trans Am. In Dawn's brief conversation with Caitlyn, they'd agreed on one thing for sure. They had to get the guys back together—and not just Owen and Kellen but the entire band. Sometimes it took a smart woman or two to straighten out the fucked-up mess a group of unsupervised men made.

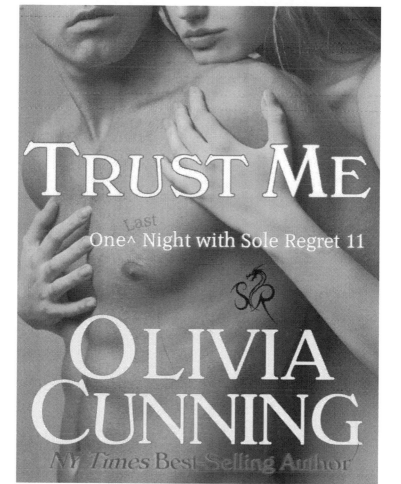

TRUST ME

One ^ Last Night with Sole Regret 11

OLIVIA CUNNING

NY Times Best-Selling Author

Trust Me

One Night with Sole Regret #11

CHAPTER ONE

GABE SAT outside the local news station waiting for his so-called best friend to exit the building. Gabe didn't have a plan. He had no idea what he would say to the jerk when he got the opportunity to confront him, but sitting around with his thumb up his ass wouldn't solve Sole Regret's problems. Every action had an equal and opposite reaction, and Jacob's action of breaking up their band—a band in its fucking prime—was unforgivable. Thus, Gabe's reaction to Jacob's selfish actions could only be explosive in nature.

Gabe had purposefully positioned his truck in the small parking lot in the front of the news station so that he had a good view of both the front entrance and the lane that led to the larger parking lot behind the building. If Jacob was still inside, Gabe would either see him leave through the front door or see his car pull out of that drive. There was no other way out. Gabe assumed the sports car owned by his band's lead singer—he still couldn't think of Jacob any other way even though the rash bastard had effectively destroyed Sole Regret—was parked behind the building. Gabe would have definitely noticed the sporty little car out front. Like the man, Jacob's vehicle was impossible to overlook.

But then maybe he'd missed Jacob altogether. Perhaps the selfish prick had left so soon after his interview—or whatever that bullshit he'd spouted on the evening news was called—that he'd been long gone before Gabe had arrived. Gabe decided to wait a while longer before trying to track him down at home. Had Jacob really moved back in with Tina? What the fuck was he thinking?

An enormous white SUV pulled to the end of the drive, and Gabe almost ignored it—Jacob drove a Tesla Roadster—until he remembered that Jacob's ex-wife drove an SUV just like that one, and Tina had been at Jacob's side throughout that ridiculous news segment. Admittedly Gabe didn't think too clearly when he was mad, and he was beyond pissed at the guy he considered his best friend—or *had* considered as such until he'd betrayed them all. Gabe caught a glimpse of the driver's mirrored sunglasses just before the SUV turned into traffic. Definitely Jacob.

"Crap," Gabe said, starting his ignition. The blast of hot air out of the air conditioner made his T-shirt stick to his sweaty chest. The evening was stiflingly hot even by late-June-in-Texas standards.

He turned onto the road, gunning the truck's big engine to cut into traffic with a loud roar. He supposed he didn't need to run Jacob off the road to talk to him. Eventually he'd stop somewhere, and as soon as he got out of his vehicle, Gabe would confront him.

His cellphone rang, and he considered ignoring it until he saw that Adam was calling. Adam. The other jerk in his band. The one who had sent Jacob over the edge in the first place. He was currently in a tie with Jacob at the top of Gabe's shit list.

"What?" Gabe answered as he accepted the call over the truck's Bluetooth connection, zooming past several slow-assed drivers until he could see the white SUV ahead.

"Did you see Jacob's interview?"

"Oh yeah, I saw it."

"What did he say?"

Gabe figured that Adam was in Dallas so had missed the Austin news segment Gabe had watched with Owen and Kellen not even an hour before. But there was this thing called the internet. Adam could have found a stream of the segment if he gave a damn or bothered to put forth any effort.

"A bunch of ridiculous nonsense," Gabe said. "Apparently he's back with Tina and wants to live in domestic bliss with her instead of in the spotlight with us."

Adam snorted. "You're joking."

"I wish I was. I'm on the road following him now. If he doesn't tell me what's really going on then I'll . . . I'll . . . " What would he do exactly? Gabe admittedly had a temper, and he'd been known to use his fists when the occasion called for violence, but never against a friend. "I'll get to the bottom of this."

"I should be the one there straightening this shit out," Adam said.

A fact Gabe would not refute, but . . . "Do you really think he'd listen to you?"

"No, but I need to try. He probably thinks I'm using again."

"Aren't you?" Gabe snapped.

He knew Adam had vanished right before their show in New Orleans because his girlfriend had been hurt pretty badly, but it would be a lot simpler to understand how someone could run off like that without telling anyone if he *were* using drugs again. Especially strong, mind-altering, life-destroying drugs like the heroin Adam had once preferred.

Adam sighed. "You'll have to take me at my word that I'm not, but you know, it wouldn't be any of your business if I were."

"Adam, you do realize that this fiasco you started and Jacob decided to finish affects more than you, don't you? You aren't the only one out of a job. What am I supposed to do? And what about Kellen and Owen? Did you ever once stop to think about how this affects anyone but yourself?"

"Madis—"

Gabe jabbed the end-call icon on the dash. He didn't give a rat's uncle about Madison at the moment. He was too pissed at her boyfriend to care that she'd fallen off her stupid horse and injured her stupid arm. It wasn't as if she was in danger of dying or anything. But based on the current reckless way Gabe was zipping around traffic to keep Jacob's SUV in view, he probably was.

He followed Jacob into the subdivision where he apparently now lived with his ridiculous ex-wife, and to a very familiar house. One of the garage doors at the front of the gargantuan five-bedroom brick-faced monstrosity opened, and while Jacob sat there waiting for it to lift, Gabe cut his engine and jumped out of his truck. Tina's white Escalade rolled into the garage, and Gabe dashed in right behind it. Jacob didn't look the least bit surprised to see him when he climbed out of the vehicle and turned to face him.

"I suppose you're here to kick my ass," Jacob said.

His sunglasses obscured his inner feelings from Gabe. Jacob had expressive eyes, and he knew of that particular weakness, hence his preference to wear sunglasses at all hours of the day and night.

"Have at it, then."

Gabe stopped advancing and squinted at Jacob to make sure he was speaking to the cocky asshole who fronted one of the biggest metal bands on the planet. The dude looked like Jacob. A defeated, tired-looking version of the typically bad-assed motherfucker who had a voice loved by millions, but the man before him was unquestionably Jacob.

"I just want to know why," Gabe said. "Why would you just . . . just *leave?*" Gabe took a step toward him, his anger flaring once again. "How could you . . . How could you leave us like that?"

Tina came around the front of the SUV to stand at Jacob's elbow. "Do I need to call the police, sweetheart?"

Gabe snarled at her, and her eyes widened. The model-perfect blonde shrank backward.

"No," Jacob said. "We need to have it out so he can move on. Go inside."

Move on? Gabe had no intention of moving on. They had to get this shit straightened out and get the band back together, because he couldn't go forward from this . . . this . . . this *disaster.* Gabe's past, his present, and his future all revolved around him being Sole Regret's drummer. He didn't have another plan. He had no idea how to proceed. He refused to give up on Jacob or the band or even fucking Adam.

"I think I'll stay to watch." Tina crossed her arms over her chest and smirked at Gabe.

He'd never in his life wanted to punch a woman until that moment. He took a deep breath and stared at the cement at his feet, trying to cool his temper. Gabe knew it sometimes got the better of him, and if he was fantasizing about knocking out Jacob's ex-wife, his ire had obviously heated to the point that he needed to take a step back. Fighting wasn't the answer. He didn't know what the answer was, but he knew it wasn't violence against Tina or Jacob.

"Daddy!" The voice of a gleeful little girl echoed in the garage. "Gramma said yous was home. Why are you staying out here for so long for?"

"Tina, why don't you take Julie inside?" Jacob nodded toward the open door that connected the garage to the house. "I'll see you in a minute."

"Can I has a hug first?" Julie asked, her small feet pattering against the cement as she rushed to his side. "I missed you."

Gabe lifted his gaze in time to witness the man melt as he scooped his daughter into his arms and gave her the squeeze she'd requested. Jacob Silverton had few weaknesses, and the adorable little blonde was responsible for all of them. He blew a raspberry on her neck, making her squeal and squirm, before setting her back on her feet.

"I need to have a grown-up talk with Gabe," he said.

"Hi, Gabe!" Julie said with a wave as she noticed him standing next to the SUV. "Daddy thinks I don't know the grown-up words, but I heard them on TV. You can say them if you want to. I won't tell Gramma."

Gabe couldn't suppress a grin. "Hi, sweetie."

"No more TV for you," Jacob said.

"Come on, Julie," Tina called from the door that led into the house. "Help me make dinner."

"What do you want to have, Daddy?"

"Whatever you're making."

"I think . . ." She pressed her index finger to her lip and looked up toward the garage ceiling. "Cupcakes," she said before skipping around the car and up the steps into the house.

"We can't have cupcakes for dinner," Tina told Julie as she ushered her inside.

"Can we has eggs? You said eggs are good for me."

"They are."

"Well, cupcakes has eggs, so that makes them good for dinner, right?"

Gabe couldn't help but grin at her cleverness. Jacob watched until the door shut behind his family before he turned to Gabe.

"I'm not going to apologize," Jacob said.

"I didn't come here for an apology. I came for an explanation and some clue about fixing this mess you've made."

"I let the band destroy my family once," Jacob said. "I won't let that happen again."

Gabe couldn't argue against that claim. Jacob's stardom had strained his marriage to the breaking point. "I thought things were going well during your visitations with Julie." Julie was the only part of his family worth saving as far as Gabe was concerned. "And aren't you dating Amanda?"

Jacob's forehead tightened with what Gabe assumed was raw emotional pain. Not that he could tell for sure with those damned sunglasses Jacob was still wearing.

"I was," Jacob said, his voice unwavering. "She decided I wasn't worth her trouble." He crossed an arm over his chest and squeezed his biceps with his hand.

"And you decided her sister was?"

Jacob moved his hand to rub his lower jaw and muttered, "Something like that."

"Is Tina blackmailing you?"

Jacob chuckled. "No. She claims she still loves me and being with her makes it easier for me to see Julie."

"But do you love her?"

Jacob shrugged. "I love Julie."

Gabe had figured as much. "And the band? Do you care about any of us?"

Jacob bit his lip, his attention fixed below Gabe's eyes. "I won't lose Julie," he said. "Not for the band. Not for Amanda. Not even for myself. Adam's disappearance was only one part of my decision to leave. Finding a new direction for myself was inevitable. I hope you can find your own new path."

Gabe didn't want to find a new path. He was perfectly satisfied with the one he was on.

"Maybe you just need a break," Gabe said. "Take a few days, get your head straightened out—"

"My head is clearer than it's been in years. And that horrible weight on my shoulders? It's gone, Gabe."

What weight on his shoulders? Jacob's job was to have a great time doing what he loved. How could he possibly consider that a burden?

"I'm not giving up just yet," Gabe said, though he took a step back. Jacob had lost his way and needed a nudge to get headed in the right direction again. Figuring out what would steer him true would take a little thought and planning on Gabe's part, but Gabe would come up with a solution. He'd always been good at solving complex problems—even ones as incomprehensible as Jacob Silverton.

"Save yourself the headache," Jacob said. "There's nothing you can do to change my mind."

Perhaps, but Gabe knew someone who might be able to.

Gabe drove by Jacob's house on his way to Amanda's and stopped long enough to yank the For Sale by Owner sign out of the yard. He tossed it into the back of his truck and forced himself not to allow his driving to match his aggressive mood as he drove off. A residential neighborhood was no place for burning up the pavement.

Amanda's car wasn't in her driveway, but he parked on the street in front of her quaint cottage and went to the door. His knock went unanswered—not that he was surprised—so he returned to his truck, tore a corner off a defunct paper map, and wrote her a short note. He tucked it under her doorknocker, hoping a gust of wind didn't send it flying down the tree-lined street. He left his number and asked her to call or text, saying it was urgent that he speak to her in person but giving no details. She'd probably guess he wanted information on Jacob, but if she'd really broken up with him, she might be unlikely to talk. Best to leave her wondering, he decided.

On his way home, he stopped by the vet and picked up his dog. His parents had planned to get Lady and take care of her at their house while he was on tour, but now that he didn't have a tour, or even a band, he'd told them not to bother. His sweet yellow Lab was so excited to see him that her tail wagging toppled her over. Her balance was a bit off due to her casted broken leg. She licked his face the entire time he carried her to the truck. Cringing, Gabe tried turning his face this way and that to escape her tongue bath as he struggled with the door handle and finally escaped her doggie breath when he settled her into the passenger seat. He gave her a belly rub, and she thunked him repeatedly with the exuberant wagging of her thick tail as she stretched out to give him free access to her tender underside.

"Good girl," he crooned, reaching into the truck to pat her head. "Are you ready to go see Beau? He'll probably drown you in slobber."

Lady released an excited whine, tail producing a rapid beat that any metal drummer would envy.

"I'm sure he misses you too." He gave her one final scratch before shutting the door and rounding the truck to climb into the driver's seat.

He supposed there was one good thing about being off tour; he could spoil his girl while she recovered from her injuries. Gabe wondered if the drunken teen who'd hit Lady with the truck he'd stolen had learned his lesson. Moron.

When Gabe pulled into his driveway, he scratched his head as he stared at the melon-orange VW Bug sitting in front of his house. Wasn't that Nikki's car? He'd ridden in the nauseatingly cute thing once with Melanie behind the wheel, but why would Nikki be visiting? He sure as hell hadn't invited her, though he knew from experience that the woman had no qualms about inviting herself.

Gabe climbed out of the truck and lifted Lady, carefully setting her on her feet and watching closely to determine if she could hobble to the house or if he'd need to carry her. A full-grown yellow Lab wasn't exactly lightweight, but he could manage if she needed help.

The front door opened, and Beau leaped clean over the wide porch to land at the bottom of the steps before racing toward his companion.

"Easy," Gabe warned as Beau danced around Lady in wide leaping circles. "You can't be rough with her."

The black Lab gave Lady's cast an interested sniff and then licked her face, whining and wriggling as if he didn't know whether to be overjoyed to see her or sad that she was hurt. A figure emerged from the large A-frame wood cabin he called home and crossed the porch to stand on the top step. All the clouds of anger and betrayal, of desperation and uncertainty, evaporated beneath her sunny smile. The door behind her framed her gorgeous body—long legs, curvy hips, slender waist—and her waist-length brown curls were as untamed as the woman was in bed.

"Surprise," Melanie said.

And what an excellent one it was

CHAPTER TWO

MELANIE HADN'T BEEN sure that arriving at Gabe's place unannounced was a good idea until she saw his face break into a relieved smile. Even his parents, who she'd talked into letting her in, had said he might not be up for company. He'd had a rough few days. So had she, to be honest, but seeing him made all her troubles less important. The only matter important to her at that exact moment was feeling his strong arms around her.

She hurried down the steps, hoping he'd start moving forward as well so they'd meet halfway. Every second he hesitated was one second she wouldn't be touching him. Eventually his feet propelled him forward, and when she collided with his hard chest, he wrapped both arms around her and squeezed her breathless. He pressed hard kisses to the top of her head as if to make sure she felt each one.

"I couldn't stay away," she said. "I'm not sure if you even want me here, but I felt that maybe you needed me."

His arms tightened. "I might."

She released a breathless laugh. "Won't even give me that much?"

"Would you think me less of a man if I admitted I need you?"

She shook her head and leaned back so she could stare up into his gorgeous green eyes. "I'd think you more of a man if you did."

"I'm glad you're here," he said.

"And?" She lifted a brow at him.

"I need you."

"Good, because I need to be here."

"Is Nikki with you?" He nodded toward the Bug in the driveway.

"Nope. I was having trouble with my car, so she let me borrow hers. She won't need it for a few days. She finally agreed to get some help, so I found a good facility and got her checked in." Facility was Melanie's nice way of referring to the high-security mental ward at the hospital. "She still doesn't feel safe, Gabe. She can't sleep, even if she's curled up with me. Maybe some intensive therapy will help her."

Gabe kissed her forehead. "We'll go see her," he said, and Melanie's heart lightened.

She knew her best friend was a pain in the ass, knew Nikki had deep emotional scars and did some really stupid things to compensate for her pain, but Melanie loved her and was glad Gabe was open to Melanie's irrefutable need to keep her friend safe, to slather her with love, and to never fail her again as she did when she'd left Nikki by herself in New Orleans.

"Really?"

Gabe shrugged. "It isn't as if I have anything more pressing to do."

"So the band's still at odds?"

He snorted on a laugh. "You might say that."

"You'll get it worked out."

"I'm not so sure," he said, "but I am sure of one thing."

"What's that?"

"You haven't kissed me yet."

She closed one eye as she teased him. "What makes you so sure?"

"Are your panties damp?"

She shook her head.

"Then I'm positive."

His kiss was deep and searching, almost desperate. She leaned into it, accepting more, taking more, until her toes were curled in her sandals and her panties were demonstrating their cotton absorbency.

A piteous whine interrupted their moment, and Gabe released her to head for the house. Lady had limped her way to the bottom of the steps, but couldn't manage to get up on the porch.

"I got you, girl," he said.

He carefully lifted the dog and set her on the porch. Apparently tuckered out, Lady lay down, her tongue lolling out of her mouth as she panted.

"Do you want to lie there or go inside where it's cool?"

Her big brown eyes fixed longingly on the front door, she whined, the sound punctuated by her jaws snapping shut.

"Well, why didn't you say so?" he asked, scooping the dog up again.

Melanie was so busy admiring Gabe's kind-hearted care of his pooch that she didn't recognize he needed help until he was practically bouncing Lady in the air to try to get a hand on the doorknob.

"I've got it," Melanie said, dashing up the steps and onto the porch. "If you need help, you can always ask."

"Hey, you got me to admit I need you. Getting me to actually ask for help?" He grinned at her and shook his head. "One step at a time, baby."

She laughed and opened the door. "I guess I'll have to read your mind and anticipate your needs."

"Works for me." He leaned over and kissed her cheek before entering the house and placing Lady on a big cushiony dog bed near the door. Beau sat beside her and then lay down, his sleek black head resting on Lady's pillow. She gave his nose a gentle lick.

"They're like an old married couple," Melanie said. And so cute and affectionate with each other, it made her ache for that level of devotion.

Gabe stroked Lady's silky-looking ears before repeating the motion on Beau. "In sickness and in health."

"And I suppose I'll have to stick with you through richer and poorer now that you're unemployed and all."

She'd been teasing, but the scowl he sent her quickly wiped the grin from her face.

"Too soon?" she asked.

"Much too soon."

He stood from his crouched position and headed toward the kitchen at the back of the house. It sprawled out into the great room, its gleaming honey-oak cabinets blending perfectly with the cabin's timbers.

She trailed after him as he made his way to the sink to wash the dog off his hands.

"If there's anything I can do to help with your band . . ." Though she had no idea how she could. She wasn't exactly an expert on getting rock groups back together.

"Just be understanding," he said, drying off his hands on a dish towel. "That's all I need from you. That and to be my guinea pig for testing out my inventions."

His smirk reminded her that she liked him best when he wasn't being so serious, and she was more than willing to be his test subject.

"I hope you mean for the sex toys."

"Are you ready for a workout? I'll probably need to up my productivity. I need to find something to keep myself busy now that I'm *unemployed*. Or maybe I'll go back to school and finish my engineering degree. Or maybe I'll wait tables. I can't stand being idle."

"Whatever you decide to do, I know you'll rock at it."

He leaned against the counter and crossed his arms over his chest, bunching up his green Yoda T-shirt that read mc^2 E is. "I really just want to be the drummer of Sole Regret."

"You do have the hair for it." Grinning, she reached up and wrapped a lock of crimson-tipped black hair around her finger. He hadn't bothered to spike his Mohawk today, so the longest of the strands at his nape were long, silky to the touch, and oh-so inviting.

"Exactly," he said, grinning. "How am I supposed to find a real job with dragons tattooed on my scalp?"

She giggled. She was used to his ink now, but corporate America might have a bit of trouble overlooking his head and body art. "Have a little patience," she said. "I'm sure you guys can work something out. It's only been a few days since Jacob left." And Gabe had ranted on the phone about it for as long. Melanie figured he needed an in-person sounding board, so that was why she'd taken a week's vacation and headed south. At least she hadn't done anything as impulsive as quit her job, though she had been working on her resignation letter so she could join Sole Regret on tour when Gabe had delivered the surprising news that the band had called it quits.

Gabe sighed. "You know, Jacob was the one who drew me into this world, and he sure as hell didn't hesitate to kick me back out of it."

"Best friends can be such pains in the asses," she said.

He chuckled and massaged his forehead with splayed fingertips. "You've got that right. Why do we put up with them?"

Melanie shrugged. "Beats the hell out of me."

"I should probably try to get ahold of one of the guys. Let them know my little chat with Jacob was a waste of time."

"So you did talk to him?"

"I didn't mention that?"

Melanie shook her head. On the phone he'd told her about his many attempts to call Jacob, which had all gone unanswered. Well, he'd ranted about it, actually. "Last I heard he still wasn't taking your calls."

"He never did. I saw him in person at his ex-wife's house. Though I guess he's living there now."

Melanie blinked and cocked her head to one side. Surely she was hearing wrong. "What? When did that happen?"

"When Jacob makes life-altering decisions, he doesn't hold back on completely altering his life."

"I guess not."

Melanie couldn't believe her ears when Gabe told her about Jacob's interview on the local news and how he'd basically given up everything so he could be with his daughter.

"His ex-wife's using their daughter to get what she wants?" Melanie shook her head. She hated bitches who did that. Tina should be glad that Jacob wanted to be involved in their daughter's life. There were plenty of *dads* who didn't give two shits about the kids they created.

"I hope those two don't scar that poor little girl for life. It can't be easy to be stuck between them."

"She's probably too young to understand she's being used as a pawn," Melanie said.

"What I can't believe is that Jacob is stupid enough to let Tina get away with it. What is he thinking?"

Gabe's eyes drifted out of focus as he stared into space over Melanie's shoulder.

"Earth to Gabriel," Melanie said when he didn't acknowledge her existence for several moments.

He started and then grinned sheepishly. "I was thinking maybe he isn't that stupid. Maybe Tina's the stupid one for letting him get close to her again."

Gabe apparently had a huge blind spot when it came to Jacob, always willing to give him the benefit of the doubt. Melanie figured the jerk was getting exactly what he wanted at the expense of his friends and fans.

"You know I can't stand the guy, right?" Melanie asked. "He's the biggest egomaniac I've ever had the displeasure of meeting."

"Once you get to know him—"

"You realize he's a user. Don't you see that?"

"If this is about his hooking up with Nikki . . ."

Melanie closed her eyes and shook her head. Jacob had annoyed her the first time she'd met him, pissed her off by using her friend for sex and promptly discarding her, and the ass hadn't earned himself a single brownie point by destroying Gabe's career. "You know what? I don't want to talk about Jacob anymore. If you want to talk about Adam or Owen or Kellen or anyone else on the entire planet, I'm happy to listen, but I came here to talk about you, to see you." She probably should have realized that by being Gabe's sounding board, she'd be hearing a lot about Jacob, but she could only tolerate so much.

"I need to talk about Jacob," Gabe said, scratching his upper lip, which was covered with a sexy length of stubble. "With someone not close to him."

Well, she definitely fit that description. And she wanted to be someone Gabe could depend on. She supposed she could suck it up a little longer for his benefit.

Gabe added, "I can't think rationally if I can't distance myself from all the emotional garbage everyone's feeling at the moment, and if I can't think rationally, I can't find a solution."

She ducked her head to hide a grin. She'd assumed he always tried to outthink his problems. She wondered if that ever worked out for him.

"I made some lemonade just before you pulled up," she said, slipping her arms around his waist and pressing her belly against his. "Let's sit out on the porch and enjoy the evening air while you torture me with tirades about Jacob Silverton."

"No tirades."

His hands slid up her back and drew her against his chest. She pressed her face into his neck and inhaled his mesmerizing scent. This was more like what she'd had in mind when she'd hurried down from Topeka.

"But I am going to talk about him."

"And I'll listen." And try to offer sound advice. But more

than likely she'd also seethe.

Gabe gifted her with a lingering kiss that made her heart pound and her skin flush with heat, and then he released her. He filled two glasses with ice, and she poured the lemonade. She carried both glasses, as Gabe decided Lady would like to hobble around the yard for a while. The happy dog seemed to get around pretty well as long as she didn't have to navigate any steps.

Once Lady was safely sniffing around the yard, Beau beside her, Gabe took the seat beside Melanie on the log porch swing, and she handed him his lemonade before taking a sip of her own. One of her eyes squeezed shut as her taste buds registered the tartness—exactly how she liked it.

"Have you thought about getting a different singer?" She hoped the question didn't upset Gabe, but it had been her idea of a solution from the moment he'd dropped the bombshell of Sole Regret's unexpected breakup.

"And guitarist?"

"Why would you need a new guitarist? Adam doesn't want to continue with the band either?"

Gabe sipped his lemonade, squeezed his eyes shut, and shook his head. "Wow, that's sour."

"You don't like it?"

After he pried his eyes open, he swallowed a gulp. "Love it."

She smiled. This could become a tradition for them—drinking sour-as-hell lemonade on the porch and talking while the sun disappeared behind the surrounding trees. Before she'd come to Gabe's house, she'd assumed Texas was all flat and desert-like, but his little slice of wilderness was rocky and wooded, and the nearby lake they'd visited the week before had been vast and pristine—all so unlike what she was used to in flat and farmy Kansas.

Gabe scratched at his jaw. "I don't know what Adam will want to do. I just assumed . . ."

"You know what happens when you assume."

"I don't think Adam can function without Jacob, to be honest."

"Has he ever been given the opportunity to try?"

Gabe chuckled. "I suppose not. Jacob rides his ass like he's trying to scale the Grand Canyon."

Melanie snorted at the visual of Jacob riding an Adam-faced

donkey up the Grand Canyon. Her lemonade burned the back of her throat as it tried to escape through her nose. "Don't make me laugh when I'm trying to swallow."

"No promises there." He grinned at her. "I love that you swallow."

She snorted again and slapped playfully at his thigh. "So getting a new singer is a possibility?"

"Maybe as a last resort," he said, "but Jacob's voice is so unique, we could never find a true replacement. The band could find a hundred drummers to replace me—"

"I honestly doubt that."

"—but not one vocalist that can fill Jacob's shoes."

"Lots of bands get new singers."

"And they're never as good as the original. Never."

"What about AC/DC?" She did pay attention to Nikki's nonstop blathering about rock music on occasion. "Van Halen?"

"Depends on who you ask."

"So maybe you'll find someone better than Jacob. You never know until you try."

"Last resort," he said, making it clear that it was not a solution he wanted to entertain.

"So what you really want is advice on how to win him back?" Melanie said, sucking an ice cube into her mouth since her lemonade was already gone.

Gabe chuckled. "You make it sound like I'm some high school girl who can't get over my crush."

She lifted her shoulders and shook her head. That sounded about right to her, but then she hadn't known any of these guys for long. Their bond must be strong to have gotten them through the challenges of becoming a successful rock band. That would be a bond worth saving. At least it was for Gabe, and if saving this band was important to Gabe, it was important to her too.

"Do you think Jacob will come back if Adam apologizes?" It had been Adam's disappearance right before a performance that had sent Jacob packing.

"I think we need to replace Adam to get Jacob back."

"Is it a good idea to accept Jacob's ultimatum?"

Didn't Gabe realize one should never, ever give in to a bully's demands? And to an outsider, Jacob's ultimatum—*Adam goes or I go*—had sounded an awful lot like bullying. Jacob hadn't let anyone weigh in on his decision. It had been his way or the highway, and in the end, he'd been the one who'd taken the highway—on foot.

Gabe rubbed a hand over his face. "I don't know. Maybe we'd all be happier if Adam were gone. He's been the center of all our problems from the start. Well, not him. His heroin addiction."

"I thought he'd gotten clean."

"He has, but the same selfish irresponsibility that led to his addiction is part of who he is. And we tolerate it because he's a talented motherfucker." Gabe released a heavy sigh through his nose and then shook his head. "Never mind. He's more irreplaceable than even Jacob. He writes our music."

Melanie's ringing phone interrupted their discussion, and she considered ignoring Nikki's call, but one of the concessions for Nikki agreeing to get help was that Melanie would answer every time Nikki needed to talk.

"Sorry," Melanie said. "I have to take this. I promised her I would pick up."

Gabe shrugged and took another drink of his lemonade before setting it aside and rising to join his dogs in the yard. She smiled at their exuberance—of all three of them—as she answered the phone.

"How are you doing?" Melanie asked.

"I'm bored. God, I'm bored. When are you going to spring me out of this place?"

"You promised you'd give it at least three days." And she'd been there just over twenty-four hours.

"Yeah, but I didn't realize how freaking boring these places are. There aren't any cute nurses to flirt with or anything."

Melanie covered her eyes with one hand. "You're not there to find dates."

"I know. I miss you."

"I miss you too." And she wasn't just saying that.

"How's Gabe? Did I interrupt anything aerobic?"

Unfortunately no, but she knew Gabe was having a hard time coping, and while inventive sex might take his mind off his troubles for a while, it wouldn't fix anything. "We were just talking."

"About me or the band breakup?"

"Both."

"Does he think I'm crazy?"

"He thinks you're troubled."

"Good, because I don't want him to think I'm crazy just because I'm locked up with real lunatics. He's still the drummer of my favorite band even though he's boinking my bestie. Tell him that they haven't made me wear a straitjacket or anything."

The man in question was currently tossing a stick for Beau to fetch while Lady sat panting at his feet. "You can tell him yourself. He said we'll come visit you soon."

"Really?" Melanie could hear the smile in Nikki's voice. "When?"

"I don't know yet. I'll call you when we make plans. How was therapy?"

Nikki blew a raspberry, and Melanie hoped her childish response didn't mean she wasn't taking her sessions seriously.

"Nikki, you promised you'd try."

"It's stupid. I already know why I'm the way I am and how I feel about the things that have happened to me. Telling some dumb psychiatrist about it doesn't help. The only thing that helps is being with you."

The familiar guilt of trying to make something of her life without Nikki gnawed at the pit of Melanie's stomach. "Nikki . . ."

"I've got to go," she said. "It seems all the cute nurses work the night shift and just clocked in."

"Nikki?" Melanie got no response.

With a heavy sigh, Melanie slipped her phone into her pocket and leaned forward on the porch swing. With her toes just touching the ground, she rested her elbows on her knees and buried her face in her palms. Gabe was a great guy. She wanted him to become a permanent part of her life, but Nikki had to be a part of it as well. She couldn't figure out how she'd ever get the three of their lives to blend, especially now that Nikki had made it clear that her affection for Melanie wasn't as platonic as she'd thought.

The swing shifted as Gabe sat beside her again. "Girl troubles?"

Melanie snorted and lifted her head from her palms. "How did you know?"

"Trouble and Nikki go hand in hand."

"I'm not sure what to do. My life was traveling a nice, neat little course until you and Nikki entered the picture."

"If I'm too much trouble—"

"You?" She shook her head and scooted closer to him so their hips were touching. "You're worth the trouble."

"And Nikki?"

Melanie released a heavy sigh. "She's worth the trouble too."

"I guess your life's course will stay a little messy, then."

She tilted her chin, her gaze holding his as she silently begged him to kiss her. "Guess I'll have to learn to live with a little mess."

He burrowed his fingers into the thick, tangled mass of her curls and closed the distance between their lips. Her body instantly ignited into an inferno of lust as pleasure sizzled along her nerve endings. Her hands slid up the back of his T-shirt seeking warm, smooth flesh, and she pressed her suddenly aching breasts into his firm chest, the hard ridge of the barbell in his nipple piercing sending a thrill straight to her core. He deepened the kiss, his tongue brushing against hers. Her moan of torment was cut off by the ring of his phone.

The muscles of his back tensed beneath her exploring fingers, and he pulled away slightly.

"Can you hold that thought?" he asked. "It's Adam. I need to take this call."

Between interruptions from her friends and his, she feared they were never going to end up naked and sweaty.

CHAPTER THREE

"WHAT THE FUCK IS GOING ON with Jacob?" Adam's idea of a greeting.

"I wish I knew," Gabe said into his phone.

"I watched his ridiculous news segment. Is he really back with Tina?"

"Looks that way."

"Of all the stupid—"

"You should go talk to him," Gabe said, nibbling on Melanie's chin so her passion wouldn't cool while he dealt with band bullshit.

"Madison is going to have surgery on her shoulder. I can't leave just yet."

Gabe bit his lip. He hadn't realized Madison's injuries were that severe. He'd assumed she'd just broken an arm. "I'm heading up to Kansas tomorrow. I could stop by Dallas on my way back to Austin."

"That would be great. I feel so . . ." Adam's deep inhale was surprisingly strangled. "Disconnected."

Which was the feeling—if history were any indication—that sent Adam reaching for a spoon of heroin, a lighter, and a syringe. "Be strong for Madison," Gabe said. "You've got this."

Adam swallowed hard enough that Gabe could hear it over the phone. "I'll try to remember that."

"There is no try. Only do or do not."

Adam snorted at Gabe's Yoda wisdom. "You're such a geek."

"A geek who is about to get laid. I'll see you soon. Hang tough." Gabe wasn't sure how encouraging such words were to an addict. Personally, Gabe had never suffered such an affliction, so could only imagine the struggle Adam endured each day.

"Madison keeps me clean. I won't falter. Not while she's around."

After they'd hung up, Gabe slid his phone into his pocket

only to have it vibrate with a text message. He checked the screen. Kellen. He was currently dealing with his band more now that they'd broken up than he'd ever dealt with them even on tour.

As he read the message, all the air evacuated his lungs. He read it again.

Owen just got some bad news. Chad was injured in the line of duty. I think it's pretty bad.

Another message from Kellen appeared below the first.

I did something stupid and now Owen won't talk to me, but he needs a friend right now. Could you call him?

Tell him I'm sorry.

Ask him to talk to me.

Please.

Gabe had never seen such desperation in Kellen before, so he was curious about what their typically calm and cool rhythm guitarist could have possibly done to make his closest friend not talk to him. They'd been chummy enough when he'd last seen them a few hours before. Gabe texted Kellen back while Melanie—no longer burning with desire for him—twiddled her thumbs beside him.

That really sucks about Owen's brother. Is he going to live? Gabe backspaced to remove the word *live*. He didn't want to put that thought out into the universe. He replaced the deleted word with *be okay* before sending the message.

I'm not sure. He's alive, but it's bad. Really bad. And Owen won't talk to me.

You mentioned that. What did you do to him?

Since Kellen's answer didn't come at once, Gabe glanced up at Melanie. "Owen's brother—he's a marine—has been injured."

Her eyes widened. "Oh my God. I didn't even know Owen had a brother. Is he going to be okay?"

"I don't know." Since Kellen still hadn't responded, he called Owen. When Owen didn't answer, Gabe left a message. "Shit, Owen. Kellen just told me about your brother. I'll be praying for him, bro. If you need anything at all, let me know. I'm here. And you should probably talk to Kellen. He wants to be there for you too."

Gabe set his phone aside and reached for Melanie. Seeking comfort in her warmth, he pulled her onto his lap and pressed his face against her neck. He didn't know Chad very well, but imagining that someone so young and so strong could be so easily ended had Gabe staring his own mortality in the face. Had him questioning his life and what was important to him. His band, yes, but also his home, his family, his . . . Melanie.

"How do you feel about shacking up?" he asked.

Melanie laughed. "Is it even called that anymore?"

"I don't know. Would you consider moving in with me?" They had never broached any serious discussions about their potential future beyond deciding that they wanted to be together. He was ready to take this step and the next. He just wasn't sure if she was.

"Move in together?"

Her voice squeaked, and he struggled not to chuckle. He had sprung that on her out of the blue.

"Don't you want to wake up beside me every morning?" he asked. "Learn all my disgusting habits?"

"Someday."

"How about now?"

She pushed against his chest so she could look up at him. "Where is this coming from all of a sudden?"

He shrugged. "You never know how many tomorrows you have left."

"Gabe . . ."

"Move in with me."

"Are you crazy? That's a huge step! I mean, staying with you for a few days is one thing, but moving in? I'm not sure we're ready for that."

He was sure. He knew Melanie was the one. Knew it with every part of his mind, his heart, and his soul. There were some truths science would never explain, and this was one of them. His knowing.

"Do you want to spend your life with me?" he asked.

"Yes," she said without hesitation.

"Then moving in with me is not a decision. It's inevitable."

"Gabe . . ."

He silenced her protests with a deep kiss. He couldn't take her rejection. Not at this rocky spot in his life. He needed something he could be certain of. He'd thought he could count on his band, thought he had a stable career, stable friendships.

He'd thought he had unlimited tomorrows, but now he wasn't sure about anything but her. He was sure about her.

He cupped her breast, squeezing gently. She moaned into his mouth and pressed her softness more firmly against his palm. He pinched her nipple, and her body jerked before relaxing into his. He became increasingly sure of her as her kiss turned desperate. She could fill a lot of holes in him, and at the moment, he needed to fill one in her.

His fingers moved to the button of her shorts. He unfastened freed the button, and pulled down the zipper before delving inside, his fingers seeking the hot wetness between her thighs.

She tore her mouth away. "Not sure why your unexpected proposition makes me want to come instead of go."

He grinned, his fingers dipping inside her. He used her slippery fluids to stroke her clit, his tempo increasing like the rising crescendo of a Sole Regret drum track. Her cries of pleasure rose as well as he brought her closer, closer, closer to her peak. She shifted her body—and he thought she might be trying to get away after all—but her shorts were suddenly on the porch and she was straddling him on the swing, struggling to free his hard-as-stone cock from his jeans. The buttons of his fly popped free, and before he could collect his thoughts enough to rationalize her sudden need for him, he was inside her.

He groaned as her heat engulfed him, sending pleasure and need spiraling through him. She must have been even closer to her peak than he realized as her body jerked and shuddered as she found release. He cracked one eye open; the sight of her face contorted in ecstasy made him groan. He lifted his hips to pound his cock up into her, but the swing shifted and he found himself at the mercy of her tempo—which had gone slow as she prolonged the aftershocks of her quick orgasm. His fingers dug into the wood beneath him as she squeezed her breasts while she rode him, completely at ease with making her own pleasure.

Once she caught her breath, her hips began to rock, churning his length inside her until his head dropped back against the swing. The slightest movement of his foot on the porch pushed him deeper as the swing swayed beneath them. His toes lost contact with the ground, and the swing tipped dizzily, unsettling him and making his heart lurch with panic. It also buried him so deep within her, not even a fraction of him was exposed. Which got him thinking about centers of gravity and sex swings with anal plugs. A short thick one for him—because it would feel amazing to have something up his ass to ground him in this rocking motion. And a longer, vibrating one for her, because why not? He loved the feel of a vibrator against his dick when he was buried inside a woman.

But she began to move faster, sending the swing swaying precariously and his thoughts shattering.

"Rub my clit," she said breathlessly in his ear. "I'm so close."

"Again?"

"Yes."

She leaned back so his hand could find her swollen nub. She had an exceptionally large clit, and he had just the suction cup to keep it overstimulated for far longer than he could manage on his own. Unfortunately, it was in the house, so he'd have to do this manually.

"Yes. Oh, Gabe. You're so good at this."

Sitting still while she did almost all the work? He was rather good at that. He sent her flying, groaning in delight as her pussy gripped him in rhythmic spasms. She collapsed against him, breathing hard, and her body went completely limp. He wrapped his arms around her, holding her close while she got her bearings.

"You didn't come, did you?" she murmured after a long moment of sitting impaled by his aching cock.

"No." He kissed her shoulder, refusing to look at the two dogs sitting at the foot of the steps watching them. "It's okay."

Apparently she disagreed. She winced as she lifted her hips, and he fell free of her delightful warmth. She settled back on his thighs and took his cock in both hands. Pleasure pulsed up and down his length with each slide of her grip. In his already overstimulated state, it didn't take her long to give him the release he craved. "Yes," he groaned, watching her catch his cum and struggling to keep his eyes open so he could see it drip over the back of her hand. "Oh, Melanie. You're so good at this."

She snorted when he threw her earlier words back at her. "Well, I'm sure I don't have as much practice as you do."

He chuckled, still twitching with the remnants of his orgasm. His jerking compounded each time her thumb rubbed over his cockhead.

"Are you suggesting that my hand is well acquainted with my cock?" he asked.

She flushed. "I meant with sex in general."

"The amount of sex I have in general will never catch up with how much I experience in my head."

Beau emitted a loud, sharp bark, and Melanie jumped. She winced and peered over her shoulder at the pair of Labradors gazing at them with obvious curiosity. "Were they watching the entire time?"

"I was too busy enjoying myself to notice." Which was partially true. He had noticed them toward the end there, but refused to let a couple of dogs ruin his good time. "I did have an idea for a new sex swing while you were giving me the ride of my life."

She lifted an eyebrow at him. "Do you always find the capacity to think when you're in the middle of the act?"

"I wouldn't call it thinking," he said, stroking both hands up her smooth back beneath her shirt. "More like sparks of inspiration. But to answer your question . . ." He bent to kiss her neck because she was every distraction he needed in his currently chaotic life. "Inspiration doesn't happen often. I just find you particularly stimulating."

"Are you going to tell me about this new idea of yours?"

"Mmm," he murmured, kissing a path to her ear and nipping the lobe. She shuddered in response. "I'd rather build the prototype and give you a demonstration."

"Not sure if I should be intrigued or worried," she said.

He wondered if she were thinking about the prototype he'd been hoping to unveil the last time she visited. They'd had to postpone its debut when it malfunctioned, but he'd got it working late last night. Tinkering took his mind off his troubles, but not nearly as well as Melanie did. And tinkering for Melanie? With Melanie? Well, that might just get him through this mess he called a life with a big smile on his face. He was tired of being angry. Tired of trying to fix problems he had no control over. Tired of feeling like his opinions didn't matter.

His arms tightened around her, and while he didn't share all the thoughts and feelings swarming through his turbulent mind, he did say, "I'm really glad you came."

"That *was* quite an orgasm," she said, her tone teasing.

"I meant—"

She squeezed him. "I know what you meant," she whispered. "I'm glad I came too. Now, if you don't mind, I'd like to find my shorts so your dogs will stop ogling my bare ass."

"Some dogs have all the luck."

CHAPTER FOUR

MELANIE KNEW she was staring, but she couldn't help herself. It was true that Gabe was the most gorgeous man she'd ever seen in profile—surpassed only by when his face was turned in her direction—but that wasn't the only reason she couldn't take her eyes off him as he drove. After making love on the porch swing, they found the rest of their evening quite normal—preparing and sharing a perfectly ordinary dinner accompanied by perfectly ordinary conversation, cuddling up on the couch with two giant dogs to watch a movie, telling each other stories about their pasts, falling asleep in each other's arms. All of it had made her heart ache with longing. She wanted this kind of life with him— ordinary, tame—and he would give anything to go back to his life as a rock star. Recognizing that he was everything she wanted in a man ignited far more than her passion. It ignited feelings she could not ignore.

I'm in love with him. She smiled as she identified the feelings within her thoughts. *I'm madly in love with him.*

After Gabe had made arrangements for his dogs to be spoiled in his absence—she couldn't help but think that guys who were good with dogs made great future fathers—the two of them had started north to visit Nikki. Most guys would have deemed her best friend too high maintenance to deal with. Melanie's last boyfriend had broken up with her for that very reason. He couldn't deal with Nikki or with Melanie dropping everything to help Nikki out of another mess. But not Gabe. Gabe cared enough about her to drive ten hours to visit the woman whose reckless behavior had already put a strain on their tender new relationship. Either Gabe was a glutton for punishment, or he cared about Melanie's happiness. Genuinely cared. Or maybe he was just antsy for a road trip because he was supposed to be touring with his band this summer.

"Take a picture; it will last longer."

He gave her a sideways look that made her toes curl.

She flushed. So he *had* noticed that she was gawking at him.

"A picture might be worth a thousand words," she said, feeling particularly sappy—maybe it was hormonal—"but it would never do you justice. A picture wouldn't smell like you, sound like you, *feel* like you."

"Taste like me?" He gave her a hopeful look.

She giggled and leaned across the small interior of the Volkswagen to kiss him. He'd left his Texas-size truck at home and opted to take Nikki's car back to Topeka, assuring Melanie that he could fix her temperamental sedan without a problem.

"A picture wouldn't kiss me back either," she said. "So I wouldn't ever take a picture over staring at the real you."

"You're so obsessed with me."

She laughed at his teasing, but he was closer to the truth than he could possibly know. "I think it's called being in love."

"What?" he said, his eyes widening.

"I love you, Gabriel Banner." Maybe she should wait for him to say it again—after all, he'd been the one to promise he'd tell her how he felt as often as she needed to hear it, and he hadn't repeated the sentiment since their hasty love confession over a week ago. But this morning her feelings were bubbling out of her like the head on an overflowing beer mug, and she couldn't contain them. She leaned into his line of sight because he was singularly focused on the road in front of him. "Does it scare you? That I love you?"

The car jerked, tires screeching as Gabe stomped on the brakes. They were on a lonely stretch of interstate somewhere in Oklahoma, so he didn't even earn a horn blare from a disgruntled driver as the Bug shuddered to a stop. Melanie pried her fingernails out of her thighs and glared at him.

"What are you doing? Are you trying to kill us?"

She jerked around in her seat to see that the road behind them was empty, but it wouldn't stay like that forever. A semi might mow them over at any moment.

"Why did you stop?" she asked, turning her attention to him.

His face had gone pale. Even his lips had lost their color. "Did you just say . . ."

"That I love you? Yes, I said it. And I'm sorry if that upsets you, but I can't help it. I love you. It's not like it's the first time you ever heard me say it." The second time, but not the first. "Now will you please go so we don't commemorate this heart-baring moment with our deaths."

The car started forward, slowly at first, and then went faster and faster until they were cruising at least thirty miles per hour over the speed limit.

"Gabe?"

He was in some sort of trance. She wasn't sure that he'd even heard her call his name. She touched his knee, poked his cheek, licked the side of his neck. Nothing. He did come out of his daze when flashing red and blue lights came up behind them and the state patrolman squawked his siren.

"Shit," Gabe said, finally coasting to a sane speed and then braking smoothly to pull over and stop on the highway's wide shoulder.

Gabe leaned across her and fumbled with the glove compartment. "Please tell me that Nikki has insurance on this thing."

Melanie couldn't help but wonder why he was avoiding looking at her, and why he was digging through the glove compartment instead of asking for her help, and why he was acting so weird just because she'd said those three little words. She'd assumed—apparently wrongly—that he still held the strong feelings he'd confessed to after their one and only huge argument, especially after asking her to move in with him last night. But maybe he was having second thoughts. Maybe she should have waited for him to tell her how he felt again before opening her big mouth. She knew how skittish some guys could be over the word *love*. She just hadn't realized Gabe was such a guy. Had she completely fucked up this relationship with premature word ejaculation? Damn it!

"She has insurance," Melanie said, though she didn't want to discuss fucking insurance at the moment. She wanted to discuss Gabe's inexplicable cold feet. "I should know. I pay for it."

"You're kidding?"

She shook her head, but he still wasn't looking at her, so she reiterated. "No joke. She's a bit short on funds at the moment. She can't hold a job. Keeps screwing around with coworkers, her boss, the janitor."

"Is she a nympho? I mean, not just promiscuous, but

legitimately has a mental condition that makes her need sex all the time?"

"No, she's not a nympho. Her shrink says she wants to belong to someone, and it's easiest for her to get that feeling by sleeping around. Of course, the feeling doesn't last long, because no one sticks around after they use her for sex." Jacob Silverton being a perfect example. Melanie crossed her arms over her chest.

"I get why you enable her."

Melanie did enable her, and she knew it. She refused to apologize for caring about someone who had no one else to look after her.

Gabe continued, "But I'm not sure it's in her best interest."

"You're enabling her too! Who decided we should go see her today?" She lifted her eyebrows at him, but he was focused on retrieving his driver's license from his wallet.

"Would you please find the proof of insurance for me?" he asked, dropping the subject.

Not unlike the way he'd dropped the subject of her love confession.

So she'd gotten a bit mushy on him. She hadn't realized he'd freak out so much over her utterance of three simple—or not so simple—words, especially since she'd told him once before. Maybe that was the problem. Maybe he'd started to doubt her feelings because she didn't say it often enough. But he was as guilty of that as she was.

"And registration," he added. "Not sure if we need it in Oklahoma."

"And we're just going to ignore what I said a few minutes ago?"

"That you pay Nikki's bills?"

She waved a hand at him, but he still wouldn't fucking look at her. He was now holding his license between his forefinger and middle finger while staring at the side-view mirror.

Melanie huffed out an exasperated breath and after finding the little wallet with the appropriate papers—Melanie knew they were in there because she'd put them inside herself—she slapped it none too gently on his thigh.

Gabe rolled the window down, and a hot blast of Oklahoman summer air entered the car.

"Can you shut off your engine?" the police officer asked in a calm but authoritative voice.

Gabe complied, and the air conditioning cut off as well. Ugh, it was already hot. This was going to be hell. Why had he been driving like a maniac? Trying to off her so he didn't have to break her heart? If he'd been joking about shacking up and if he didn't return her love, he should just tell her. She was a big girl. She'd been dumped more than once. It wasn't ever fun, but it hadn't ever killed her either. This oppressive heat, on the other hand, just might do her in. She tried rolling down her window, but the ignition was completely off, so the glass stayed shut tight. She lifted the heavy mass of her hair off her nape and held it against the back of her head as she used her free hand to wave hot, thick air into her face.

"License, registration, and proof of insurance, please."

The officer's voice drifted down into the car. Melanie couldn't see anything but the man's middle, which included a holstered pistol.

Gabe handed the cop the required documents. "How fast was I going, sir?"

Melanie scrunched down so she could see the officer's face. He was a bit thick around the waist, but not overly fat. A pair of dark sunglasses hid his eyes, but when he glanced at Gabe's license, Melanie saw him do a double take before he looked down at Gabe. He even held the license next to Gabe's face to make sure it was the same guy. Apparently he'd never seen a highly tattooed, Mohawk-sporting hunk of a drummer driving a melon-orange VW Bug before.

Gabe took off his ball cap, revealing the dragon tattoos on his scalp that must be visible on his license. They didn't allow ball caps in Texas driver's license photos, not even Texas Rangers ones. "Yep, that's really me."

"I see that. I clocked you at ninety-six."

Ninety-six? Holy shit!

"Huh," Gabe muttered. "I had no idea this little car could go that fast."

"Just because there's no traffic doesn't mean you should test the limits of your—" The officer choked on a laugh as he eyed the adorable Bug. "—vehicle."

"That isn't what I was doing," Gabe said. He flicked a hand in Melanie's direction. "She just told me she loved me."

So he *had* heard her.

The officer leaned slightly to peer into the car. Hot in the face, Melanie offered him a little wave.

"Does your daddy know who you're dating?" the man asked.

Her slight embarrassment turned into heated outrage.

"My daddy has no say in who I love," she snapped.

Gabe giggled and pressed the backs of his fingers to his nose. It was a sound Melanie hadn't realized he could produce, and one she never wanted to hear from him again.

The officer flicked the car's registration against his thigh. "I'll just run this to make sure everything checks out and write you a very large ticket. Are you Nicole Swanson, ma'am?"

Melanie shook her head. "No, that's my roommate. She let me borrow her car because mine's in the shop." Technically it was sitting in the parking lot of her apartment building collecting bird poo, which in her opinion was all it was good for at the moment.

The officer returned to his vehicle, and Gabe sat stone still, staring straight ahead as if she were a T-Rex who wouldn't notice he existed if he didn't move. Was the thought of her telling him she loved him really that terrible? Did he find her feelings humorous or just pathetic?

"Gabe, I didn't mean to make you uncomfortable."

"I'm not uncomfortable."

"Then why won't you look at me?"

"Because."

"Because why?"

"I feel like my heart is going to explode as it is. If I look at you now, I don't think I'll survive."

"It's not like I've never said it before."

"But that was after an argument. It doesn't count."

What the hell? So when he'd returned her hastily spewed loved confession after their argument about Nikki, he hadn't meant it? Her heart twisted so hard, she covered her chest with a fisted hand.

"It counted," she said, her voice tight with a mix of hurt and anger. "Of course it counted. I don't say such things to every guy who comes along, you know."

"I didn't mean it that way," he said. "I just . . . I believed it more this time. Last time it felt like we were just trying to soothe wounds inflicted by arguing."

"So you're not upset that I said I love you?"

He emitted a slight whine. "Please don't say it again until we're alone in a relatively safe location. I'm dying to pull you into my arms and show you that I feel the same way."

Her heart lightening with relief, eyes brimming with tears of happiness, she said, "I know we were planning to drive the entire way to Topeka in one day, but I'm a bit tired. I think we need to find a nice hotel soon."

"I'm a bit tired myself."

"Ten hours is much too long to sit beside you without you buried inside me."

He cleared his throat and nodded, still not looking at her. "I completely agree."

"Will it be okay for me to say I love you when our bodies are one?"

He bit his fist and groaned.

She laughed. "I do love you, Gabe Banner."

He turned in his seat to check out the state trooper behind them. The officer sure was taking his sweet time.

"How big will my ticket be if I leave for the nearest hotel right now?"

She slid a hand over his thigh to nestle between his legs. Though she wasn't close to touching his cock, he squirmed beneath her touch.

"You can wait," she whispered close to his ear.

"Nope," he said, and started the car. "Waiting is not an option."

Before he could put the car in gear, she turned off the ignition. "Getting pursued by the law in a high-speed car chase is not going to get you laid faster."

"Damn, you're right." He smoothed his hair back and yanked his ball cap back into place. "Maybe you should look up a nearby hotel on your phone and get us directions. I'd hate to get two tickets in one day."

"Promise me you will not speed to the hotel no matter how fast this Bug can go."

"The second ticket won't be for speeding." He gifted her with a devastatingly naughty grin, and her heart fluttered. "It will be for public indecency."

She grinned. She'd be more than willing to pay that fine.

"God, I want you right now, Mel," he said.

"I love you," she said again, just to watch him twitch. And maybe she was hoping he'd say it back to her, but he left her wanting.

CHAPTER FIVE

GABE KNEW a man wasn't supposed to feel gloriously happy when a chick he'd met less than two weeks before declared her love. He was supposed to run. But Gabe wasn't running. He wasn't even considering it. He'd already decided Mel was his one, and knowing that she felt the same way gave him no choice but to be ecstatic. He'd wanted to tell her how he felt again a thousand times over the past week, but she'd never said the words after that one time backstage in New Orleans, so he'd decided it best to keep his own words locked inside. And now that she'd said them again—each utterance a moment of pure joy for him—he felt it would be a bit canned to repeat them to her like a fucking parrot. But he would tell her how he felt. Soon.

Unfortunately, the nearest decent hotel was about seventy miles away. If he committed to doing the speed limit, it would take them over an hour to get there. Even though he'd just gotten a speeding ticket—not his first, but his first in Oklahoma—he was having one hell of a time not slamming the gas pedal to the floor. Because he wanted her body, yes, but his urgency to be alone and naked with her was more than just sexual. He wanted to bare his heart to her. He trusted her to treasure it.

"Are we there yet?" he asked. Melanie laughed.

He loved the sound of her laugh. Every time he heard it, he couldn't help but smile.

"We're about two minutes closer than we were the last time you asked."

"You have got to keep me distracted. I'm dying over here."

"What kind of distraction did you have in mind?"

The kind he had in mind would likely get him that public indecency charge. Besides, he doubted he could drive at all with her gorgeous mouth sucking at his cock. And if they pulled over . . . He shook his head to clear his thoughts. He felt like a teenager around her. Horny, confused, emotional, fixated, yet at the same time distracted and a bit giddy. But yeah, mostly fucking horny.

"Tell me about your parents," he said. "That ought to keep me from discovering how well I can drive while you suck my cock."

"Parents?" She crinkled up her nose. "I prefer that second distraction for sure."

She unfastened her seat belt and reached for the top button of his fly. He caught her hand. His heart was thundering so hard in his chest, he thought someone might need to call the paramedics. Having such an intense response before she even touched him did not bode well for his ability to be sucked and to drive simultaneously.

"You don't want me to?" she asked, looking up at him from where she was partially leaning across his lap.

His cock jerked in his jeans. Her looking up at him like that, with a naughty question in her hazel eyes, had him out of his mind with lust. Christ, she had to be the most beautiful thing he'd ever seen.

"Of course I want you to," he began, his voice husky to his own ears. "But—"

She didn't let him finish. Instead, she unfastened his pants and gently pulled his cock free. His seated position didn't allow for much maneuvering of his underwear, so his length was pressed up against his belly. He knew he should have gone commando that morning despite the discomfort of sitting in a car all day.

"If you don't think you can drive while I suck you off, then I'll just lick it a little. Okay?"

Her cool hand gently pressed against the underside of his cock, and her thumb brushed the throbbing head.

"Mel," he gasped.

"Okay?" she asked again.

"Please." He wasn't sure if it was a plea for her to stop— surely not—or a plea for her to begin, but she took it for the latter.

When her tongue caressed him so gently his balls ached and his belly tied itself in knots, he praised genetics that he was gifted with long legs so that there was plenty of room between his lap and the steering wheel. He also praised the engineer who'd invented cruise control as he set his speed exactly on the posted limit. He concentrated on keeping his eyes open and focused on the straight stretch of road before him, but it was damned hard when Mel's tongue was teasing him beguilingly.

"That feels so good," he whispered, squeezing his eyes shut for a heartbeat, allowing himself the tiniest moment of pure bliss before he forced his attention back on the road. There was something about trying to squelch the pleasure rippling through him that intensified it.

Melanie's hand slid against his belly and pushed his cock away from his body so she could lick the neglected top of his cockhead. She drew an inch of him into her mouth and sucked, her tongue teasing his rim, and then pulled back to blow cooling breaths over his wet tip.

He shuddered in torment. Worried that he'd hit the ditch running along the highway if he took a hand off the steering wheel to burrow into her thick hair, he tightened his grip until his fingers ached. She repeated the motions—lick, suck, blow—and his eyes rolled back. He swerved just enough to hit the warning rumbles on the edge of the pavement, which caused him to jerk out of his lust-induced stupor and right the car again.

"Fuck, woman," he growled. "You're going to have to stop. I can't see straight."

"You can't *drive* straight either," she said with a chuckle.

The huffs of air her soft laugh produced tickled his highly sensitive and still-wet tip.

"Of course I can't drive straight. You give great head."

He chanced touching her sleek curls, but only for a second, as that increased the tenderness he felt for her and completely shattered him.

She'd said she loved him. She'd said it. Without prompting. Not as some sort of apology or to make amends, but just because.

And she really did give great head.

She smiled up at him and seemed determined to prove his compliment correct when she took the tip of him into her mouth once more.

Just stay on the road, Gabe. Stay on the goddamned road. He groaned when her free hand, which had been resting on his thigh, brushed up against his balls. Her other hand was curled gently—

unmoving—around his shaft.

"Do you want to come?" she asked.

His belly clenched at the sound of her sexy voice, and his cock jerked in her hand. "Yeah. Inside you. In about thirty minutes."

"Should I stop? Are you close?"

Probably and *definitely*, but he said, "Keep doing that just a little longer."

She kept him on the brink of orgasm for miles. He fought to stay focused on the road, fought to keep from filling her mouth with the heaviness pooling in his balls, fought not to shove her head down and fuck the back of her throat.

When the hotel-directed GPS on Melanie's phone announced *prepare to turn right in two miles*, he was sure the robotic voice belonged to an angel of mercy.

Melanie sat straight in her seat, her face flushed, lips swollen from working him over. She wiped a bit of saliva from the corner of her mouth, and he groaned, his overexcited body unable to take the added visual stimulation of the sexiest mouth he'd ever seen or felt. Or tasted.

When they got to that hotel room, he planned to devour that sweet, dirty mouth of hers while he pounded her pussy raw. He knew he wouldn't be able to take her slow, to show her care or how much he loved her. Not this time. But he would countless times in the future. Because he wanted her in his life permanently, and he wasn't afraid to let her know it.

Melanie tried rearranging his cock in his jeans, which made him double over in agony.

"God, you're hard," she said.

"I wonder why," he snapped, but he wasn't angry. Far from it. He was, however, going to die if he didn't fuck her within the next five minutes.

"You know, I heard that cars will be driving themselves in the next ten to twenty years," Melanie said.

"Normally I'd enthusiastically discuss the particulars of self-driven cars, but I think I need to concentrate on breathing until we get to the hotel."

"I wonder how people will keep themselves entertained on long road trips if they don't have to pay attention to the road."

He immediately caught on to her implication. "I'm liking the idea of a computer being in charge of my vehicular safety more and more."

She laughed and tried forcing his rigid length back into his pants again. "Still too hard. Are you going to make it to the hotel?"

He spotted the hotel's sign and imagined it was pointing the way to nirvana. He was more than ready to find his way there with Mel.

It was a typical chain hotel, but newer and nicer than he'd expected. Melanie had to go inside to check in because Gabe was still at the whim of the hardest dick he'd ever owned. By the time she exited to stand beneath the portico where he was waiting in the car, he'd managed to get himself to a state of semi-hardness by forcing himself to think of post office lines and filing taxes. Yet the second she smiled and brandished a room card at him, he was hard as stone again.

"Calm the fuck down," he pep-talked his dick. "It isn't as if you've never been laid before."

But with Melanie, every time carried the excitement, the longing, the curiosity and wonder of his first time. The main difference was he had a few more skills now than he'd had when he'd gratefully lost his virginity in college.

Melanie climbed back into the passenger seat. "The entrance we want is around back. Unfortunately, check-in time isn't until four."

A spike of panic thrust through his chest. He couldn't wait two hours. "What?"

"I convinced them to let us check in early." She grinned. "I told them you aren't feeling well—probably have a case of food poisoning—and that you really needed to use the bathroom before you lie down for a nap, so no one will be suspicious if you have to walk in all doubled over."

"Now, Miss Anderson, why would I have to walk in doubled over?"

Her hand slid to his lap, and he groaned when she discovered he was as hard as ever.

"I don't know, Banner. Why would you?"

"You're evil."

"Get used to it."

Luckily, the back parking lot was empty except for a single

semi-truck parked far off to the side. Gabe snagged the parking spot next to the alternate entrance and shut off the car. He glanced up at the nondescript beige multi-floor box of a hotel, hoping their room wasn't far from the door.

"We're on the first floor," she said as if they shared a brain. "So you won't have to hobble up stairs or wait for an elevator."

She was enjoying his misery far too much. Though elevators had possibilities, he was grateful the room wasn't too far away. He silently pledged that after he filled her with his cum—and probably took a long nap—he'd make her want him as much as he currently wanted her.

"Give me a minute, and I think I'll be able to stand," he said.

Melanie leaned over and nibbled on his ear. "I sure hope so. I was hoping you'd take me up against the wall."

His face tightened in agony. Was she trying to kill him? "You like this power you have over me, don't you?"

She grinned. "You have it over me too. That's why I wanted you to drive today."

He closed his eyes and laughed. Yeah, if she'd been driving, he'd have had no choice but to put her in a similar state of arousal.

"You're driving the rest of the way, then," he said.

"I plan on it."

She kissed him—rather chastely—and opened her door. She looked at him over her shoulder, the question in her eyes turning him into a smoldering kettle of lust. What was it about that look that reached deep inside him and pushed all of his triggers? He watched her pass in front of the car like he was some sort of creepy stalker rather than her boyfriend, but he could not for the life of him get his body to move from the driver's seat.

"Are you coming?" she called when he just sat there in the stupid car, staring at her through the windshield.

"Almost," he whispered to himself.

He was pretty sure he was drooling, but couldn't help it. She was everything he wanted. Not just physically, though that was at the forefront of his mind at that particular moment, but everything he wanted and needed in his life. He knew he'd never love another woman as much as he loved her. Until Melanie, he'd never known he could be completely sure of anything. Having a keenly scientific mind, he automatically questioned everything—fact or theory—extensively. But not his feelings for Mel. With her, he just knew. Was this what it felt like to have absolute faith? If so, he envied those that faith came to naturally.

"If you don't hurry, I'm going to have to take care of myself," she said. "My panties are uncomfortably damp and—"

He threw open his door, jerked against his still fastened seat belt, cursed the infernal device as he fumbled with the clasp, and finally unfolded his long body from the confines of the Bug. He slammed the door and met Melanie at the hotel entrance. She was moving as swiftly as he was. Expecting the card reader to waylay their plans, he actually said, "Fuck, yes," when the light turned green and the mechanism unlocked on her first attempt.

He followed her into a small foyer, and she glanced from the number written on the cardboard folder of her keycard to the small plaque on the corridor wall. "This way," she said.

Gabe couldn't keep his hands off of her for another second. He wrapped an arm around her shoulders and pulled her up against his side, leaning in to steal a kiss. And once he tasted her sweet lips, he couldn't stop. He was only vaguely aware that they were still moving down the hall toward their little sanctuary. Melanie's soft lips had his full attention.

She turned her head and eyed the number next to a door before turning back to his kiss and luring him past the next few rooms. By the time they reached the end of the corridor, his hand had developed a mind of its own and was massaging her soft breast. Her nipple was distractingly hard against his palm. He needed his lips on it, his tongue on it, his teeth . . .

"Just let me open the door," Melanie said.

Her voice was husky, but she could still form words. She wasn't nearly as turned on as he was if she could speak a complete sentence. He planned to take that ability from her at once. She turned toward the door, and he moved to stand directly behind her, his dick pressed into the soft swell of her ass, one hand roughly rubbing her tit, the other seeking the heat between her legs. She gasped when his mouth found the point where her neck met her shoulder.

"Gabe," she said, his name a breathless whisper. "I can't open . . . door . . . You . . ."

She shifted her hips, rubbing her sweet ass against his

aching, throbbing cock. She could still speak in recognizable words, so she wasn't at his level of desire just yet. He pinched her nipple, and she shuddered, flattening herself against the door, her legs spreading for him as if she was perfectly okay with him taking her right there in the hotel corridor. Satisfied that she'd be ready for him the instant her panties hit the floor, he slipped the keycard from between her fingers and stuck it into the slot. It blinked mercifully green, and when he pushed the handle down, the door sprung open. Melanie stumbled forward, and he allowed the few inches of separation between them, but only until they were both inside the room and the door clicked shut behind them. He yanked off her shirt while she kicked aside her shoes. He jerked open his fly while she shimmied out of her shorts. Jeans around his ankles, he caught her around the waist and turned her so that her face was pressed against the wall and her gorgeous bare ass was tilted upward. He grabbed his cock, rubbing the tip through the wetness he knew he'd find. He slipped into her swollen pussy with a groan of part triumph, part agony and pushed forward until he was buried to the root. She whimpered, her hands curling into the wall on either side of her face.

He pulled back and pounded into her again and again. He held her hips in a solid grip as he pulled her into him while he thrust forward. Her flesh rippled with each forceful invasion.

"When you tease me like that," he growled, "I have no choice but to punish your naughty pussy."

"Deserves good pounding," she slurred.

Her hand moved down to where their bodies were joined, and her fingertips brushed his length every time he moved within her. Enjoying the sensation, he slowed his thrusts, pushing back his mindless need to attain release. When his instincts retreated and he located a sliver of reason in his lust-clouded thoughts, he gently slid his hands around Melanie's body and cupped her soft breasts. He kissed her sweat-damp shoulder and brushed her hair back with the side of his face as he kissed his way to her neck.

She moaned, churning her hips to meet his much slower but still deep thrusts.

"Kind of lost myself there for a moment," he whispered, fingers tugging at her nipples. "I almost forgot it's better to give than to receive."

"You're always . . . Oh!"

He grinned at her reaction to his rough treatment of her stiff nipples. "What were you saying?" he asked.

Jeans around his calves, his shuffled toward the bed, still joined with Melanie. "You're always giving, Gabe. It's okay to take. I want you to take. Take all of me."

So he bent her over the bed and took and took and took until he exploded inside her. When he collapsed onto her back, breathing hard, his balls quivering from the merciful release, he had no idea if she'd enjoyed it, if she'd reached orgasm, or if she wanted to do nothing more energetic than sleep for the next few hours. But he knew all those things were true in regard to himself.

"You okay?" he asked, face squashed against the middle of her back.

"Never better."

He hoped she wasn't just saying that. He wanted their relationship to be built on trust and no lies. If his bedroom skills lacked in any way, he wanted her to tell him so that he could improve. Even if that meant they had to accessorize with new devices.

"Did you come?" he asked.

"Twice." Her hand, resting on the bedspread beside her head, curled, and she extended two fingers. They were shaking.

So it hadn't been a total failure on his part.

After a moment, he found the will to stand. He gently caressed her back with both hands and watched his softened cock slip from her pussy. If he hadn't just come, the sight of their combined cum dripping down her thighs would have made him instantly hard for a second round, but he was completely spent. He kicked off his cumbersome jeans, pulled back the covers and climbed between them.

"There's a spot right here for you, baby," he said, holding the covers up in invitation.

A look of longing on her face, she glanced toward the suite's bathroom. "Hold that thought."

He did until she returned a few moments later with a warm, wet washcloth.

"I want you to sleep comfortably too," she said, and handed

the cloth to him.

He wiped the stickiness from his dick, overwhelmingly touched by her completely unembarrassed meeting of his needs. The simplicity of the gesture reminded him of her earlier confession. He dropped the cloth to the floor and wrapped the covers around her when she slipped between them. Spooning up against her back, he brushed her hair aside with one hand and kissed the delicate curve of her jaw.

"There's something I've been wanting to tell you every time I look at you," he said, his heart now thudding a rapid staccato. "Or even think of you."

She turned her head, that questioning look that laid waste to all rational thought on her beautiful face. "What's that?"

"I love you." He half-expected a comet to strike the planet and end the world at that moment, but the only thing that happened was the room air conditioner kicked on.

"Are you sure?" she asked, the question clear in her eyes. "You don't have to say it again just because I said it."

"Trust me."

She rolled over in his arms and palmed his cheek in one hand. "I do."

Two words even scarier than the three he'd just said, but he smiled at hearing them. He planned to hear them again from her in a more formal setting in the future. "Good," he said. "Because it's true. I love you."

All the questions left her face, to be replaced by a radiant smile. "I love you too, Gabe. Crazy as it sounds."

"Didn't think you'd ever fall for a tattooed metal drummer?" He lifted a teasing eyebrow.

"Well, no, but that's not the crazy part. What's crazy is how fast it happened."

"Mass remaining stable, the faster the acceleration, the greater the force."

"And Force is with me on this?"

He laughed at her use of his nickname and kissed her. "Force will always be with you." He kissed her again. "But please leave the corny Star Wars references to me."

She shook her head. "I want to share everything with you," she said, her fingers sliding through the strip of hair at the center of his scalp.

He had no idea what had happened to his ball cap, but was glad they were completely bare to each other—inside and out—at that moment.

"I want to share my body, my heart, corny Star Wars references." She blinked, but then held his gaze. He could feel her heart thudding against his. "My life."

"I guess if corny Star Wars references come with the rest of those amazing perks, I'll allow them."

She scowled at him. "Perks?"

"I said they were amazing."

"But do you want the same thing?" she asked, her hand now moving to his cheek.

He melted into her palm, sorry he'd made her doubt his intentions. "I want to marry you, Melanie Anderson. Is that what you had in mind?"

The blood drained from her face. "It's much too soon for that. I was talking about moving in together. I've been thinking about it, and I'm ready."

He caught her wrist and drew her hand to his mouth, tenderly kissing her palm. "I'm glad. But . . ."

"But? I thought that's what you wanted."

"It is. But . . ."

She stared at him, waiting for him to continue. Moving in together just wasn't enough.

"I know I don't look it, but I'm rather traditional."

She snorted.

"I mean that," he said. "I might move in with a woman I wasn't sure about, but I'm sure about you, Mel. You're my one. My forever. My only. I want you to be my wife."

Her eyes widened, and she stared at him for a full minute before she blinked. "Do you really mean that?"

His kiss moved from her palm to her wrist, where her pulse beat rapidly against his lips. "I've never meant anything more in my life."

She grinned. "Your acceleration is a force to be reckoned with, Force."

He laughed. He actually liked that she teased him about his nickname. "Is that a yes? You'll marry me?"

Her smile brightened, and she cupped his cheek in one hand. "Yes."

The air conditioner kicked off. A comet didn't strike the planet. But he was pretty sure his world had just ended. It had brightened into a new one with the promise of this woman by his side. Always.

CHAPTER SIX

MELANIE DIDN'T KNOW how Gabe could sleep at a time like this. Had he really just asked her to marry him? Not moving in together or how she felt about marriage, but a genuine proposal? And had she really said yes? She felt no regret over her hasty decision. Not even a trace of regret. But how could he cement their lives together and then casually roll over and take a nap? Must be a man thing.

Practically vibrating with excited energy, Melanie kissed Gabe's bare shoulder and allowed herself the pleasure of running her hand down his perfectly defined chest, pausing to toy with the sexy barbell piercing his nipple before continuing over the eight perfect bumps that defined his abs. As she copped her feel, she dwelled on the reality that this magnificent, albeit sleeping, man was all hers, and then, unable to keep that reality to herself for a single second longer, she hopped out of bed. She found her shorts, fished her cellphone from the pocket and then quietly shut the bathroom door so she didn't wake her sleeping fiancé. Fiancé? Holy shit, she was engaged!

"Mental Health Services," a receptionist answered her call. "How can I help you?"

"I need to speak to Nicole Swanson, please. She's a patient."

"Oh yes, we're all *very* familiar with Nikki," the woman said.

What, exactly, was that supposed to mean? "Can I talk to her?"

"Let me see if she's available."

While Melanie was on hold, she stared at herself in the enormous mirror over the sink. She didn't look any different from the way she'd looked that morning, but she felt like an entirely new woman. An obscenely happy one. Perhaps Nikki wasn't the best person to share this news with first. She might not take it well. Maybe Melanie should have called her mom first. Her mom would be happy about her exciting news until she learned it meant her only daughter would likely be moving to Texas. Melanie normally saw her parents a couple of times a week. Her leaving Topeka would be an adjustment for all of them. And if she and Gabe had babies—her heart thudded with a mix of excitement and dread at the idea—she figured her parents just might find a way to move south to spoil those future grandchildren. But Melanie was getting ahead of herself. She and Gabe had talked about having babies only once, and it had been in regard to that pregnant groupie, Lindsey. Melanie wasn't sure if she could handle the idea of another woman carrying Gabe's baby. "Please don't let it be his," she murmured to herself.

"Please don't let it be his *what?*" Nikki asked in her ear.

"Guess what?"

"You'll be here in a couple of hours to bust me out of this hellhole."

"Uh . . ." That had been the original plan. "We won't be there until tomorrow, sweetie. Something came up."

"Let me guess. Gabe's dick came up, so you had to stop at a hotel and take care of that for him."

Melanie laughed. "Lucky guess."

"More like inevitable situation. You two are on fire for each other. Putting you into a car alone together could only lead to one thing."

"Two things, actually."

"You stopped at two different hotels? You *are* insatiable. Meow."

"No, just the one. The other thing is . . . Can you keep a secret?" Melanie wasn't sure if Gabe wanted her to keep their spur-of-the-moment engagement a secret or not, but just in case . . .

"You *know* I can't keep a secret, Mel."

"Well, try. I can't keep this to myself. It's too wonderful."

"I'm locking my lips. Throwing away the key."

Knowing Nikki, Melanie pictured her pantomiming the actions as she said them.

"Okay." Melanie took a deep breath, her belly fluttering with butterflies. She was half-convinced she was dreaming, but telling Nikki made it more real. "Gabe wants to get married."

"To who?"

Melanie rolled her eyes at herself in the bathroom mirror.

"To me, silly."

"You're going to marry Gabe?"

"I know it's a little fast—okay, it's a lot fast—but I also know he's the one. Is it possible? To just know? I never believed falling in love could really happen this way. I always thought love had to develop over time to be strong enough to withstand marriage, but with Gabe—"

"You're going to marry Gabe?" Nikki interrupted.

"Yeah." Melanie smiled at her reflection with complete confidence. "I'm going to marry Gabe."

"Oh my God! You, Melanie from Kansas Anderson, are going to marry Gabe Force Banner, the motherfucking drummer of Sole Regret!" And so now the entire top floor of the hospital knew Melanie's secret.

"Way to keep your mouth shut, Nik."

"This is so freaking great! I get to be your maid of honor, right?"

"Well, I hadn't thought that far ahead."

"Right?"

"Of course." She couldn't deny Nikki that central role at her side on the most important day of Melanie's life. Nikki was her best friend. Melanie's parents had never liked Nikki—*she's a bad influence on you, sweetheart*—but that didn't matter. If they thought Nikki was a bad influence, she couldn't imagine how they'd react when they met Gabe. Conservative wasn't just her parents' middle names, it was their first and last names too. But she'd worry about their reaction to her fiancé later.

"Yes!" Nikki shrieked, her enthusiasm making Melanie smile. "I'm going to throw you the most amazing bridal shower and the bachelorette party of the century! When's the big day?"

"We haven't set one yet. Calm down a little. You'll have plenty of time."

"I'm going to start looking online for ideas. Oh, but I can't do that here. I wish I had my phone. Then you could send me a pic of your engagement ring too."

"Uh, well, I don't have one of those." And frankly a ring wasn't that important to her. She wanted the man, not the diamond.

"Are you sure he proposed?"

"He asked and I said yes."

Nikki cleared her throat. "Were you in bed at the time? Had he just had some crazy-hard orgasm right before he asked you?"

"Well, yeah, but—"

"Oh, Melanie, I'm so sorry. And you were so excited about it too."

Melanie sat on the toilet because her knees were suddenly wobbly. "What are you saying?"

"Those after-sex proposals don't count, hon. If I married every guy that proposed marriage to me after he blew a load, I'd have more husbands than Zsa Zsa Gábor and Elizabeth Taylor combined."

"It wasn't like that. We discussed it. He asked me. It was real."

"Did he roll over and fall asleep afterwards?"

Melanie glared at her phone. Did Nikki have the place bugged? How could she know all that? Of course, Nikki had a lot more practice with men that Melanie ever would, but what Melanie had with Gabe wasn't like anything Nikki had ever experienced.

"Yeah. He's asleep."

"If he doesn't remember it when he wakes up, you have to give him an out. Sometimes good pussy makes guys say things they don't mean."

Melanie's balloon of elation didn't deflate, it burst. She swallowed the lump in her throat, glad she hadn't been stupid enough to share the news with her mom before Nikki had set her straight.

"We'll, uh, be there tomorrow," Melanie said, blinking back the ridiculous tears in her eyes.

"Oh, please don't cry, Mel. I didn't mean to upset you. Maybe he really meant it."

"I'm not crying." And now she was a liar. She unrolled some toilet paper and dabbed at her eyes, fighting the urge to sniff, which would give away her deception.

"I'm sure he meant it, Mel. Who wouldn't want to marry the sweetest, most caring and most generous, smartest, funniest, sexiest woman alive?"

"I'll see you tomorrow."

"Mel," Nikki whispered, "my heart is breaking for you."

"I'm okay."

She hung up and sat there trying to recall all that had been said and done when Gabe had asked her to be his wife. She'd believed his sincerity at that moment, so why was she doubting him now? She stared down at her bare left ring finger and jerked when a knock sounded on the door.

"Are you okay in there?" Gabe called.

"F-fine," she said, wiping away a fresh batch of tears.

"I woke up to snuggle with my beautiful fiancée and found her missing."

Fiancée? So he hadn't forgotten? It hadn't just been something he'd said because he'd blown his load—as Nikki had not-so-delicately put it.

"Can I come in?"

She stood from the toilet and checked herself in the mirror. Would he be able to tell she'd been crying? And all because she'd doubted him so easily. God, she felt absolutely wretched for her lack of confidence in his words. She looked almost as bad as she felt. Should she tell him? Or would her lapse of faith hurt him? The last thing she wanted to do was hurt him. But she didn't want to lie to him either.

"Do you really love me?" She felt stupid in her insecurity, but there it was staring her directly in the face through her own damned reflection.

"Yes, I love you."

Her heart swelled. She closed her eyes and took a deep steadying breath, but she never felt steady when it came to Gabe, so wasn't sure why she bothered. "Then you can come in."

He opened the bathroom door, took one look at her, and stepped forward to drag her into his arms and hold her securely against his chest. "Why are you crying?"

He smoothed her hair with one hand, the other pressing her close against him, and kissed her head.

"Was," she said. "I'm not crying anymore. Everything's fine now."

"Why were you crying?" he rephrased his question.

So she told him her entire conversation with Nikki. And it felt good to confide in him. To not have to hide her concerns, her insecurity.

"You know what your problem is?" Gabe said when she'd finished her spiel.

She leaned back and lifted an eyebrow at him. If he thought she'd let him use her insecurity against her, the man was mistaken. "*My* problem?"

"You don't have a ring." He scooped up her left hand and brought it to his lips, kissing the bare knuckle of her ring finger.

"I don't need a ring, Gabe. I just want you."

"You do need a ring. One that says my man loves me so much he emptied his bank account to buy a shiny lump of carbon atoms organized by nearly unbreakable tetrahedron covalent bonds."

"You mean a diamond," she said, giggling because his inner nerd was showing.

He nodded with a grin. "A great big one."

"How about a tiny one?" She pinched her fingers together and held them up. Only a sliver of light shone between their tips.

"How about I surprise you? When I propose for real."

"For real?"

He winked at her.

"Gabe? You aren't planning on embarrassing me, are you?"

"Delighting you."

"Just promise not to empty out your bank account."

He scowled. "You're not worried that I'm broke, are you?"

She was an accountant, so it had crossed her mind. He'd mentioned the possibility that the band would be sued for canceling their tour and not fulfilling their record contract. She didn't care if he didn't have two dimes to rub together—she'd love him regardless of the number of digits in his bank balance— but she didn't want to contribute to his financial worries because he thought she needed a ridiculously expensive ring.

"Just be practical about it. I don't need a ring at all, but if you insist, I'd be happier with something small."

"I'm getting married to my one," he said, and his delighted smile made her heart fill to bursting. "Practical will not be a variable in this equation."

"Obviously." Their relationship was progressing at the speed of light. Neither of them was being practical about being together, though both of them were typically practical people. "We haven't even talked about the important things."

He lifted a brow. "Like what?"

"Living arrangements, dates . . ." She felt her face flush

before the next word even escaped her lips. "Babies."

He blinked and licked his lips. She got the feeling he wanted to bolt, but instead he took a step back, tugging her forward by the hand he still held. "I think we should discuss this in bed."

"Bed?" Though she doubted anything requiring reasoning skills could ever be accomplished when the two of them were in bed, she followed him out of the bathroom. "I don't think I can make important decisions in bed."

"Then I'll state my case, you state yours, and we'll compromise."

She did love that he was as levelheaded as she was. Well, he was levelheaded except when he was angry. And in love.

He sat on the edge of the bed and grabbed her ass to pull her to stand between his open legs. She stared down into his dreamy green eyes.

"Would you rather go first, or should I?" he asked.

She traced his lower lip with a fingertip, still trying to wrap her head around the idea that this man was hers. Not for one night—as had been her original plan when they'd met—but always. "You go first."

"Okay. I want you to live with me in Texas. We should get married as soon as possible. I have no preference on the where or the how, but soon." He swallowed and glanced away for a second before meeting her eyes again. "I do want children, but I'd rather wait four or five years. Mostly so we can have an extended honeymoon."

The grin he offered made her toes curl into the low-pile carpet.

"But also because my career is a little rocky and I'd want to be settled before we expand our family."

"What if Lindsey's baby is yours?" There, she'd asked.

"Not likely," he said, "but . . ."

He rubbed his lips together, and she could practically see the cogs turning in his head. She hoped he wouldn't say what he thought she wanted him to say just to please her. This relationship would be built on trust, and that had to start with being truthful even if the truth hurt.

"I'd still want things the way I just described, but I'd have to be a dad too. I couldn't ignore any child I fathered. Now, what do you want?"

To be the first woman to mother your children. And to create those children out of love not lust. "A real wedding, surrounded by family and friends. It doesn't have to be huge. Actually, I prefer something small. But I don't want to elope. I want to share the celebration with everyone I love."

"When?"

"As soon as possible."

He grinned. "Glad we agree on that. Are you okay with moving to Texas? I know all your family lives in Kansas. Are you close?"

She nodded. "I see them a couple of times a week, but I would love to move into your house in Texas. I'm not overly attached to my job or my apartment." And then she remembered someone she was attached to. "I can't leave Nikki there by herself."

Gabe squeezed his eyes shut. "I'm probably going to regret saying this, but we have plenty of room at my place. She could . . ." His lids squeezed even tighter. ". . . stay with us."

"You mean it?" Melanie grabbed him around the head and pressed his face against her chest.

"Trial basis," he said, his voice muffled by the boob against his lips.

"Of course. She'll be on her best behavior." Why did it make her love him more when he was good to Nikki? She supposed it was because in her eyes, his tolerance of Nikki made him a good person. And given time, maybe Nikki and Gabe could become close friends. Assuming Nikki didn't try to seduce him or something. That would end her trial-basis living arrangements right there.

Melanie released his head and kissed his forehead. "I do love you."

"Does that mean you want to have my babies?"

"I want to be the first and only woman to have your children."

"Two or three?"

"If they're like their father, I'd have a dozen." When his face went ashen, she laughed. "I think three is a good compromise."

"Let's see how the first one goes before we add to the brood."

"Good plan."

"And you're okay with waiting?"

"I'd start tomorrow if I could," she admitted. She couldn't wait to hold a little one that she and Gabe had created together.

"This will require some compromise," he said. "How about three years? I should be able to figure my future out by then."

"I thought I was your future."

"You are," he said. "But I thought you might like to have a roof over your head and food in your belly."

She nodded, understanding his need to provide. "I can help with that, you know. How about we wait a year?"

"I'm okay with that if the band is back together and stable."

"And if it's not?"

"I don't know if that will give me enough time to finish my degree and find a good job. I don't know if I'll be as stable as I'd like."

She stroked the soft fuzz that was already starting to grow on the sides of his scalp. "There's no way to predict that, and if we wait too long, it might never happen. I can easily get a good job. My skills are in high demand. I can work as either an accountant or a business manager. I have plenty of experience in both."

"We could always play it by ear," he said.

Their eyes met, and they both laughed. They were a pair of planners, that much was clear. Playing anything by ear was highly unlikely.

"When will you know if Lindsey's baby is yours? That will likely throw a few more wrenches into our plans."

"Owen said something about her getting a blood test to determine paternity. We could know within a week."

"That soon?" Would that give her time to mentally prepare for the possibility that Gabe was going to be a father outside of their proposed timeline? But it was probably best to know as soon as possible so they could plan for a baby's arrival, even if it wasn't hers. Could she love a child that Gabe had fathered with another woman? Her heart froze over in ice at the very thought, but if confronted by a perfect tiny human that was half Gabe, she figured it would thaw instantly.

"Do you think I'd feel some sort of attachment to Lindsey if she's carrying my child?" Gabe asked, his fingers tracing lazy patterns on her lower back. "I feel nothing for her. No affection.

No animosity. Not even pity. Just a big hazy void of nothing. Maybe a touch of concern, but on her behalf, not mine. I don't feel like it's mine. There's no connection."

"But you'd feel a connection with the baby if it's yours, wouldn't you?" Melanie asked. "Once it's born, I mean."

He shrugged. "I assume so. It's not something I have any experience with."

"Let's worry about that bridge when we come to it." Their eyes met, and they both laughed again. Being planners also made them both worriers. "Let's try not to worry about it too much in any case."

"I'll do my best."

His hands slid from her lower back to cup her ass. He gave both cheeks a tight squeeze that made her ache for him.

"So now can we use this bed for something other than important discussions of our future?"

"What did you have in mind?" As if she didn't already know.

"We need to practice our baby-making skills."

She nipped his lip and straddled his lap. The tip of his cock pressed against her lower belly near the small diamond that dangled from her pierced belly button, and her breath caught as a knot of lust uncoiled within her. Would she ever be able to be in this man's presence without wanting him buried balls deep inside her? She hoped not.

"I do think I need a refresher course." She giggled when he tumbled her onto the bed.

"At some point tonight we'll need to get our luggage out of the car. All of my hardware is in there."

"I think you'll manage to get the job done without it." She wrapped both arms around his neck and pulled him down for a toe-curling kiss. His mouth moved along her jaw toward her ear.

"How do you feel about sex swings?" he asked, his voice low and at almost a whisper.

"Never been in one."

"With anal attachments. For him and her."

She laughed. "Only you would come up with something like that."

"You can't hold it against me. *You* inspired the idea."

"Then I guess I'll have to try it."

"We're going to have to put something in our wedding vows about prototypes."

She snorted, wondering how she could be turned on and amused at the same time. "About you inventing them or me using them?"

"Both."

"If we do, I'm not inviting my parents to the ceremony."

He nipped her earlobe, which sent a spike of pleasure down the back of her neck. "I wanted to elope anyway."

"I want a real wedding, Gabriel," she said, not willing to compromise on that particular point.

"Oh no," he said, grimacing. "She already knows how to get her way by using my full name."

It was that easy, was it? In that case . . .

"Oh Gabriel."

"Yes, Melanie?"

"My clit has a date with your tongue."

He grinned crookedly. "Well, my tongue sure doesn't want to be late for that."

CHAPTER SEVEN

THE NEXT AFTERNOON, GABE HELD Melanie's hand as they made their way to the psych unit of the hospital. He'd been serious when he'd said that Nikki could stay with them, but as they left their cellphones in lockers and were checked for "potentially dangerous objects" before even being allowed on her floor, Gabe wondered if they were getting in over their heads. Maybe Nikki needed more than just a safe place and unconditional love. Maybe she needed intensive therapy. And padded walls.

Nikki came out to meet them in a secure common area. When her gaze landed on Melanie, her expression transformed from misery to elation. Gabe smashed down an unwarranted pang of jealousy when the women embraced. He knew Melanie wasn't interested in a relationship with Nikki, but he wasn't so sure that Nikki would abide by that boundary.

"I'm so glad to see you both," Nikki said, reaching out of the hug she was still sharing with Mel to squeeze Gabe's arm. "I hear you popped the question."

Gabe felt his face turn hot. Nikki never beat around the bush. He actually liked that about her. "I did."

"And you're not going to back out?"

Melanie's jaw hardened. "Nikki."

"No," Gabe said without hesitation.

"You'd better not. Because if you break her heart—"

"I won't."

Melanie leaned back to take a hard look at Nikki. She touched the nearly faded bruise on her cheek—the last visible reminder of what that fucking asshole in New Orleans had done to her. Gabe couldn't keep his hands from balling into fists as a fresh surge of rage flooded him. That hollow look in her blue eyes—lessened only when her gaze was fixed on Melanie—might not ever fade completely.

"So what have the doctors been saying?" Melanie said, drawing Nikki into a chair and sitting beside her. She held one of Nikki's hands between hers.

Nikki ducked her head. "Sex addiction and compulsive risk-seeking behavior. Both remnants of what Daddy did to me."

Gabe swallowed and sat across from the two women. He didn't know what Nikki's father had done to her, but he could guess. He didn't want to know details. Wasn't sure he could handle them.

Nikki continued talking, her voice so low that Gabe had to strain to hear her clearly.

"Also having PTSD episodes because of what happened last weekend. My symptoms might get worse before they get better." She looked up at Melanie with tears swimming in her eyes. "I don't want to stay here. I miss you."

Melanie smoothed the silky brown hair from Nikki's face and tucked it behind Nikki's ear. "Honey, if this is the best place for you—"

Nikki's head snapped up, blue eyes flashing fire. "It isn't. I feel worse here. I want to go home."

"I'm not leaving you in the apartment by yourself," Melanie said.

Nikki glanced at Gabe, and he expected animosity in her gaze, but she smiled at him. "I get it. I'm the third wheel to your bicycle built for two."

"If it's okay with your doctor," Gabe said, "we want you to come hang out with us in Austin for a few days." He didn't want to offer her a permanent home just yet. He and Melanie had already discussed Nikki's trial period, but he couldn't in good conscience separate the two of them. It was obvious that Nikki needed Melanie's unconditional love, and Melanie needed to nurture her friend almost as much. Melanie would make a great mother, he thought with a unexpected feeling of longing in his gut. Assuming the soft-hearted woman didn't spoil their kids too much.

"Why does he have that goofy look on his face?" Nikki asked.

"Probably inventing something in his head."

"Actually," he said, "I was thinking you'll be a great mother."

Nikki squealed. "Oh my God, are you preggers, Mel? Is that why he proposed?"

Melanie shook her head. "We've just been talking about our future."

Nikki grabbed Melanie in another hug. "I'm so happy for you. And you." She extended a leg and poked Gabe in the shin with her toe. "You're one lucky son of a bitch. Do you have any idea what a prize she is?"

"I'm seeing it more and more," he said, his eyes glued to his prize. "Can I go talk to Nik's doctor about discharge or—?" He shrugged and shook his head, at a loss as to how they should proceed.

"I'll have to," Melanie said. "I'm on all her paperwork as her medical contact person."

"She's responsible for me," Nikki said.

Gabe could see that. And Melanie didn't take that responsibility lightly. While Melanie and Nikki went to talk to someone about her release, Gabe tried to sort through all the new complications in his life and prioritize.

Melanie hadn't mentioned meeting her parents, but since they were in Topeka, they should probably break the news about their engagement in person. His parents had already met—and loved—Melanie, so he wasn't worried about their reaction. From what little Melanie had said about her parents, they seemed the strict and conservative type and obviously loving and protective of their daughter. He wasn't sure they'd warm up to the idea of her getting hitched to a tattooed rock musician currently out of a job. He rubbed a hand over his face, a bit nervous about the prospect of breaking the news to them. He definitely needed to get a ring on that woman's finger to show he was serious about their future together.

He planned to stop in to see Adam on his way through Dallas, which would likely be tomorrow. Or the next day if Mel and Nik needed more time to get their things together. He didn't want Nikki to know they were considering her as a fulltime roomie just yet, though, so they should be able to pack a few things and leave tomorrow.

And Amanda still hadn't called him about Jacob's confusing emotional state, but he wasn't sure if she'd gotten his message, so he'd have to track her down when they got back to Austin.

Apparently Owen and Kellen were having a few issues of their own. If he couldn't rely on the stability of that lifelong relationship, what could he rely on? He also needed to get that paternity test. What the fuck was he going to do with a baby he didn't want? Round and round his thoughts stirred until Melanie returned to his side. As usual, when she was near, all his problems seemed like minor obstacles easily overcome. She was everything he'd been looking for to complete his life, and he hadn't even known anything had been missing.

"They can't keep her since she checked in voluntarily," Melanie said, "but they advise against her leaving."

"We have to do what's best for her," Gabe said, squeezing her hand. He could tell it was hard on Melanie to make the decision.

"She'll check out on her own if we don't take her with us."

"Then we take her with us."

"I'm not a psychiatrist. I don't know what to do if she starts acting promiscuous or seeking trouble. Do I put ultimatums on her behavior? I don't want to threaten her. I want her to feel safe to be herself when she's with me."

Gabe lifted her hand and brought her wrist to his lips, kissing her pulse point. "You do what you've always done for her—love her unconditionally. I'll be the bad cop. I'll try to keep her in check with some rules."

Melanie snorted. "Nikki doesn't like rules."

"If she wants to live under *my* roof, she'll follow my rules." God, he sounded like his father.

"I guess we can try it, see how she responds."

She grinned at him then, and he knew everything would work out because they had each other's backs.

"I bet she never imagined the drummer of her favorite metal band would become her surrogate father."

Speaking of her father. "Did her real father abuse her?"

Melanie glanced away, her eyes brimming with tears. "That's a nice way of putting it."

Nikki came into the waiting area before Melanie could say more, and Gabe stood up. He approached her, but gave her plenty of personal space. She didn't seem to want it as she immediately slipped her arm through his and leaned her head against his shoulder.

"I'm so happy you came with Mel."

Gabe cleared his throat and spoke in a firm voice. "Before we leave for home, I have a couple of rules you have to abide by or we're bringing you back here immediately."

Nikki tilted her head back to stare at him with wide eyes. "Rules?"

"No one-night stands with men."

"What about with women?"

Even the challenge in her gaze was sexually charged. He wasn't sure she could function without sexualizing everything in her life.

"No women either."

"But if I go on dates and plan to make a relationship, then . . ."

"Why don't you try not dating or hooking-up at all for a month? See how that goes."

"A month? I'll dry up like an old nun."

Gabe laughed. "I seriously doubt that. If you have an addiction, the best way to break it is to quit cold turkey."

"My therapist thinks I can talk my way through my sex addiction."

"How's that going for you?"

"It makes me horny to talk about it. He was very professional when I tried to seduce him. The night charge nurse was a bit easier to manipulate."

So this place obviously wasn't helping her.

"There's always that treatment center in Florida," Melanie suggested.

Nikki released Gabe's arm and reached for Melanie, who didn't hesitate in giving her the hug she sought.

"I want to be with you and Gabe," Nikki said, her tone reminiscent of a compliant child. "If that means I have to give up sex for a month, then I think I can do it. Let me try. Please. I won't let you down."

Melanie glanced up to meet Gabe's eyes. There was a hint of triumph behind her gaze. This plan might actually work. At least Nikki was being cooperative. And maybe they were manipulating her, but hopefully their ploy would help her regain control of her life, because she was currently in a tailspin.

"We'll let you try," Melanie said. "Right, Gabe?"

"If she breaks my rules, she's out," he said, dutifully sticking to his tough-cop routine.

"I won't."

"She won't, Gabe."

Nikki smiled at Melanie's vote of confidence, her adoration for her friend evident on her entire face.

"I have one more rule to lay out before I agree to this," Gabe said.

The women looked at him expectantly.

"Nikki will make no further sexual advances toward my fiancée."

Nikki glanced at Melanie. "I told you what my doctor said about that. Didn't you explain it to him?"

"I didn't know you wanted me to," Melanie said.

Nikki turned to Gabe. "I was confusing platonic love with sexual love. I have a hard time understanding that there's a difference, because . . ." She licked her lips. " . . . my father . . . should have been platonic, but was . . ." She closed her eyes and took a deep breath.

Gabe's stomach turned at the very idea. He didn't think he could stand to hear her actually say it. "So you're not confused anymore."

"I'm totally confused," Nikki said, "but now that I know what I was feeling for Melanie is part of my condition and not real attraction, I can handle it. I won't try to jump Mel's bones again." She made a cross over her heart. "Hope to die."

Gabe wasn't so sure Nikki was confused about her feelings for Melanie, but he would give her the opportunity to prove herself. Regardless, he trusted Melanie not to fuck around on him with Nikki or anyone else.

"All right, let's shake on it." He spit in his palm and extended his hand toward Nikki.

Her cute nose crinkled up. "You're so gross."

"That's not what your friend thinks."

"Maybe she's wrong about you."

Melanie laughed as Nikki spit into her own hand, cringing the entire time her wet palm was pressed against Gabe's as they sealed the bargain with a firm spit-coated handshake.

"Are you two ready?" Melanie asked.

Staring hard into Nikki's eyes, Gabe nodded. Without looking away, Nikki mimicked the motion.

"Let's head to the apartment and pack a few things," Melanie said. "We can start for Texas in the morning."

"I'll take a look at your car while we're here," Gabe said, unable to ignore his urge to tinker with a machine.

"That would be fantastic," Melanie said.

Gabe wiped the spit off his hand on the leg of his jeans and took Melanie's hand. She didn't flinch or make a face. He was glad she didn't think he was gross. "I'd like to do one more thing before we leave tomorrow," he said as they headed out of the hospital unit, Nikki leading the way.

"What's that?"

"Meet your parents."

Based on the look she gave him, maybe she did think he was gross after all.

CHAPTER EIGHT

MELANIE HELPED Nikki sort through her clothes to find appropriate attire to wear on what Nikki thought would be an exciting mini-vacation to Austin. Gabe was down in the parking lot tinkering with Melanie's stupid car.

"Does Gabe have a pool?" Nikki asked.

"No, but he'll probably take us to the lake on his boat."

Nikki tossed a neon-pink string bikini into her open suitcase. Melanie didn't comment. She would only wear a swimsuit like that to attract male attention, and in the past Nikki had thrived on that kind of attention, but she wanted Nikki to make her own choices. If she could manage to strut around in that bikini without initiating sex with the admirers that were sure to flock around her, more power to her. Melanie just hoped Gabe was impervious to Nikki's blatant sex appeal. Crap. She'd forgotten the man had eyes. Of course he'd find Nikki attractive. What had she gotten them into?

Melanie took a deep breath. This wasn't like situations in her past. She and Gabe were partners. Nikki wouldn't take him away or seduce him, because he understood her risky behavior was part of her psychological condition. At least Melanie believed he understood that.

Her phone dinged with a text from Gabe. *Got it started. Going to take it for a test drive.*

"He got my piece-of-shit car started," Melanie said, smiling at his genius.

"I'm not surprised," Nikki said. "He's pretty handy. Did you call your parents and ask them to dinner yet?"

Melanie's heart took a dive to her feet. "I think I'll just tell him that they couldn't come."

"So you haven't asked them yet."

"What if they don't like him?"

"It doesn't matter. *You* like him."

"I *love* him."

"Right. That's what I meant. And if you love him, they'll love him."

Melanie was pretty sure it didn't work that way.

"They thought Anthony was too wild for me."

He was an accountant she'd dated a couple of years ago, one of her many boyfriends who'd ended up sleeping with Nikki. Her parents had thought him wild because he owned a motorcycle. He'd rarely ridden it, but just the owning of the dangerous thing had made him wild. If Anthony had been wild, then Gabe had been raised by wolves.

"Anthony was a dick," Nikki said. "You know he came on to me, not the other way around."

"I know."

"I could have said no." Nikki offered her a regretful frown and then looked into her suitcase. She removed the pink bikini and replaced it with a black one piece.

"Saying no is hard for you."

Nikki nodded slightly. "Still not a good excuse. I'm sorry for all those times I messed up your relationships."

"If it weren't for you, I'd have never met Gabe."

Nikki lifted her head and met Melanie's eyes. She smiled. "So I guess that makes up for all my wrongs."

Not even close, but Melanie nodded. "We're square. Just don't try to take him away from me."

"I'd never. Not someone you actually loved. I've seen the way you look at him." Nikki smacked Melanie in the gut with a bed pillow.

Melanie had thought she was in love with Anthony. Now that she was with Gabe, she knew better. He made her feel far more deeply than she'd ever experienced with anyone. So maybe all that heartache was a blessing in disguise. It allowed her to recognize the depth of her feelings quickly, allowed her to act on them, and to believe in them.

"I don't know why you keep taking me back," Nikki said, tracing a stripe on the comforter on her bed. "I've done some truly awful things to you."

"I like to be needed."

"Then I'm perfect for you. I have boundless need."

Melanie laughed and hugged her.

"Go invite your parents to dinner," Nikki said, "or I'm going to call them. I'm sure you remember how well that went the last time I called."

Her parents had called the police, convinced that something terrible had happened when Nikki wouldn't let them talk to Melanie. Melanie had been taking a nice leisurely bath. Nikki had called them to ask if they'd lend her the money to buy Melanie a birthday cake, which they thought was some code for drugs. Yeah, her parents were a bit overprotective and judgmental. She could only imagine their reaction when she introduced them to a man with a crimson-tipped Mohawk and dragon tattoos on his scalp. They'd probably think he'd pass those traits directly to their grandchildren.

"If Gabe finds out that he's marrying into crazy," Melanie said, "he'll break off our engagement."

"Your parents aren't crazy," Nikki said, but then she lifted her hands in surrender. "Okay, your parents are a little out there, but it's only because they love you so much. I'd give anything to have parents like yours."

Melanie snorted. "You wouldn't say that if they were yours."

Nikki yanked Melanie's phone from her hand and managed to dial Melanie's mother before she could get the device away from her. Melanie ended the call and shoved her phone back into her pocket. She had her mouth open to chastise Nikki, when her phone rang. She didn't have to look at caller ID to know it was her mother. She closed her eyes and took a deep breath, then answered. She didn't want the police to show up at her place because she didn't pick up.

"Is everything okay, Melanie? You called but I wasn't fast enough to answer."

Melanie imagined her mother practicing speedy call acceptances like she was a Western gunslinger trying to perfect drawing her weapon.

"Everything is fine, Mom. I just butt dialed you. Sorry."

"That's okay. I haven't talked to you for days. How's work?"

"Uh, well, I took some vacation days."

"Then why haven't you visited? Your dad made this great new beer. He's been dying for you to come try it out."

Nikki was giving Melanie a blend of the evil eye and a look of chastisement.

Melanie pivoted to the wall. "Actually, I did want to call and ask if you and Daddy wanted to join me for dinner. I . . . uh . . . have someone I'd like you to meet."

"A new boy?"

Melanie rolled her eyes. Would she be perpetually twelve years old to her parents? "Not a boy, a *man*," Melanie said. "And he's incredibly important to me, so I don't want you to act all overprotective when you meet him."

"So it's serious? How come you haven't mentioned you've been seeing someone?"

She hadn't had the time. "Because I wanted to be sure he was impervious to criticism before I introduced him to you and Daddy."

Mom snorted. "Mel, we aren't that bad."

They were that bad. "So, dinner?"

"Dad's been working on a rack of ribs for hours. Why don't you bring your little friend here? Around seven?"

Her little friend? Gabe was far from little and was much more to her than a friend, but Melanie said, "Okay, but if you start acting like jerks, we'll leave, and you might not ever see me again."

"Why would we act like jerks?"

"Because . . ." How should she put it? "Because he's not an accountant."

Her mother laughed. "That's probably a good thing. I remember how well your last relationship with an accountant went."

"You're being a jerk," Melanie pointed out. "See you at seven." She hung up before she changed her mind. Perhaps she should have asked Gabe if he was okay meeting her parents on their turf. They'd have to be more civil to him in public. But maybe she was worried over nothing. Except for the overprotective-bordering-on-oppressive thing, her parents were wonderful people.

She sent Gabe a text. *How's the car doing? We're having dinner with my parents at seven. Hope you're not stuck on the side of the road somewhere. Let me know if you need a tow.*

He didn't respond immediately—she hoped that meant the driving was going well—so she continued to help Nikki pack while Nikki prattled on about various times she'd gone head to head with Melanie's parents. They treated Melanie like a princess. It was anyone who dared cause their princess grief that they turned on. And Nikki had caused Melanie plenty of grief in the past. Melanie kept them separated these days. She loved her parents dearly, but Nikki was an important part of her life too. If Mom and Dad had issues with Gabe, she supposed she could just keep them apart as much as possible.

A message from Gabe came at about six. *Just now saw this. I'm on my way back to the apartment. The car is running fine. See you in a few.*

"I thought maybe he'd chickened out and headed back to Texas," Melanie said as Nikki helped her pick out something to wear to dinner.

"He's the one who wanted to meet them," Nikki said, holding a slinky red dress up to Melanie's front.

"Uh, I'm taking my fiancé to meet my parents, not picking up johns on a shady street corner."

Nikki rolled her eyes. "You're so gorgeous, yet you never show off the goods."

"I show them off plenty to Gabe. He's the only one who needs to see them."

Melanie shoved the red dress back into the closet and pulled out a soft wholesome-looking green sundress that she knew her father liked. She paired it with flat sandals and a light sweater. The only make-up she applied was the lightest dusting of powder, some mascara, and a blush-toned lip gloss. Maybe by looking fresh-faced and sweet she'd counter some of Gabe's overstated alternative look. She liked how he looked. In fact, his tattoos, piercings, and Mohawk turned her on, but it wasn't the kind of look her parents would appreciate. She wasn't going to insist he dress in any particular fashion when he met them. If he wanted to wear leather, a T-shirt that read FUCK AUTHORITY, and his Mohawk spiked straight to the sky, she wouldn't have a problem with that. Whatever made him comfortable was fine with her. She'd love for her parents to accept him, but if they didn't, it wasn't a deal breaker. She loved him and didn't care who approved or disapproved of their relationship.

Yeah, she told herself all that. But in her heart she'd be overjoyed if they approved of him.

A few minutes later, Gabe knocked on the door. She smiled at him, took from his hand the bouquet of white lilies and pink roses that he told her were for her mom, and kissed his cheek. He was filthy—hands covered in oil, grime, and general filth—and she had to admit he'd never looked sexier.

"Hope I have time for a shower," he said, pulling his shirt off over his head as he headed for the apartment's single bathroom.

Nikki offered his shirtless body an appreciative whistle before he closed the bathroom door.

"Aww, he bought you flowers?" Nikki said, touching the silky white petal of one of the lilies.

"No, he's even sweeter than that. He bought my *mother* flowers."

The shower kicked on, and Melanie stared at the closed door, wishing she had time to join him in there. She loved the dirty, sweaty version of Gabe, but might admire his wet and naked version even more. She couldn't be sure unless she got an eyeful for comparison.

"If they don't absolutely love him, they're idiots," Nikki said.

"Let's hope they can get over their prejudices. If not, they're the ones who'll miss out."

"Are you going to tell them that you two are engaged?"

Melanie lifted her left hand to show Nikki her naked ring finger. "Don't see why I should. He hasn't put a ring on it yet."

"He hasn't had time to put a ring on it."

"I'm not upset about it," Melanie said, staring longingly at the bathroom door. How late would they be if she stripped off her dress and joined him? "I figured we'd let them adjust to the idea of my new boyfriend before we force them to consider him my future husband."

"Hey, if I was engaged to that delicious man, there wouldn't be a person on the planet that I wasn't proud to tell."

Melanie grimaced, appalled by the connotation in Nikki's words. "Does it seem like I'm ashamed of him?"

Nikki shook her head. "No, just that you *expect* others not to accept him for who he is."

It was practically the same thing. She needed to get that vibe under wraps. If her parents picked up on it, they'd run with it. "I wish everyone saw him the way I do."

"As a hot-as-fuck and talented badass with a great body and

amazing green eyes?" Nikki snorted. "Trust me. Everyone sees him that way."

But that wasn't all that Melanie saw when she looked at him. "I see him as heroic, tender, a little hot-headed if he's been wronged, but ultimately a good person."

"I assume you're talking about me."

Gabe's deep voice made Melanie jump.

Nikki giggled. "He caught you waxing poetic about him."

Melanie turned to find him wearing nothing but a towel, his exposed chest and belly glistening with water. The fresh, clean scent of soap on his recently scrubbed flesh had her knees a bit wobbly. "If he hadn't interrupted, I would have added that he's smart, adventurous, talented, and devastatingly inventive."

Gabe crossed his arms over his chest, his towel slipping an inch lower as he stood straight. "Do go on," he said.

"He's also a bit cocky. I'm not talking Shade Silverton's level of cocky, but he's not lacking in self-confidence."

"Shade is perfectly cocky," Nikki said. She moaned as if being tortured. "He also has a perfectly huge cock."

"Gabe," Melanie said, "you might want to keep your gorgeous body concealed from the recovering sex addict. She's already thinking of Shade as a viable option."

"Shade is always a viable option," Nikki said, taking in an eyeful of Gabe. "He stops when you say stop, but who the hell would want him to stop?"

"Who would want him to *start*?" Melanie countered. She honestly didn't understand Jacob's appeal. He was good looking, but she just didn't recognize him as having any substance, and now that he'd left Gabe and his bandmates high and dry just because he felt like it, she liked him even less.

"How long do I have before we're supposed to be at your parents' house?" Gabe asked.

Melanie glanced at the clock on the wall. "About three minutes."

"Shit!" He disappeared into Melanie's bedroom and shut the door.

"I hope they don't use our tardiness against him," Melanie said, figuring they'd use any negative as ammunition.

"He really is a good guy," Nikki said. "But admit it. If you'd realized who he was before you started talking to him, you never would have come to know who he was, because you wouldn't have given him a chance."

"Exactly, and where do you think I picked up that horrible bias?"

"Your parents."

Melanie nodded. "It will do me good to get out of Kansas."

"Not sure how much a week in Austin will free you from their shelter."

Melanie opened her mouth to remind her that she was moving to Austin for good, but remembered in time that they hadn't told Nikki the move would be permanent. And that would be another weapon in her parents' arsenal against Gabe. He was taking their baby girl far away from them. She predicted the evening was going to be a total disaster.

Gabe hurried out of the bedroom a moment later, looking mind-bogglingly attractive in a pair of black slacks and a white button-down dress shirt. She stared at him, mouth agape, for a long minute before realizing he was asking for assistance in buttoning his cuff sleeve. He'd applied a splash of cologne, which she could only smell when she was really close. The scent made her want to bury her face in his neck and breathe him in.

"Should I wear a hat?" he asked.

Melanie tilted her head back, her heart throbbing with excitement. Why on earth would he want to shade those gorgeous green eyes beneath the brim of a hat?

"I don't have time to grow my hair out," he added.

"Wear whatever makes you comfortable," Melanie said. She was too far gone over the guy to give a fuck what her parents thought.

Gabe licked his lips. "Trust me when I say a man is never comfortable when he meets his future in-laws."

"Her parents are ultraconservative," Nikki said. "You should probably wear a Ronnie Reagan mask if you want them to like you."

Gabe blew out his cheeks. "Hat, it is."

He slipped back into the bedroom and reemerged wearing a trendy black fedora. Melanie let out a low whistle.

"Why didn't you tell me you clean up so well?"

"Because I prefer to be dirty." Gabe winked at her and extended his arm to take her hand. "Ready when you are."

He let her drive since she knew the way. The flowers he held clutched in one hand were shaking slightly, but she didn't let him know she noticed. She did let him know that he was flipping brilliant. Her car ran better than it had in years.

"I thought fixing new cars was impossible for anyone but a technician with all sorts of diagnostic equipment," she said.

"You had a vacuum hose leak. Easy to fix."

"My car has a vacuum? Can't tell with all those crumbs under the seats."

He laughed and picked up her hand. His palm was a bit damp, but she didn't point that out either.

"Just so you know," Melanie said, "if they don't love you—and I'm not sure how they couldn't, you're amazing—I love you. Their opinion won't change my mind."

"Just like their opinion didn't make you afraid of tattoos and men who have them?"

"I was an impressionable child at the time. I didn't think my parents could be wrong about anything. They were wrong to exacerbate my fear into a phobia. I see that now. You helped me see that. Now it's their turn to get over their stupid prejudices against tattoos. Tattoos are mainstream. I'd say half the people our age have at least one."

"How many of those have them on their scalps?" Gabe pointed to his head.

"Just the best ones. I plan to get one to match."

He laughed and squeezed her hand. She had been joking, sort of. She did want to get a tattoo, mostly to prove that she wasn't afraid, but also because she was starting to think of them as sexy, and she wanted to be sexy for Gabe. She didn't have plans to add one to her scalp, however. That had to hurt. She was thinking of something like a butterfly on her shoulder. Nothing too over the top. In any case, she'd hoped her little spiel would make him feel better, but he still looked green around the collar.

She pulled up into her parents' driveway, the brick ranch house looking much the same as it had her entire life, and put the car in park. "Just remember you're the one who wanted to meet them. I did not force this on you." She kissed him on the lips and opened her door. After a few seconds, Gabe climbed out and adjusted his hat, tugged at a shirt sleeve, and smoothed a nonexistent wrinkle in his pant leg. Her warnings had the poor guy entirely nervous. Perhaps she shouldn't have told him about her parents at all. Maybe it would have been easier to surprise him the same way she was surprising them. She linked her elbow through Gabe's and urged him forward.

"Last I checked, they don't have rabies," she said, leaning close to him and catching the scent of his sweet and woodsy cologne. "They won't bite. Their schnauzer, on the other hand, has been known to take a nip out of a kneecap or two."

"Maybe I should wait for you in the car."

Their arrival was announced by Lucy's vigorous barking. Melanie opened the front door, and the barking morphed into an excited howl. She squatted to pet the pooch, but Lucy had spotted Gabe. Her growl of warning made Melanie cringe. Undeterred, Gabe squatted next to Lucy and made no threatening moves while the dog sniffed him.

"What's his name?" Gabe asked.

"Her name is Lucy."

"Hello, Lucy," Gabe said, taking on his higher-pitched dog-speaking voice. "Are you a good girl?"

He extended his hand slowly, gauging the dog's reaction, and she gave it a sniff before licking him and accepting him as a new member of her pack. Gabe scratched behind her ear, and she wagged her tail.

Melanie smiled as she watched the pair bond. "Good at fixing cars and charming cranky little dogs. I picked a winner."

Gabe laughed and stood straight.

"Is that you, Melanie?" her mom called from the back of the house. "We're out on the deck. Dad's grilling ribs."

"Dad makes great ribs," Melanie said, her belly rumbling at the thought of scarfing some down. She was a little surprised the pair of them weren't standing at the front door in anticipation of meeting her new boyfriend. Maybe they'd mellowed since they'd celebrated the loss of her last one.

"I love ribs," Gabe said.

When they entered the kitchen, her mom was removing cold dishes from the refrigerator and setting them on the counter. "Could you give me a hand, Melanie?"

Melanie rushed forward to take the huge bowl of coleslaw out of her mom's hands. Which was a good thing. Mom had just spotted Gabe, and her grip went slack. If Melanie hadn't had a hand on the bowl, it would have dropped to the floor.

"This is Gabe," Melanie said, feeling all sorts of awkward. "My mom."

"Nice to meet you, Mrs. Anderson."

Mom's hand fluttered near her neck, and she pressed it hard against her chest. "You too."

"I brought you some flowers. I hope you like lilies and roses."

Gabe handed over the bouquet. Her mom couldn't take her eyes off him. Not even when she accepted his gift. Melanie was pretty sure her mother had gone into shock. While Melanie grabbed a vase from a nearby cabinet and filled it with water, Gabe attempted small talk.

"You have a lovely home, Mrs. Anderson. Uh, and a great dog."

"Lucy?" Mom asked, glancing down at the gray-mustached dog at Gabe's feet who was staring up at him adoringly. "Lucy hates strangers."

"Well, she obviously loves Gabe," Melanie said, taking the flowers out of her mom's hands and sticking them in the vase. "He has a couple of Labradors."

"Is that right?" Mom said, finally allowing her eyes a swift blink.

"Lady and Beau," Gabe said.

"Could you carry this out to the deck?" Melanie asked, handing a bowl of potato salad to Gabe. He took it and turned, looking for the way out to the deck. Visible through the sliding doors, a big plume of smoke billowed from the grill as Dad manned the fire with his back to them. Gabe headed in that direction, Lucy on his heels, and Melanie reached for the bowl of coleslaw. Mom lifted a pitcher of lemonade and grabbed Melanie's arm.

"You didn't warn me that he was gorgeous," Mom said, leaning close to whisper in Melanie's ear. "I made a fool of myself."

Melanie blinked at her. That was why she'd been staring at Gabe like that, because she thought he was good looking? Melanie laughed. "Hey, Mom," she whispered so Gabe didn't overhear, "my new boyfriend is very easy on the eyes. Don't step on your tongue."

"Mel!" she admonished, but then she laughed. "Actually, that is a possibility."

Gabe slid the door open and waited for both women—and the dog—to exit before he followed them out.

"Thank you for the flowers," Mom said to Gabe as she passed him. "They're lovely. And please, call me Linda."

"You're very welcome, Linda," he said, pulling the glass door closed behind them.

Melanie couldn't stop herself from touching his arm as she stood beside him.

"You look just like your mom," Gabe said.

"Everyone says that," she said, "but I have my dad's eyes." She set her bowl on the rectangular table, and Gabe followed her lead with his bowl.

"Daddy?" she said, wondering why he hadn't turned around. He had to know they'd come outside. Lucy was standing on her back legs right beside him, begging for a rib.

"Just about ready," he said, closing the lid on his smoky charcoal grill.

He took a deep breath, squared his shoulders, and then turned. She watched Dad search Gabe's face, the sides of his head that the hat didn't conceal, and the little hint of a tattoo at his collar, and then narrow his eyes at the tattoos peeking out at each wrist.

"I assume you're wearing long sleeves in late June to hide something," Dad said, his hazel eyes boring into Gabe's emerald green ones.

"Out of respect, actually," Gabe said, not breaking eye contact.

"Mark," Mom said, moving next to him and kissing her perturbed-looking husband on the cheek. "You promised."

"I promised I wouldn't castrate him on sight."

"Daddy!" Melanie said, laying a hand on Gabe's back to let him know his junk was safe. If necessary, she'd defend his nether parts with her life.

"I didn't promise to like him," Dad added.

"You haven't even given him a chance," Melanie said.

"If Melanie were my daughter, I wouldn't have let me in the front door," Gabe said with a disarming smile.

Dad seemed to like his answer. He actually laughed and

offered his hand for a measuring handshake. He seemed to like the handshake as well, because it was accompanied by a hard clap on Gabe's opposite arm.

"I hope you like ribs," Dad said, turning back to the grill and opening the lid. A fragrant plume of smoke puffed toward the cloudless sky, and tongs in hand, Dad removed the ribs from the grill and placed them on a huge platter.

"If they taste half as good as they smell, I'm in for a treat," Gabe said.

"They're always delicious," Melanie said, sidling up to her father to kiss his cheek. "How was your week?"

"Just fine," Dad said. "We missed you Wednesday night."

She usually had dinner with them at least once a week, but had been dealing with Nikki's admission into the hospital most of the day on Wednesday. She hadn't told her parents why she'd turned down a home-cooked meal, just that she was busy.

"Haven't seen much of you for the past couple of weeks, to be honest. Does this fella have something to do with that?" Dad nodded toward Gabe, who was helping her mom fill glasses of lemonade.

"He might," she said. "He's important to me, Daddy, or I wouldn't have brought him to meet you."

"Not sure how you got him to agree to that."

"It was his idea."

"That so?" Dad assessed Gabe even more closely as he added the platter of BBQ-sauce-encrusted ribs to the center of the table.

"Family is important to me, sir," Gabe said.

There was no doubting his sincerity.

Dad's eyes narrowed marginally. "That so?"

"I've met his parents already," Melanie said. "You'd like them. They're both doctors. His sisters are also doctors. I haven't actually met them yet, but I'm sure they're as awesome as the rest of his family. And he's great with dogs. You know what they say about men who are good with dogs. They make great fathers. Not that I'm pregnant or anything. I just wanted to assure you that family really is important to him—he wasn't just saying that to impress you—and . . . I'll shut up now." She didn't know why she was babbling. Probably because she so wanted her parents to accept the man she loved. She didn't want to have to give up her close bond with her family to be with Gabe, but she would. At least Mom seemed to like him. Based on her appreciative stare, perhaps a little too much.

"So," Dad said, taking a seat in his usual spot at the head of the table. The rest of them found chairs as well, with Gabe across from him, and his women at either side. "Family of doctors, huh? What do you do for a living?"

"I'm not sure at the moment."

"He plays drums for a famous rock band." Melanie squeezed his hand under the table.

"Of course he does," Dad said with a frown.

"The band's on rocky ground right now," Gabe said in a tone far calmer than he usually used when talking about Sole Regret's troubles. "I'm currently trying to decide my next move. Start a business. Go back to school. Try to get my band straightened out." He shrugged and scooped a pile of potato salad onto his plate.

"I dated a musician right after high school," Mom said, her chin in her hand as she gazed at Gabe.

"You see how well that turned out," Dad said, sawing between ribs with a huge chef knife. Gabe eyed the sharp instrument warily.

"I never knew that," Melanie said. "I thought you and Dad were high school sweethearts."

"We were," Mom said, "but we broke up for a few months before we came to our senses and decided it was meant to be."

Dad reached for her hand and squeezed it. "I'm glad you came to your senses."

"Me too, but those three months with Darryl sure were fun."

Melanie blinked at her mother. How come Mom had never told her that she'd dated some musician named Darryl?

"He played guitar," Mom elaborated. "In the backup band for a country singer. I think he still does, but I'm not sure. We lost touch long ago."

"He wasn't right for you, Linda," Dad said, and Melanie recognized bitterness in the tight press of his lips.

"No, he wasn't." Mom leaned closer to Gabe to whisper, "But he was a lot of fun."

As Mom leaned away, her eyes focused on the side of

Gabe's head where a hint of dragon claw was visible beneath the brim of his hat.

"Do you have something on your head?" she asked.

Gabe went entirely still, a forkful of coleslaw halfway to his mouth. "Uh, just a little ink."

Mom grinned. "You do know that if you don't show me, I'm going to look you up on the internet and find out just what kind of rock star my daughter is tangled up with."

Melanie had already googled him and knew there wasn't much incriminating evidence out there about Gabe. Compared to what she'd read about Jacob and Adam, Gabe was relatively boring. But there was a lot of commentary on his dragon tattoos.

"You might as well show her," Melanie said.

After a few seconds of hesitation, he removed his hat and set it on the table beside him before picking up a rib and gnawing off a bite.

"You're such a nice-looking young man," Mom said, "Why would you permanently ruin your looks?"

Gabe turned to offer her a hard stare, and she shrank back into her chair with her hand over her chest as if he'd threatened her. He then smiled, and her shoulders relaxed.

"That's why," he said.

"I still don't get it," Dad said. "Or the red hair dye. What are you thinking, boy?"

"It's part of his image," Melanie said. "For the band. It toughens him up."

"And if he ever wants to lose that image?" Dad asked.

"I'll grow my hair out."

Just in the few days he'd been off tour, a fine layer of dark brown hair had started to fill in the sides of his Mohawk.

"Now that I'm used to them, I like your dragons," Melanie said. She touched a spot just behind his temple where the tips of flames from the dragon's mouth extended a few centimeters beyond his hairline. "I'm not sure they'll be entirely covered anyway."

"For the most part they are. I always let my hair grow out when I'm not on tour. It's a total pain in the ass to have to shave your head every day."

"You might be able to get a real job, then," Dad said.

Apparently the man was already comfortable enough around

Gabe to offer parental criticism.

"I might," Gabe said.

Melanie supposed he got similar talks from his own parents. Maybe he was used to this kind of thing, but it still annoyed her.

"I didn't start going out with him because he's a rock star," Melanie said, "but I'm proud to be his."

"That sounds pretty serious," Mom said, her gaze darting to Gabe's head whenever he was looking the other way.

"We are serious," Gabe said. "And I was going to wait until after dinner to do this, but now seems like a good time."

Gabe stood and slid his hand into the front pocket of his slacks. He went down on one knee beside Melanie's chair, some small object in his hand. She smiled at the look of love in his eyes and was sure a similar look was showing on her face as well.

"I planned to ask permission, but I doubt your parents will grant it, so I'll just make this official." He took her left hand in his and slipped a dazzling diamond ring onto her finger. "You already said yes once, but I'll ask again anyway, this time with witnesses and a ring. Melanie Anderson, you are my one. I promise to love you as you deserve to be loved every day for the rest of my life. Will you do me the honor of marrying me?"

His face blurred behind the sudden rush of tears in her eyes. "I meant it when I said I would. Ring or no ring, my answer will be the same even if you ask me a thousand times. Yes, Gabe Banner, I will marry you."

Her mother produced a barely perceptible squeak. Melanie forced her eyes from Gabe's smiling face to make sure Mom was okay.

"Oh, sweetheart," Mom said, climbing from her chair to circle the table and wrap her arms around Melanie. "I'm so glad you found someone to love." She kissed the top of Melanie's head, nearly smothering her against her chest.

Melanie felt some of the strain in her spine ease. She hadn't realized how worried she was about her parents' reaction until her mom so easily accepted the inevitable. There was still a bit of tension in her body as she turned to her father. His face was nearly purple.

"No daughter of mine is marrying a . . . a . . . a *thug*."

And here was the man she knew as her father. She'd wondered where he'd been hiding.

"He's not a thug," Melanie said, her spine stiffening defensively. "He's the greatest man I've ever known next to you." Dad didn't take that as a compliment. "Musicians are all alike—head in the clouds, impractical, self serving destroyers of virtue."

Melanie didn't know which part to laugh about. Gabe was none of those things—except the musician part—and Melanie had been far from virtuous when she'd met him.

"Mark," Mom said softly, "this isn't about me and Darryl. This is about Melanie and Gabe."

The flush on Dad's face seemed to be embarrassment rather than anger as he ducked his head and then stood. "I need a beer. Melanie!" he said sharply as he headed for the garage where he'd set up the little microbrewery he was so proud of.

Melanie cringed. She was very familiar with that tone; in the past it had meant she was about to be grounded. And even though she was fully grown, living on her own and now engaged, she never wanted to disappoint her dad.

"I'll be right back," she said to Gabe as she stood.

She rubbed the unfamiliar band on her left finger and took a second look at her new diamond. She smiled, her heart brimming with happiness. The ring was perfect. Not too big, but not tiny. Like the man, it was perfect. When had Gabe found the time to get her a ring? When he'd been out test driving her car, she realized with a rush of pleasure. She glanced over her shoulder and offered him a courageous smile before entering the overwarm garage. Dad shut the door behind her.

"What are you thinking?" he said, taking her firmly by one arm. "You cannot marry a guy like him."

"A guy like who? Like Gabe? I'm lucky to have him. He's the best thing that's ever happened to me."

"You said that about the last guy."

She didn't remember ever saying that about any of her previous boyfriends, but it didn't matter. "This will be my last guy. Gabe will be my husband. You'd better get used to the idea."

Dad shook his head. "I'll never get used to the idea. Will you look at him?"

"Will you?" Melanie said, tugging her arm out of his grasp and going to the small refrigerator where Dad kept his various home brews. "Look at him, Dad, not at what's on the outside."

Though she was undeniably attracted to that part of him as well. "But what's on the inside. I guarantee he will surprise you."

"He surprised me all right," Dad said. "At first glance he looks ordinary. But underneath?" He shook his head as if unable to believe that Gabe was real.

"He's anything but ordinary, Dad. He's remarkable. I see it, and I hope someday you'll see it too. I'm moving to Austin to live with him." She opened the refrigerator and peeked inside. "Which beer should I try?" Maybe that question would distract him from her previous statement.

"You're not moving in with him."

"I am. And I'm marrying him. There isn't anything you can do about it. I'm a grown woman."

He closed his eyes and bit his lip. After a moment, he said, "But you're not. Not to me. To me you'll always be my little girl."

"Would you give beer to a little girl?"

He laughed and opened his eyes. She'd never seen her father cry, so the mistiness in his eyes made her own tears well up.

"You've always been clever. Do you know how exasperating that is?"

"I get that from Mom, and you must like it if you married her."

"Take a beer to your friend and give me a minute to compose myself," Dad said. "And you might want to hide the knife before I return to the table. I might find a new use for it."

"Daddy!" She pulled two beers from the fridge, closing the door with her hip. "You aren't going to stab anyone."

"I believe I have a castration on my agenda."

"Then you'll never get to be a grandpa." She kissed his cheek on her way past him. "I'll give you a few minutes. If you're not back, I'll send Mom in here to find you."

He cringed. "She'll chew me out."

But Melanie knew better. Her mother was her father's perfect complement. And she hadn't realized it until that moment, but her parents had the kind of relationship she wanted for herself. A lasting, strong partnership strengthened by love and honesty.

"For your sake, I'll ask Gabe to put his hat back on." She kissed her dad's cheek as she passed him and left the stifling heat of the garage behind.

"How did that go?" Mom asked when Melanie returned to the table.

"He let me escape with two of his precious home brews," Melanie said, handing one over to Gabe. "No matter how terrible it is, you have to say it's the best you've tasted."

"You'd have me lie?"

"To spare my daddy's feelings?" She twisted the top off and took a sip, surprised that it was actually good. Dad's early concoctions hadn't been fit for consumption, but he had certainly improved with practice. "You bet I would."

"She's a bit of a daddy's girl," Mom said. "Always has been."

"This one is actually pretty good," Melanie said, inspecting the blue and gray label that read Anderson's Secret Ale. "You won't have to lie."

A few minutes later, Daddy returned with a beer for himself. Her mother never drank, but was ever supportive of his various hobbies. As soon as Melanie spotted her dad, she nonchalantly placed Gabe's hat on his head, slipped the chef knife from its position next to her father's plate and hid it under the table. Gabe offered her a confused look before he smiled at her dad.

"Great-tasting brew, Mark," he said. "How long have you been working at it?"

"Couple of years," he said, tossing back a long swallow of his latest invention. "Everything I brewed at the start tasted like goat piss, but Melanie liked it for some reason."

Melanie choked on her swallow of beer and set it aside, wiping her mouth with the back of her hand as she struggled not to cough up a lung. "It was horrible," she said after she caught her breath. "I didn't want to hurt your feelings."

"She's very sensitive to other people's feelings," Gabe said. "Well, except for Jacob's. She has a blind spot with that guy."

"He's a jerk," Melanie said.

"Biggest softie on the planet," Gabe said. "You just have to see him around his daughter to recognize it. Kind of like your old man here."

Melanie scowled at him. "My daddy is nothing like Jacob Silverton."

Gabe's knowing grin had her seeing red.

"Jacob is the lead singer, right?" Mom asked.

How did she know that?

"I filled her in while you were in the garage," Gabe said to Melanie. "I think you'd like him, Linda."

"I'd love to meet him. Actually, I'd love to meet all your bandmates. They all sound so interesting."

"That's one way to describe them." Gabe laughed and patted Mom on the arm.

Dad didn't seem to appreciate their chumminess, but Melanie's relief was absolute. If Mom liked Gabe, she knew it wouldn't be long before her dad came around. Mom had never taken a liking to Melanie's past boyfriends, so she couldn't help but take her obvious affection for this one as a positive.

"So how's Nikki?" Mom asked, pushing her empty plate toward the center of the table.

"She seems better now that she's out of that hospital," Gabe said.

Melanie squeezed her eyes shut. She'd forgotten to warn him about her mother's intense dislike for one Nicole Swanson.

"Hospital?" Mom asked.

"She went voluntarily," Gabe said.

"How about dessert?" Melanie hopped up from the table and grabbed Gabe by the wrist. "Mind giving me a hand?" she asked, but she wouldn't give him the opportunity to refuse.

"I thought Nikki was out of your life for good," Mom said.

Gabe's eyebrows drew together, and he glanced at Melanie.

"She was in need of a friend," Melanie said, tugging on Gabe until he finally stood.

"That girl is always in need of something." Mom exchanged a knowing look with Dad.

"Melanie's too kind-hearted to turn away anyone as broken as Nikki," Gabe said over his shoulder as Melanie towed him to the house.

"Too gullible, you mean?" Mom said.

Gabe didn't have the opportunity to answer because Melanie tugged him into the house through the sliding door and closed it behind him.

"Is it common for you to hide things from your parents?" Gabe asked.

"Certain things," Melanie admitted. "They really don't like Nikki."

"I gathered as much. Can I ask why?"

"They think she uses me."

"She totally uses you."

"I know, but I'm okay with that. They're not. They think it's best if I don't associate with her at all."

"A week ago, I would have agreed with them, but Nikki needs someone like you in her life."

Melanie nodded. "They'll never see it that way. It's best to just not talk about her around them. They both get all riled up."

"*Now* you tell me."

She wrung her hands, and her engagement ring caught her eye, which reminded her . . . "I told my dad I'm moving to Austin."

"I'm sure he took that well," Gabe said.

"I don't think he's processed it all yet. Maybe we should escape before he does."

The door slid open, and Mom looked into the kitchen at the two of them. "Your father tells me that you're moving in together. In Austin."

Too late for escape.

CHAPTER NINE

GABE'S FIRST MEETING with his future in-laws could have gone better, but it also could have gone a lot worse. At least he hadn't been chased off their property with a shotgun. Melanie was obviously upset, oscillating between hurt and rage over the argument she'd gotten into with her mother before she'd slammed out of the house with Gabe having no choice but to follow. Oddly, the argument had been over Nikki, not himself. Her parents were more onboard with her marrying a tattooed, unemployed rock-star *thug* than living with the train wreck that was her best friend.

"So I take it they don't know Nikki lives with you now," Gabe said, instantly wishing he could keep his mouth shut as Melanie leaned so far against the passenger door he feared she might roll right out onto the side of the freeway.

"Of course they don't know. You saw how they reacted."

"Is there a reason why they don't like her? Well, besides the fact that she's unstable and uses you. Your parents don't seem like the type to turn on someone in need."

Melanie sighed. "You remember that story I told you about the tattooed bikers who harassed me as a girl?"

He nodded and took his eyes off the road long enough to glance at her. Her hands were shaking as she knotted her fingers in the hem of her sundress.

"Nikki was flirting with them and called me over."

"Weren't you like *twelve?*"

"Thirteen."

"That's no better. Was *Nikki* . . . ?" He couldn't bring himself to ask if a little girl—and a thirteen-year-old was definitely a girl—had been promiscuous.

"Sexually active?"

Gabe winced and nodded. It would be bad enough to think of such a young girl fooling around with boys her age, but those bikers Melanie had described to him had sounded like grown men.

"Her father's abuse started in elementary school."

Gabe swallowed the nausea rising up his throat. "And your parents hold that against her?"

"What?" Melanie blurted. "Of course they don't. She put me in what could have been a very dangerous situation, and they never forgave her for that."

"I'm sure it wasn't intentional. She probably thought you'd like the attention, because she likes it." He could understand wanting to protect a daughter at the expense of someone else, but the more he learned about Nikki, the more he wanted to protect her—not only from those who might hurt her, but from herself. Someone needed to. He realized that Melanie had been doing that long before he'd come along.

"I know it wasn't intentional. I don't think most of the things she does that hurt me are."

"What kinds of things?" He took her hand, smiling as the diamond he'd bought only hours ago dug into his palm.

Melanie shrugged. "Things."

"I thought we were going to be honest with each other. Trust each other."

"She sleeps with my boyfriends. Not all of them." There had been that one who'd turned her down.

"You don't have to worry about that with me," he said, lifting her hand and kissing the inside of her wrist. "I'm a one-woman man and you're my one."

She smiled, her eyes misty. "Am I stupid because I keep taking her back? She always worms her way back into my life no matter how hard I push her away."

"I don't think you're stupid at all," he said, pulling into the parking lot behind her apartment building and putting the car into park. He was glad he was finished driving so he could brush her hair out of her lovely face and kiss the worry out of her expression. "You have a generous heart, Mel. Enough for Nikki and for me, for your parents and for all our future children."

She lowered her eyes, which surprised him. He figured she'd take that as a compliment.

"Gabe?" she said after a moment. "If that groupie's baby turns out to be yours, I . . . I don't think I can love it." She grimaced as if she'd said she wanted to harm the child.

Gabe hadn't given Lindsey or her unborn baby a single thought for days. "Will you be jealous if I love it?"

She looked up, and the turmoil in her hazel eyes cut him so deep, he felt it through his entire chest. She nodded and closed her eyes, sending a single tear coursing down her cheek. She dashed it away.

"I don't know why I feel this way. It's not the baby's fault. And if it's part of you . . ." She reached for the door handle and tried to escape the very uncomfortable conversation she'd initiated. Gabe grabbed her hand to make her stay put.

"Finish what you were going to say."

"If it's part of you, I *should* love it. I know I should. I just . . . can't."

Gabe wasn't sure what to say to that. He felt no connection to Lindsey's unborn baby, but he would be a good father to the child if it was his. He'd already told Melanie as much. He wasn't going to take back that vow just to make her feel better, because he'd meant it. He had no doubt that she'd come around if his newborn baby was staring up at her. She wouldn't be able to hold a grudge anything so innocent and pure. He knew she wouldn't. But they'd cross that bridge *if*—and in his mind that was a big fucking *if*—they came to it.

"If that's the way you feel . . ."

"But I *hate* feeling this way. I'm a terrible person for wishing a baby didn't exist."

"You're not a terrible person," he said. "You just have a terrible wish."

She jerked free of his grasp and opened the door. She climbed out and slammed the door behind her, clutching her stomach and breathing hard, as if she'd just played Sole Regret's set list with one drumstick. This was really tearing her up inside. He climbed out of the car and moved to stand beside her, pulling his cellphone out of his pocket and dialing Owen. The continually silent bassist didn't answer Gabe's call, so he left a message.

"Hey, Owen. I hate to ask anything of you at a time like this. I know you must be having a hard time with your brother's situation." God, Gabe felt like an ass for even bothering him. "I know it's probably not something on your mind right now, but I was wondering when Lindsey is going to have that paternity test. I'd like to know if her baby is mine as soon as possible. I'm getting married, you see, and it's something I need to know before I make this wonderful woman pledge her forever to me. So if you have any details on that test, please call or text. And if you need anything—absolutely anything—don't hesitate to ask. I'm here for you. Take care, bro. I'll stop in to see you when I get back to Austin in a couple days. And if you haven't made up with Kellen yet—I still don't know what he did—but for fuck's sake, dude, give the guy a break. You know he's your anchor. Always has been."

Feeling stupid for leaving such a long and sappy message for a *guy* while Melanie listened in, Gabe disconnected the call and tucked his phone back into his pocket.

"I'm not sure if I should be glad or afraid that you did that," Melanie said.

"I thought you wanted to know if the baby's mine."

"I do," she said. "But what if I'm not ready?"

"Will you be ready in three months when the baby is born?"

She sucked in a laugh. "Probably not."

"I don't want this hanging over us. We need a plan of action."

"I thought rock stars always went with the flow," she said, linking her arm through his and tugging him toward the apartment.

He cocked his head to one side. "Have you met me?"

She laughed. "Fortunately, I have, and I never once took you for a rock star."

For some reason her jest wiped the smile from his face.

THE NEXT MORNING, GABE FILLED the trunks and back seats of two cars with a bunch of what he considered useless girl stuff that would soon be cluttering up his house. He was a little cranky because his mattress-time with Melanie had been interrupted by Nikki forcefully inserting herself between them so she could sleep. This entailed her cuddling with Melanie, or rather, wrapping herself around Melanie like a starving python. There was no way in hell Gabe would put up with that bullshit when they reached Austin. If Nikki got scared in the night, she would just have to sleep with a pair of hot, smelly, slobbery, oft-times gassy Labradors.

"Are we stopping for breakfast?" Nikki asked, sweeping her hair back with the pair of white-rimmed sunglasses on top of her head.

"Not if we're going to make it to Dallas by three," Gabe said. That was when he'd told Adam to expect them, and Gabe wasn't typically late for the appointments he made.

"But I'm hungry, and Melanie drank the last of the milk."

"I asked you if you wanted some," Melanie said, but she opened the trunk and rummaged around in bags until she came up with a box of granola bars. "Enjoy," she said, handing a bar to Nikki.

Nikki immediately opened the wrapper and took a bite. "You're riding with me, aren't you?" she asked with her mouth full.

Gabe hid a self-satisfied grin. He'd deliberately crammed several heavy boxes, a thick comforter, and several extra pillows in the front seat of the Bug so Melanie would ride with him in her Toyota.

Melanie lifted a brow at her friend. "Would you ride with you if you had the chance to ride with him?" She jabbed a thumb in Gabe's direction.

"Good point," Nikki said. "I'll ride with Gabe. You drive my car."

For a second, Gabe thought Melanie was going to agree to that arrangement. He opened his mouth to protest, but Melanie said, "If this is going to work, you have to recognize that Gabe is my top priority. If you want to come, you will drive your car and I will ride with Gabe in mine, got it?"

Nikki crinkled her nose at Gabe, but took another bite of her granola bar and swung open the door of the Bug. "I'm stopping with you in Dallas," she said as she climbed into her frivolous melon-orange car. Unlike Gabe, she actually looked good behind the wheel. "I want to say hey to Adam."

She closed her door and started the car's engine. Melanie knocked on the glass, and Nikki rolled down her window. "I'll be careful."

"Good, but I wanted to tell you that we'll stop for a quick

lunch, so don't get too far ahead of us. I'll call you when it's time."

Nikki polished off the last bite of her granola bar, crinkled up the wrapper, and stuck it in Melanie's hand. "See you at Waffle House."

They always stopped at Waffle House on their way south. The restaurant didn't have any locations in Topeka or even Wichita, so eating there was a rare treat for them.

"I'm not sure if Gabe likes Waffle House," Melanie said, but Nikki was already backing out of her parking spot and waving out the window.

"Waffle House is fine," Gabe said.

"I don't think we should let her get her way. She's testing her boundaries to see what she can get away with."

"She's a grown woman, not a new puppy."

Melanie stuck the empty wrapper into his hand. "Are you sure about that?"

He grinned and kissed her. "The only thing I'm absolutely sure of is you."

When he started to move away, she wrapped both arms around his neck and drew him down for a lengthier kiss. The wrapper crinkled as he moved his hands to her hips to draw her closer.

"Love you," she murmured against his lips.

He'd never tire of that sentiment and was glad they said it freely to each other now. "Love you."

She pulled away slowly, lips lingering on his, and opened her eyes. "Maybe we can fix up a pile of hay in the barn for her."

Gabe chuckled. "Now there's an idea."

To pass the time they played a game of Google Feud on Melanie's phone while they traveled south. Nikki was a few miles ahead of them, so they didn't see her. She did call several times to complain that she was bored. Gabe could hear Sole Regret's last release blaring in the background as she asked questions about his house and her would-be room and the nearest night club and his boat. It made Gabe sad that the album she was listening to might be Sole Regret's last. Surely he could convince Adam to make amends with Jacob. They were giving up more than a career. Music was their life. He knew he wasn't the only member of the band who felt that way.

"What's bothering you?" Melanie asked when he didn't respond to her next Google Feud search prompt.

"Just hoping I can talk some sense into Adam so he can talk sense into Jacob."

"You miss them, don't you?"

Gabe couldn't deny that reality, so he nodded. "I know it sounds odd, but I spend most of the time on the tour bus reading, not goofing off with the guys. But even though I'm off in my own world, they're there, you know. If I do decide to bullshit with them, they're there. And now . . ." He shook his head. "They're not there." He couldn't explain the tightness in his chest. He rubbed at it impatiently.

"You can bullshit with me," she offered, her smile hopeful.

"I plan to," he said, not wanting to hurt her feelings by pointing out that it wasn't the same. He didn't want to bullshit with her. He wanted to love her.

At brunch, Gabe tried to find something worth eating on the Waffle House menu. Both of his companions ordered waffles, but he feared he'd go into a carb coma and drive off the road if he attempted that kind of breakfast, so he opted for eggs and sausage instead.

Nikki continued with her string of questions about their destination. She was definitely a talker, while Melanie was more of an answerer and Gabe definitely a listener. The three of them got along well until Nikki broached the subject of Sole Regret's breakup.

"So how do we go about getting the band back together?" she asked, dipping her bacon in maple syrup and taking a bite.

Gabe lifted a brow at her. "We?"

Nikki caught his eye and nodded. "I know Shade pretty well. Maybe he'll listen to me."

Gabe snorted. "You had a one-night stand with him. You don't know him at all."

"More of a one-night, one-morning stand, but I do know him. He does talk to the women he sleeps with, you know. He was worried that he was going to miss his daughter's birthday. Said his ex-wife told him not to show up at their house unless it was one of his visitation days."

"He saw her on her birthday," Gabe said. At least he was pretty sure he had. Gabe had been in such a rush to spend time with Melanie that he hadn't paid much attention to what was going on with Jacob that weekend. He knew for a fact that it was a visitation weekend, though, because their entire tour had been scheduled around having every other weekend off for that very reason. When he brought that up to Melanie and Nikki, they both looked heartbroken.

"Poor guy," Melanie said. "Is there any way that Julie can go on tour with the band? He obviously doesn't get to see her often enough."

"He does now that he's back together with his praying mantis of an ex-wife."

"If he stays with her, Sole Regret is finished," Nikki said.

"I think you're right about that," Gabe said, taking a sip of coffee and staring down at his nearly empty plate. "I really thought he and Amanda had a shot."

"Who's Amanda?" Nikki asked.

"His ex-wife's sister," Melanie said.

Nikki let out a low whistle. "Well, that would never work out."

"Why not?" Gabe happened to think Amanda was perfect for Jacob.

"Can you imagine how awkward the holidays would be?"

Melanie laughed. "That would be awkward."

"But she already loves his daughter," Gabe said, "so adjusting to being a nuclear family would be easier on the three of them. It would be everyone else that would have issues with it, not those three."

"Well, his ex would definitely have an issue with it," Melanie said. "Does she know that Jacob and Amanda were together?"

Gabe shrugged. "I hope not. She'd probably beat the snot out of him." Which might explain the bruise on Jacob's forehead when he'd had returned to the tour after his weekend with Julie. Gabe wished he'd been paying better attention to what had been going on with Jacob that day, but then he'd had his own worries to deal with that weekend. And all of his problems had centered around Nikki. He scrutinized her closely as she waved the waitress over for a refill on her glass of milk. She looked so perfectly harmless.

"If my ex-husband was sniffing around my sister, I'd definitely bust his balls," Nikki said. "Not that I have an ex-husband. Or a sister."

"I might be okay with it," Melanie said, "if they genuinely cared about each other and my ex and I had parted under friendly terms."

"If you're friendly, why would you part?" Nikki asked.

"People grow apart. Maybe they shouldn't be married anymore, but it's possible to still get along."

Gabe snorted. "Tina and Jacob are anything but friendly. That's why his getting back together with her makes absolutely no sense. None."

"I'll talk to him about what's going on," Nikki said. "Maybe he'll open up to me. I'm a good listener."

"When you're asleep," Melanie said with a laugh. "Maybe. Sometimes you even talk then."

Nikki stuck her tongue out at her.

After paying for brunch and gassing up both cars, Gabe called Adam to make sure he remembered that they were stopping by the hospital in Dallas for a quick visit.

"I'll be here," Adam said. "I don't have anywhere better to be."

"Have you heard from the other guys?" Gabe asked.

"Just Owen. He said once his brother is stable, they're shipping him to an army hospital at Fort Hood. He wanted me to ask the doctors here if that would be in Chad's best interest."

"Does Owen know more about Chad's injuries now?"

"Not much more. But he did say they take those with the most severe injuries to San Antonio, so maybe them sending him to Fort Hood is actually a good sign."

"I hope you're right." Gabe wished he knew more about such things. It was no wonder Owen had never returned his call about the stupid paternity test. The guy definitely had more important worries. Gabe wouldn't bother him again. "I'll see you in a few hours. Do you want to meet me down in the lob—"

"I'm not leaving Madison's side," Adam interrupted.

"Is she okay with company, then? We could come up to her room."

Adam mumbled something, and then he laughed. "She says she'd like to see a new face about now. I guess she's tired of looking at my ugly mug."

Gabe could hear Madison's protests in the background.

"I know you don't think I'm ugly," Adam said to her.

"I'll see you in a few then," Gabe said, wanting to get back on the road. Melanie was sending him questioning looks through the windshield as he stood in front of the car on his phone.

"See you."

For the first time in his experience, the traffic around Dallas wasn't bad, but finding parking at Baylor was a nightmare. Nikki had somehow snagged a prime spot near the entrance to the main hospital and waved at them as they drove past. By the time Gabe found a spot, she'd already found a new friend to talk to. Well, the guy was mostly talking at her boobs—which he was quite obviously ogling—but she didn't seem to notice. Gabe moved to stand beside her, wrapped an arm around her shoulders, and kissed the side of her head. "Hey, sweetie, sorry to make you wait. Is this guy bothering you?"

"No," she said. "He's a med student."

Gabe offered the young man an unrelenting stare. "A future gynecologist, I presume, since he's doing such a thorough examination of your breasts."

The guy had the decency to blush and back away. Nikki giggled in delight. Melanie rolled her eyes and shook her head at them both.

"We're trying to find a patient," Gabe said to the endearingly awkward guy. "Where would we go for information?"

After pointing them in a general direction, the med student adjusted his wire-framed glasses and turned to go, but then he stopped and faced Nikki again.

"It was nice talking to you, Wilma. I wish you had told me you had a boyfriend." He released a full-body sigh, looking as if he'd just said goodbye to his soul mate, and then walked away.

"Wilma?" Gabe asked before releasing his proprietary hold on Nikki and taking Melanie's hand.

"He said his name was Fred," Nikki explained. "I told him we must have been fated to meet because I was Wilma."

Melanie snorted.

Gabe shook his head at the two of them. "You shouldn't get a guy's hopes up like that. Do you know how to flat out reject a guy? That whole let-him-down-easy thing you women do just makes it harder on us in the long run because then we have hope."

"Do I know how to reject a *guy*?" Nikki asked. "Sure. Do I know how to reject a sweet, cute future doctor named Fred? Not so much."

"Since you're not supposed to hook up with anyone this month, you're bound to find the man of your dreams," Melanie said. "It's poetic justice. Karma. Whatever you want to call it."

"If he's the man of her dreams, he can wait," Gabe declared. "In fact, any man worth your time and affection can wait until the time is right for you, no matter how hard he tries to convince you otherwise."

"Oh, Gabe," Nikki said, poking him in the ribs. "You're such a romantic."

It took them a while to find their way to Madison's room. They stopped and picked up some flowers at the gift shop, and Nikki insisted on a Get Well Soon balloon to go along with the bouquet of cheerfully bright daisies. As they walked down a long sterile hallway, Gabe noticed how Nikki began to cling to Melanie. He wondered if it would be better for Nikki to talk about her obvious fear, or if that would make her feel worse.

He opted for middle ground to give her the opportunity to speak freely if she felt like it. "You okay, Nik?"

She looked up at him and nodded with a slight smile on her lips. Melanie lifted Nikki's hand and pressed it to her chest.

"Hospitals remind her of all the reasons she's been in one," Melanie said. "None of them good."

"A few of them good," Nikki corrected. "Like when my cousin's baby was born."

"I apologize. I shouldn't have spoken for you," Melanie said.

"That's okay."

"You just looked a little nervous," Gabe said. "I was worried about you."

At his declaration, Nikki beamed. "I am nervous. We're going to see Adam Taylor. I wonder if he'll even remember me. Did you see the sketch he drew of me? Pretty cool, huh?"

Gabe chuckled. "Very cool. And I'm sure he'll remember you."

He had seen the drawing Adam had done, and recalled that Jacob had been upset that half of Nikki's beautiful face had been depicted as decayed to bone in Adam's artwork. Jacob tended to take things a bit too literally, while Adam was pathologically artistic. They never saw eye to eye on anything, and that was exactly why Sole Regret needed them both. Having a band made up of like-minded individuals would have made for some uninspired, passionless music.

Which was why he was there. To remind Adam—and himself—that no matter what obstacles appeared in their path, their friendship, their band, their *music* was worth fighting for.

When they reached Madison's room, Gabe knocked on the open door and called loudly, "Are you decent in there?"

"I wouldn't call myself decent," Adam replied, "but you can come in anyway."

Gabe was surprised that while Madison had been the one injured and had recently undergone surgery, she looked a hell of a lot better than Adam did.

"When was the last time you slept?" Gabe asked him while the women crowded around Madison to give her flowers and to hear her story about a rattlesnake spooking her horse.

"Can't remember," Adam said, swaying slightly in Gabe's direction.

Gabe caught him by both shoulders. "You won't be able to help her if you collapse from exhaustion."

"I keep telling him that," Madison said. "That he should get some rest while I'm stuck in here, because when I get out and he goes back on tour, he's going to be too tired to perform. If he thinks Jacob is mad at him now . . ."

Gabe winced, but before he could open his mouth to comment, Adam grabbed him by the arm and tugged him toward the hall.

"Be right back, babe," Adam called to Madison. "You ladies take good care of her while I'm gone."

Adam closed the door softly and turned to face Gabe. Adam couldn't meet his gaze, however, standing there hands on hips, eyes focused downward.

"You haven't told her?" Gabe asked. "About the band breaking up?"

Adam shook his head. "She'll feel like it's her fault. I don't want her to feel that way. It's my fault."

Gabe licked his lips. He wasn't going to give Adam an out.

The band's breakup *was* at least partially his fault, and Adam had never been the type to claim responsibility for anything. So to hear him say that he was taking the blame gave Gabe hope. Gabe knew that was what Jacob had always wanted out of Adam, for him to claim responsibility for something—for *any*thing. This was a big step in the right direction. But would it be enough?

"So what are you going to do to fix it?" Gabe asked.

Adam finally met his eyes. He really did look like hell— wrinkled clothes, a scruffy growth of beard, dark circles under both eyes, and his messy-by-design hair was extra-disheveled. He was even missing a few of the chains he usually wore.

"There's no fixing this. I fucked up too big this time."

"You did fuck up big," Gabe said.

"Sorry."

God, Jacob should be here witnessing this change in Adam. Though it might not matter. Whenever the two of them were in a room together, their alpha supremacy bullshit began.

"But we can fix this," Gabe said.

"How?"

"Oh my God!" Madison squealed inside the room.

Before Gabe could blink, Adam had bashed open the door and was at her bedside. "What is it? Where does it hurt?"

"I'm fine, sweetheart," Madison said. "It's just . . . Melanie and Gabe got engaged too!", She held up her left hand next to Melanie's to show they both had sparkly new engagement rings.

Adam covered his chest with one hand. "You scared the hell out of me."

"I'm sorry." She shifted forward as well as she could, given that the cast covered her entire right arm, shoulder and chest, and puckered her lips for a kiss, which Adam supplied without hesitation. The metal bar holding her unwieldy appendage out at a ninety degree angle bumped against the bed rail and made her wince.

"Stop moving around so much," Adam said, kissing her again.

"I hate this freaking cast," Madison said. "My elbow is itching like crazy." She looked up at Melanie and beamed. "Hey, maybe we should have a double wedding."

"Yes!" Nikki said, bouncing on her toes. "That would be so much fun! I get to help organize it all, right?"

"Hey, Nik," Adam said with a tender smile. "How've you been?"

"Great," she said. "Except all my favorite rock stars are getting hitched. First Jacob gets back with his ex-wife, and then Gabe and Adam get engaged. Who's next to fall—the consummate playboy, Owen? So not fair."

"Did you say that Jacob was back with his ex?" Madison glared at Adam, who was toying with a strand of her hair and watching the action of his fingers. "Did you know about this?"

"I was hoping it wouldn't last long," Adam said.

"You and me both," Gabe said.

"You aren't hiding things from me again, are you?" Madison asked.

"Of course not," Adam said.

Lies came so easy to him. Gabe wondered if Adam would be able to break that habit, even for someone he so obviously loved.

"I think you need to get some rest, babe," Adam said, "and I'm getting hungry, so I'll walk these guys out and pick up something from the cafeteria on my way back upstairs. Do you want me to bring you anything?"

His gaze lifted to meet hers, and Gabe watched her practically melt into her pillow.

"I don't need anything, but I am a little tired. They have me on some very nice pain meds."

Adam kissed her gently and jerked his head at Gabe to get him to follow.

"Hope that arm heals up fast," Gabe said in parting, reaching over to give Madison's good shoulder a gentle squeeze. "You'll need it to keep this guy in line."

"He's not as tough as he looks," Madison said with an admiring grin at her new fiancé.

Gabe followed Adam out into the hall again while Melanie and Nikki said goodbye to Madison. He was pretty sure they were all exchanging numbers so they could work on those plans for a double wedding, which sounded like a nightmare to him. But if it made Melanie happy, he'd put up with it.

"I hope they don't have their hearts set on a double wedding," Adam said. "Ain't happening."

Gabe chuckled. "It will if they want it to."

"Your woman might boss you around, but mine—"

"Has a more subtle means of control." Gabe smacked him in the center of his back, and Adam laughed, nodding slightly.

"When are you going to tell her about the band?" Gabe asked.

"After I talk to Jacob. If I can straighten this mess out, she never needs to be the wiser."

"Do you really think that's the best way to start a relationship with your partner for life, keeping her in the dark about everything that might upset her?"

"I don't want her to be upset. Ever."

"Yeah, but—"

"Guys, wait up," Nikki called from behind them. A nurse shushed her, but that didn't deter her from racing down the hall. Gabe stopped to allow Melanie, who was walking at a fast clip as quietly as possible, to catch up. Nikki zoomed right past him and careened into Adam, laughing when he caught her by both arms.

"Easy there," Adam said. "I'm not exactly in top form at the moment."

"You look great to me," Nikki said, linking her arm through his and leaning into his side.

Gabe offered Melanie a smile and took her hand, falling in step behind the chatterbox that was her best friend and the broody musician that was one of his.

"So you're going to fix Sole Regret, right?" Nikki asked. "Because I'll be devastated if I have to start listening to Nickelback again."

"I'll do my best," Adam said. "Once Madison is out of the hospital."

"Are you taking her back to your place?" Nikki asked.

"That's the plan."

"So I'll be in Austin for a while too. I can come help you out if you need me to." She leaned close to his ear and whispered loud enough for Gabe to hear, "I'm sure the lovebirds will want some time alone, if you catch my drift."

When they passed a waiting room near the elevators, Madison ran up to Adam and grabbed his sleeve.

Wait? How could Madison be there with a fully functional right arm when they'd just seen her in that hospital bed with a cast that went on for miles? Gabe exchanged a look with an equally baffled Melanie.

"Will she see me yet?" uninjured Madison asked Adam.

"You might as well go home, Kennedy. She's not ready to forgive you yet."

Kennedy? Gabe actually said *oh* aloud as he recalled Adam mentioning at one time or another that Madison had an identical twin.

Kennedy's eyes brimmed with tears, and she pressed trembling lips together. "I'm not going home until she talks to me."

"She'll talk to you when she's ready."

"Are you leaving?" Kennedy glanced longingly down the hallway.

Adam sighed. "I guess not." He turned to Gabe. "Thanks for stopping in."

"I thought you were hungry," Nikki said, squeezing Adam's arm and gazing up at him adoringly. It wasn't the same kind of look she gave Shade. This look was more of a hero-worship thing than a "whoops my pants fell off, what are you going to do about it" kind of look. Gabe didn't even get bestowed with her hero-worship look. What was up with that?

"I'll be fine," Adam said. "I had some of Madison's tomato soup earlier."

"I'll get you something," Nikki said, and Gabe was at once reminded of the fangirls who jumped to do Adam's bidding. And then it occurred to him that Nikki *was* a fangirl.

"How is she feeling?" Kennedy asked. "Is she getting enough rest? You aren't eating all of her food, are you? She needs to keep her strength up."

"As good as can be expected," Adam reported. "She's about to take a nap now. No, she's eating plenty. She didn't like the soup so she gave it to me."

"You're Madison's sister, right?" Melanie asked.

Kennedy nodded.

"Why doesn't she want to see you?"

Adam lifted his eyebrows at Melanie, and she lowered her gaze.

"None of my business," she said under her breath.

"I . . . uh . . . sort of told her boss that she was dating a client," Kennedy said, cringing.

"Hoping that Madison would dump me," Adam said. "But it backfired, didn't it, Kennedy?"

Kennedy scowled. "I'm sure I can help her get her job back."

"She'll find a new job," Adam said. "In Austin."

The elevator opened and several people emerged.

"Don't bother her while I'm downstairs," Adam said, "or I'll call security to have you removed."

"You wouldn't!"

Adam's jaw was set in a hard line and his gray eyes were as cold as arctic steel when he said, "Try me."

He stepped onto the waiting elevator, and the rest of them scrambled in after him before the doors shut. Adam leaned against the interior wall of the elevator and rubbed both eyes with the heels of his hands.

"Madison has to forgive her eventually," he muttered. "I don't like having to play the bad guy and keep them apart."

"So Kennedy got Madison fired because she dated you?" Gabe asked, having connected some dots.

"Yep," Adam said. "I'm okay with it—one less string to tug her away from me—but it really did a number on her ego. She's good at what she does and makes a huge difference in the lives of a lot of people who don't know how to function without medicating. Just look what she did for me."

Gabe had to admit that Adam was almost a fully functional human being these days.

Nikki fingered the sleeve of Adam's leather jacket. "You know her sister is going to go check on her now that you're going downstairs with us, don't you?"

Adam smiled slyly and cupped the back of Nikki's head, roughhousing with a little shake, as if she were his exasperating little sister. Nikki's smile was breathtakingly joyful.

"Of course I know that, silly. I'll just give Kennedy a few minutes to sneak a peek at her sister. She'll be quiet. I know she doesn't want Madison to get upset. She's just worried about her."

"So why did you bother to threaten her?" Gabe asked.

Adam pressed one hand to his chest. "Playing the bad guy, remember?"

"So that Madison doesn't have to," Melanie said, squeezing Gabe's hand.

He supposed that Adam taking the brunt of the blame for the rift between the sisters was one way he showed he cared. Gabe assumed that Madison would prefer to be told the truth, but what did he know? Just because his relationship worked better based on mutual trust and honesty didn't mean every relationship worked that way. Maybe Madison *liked* that Adam hid things from her. But Gabe doubted it.

When they exited the elevator, Adam said goodbye and turned toward the cafeteria.

"I'm hungry," Nikki said to Melanie, her gaze following Adam's retreating back. "Actually, I'm starved. Why don't we join him? Then we won't have to stop later."

How could she be starved after eating her weight in waffles and syrup-covered bacon less than three hours before?

"He's engaged, remember?" Melanie shook her head at Nikki.

"I don't want him that way," Nikki said. "I just like to be around him. He gets me without trying to."

"I get you," Melanie said.

Gabe snorted, but Nikki smiled. "Because you try so hard. That means the world to me, you know." Nikki looped her arm through Melanie's free one and leaned into her side, hugging her arm. "Please. I'm sure Gabe has more to say to him."

Gabe had a shit ton of stuff to say to Adam. "I could eat," he said.

"Outnumbered," Melanie said with a resigned sigh. "I'm not hungry, but I could definitely go for a cup of coffee."

Nikki squeezed her arm again and took off down the corridor after Adam. Gabe and Melanie followed at a much more sedate pace.

"You're not really hungry are you?" Melanie asked just as Nikki caught up to Adam and nearly knocked him over by jumping on his back. Rather than look pissed—which is what Gabe expected his reaction to be to such an assault—Adam laughed, looped his arms around her long legs at his waist, and gave her a piggyback ride toward the cafeteria.

"Stuffed," he admitted. "But I like to see her happy, and for whatever reason, Adam does that for her."

"Do you think I try too hard to understand her?"

"Nothing wrong with that," he said. "You're empathetic. It's one of the things I love most about you."

She leaned into his side and gazed up at him with a look of adoration that made his heart flutter stupidly.

"It's a quality we share."

Gabe wasn't so sure about that, but he accepted her compliment and got in the cafeteria line behind Nikki and Adam. Nikki was asking Adam about his music-writing progress and if he'd drawn any more pictures of her. Gabe was surprised by how open Adam was about himself when he talked to her. Adam had always been secretive about his personal life, but with Nikki, he held nothing back. Perhaps she got him the same way he got her. Gabe didn't get either of them, but that didn't stop him from enjoying their company. Especially when they were together.

"So what you need to do," Nikki was saying to Adam as she munched on the salad she'd selected from the cafeteria cooler, "is show Jacob all the work you've been doing. He'll get all excited about it and want to get the band back together."

"It's not that good," Adam said, dipping a fry in ketchup, his eyes trained on his task.

"Everything you write is good," Nikki said. "And most of what you write is excellent."

"That's true," Gabe said. He took a sip of his eyeball-peelingly strong cup of coffee and pulled a layer off the stale cinnamon roll that he and Melanie were sharing.

"You haven't seen everything I write," Adam said.

"I saw the lyrics you wrote about you and me," Nikki said. "One wounded beast recognizes another…"

Adam rolled his eyes. "Those lyrics could be about anyone." He stuffed several fries into his mouth. "Or no one," he added around his mouthful of fries.

"But that song wasn't about just anyone. You wrote it about me. I was right there when inspiration struck. I saw it awaken in you. It was so freaking cool!"

"I'm usually inspired by dark things," Adam said, pointing at her with a French fry. "And you, darling Nikki, are dark."

Gabe stared at her, trying to see in her what Adam saw, but to him, Nikki was a pretty girl with gorgeous eyes and an infectious smile who seemed to live without a care. He knew better, but yeah, he didn't see her dark side at all. She was too good at hiding her true feelings and covering them with bubbly bullshit. Apparently Adam could easily see through all her false normality. He'd always been a deep and complicated sort of guy, and though he'd nearly driven them all mad with those complications, Gabe was glad he was a part of his life. Being around Adam today reminded Gabe how much he'd lost when Jacob had walked off their tour bus outside of New Orleans.

"When we get the band back together," Gabe said, "you could bring Madison on tour with us while she recovers."

Adam paused with his dry-looking poor excuse for a cheeseburger halfway to his mouth. "Do you honestly think this is going to work out?"

Gabe's heart skipped a beat. He had not only thought it but *believed* it. But if Adam didn't think it was possible, then how could the rest of the band rely on him to set things straight with Jacob? Hell, when had they ever been able to rely on Adam for anything?

"What are you going to do with the rest of your life, if it doesn't?" Gabe asked, his pulse thrumming hard in his ears. He still didn't have a plan B, which frankly freaked him the fuck out whenever that fact came to mind.

Adam shrugged. "Wing it." He bit into his cheeseburger.

"It's the only way to live as far as I'm concerned," Nikki said, a bright smile on her face.

Melanie stiffened slightly and reached for Gabe's hand. Well, at least one person at the table understood Gabe's terror. Wing it? Was Adam fucking kidding him?

"You are going to try to talk to Jacob, aren't you? Me, Owen, Kellen, we're all counting on you."

Now it was Adam's turn to stiffen. He dropped his burger and pushed his tray away. "You should know better than to do that," he said quietly. He stood. "I have to check on Madison." And without so much as a goodbye, he stalked off.

"He's not going to fix this," Melanie said when Adam was out of earshot. "It's as if he doesn't give a shit about how this affects the rest of you."

"He's always like that," Gabe said, tossing the remains of their demolished cinnamon roll onto Adam's abandoned tray. "If responsibility so much glances in his direction, he takes off."

Nikki rose from the table to discard their trash. Her face was flushed, but Gabe couldn't read her. He didn't *get* her, and he sure as fuck didn't get Adam Taylor. Gabe might as well call Owen and Kellen and tell them both to find a new life, because the old one's champion refused to even suit up for the battle.

CHAPTER TEN

MELANIE CLIMBED out of her car and stretched the aches out of her limbs, back, and butt. She was so glad to be home, and as she gazed up at the big A-frame log cabin surrounded by woods and nature, it hit her. This beautiful place really was her home now. Gabe hurried up to the house to let the dogs out. His regular dog-sitter had taken care of them while they'd been gone. Beau was instantly jumping for joy on the porch beside him. Lady limped out, her ears droopy and her big brown eyes sad.

"Last trip for a while," he said to her, scratching her head. "I promise."

Melanie grabbed an armload of her stuff from the trunk and was halfway to the porch when Nikki's Bug pulled up behind Melanie's car. Nikki stepped out of the little melon-orange car and stood with her hands on her hips, assessing Gabe's gorgeous home.

"I thought rock stars lived in mansions," she said.

"It's my castle," Gabe said, helping Lady off the porch while Beau went to investigate the newcomer.

"It's a beautiful house," Melanie said. "I absolutely love it."

"Because you have great taste." Gabe offered her a wink.

"Doggie!" Nikki said, practically launching herself on top of Beau, who backed off with his tail between his legs before leaping forward again to give Nikki a full-face tongue bath. They rolled around in the dust for several minutes like a pair of rambunctious puppies before Lady went to check out the potential new member of their pack.

"Oh, you poor thing!" Nikki reached a hand in Lady's direction. Lady gave it a sniff and then a timid lick. Soon she was lying on her back, wagging her tail and getting a vigorous, apparently much appreciated, belly rub.

"Lady will never leave her alone now," Gabe told Melanie, his face bright with mirth. "That dog is addicted to belly rubs."

And that was how Melanie and Gabe ended up unloading both cars while Nikki became well acquainted with the dogs.

Later, Nikki sat perched on a stool at the breakfast bar while Melanie and Gabe worked to throw a meal together. Nikki's new furry friends sat on either side of the stool with their faces pressed against her outer thighs.

Nikki sighed. "You two belong together," she said. "Just look at you. Cooking without arguing. Road trip without arguing. Pick up crazy friend from the loony bin without arguing. Do you two ever argue?"

Melanie smiled at Gabe, recalling that the last time they'd had a disagreement had been because Nikki had kissed Melanie and made it clear that she wanted her. "Not often."

"So can the dogs be in the wedding?" Nikki asked, reaching down to scratch each behind the ears. Puppy love was totally a thing, and both of Gabe's dogs had it bad for Nikki.

"I don't see why not," Gabe said as he added more olive oil to the fresh salad dressing he was mixing.

"Wouldn't that be a recipe for disaster?" Melanie was immediately imagining a doggie tug of war with her veil and dogs marking their territory on pews.

"My dogs are well behaved," Gabe said, but Melanie was far from convinced.

"I'll put together some ideas and we'll vote," Nikki suggested.

"As the bride, my vote counts double and breaks all ties."

Gabe smirked at Nikki. "In other words, no dogs."

Dogs should take puppy-dog-eyes lessons from Nikki. If a pooch sported the current look she was giving Melanie, he'd easily get any treat he desired. But Melanie didn't fold. She added another layer to the lasagna to avoid Nikki's pleading stare.

"How about a skydiving wedding?" Nikki asked.

Melanie sprinkled parmesan cheese on top of the final thin layer of sauce. "Absolutely not." She lifted the ceramic dish and turned to the preheated oven in the wall, which Gabe opened for her.

"Beach wedding?"

"How about we have it here?" Gabe asked.

Melanie stole a kiss. "Fabulous idea."

"In the trees?" Nikki asked. "Where will the guests sit? The dusty driveway?"

"No one ever said chairs have to be set out in perfect rows," Melanie said. "Just scatter them about the forest."

Gabe snorted. "I never knew you were such a rebel."

He swatted her butt playfully, which somehow turned into a rear-end-massaging embrace fueled with a passionate kiss. He pressed his rapidly hardening cock into her hip, and her knees buckled. If he found scattered chairs sexy . . .

"The dogs would be more comfortable here," Melanie said, wondering what she was getting into, but she decided the smile Gabe gave her was worth a slobbery ring-bearer pillow.

"You hear that?" Nikki said. "Your daddy's getting married and you're invited."

Lady barked, and Beau echoed her—the low but loud sound making Melanie jump.

"How long does that lasagna need to bake?" Gabe murmured in Melanie's ear.

"At least forty-five minutes," she said.

"Hey, Nik," Gabe said, "if I'm not done devouring your friend in forty-five minutes, could you take the lasagna out of the oven?"

Nikki grinned. "You got it."

Melanie tripped over a squeaky toy as she trailed after Gabe, already anticipating all the delicious things he'd do to her body. She supposed Nikki being there did have a few advantages. Not burning the lasagna, for one. Entertaining Gabe's fur babies, for another. She was sure she'd think of more advantages later.

At the door to the master bedroom, Gabe made an unexpected detour to a separate door just to the right. Melanie wondered why they were going into a closet—at least that was what she assumed the unexplored area behind the door led to—but was surprised to find it was a very small bedroom, perhaps designed as a nursery since the rest of the bedrooms were on the opposite side of the house. Her heart warmed at the thought, but then her entire body flushed when she realized that instead of a cradle or crib, the only object in the room was something that reminded her of a small mechanical bull with various straps and gizmos attached, and what she could only describe as a giant dildo in its center.

"What the hell?" she said under her breath as he tugged her

into the room and shut the door.

"I was going to wait to show you this after dinner," he said, "but knowing it's here, finally ready to ride, I just couldn't wait."

"Is this what I think it is?" She edged closer, approaching slowly as if the contraption might spook, rear up, and kick her in the face.

"I've been working on it for years, but ultimately abandoned it until recently," he said, his eyes full of excitement. "I wasn't sure what it was missing until I woke up in the middle of the night a few nights ago and knew that the failed prototype I had planned to try out on you last weekend was the missing link."

Melanie cringed. The thing looked—well—*violent*. It was black, covered in faux leather, with studded straps, buckles of various sizes, and a few ropes. Red satin sashes dangled from the rear like a kinky tail.

"The, uh . . . man part . . ." She licked her lips and swallowed. "It's a bit *large*, don't you think?"

"Fully adjustable," he said with pride in his voice. "It starts out small and you use this . . ." He handed her a remote control with at least twenty buttons. ". . . to increase the length and girth to your liking."

She pushed a button, and the shaft began to piston up and down. Despite her trepidation, Melanie felt a tingle of excitement between her legs. Gabe took the remote from her and shut off the thrusting cock.

"I think all single ladies need one of these," she said, "but if you have a partner . . ."

Gabe smirked. "He gets the remote."

In her experience, men did love to fiddle with remote controls. With her heart thudding, she wondered what "channel surfing" would feel like while strapped to this crazy, yet intriguing, invention of Gabe's. His gadgets and devices had never failed to send her soaring, so this, his magnum opus, would undoubtedly be phenomenal.

"Show me more," she said, running her hand along the side of the pommel. The material was cool and smooth.

"You need to be naked for that."

"I'm not sure I'm prepared to climb on board," she said.

"Oh." His shoulders sank as she knocked the wind out of his sails.

"I don't mean never. I just mean . . ."

He took her by the hand and led her to a big black case sitting in the corner. "At least come see the attachments."

He knelt and opened the case, and she dropped to her knees beside him for a closer look.

"These are skins," he said. "They fit over the dong."

She giggled at his use of the word dong, but had to admit the skins were fascinating. They were all made out of the same surprisingly supple grayish material that was shaped to fit over the phallus and stretch to accommodate the lady's size preference. The surfaces varied from smooth to lightly textured to bumpy to having various tickly-looking strands at the tip. There were skins with ridges, knobby projections, and rows of bumps along one side or the other.

"Why so many different textures?" She'd already picked out one that looked like it would rub her front wall in just the right spot, but she wasn't about to tell Gabe that. Not yet.

Gabe grinned at her. "Every pussy is different. What feels good to one woman might hurt another. Do you think the gray color is a turn-off? I could add pigments to the polymer to make the skins more interesting or create various flesh tones or . . ."

"I don't think the color matters. I always wondered why vibrators were purple and red. Like that's hot in any way."

"Must be a reason," he said. "I'm sure there are people whose job is to determine which color is most likely to increase dildo sales."

Melanie giggled, wondering what such an employee's resume looked like, but knew Gabe was right. That was totally someone's job.

"So gray is okay?"

"Let's slide a skin on and see how it looks." She nonchalantly handed him the skin she most wanted to try out.

He kissed her under her ear. "That one's going to make you squirt."

Exactly. She loved how this man understood her anatomy and how he was unashamed to take the time and ask the questions required to figure out what gave her the most pleasure. So many men just went at it, hoping by some miracle that they were doing it right, and if not, oh well, must be something wrong with the woman.

He helped her rise and used the remote to decrease the length and girth of the phallus before showing her how to stretch the skin over it and snap the dildo's wide square base securely into place in what she could only describe as the saddle.

"The gray looks good with the black leather surrounding it." And staring at that now-small phallus with that big bump on the top—that she could get in exactly the right spot by altering the size and girth of the shaft—had her pressing her thighs together to calm her irrefutable excitement.

Gabe pushed on a spot behind the phallus, and a smaller, more slender dildo shifted into position behind the first.

"Optional anal stimulation," he said before uncovering a ridge in front of the main phallus. "And clit vibration. What do you think about adding suction?"

Her breath stalled in her throat. "Yaaaassss," she said as she forced the breath out. "That clit-sucky thing you made . . ." She produced a full body shudder. "Dear lord, every woman needs that thing in her life."

He chuckled and pulled her into his arms, her breasts pressed firmly into his hard chest. Which reminded her of another gadget he'd invented that had rocked her world.

"What about those buzzy nipple clamps?" she asked. "Could those be an attachment?"

"Already are," he murmured, lifting the hem of her shirt and caressing the bare skin of her lower back with both hands. "So what do you say? Are you brave enough to take it for a ride?"

"Fuck yeah, I am," she said, yanking her shirt off over her head.

He pulled her back into his arms, cupping her bottom in a strong grip and kissing her senseless. "I love you more with each passing second," he said when he finally drew away.

"I know the feeling," she said, breathless and giddy and more than a little anxious to climb aboard his . . . "What do you call this thing, anyway?"

"Haven't named it yet." He scowled in concentration. "How about the Pleasure Pump?"

Melanie winced and shook her head. "So not sexy. You can do better."

"Maybe inspiration for a name will strike me while I watch you get off on it."

She grinned. He seemed as excited to start her maiden voyage as she was. His fingers moved to unfasten her jeans, and he kissed her deeply while he slipped her pants and panties down her thighs as far as he could reach. She moaned a protest when he broke the kiss, but groaned in pleasure as his lips began to journey down her neck, along her collarbone and down her chest so that he could push her clothing lower. Her jeans were at her knees when he latched on to one nipple, sucking so hard through the lacy fabric of her bra that she had to cling to his shoulders to keep her balance.

He helped her out of her pants and slid one strong hand up the inside of her thigh, stopping just short of touching the parts of her so molten with desire for him that she was in danger of catching fire.

"Gabe," she murmured, her thighs trembling with need. "Please."

"I have some lube," he said. "Or we can do this the old-fashioned way."

"What's the old-fashioned way?"

He dropped to his knees and scooted closer. "Allow me to show you," he murmured, a wicked gleam in his eye. He looped one of her legs over his shoulder, grabbed her ass and pulled her already throbbing pussy to his mouth.

"Ah yes, I definitely prefer this. Guess I'm an old-fashioned kind of girl," she said, her hands holding on to his head, fingers tangled in the long silky strands of his strip of hair.

His soft laugh teased her sensitive and already slick skin before his tongue and mouth went to work on her clit. The way he roughly massaged her ass cheeks was equally responsible for getting her juices flowing. Her head dropped back as she lost herself to the feel of his mouth and fingers, all tugging at her in ways that quickly increased her excitement. He released her ass with one hand and slipped two fingers inside her. She cried out and then gasped in surprise when he pulled them out and moved them to her ass. Oh yes, this was far better than lubing up with an artificial product. When he decided she was wet enough—was the ocean wet enough?—he eased her back to standing on her own—an incredible feat on her wobbly legs—and then showed her where to put her foot to mount his invention.

He became weirdly businesslike as he positioned the

pathetically small and slightly flaccid dildo inside her. She was so turned on that it actually felt good, and she rocked against it impatiently, wishing it were larger, harder, and pistoning into her like she'd seen in Gabe's earlier demonstration. Next, he fastened a bunch of straps to hold her legs in position, which shifted her clit against that intriguing ridge he'd showed her.

"Hold here," he instructed, pointing out two handle grips on either side of the saddle-shaped center of the device.

She complied, her anticipation building with each added component. The straps around her thighs were incredibly sexy for some reason.

"Anal stimulation?" he asked, as if he were asking if she wanted ketchup with her fries.

"Do you really need to ask?"

She squeaked when he messed with something behind her, and then he abruptly walked away. She turned her head to watch him remove several somethings from the case of skins.

"What kind of shape do you want?"

She laughed. "For my butt?"

"I don't have as many varieties yet. I've been focusing mostly on vaginal stimulation, but I know you like a little tickle in the rear."

"You pick," she said, not sure if she was flushing with embarrassment or excitement. "Just hurry."

He returned and without showing her what he decided on, he attached it with an audible snap and then shifted her slightly. Something pressed against her rear entrance but didn't penetrate her.

"Do you want the nipples clamps too?" he asked.

Jeez, she'd be ready for the nursing home by the time he got her hooked up to the thing.

"I'm all in," she said.

He bit his lip. "I think that might be a bit much to start you with. Maybe next time."

He was probably right, but she couldn't help but be disappointed.

He stepped back and looked her over, adjusting a strap here, tightening a rope there, until he seemed satisfied. Melanie decided she was either in for the ride of her life or would soon be having the most embarrassing trip to the emergency room in the history of sexual deviants. But she didn't have time to worry because Gabe pushed the first button on his remote control.

The small phallus inside her began to churn, and she got a great lesson in how it's not all about the size, but how he uses it before it began to enlarge—first in girth, until she was moaning at the delicious stretch, and then in length until that enlarged bump she'd first been drawn to hit her in a spot that had her screaming in pleasure. And *then* the thing began to thrust. While it was still churning. Holy fuck! Melanie gripped the hand holds with all her strength as an intense vaginal orgasm shuddered through her. That was when Gabe decided to turn on the anal stimulation, which sent her soaring even higher. She couldn't help but rock against the saddle, working against both the ingenuous dildo and the small bead popping in and out of her ass.

"Hold still, baby," Gabe said, his hand touching her shoulder. "Let it do all the work."

She tried staying still, but it was instinctual to move.

"Let's see if this helps," he said, pushing yet another button.

A hard, oscillating vibration buzzed against her clit and while it didn't help her fight her instincts to fuck the ingenious machine, it made her body shudder with an instantaneous clitoral orgasm.

"Gabe," she called, sobbing from the intensity of her pleasure.

"One more, baby," he said. "I need to make sure full functionality doesn't overload the system. Do you think you can handle just a little more?"

More? How could there be more?

He unhooked her bra and let it dangle from her arms before he reached for the slender cords hanging from the pommel in front of her. She moaned as he licked her nipple to wet it and carefully attached one clip. She was lost in a second clitoral orgasm when he was repeating the action on her other breast.

Before she could tell him that she believed it was indeed possible to *die* from too much pleasure, he pushed a button on his remote and a tingle zinged through both nipples, making her insides tighten with breath-stealing rhythmic spasms. The overwhelming force of her release ripped a scream from her throat.

"What in the hell are you doing to her?" Nikki asked from outside the door. "It sounds like she's dying."

She was dying. If dying felt like every cell in your body was having an orgasm simultaneously.

"Just trying out a new prototype," Gabe said. "She's fine. Tell her you're fine, Mel."

"Turn it off," Melanie cried. "Can't take . . . another orgasm. Oh God, I think . . ." She came again, not sure how it was possible when she was still coming from nipple stimulation. But all the things going on in her pussy had pushed her over another edge, and the motion in her ass and the vibrations in her clit drove her beyond yet another height.

"We're going to back you down slowly, babe," Gabe said. "I'll turn off the clit massage first."

"Clit massage?" Nikki was suddenly beside Melanie, trying to see under her thigh.

As soon as the vibration stopped against Melanie's clit, she found the frame of mind to take a breath. And then another.

"What are these things on your nipples?" Nikki asked, touching Melanie's breast.

"Nikki," Gabe said, "I think the lasagna is burning. Let me bring Melanie down, and we'll show you how it works later."

"I get to ride it?"

"Well, no, it's just for Mel, but you can look at it."

"Look at it? But I wanna—"

"Will you two stop arguing and get me off this thing?" Melanie shouted.

"Does watching her get off on a machine turn you on?" Nikki asked. "You're pitching quite the tent there, Force."

"Get out!" Melanie said. She released a sigh of relief when she heard the door close and loosed a second relieved breath when Gabe locked it.

"Should have locked the door earlier," Gabe said. "Sorry about that. I didn't think."

The bead driving her ass crazy popped out one final time, and the tingling stopped in her nipples. Her pussy was mostly numb from all the stimulation, so it took her a minute to realize the dildo inside her had stopped dancing and was slowly decreasing in size.

"She probably thought you were murdering me," Melanie

said, collapsing against the front of the pommel even though doing so pulled at her still-bound legs. "I'm sure I was screaming."

"Was it hurting you?" Gabe said. "I thought you liked it, but maybe I was reading you wrong."

"If you thought I *liked* it, you were definitely wrong. I fucking *loved* it. I do think I might be permanently maimed, however. I can't feel my feet."

"Why didn't you say something?" Gabe said, hurriedly unfastening several buckles.

"Because I was coming too hard to notice at the time." She whimpered when her leg dropped free and her muscles protested at the sudden movement.

"Maybe I need to rethink the restraints," he said, hurrying around to her opposite side to release her other leg.

"I'm not sure I could stay on it without them," she said, pushing herself upright so she was no longer straddling the saddle at an angle. "And you'd have to redesign the clit massager; it wouldn't be at the right angle. Maybe some sort of cushion to rest my belly against would work better. My muscles feel like jelly."

"So you like the current angle?" Gabe asked, his gaze searching hers.

She was surprised he wasn't jotting down notes.

"It's perfect. The whole thing, perfect."

He smiled.

"Its inventor?" She rolled her eyes to the heavens. "A fucking genius."

She wrapped her arms around him and pulled herself off the device. Gabe moved her closer, so that her toes were barely touching the ground and her front was pressed securely against his. She shifted her gaze left and then right when she became aware of something hard pressed into her lower belly. "Is that a drumstick in your pocket or are you just happy to see me?"

"It's the one problem with making your woman get off without you."

She squirmed out of his grasp. "That's one problem I have the solution to."

She backed him into the door and yanked open the fly of his jeans before sinking to her knees and doing her best to make

Force lose mass with rapidly accelerating friction.

CHAPTER ELEVEN

By the time Gabe came to his senses, Melanie's homemade lasagna dinner was undoubtedly cold. The cook was lying on the floor beside him, staring up at the ceiling. Every ten seconds or so, she'd look over at his invention, get a silly look on her face, and then go back to staring up at the ceiling. He hoped he hadn't invented himself out of a lover by creating the ultimate pleasure machine.

"We should probably go eat," he said, tugging his pants up his thighs and fastening them.

"I am hungry," Melanie said, and rolled over onto her knees, searching the floor for her discarded clothing.

Gabe climbed to his feet and retrieved the articles she couldn't reach, dropping them beside her so she could dress. Her legs were shaking so bad, she had a hell of a time putting on her panties.

"Need some help?" he asked with a grin. Watching her dress was a simple pleasure he would never deny himself.

"I think what I really need is a nap." She tipped over onto her back and put her jeans on while lying down. "We need a bed in here. Or you could be a gentleman and carry me to your bed after your machine does its thing."

"Next time," he promised, going over to the device to remove the two skins.

"I can clean those," she said. "As soon as my body remembers how to move when I tell it to, I'll get right on it."

"They're dishwasher safe."

He had to laugh at her mortified expression.

"You're not going to put those in the dishwasher next to the supper dishes, are you?"

"I'll prewash them in the sink," he said, "but yeah, they should be sanitized in the dishwasher after every use."

He used his free hand to help her off the floor and waited

for her to struggle into her bra and shirt. He supposed he could have helped her, but he found her efforts to dress herself endearing. Like watching a toddler try to figure out socks.

"So can we call the invention a success?" He'd put a lot of thought and years of work into the final product. For whatever reason, he needed her validation.

"A success? Yes, you can call it that. You need to put that thing into mass production tomorrow, so the world can be full of very happy women."

"You look more zonked out than happy," he said.

"Trust me, I'm happy. I'm just too disoriented to figure out how to smile."

She did smile, though, when she finally got her shirt on. It was wrong-side out, but he didn't have the heart to tell her.

When he and Melanie meandered into the kitchen, Nikki was sitting at the breakfast bar staring at the pan of lasagna like Garfield the cat, and both his dogs were watching her like she might toss the yummy-smelling dish in their direction at any moment.

"Can we eat?" Nikki asked. "I'm starving."

Melanie collapsed onto the stool beside Nikki while Gabe went to the sink to clean the skins.

"You could have started without us," Melanie said. "We didn't mean to keep you waiting."

"The lasagna's been done for like an hour."

"An hour? Surely we weren't in there that long."

"You were. And all that noise you were making was scaring the dogs."

Gabe grinned to himself as he listened to their conversation.

"When do *I* get a turn on the Sex Stallion?" Nikki asked.

Gabe went perfectly still, and then turned to catch Melanie's eye. "I think we have a name for it."

"Good one, Nik," Melanie said. She laid her head on the counter.

"Well?" Nikki said, both eyebrows raised. "You didn't answer my question. When do I get a turn?"

"The Sex Stallion is for Melanie's enjoyment and hers alone." Gabe opened the dishwasher and placed the washed yet not sanitized skins next to a few dirty glasses and bowls on the top rack.

"That's so not fair."

Melanie lifted one arm and rested her hand on Nikki's back. "Guess you should have seduced the drummer instead of the lead singer after you lied our way backstage."

"I didn't lie. I totally would have had a threesome with you and Shade. You were the only unwilling variable in that equation."

Melanie laughed wearily. "Still unwilling."

Gabe cut the lasagna and shoveled it onto plates with a small spatula. Their meal was still warm, but not exactly hot. "Are we going to eat at the table?"

"Does that require me to move?" Melanie asked, lifting her head just enough to look at him.

"Maybe eating will give you some energy," he said, more than a little proud of his Sex Stallion for satisfying her to exhaustion.

"I bet that thing wouldn't make me tired," Nikki said, drawing a plate toward herself and digging in. "Melanie doesn't have the sexual stamina I do."

Gabe decided teasing Nikki about her extensive sexual practice was inappropriate considering her difficulties with sex addiction, but the joke did cross his mind, even if it didn't escape his lips.

"Sit," Melanie said, patting the stool beside her. "We can eat at the table next time."

Her assurance that there would be a next time made him smile.

"You're so wobbly, I'm afraid you'll fall off your stool," he said, sliding one plate in front of Melanie and the final one in the empty spot next to her.

"I'm not *that* wobbly."

Nikki gave her a playful shove and immediately had to grab Melanie's shirt to rescue her from falling off her stool.

"God, I want to ride that thing," Nikki said once Melanie had regained her balance.

The blush on his bride-to-be's face was so utterly charming that Gabe couldn't resist kissing her before taking the stool next to her.

"I guess I do need to work on my sexual stamina," Melanie said.

"I suggest daily workout sessions," Gabe said. "With me."

"I think I might need twice-daily sessions," she said with a smirk. "I want to be in prime condition as soon as possible. I take my prototype-testing duties very seriously."

"I can take some of the responsibility off you," Nikki offered.

"Sorry, Nik. I'm going to have to be entirely selfish in this case."

Nikki scowled and bit into a piece of garlic toast.

Gabe picked up his fork and took a bite of his lasagna. What his woman lacked in Sex Stallion– riding stamina, she sure made up for in cooking. "This is delicious, babe."

"Glad you like it." She used the edge of her fork to cut into her saucy, cheesy layers of noodles, but couldn't seem to find the energy to put it in her mouth.

"Please, can I ride it?" Nikki asked. "Pretty please with my cherry on top."

Gabe snorted and choked on his mouthful of lasagna.

Beau suddenly turned toward the front door and released a loud bark before scrambling off to investigate. He only did that when a vehicle pulled into the driveway.

"Someone's here," Gabe said, rising from his stool. Lady limped after him as he made his way to the front door. He peeked out the window and recognized his father's truck in the drive. When his oldest sister climbed out of the passenger seat, his heart filled with joy. It had been months since he'd seen Leslie. She was always so busy with her residency in Boston that she rarely made it back to Texas. And his plans to visit her when the band's tour took them through the New England states had obviously fallen through.

Mom was the next to shift out through the passenger door, carefully holding a plate of her latest foil-covered food offering in one hand. She smoothed her free hand over her short light-brown curls and slammed the truck door. Dad brought up the rear, walking slower than the women as he used his cane to assist his stiff left leg. When Gabe opened the door, Beau ran out to greet their latest guests. Lady got only as far as the top step, but based on the enthusiasm of her tail wags and her high-pitched bark, she was happy to see them too.

"I didn't know you all were coming," Gabe said. They'd

been warned about just showing up more than once, but the warnings did no good. Not that he really minded unexpected visits. But now that Melanie was living with him, his family might catch them in a compromising position or three, especially if they happened by his house during prototype runs.

"I texted you over an hour ago," Leslie said. "You never responded, and since we were in the neighborhood . . ." She grinned, her green eyes flashing with familiar teasing.

"Mom and Dad live next door," Gabe reminded her, though next door was almost a mile away. "They're always in the neighborhood."

Leslie climbed the porch steps and hugged Gabe. "You're the fool who thought it was a good idea to live within spitting distance of them," she said quietly.

"Not everyone wants to move to Boston to become some fancy brain surgeon." He gave her an extra tight return squeeze as pride swelled in his chest.

"About that . . ."

"How's the ol' girl doing?" Dad interrupted, bending over to give Lady some attention. "You didn't have to rush home, son. We could have taken care of her."

"What's going on with the band?" Leslie asked. "Daddy said you guys broke up, but that can't be right. How can I tell my friends that my hot little brother is a rock star if your stupid band breaks up?"

Gabe shoved her. "It's all about you, isn't it?"

"Of course it is." She grinned and peeked around Gabe's back. "So is she here? Your new girlfriend?" Her final question was spoken at a whisper.

"She's here. We just sat down to eat dinner, but come on in." He held the door open for everyone, and his cozy dinner instantly became a party.

"There's Melanie," Mom said, rushing over to the kitchen area as if she were greeting her best friend of fifty years. She smooched Melanie's cheek before setting her foil-covered plate on the counter. Gabe would bet his favorite drum kit that Mom's infamous lemon bars were under that foil.

"So good to see you, Kathy," Melanie said, and it warmed Gabe's heart that she actually seemed to mean it. "This is my friend Nikki. She's visiting from Kansas."

"You mean people still live in that state?" Leslie asked.

"A few," Melanie said. "You have to be one of Gabe's sisters. You look just like him. That Mohawk of yours is a dead giveaway."

Leslie's eyes popped wide before she realized Melanie was obviously joking about the Mohawk, and then she laughed. "I love you already," she said. "I'm Leslie, since my brother is too rude to introduce me." She scowled at Gabe, who was standing behind her, waiting for an opening.

"Not rude," Gabe said. "Just can never get a word in when the room is full of Banner women."

"You got that right," Dad said, offering him a high five.

"So are you the doctor doctor or the professor doctor?" Melanie asked, eyes narrowed slightly as if she were trying to read Leslie's mind.

"The doctor doctor." Leslie elbowed Gabe in the ribs. "What have you been telling her about me?"

"Nothing," Gabe said, and he wasn't lying. He didn't talk about his family much, and suddenly wasn't sure why. They were pretty terrific people.

"Are you hungry?" Melanie asked. "I made lasagna. There's plenty for everyone."

"We already ate," Dad said, "but I never say no to lasagna. Especially when these two think I can live on salad."

"It's good for you, Daddy," Leslie said, but she took one look at the deep dish lasagna on the counter and got in line.

The Banners filled their plates, and they all moved to the dining room, which could easily seat twenty people. Gabe was suddenly imagining holidays with his family, his wife, and future kids. When had he become so domesticated? As he watched Melanie talking to his parents and his big sister as if they'd known each other forever, he realized it had happened the moment he'd met her.

"Melanie and I have an announcement." Gabe broke into their conversation about Leslie's high school frog dissection.

"I was wondering when you were going to explain that ring!" Mom said.

He could never get anything past the eagle-eyed heart surgeon.

"Uh, yeah," Gabe said, his announcement now more of a

confirmation. "We've decided to get married."

"And I get to help plan the wedding," Nikki said.

"I knew you two were the real deal," Mom said. "From the moment I first saw you together, I knew it."

"Is that why you practically skipped out of my house the night you met her?" Gabe teased.

"I do not skip," his mom said.

Gabe snorted. "Yes, Dr. Katherine Banner, you do."

"Don't tease," she said, reaching over to slap him playfully. "I thought I'd end up dead before I was blessed with grandchildren."

"Oh, I'm not pregnant!" Melanie blurted.

"But you do want babies, don't you?" Mom asked, actually looking depressed.

Melanie exchanged an uncomfortable look with Gabe. Way to put her on the spot, Mom.

"In a few years," Gabe answered for her.

Mom brightened. "I think I'll still be alive then."

"Oh, stop," Leslie said. "You're still young, Mama."

"And you're well over thirty," Mom said to her eldest daughter, giving her an appraising look. "Your eggs are starting to spoil."

"Katherine, we didn't start having children until you were older than she is," Dad reminded her.

Mom glowered at him. "Because . . ."

"The exact same reason she hasn't settled down," Dad said. "Becoming a surgeon is hard, and you have to dedicate your life to it, especially in the beginning."

"And how hard do you think it is to find a nice normal girl when you're a musician?" Mom countered.

"Since when is Gabe the star child of this family?" Leslie asked.

Gabe chuckled. He and his sisters were highly competitive for parental approval. Only recently had he realized his parents loved them all no matter their faults and real or perceived level of accomplishment. But he got where Leslie was coming from. When both your parents were highly successful, brilliant, and hard-working, it was hard to live up to their standards. Even if those standards were mostly imagined.

"Since I convinced this wonderful woman to be mine,"

Gabe said, reaching for Melanie's hand and kissing it just below her new diamond.

"Didn't take much convincing, to be honest," Melanie said, leaning in to steal a proper kiss from his lips.

"I'm responsible for them meeting in the first place," Nikki said.

"Oh?" Mom asked. "And how do you know Gabe?"

"I'm a huge Sole Regret fan," she said, her face slightly flushed. "I convinced Melanie to go backstage to meet the band. She had no idea he was the band's drummer when she started talking to him."

Melanie cringed. "I think I even insulted the band at one point."

Gabe's family thought that was hilarious. He laughed along with them because it had been Melanie's *not* knowing he was famous that had inspired him to pursue her initially.

"So no romantic prospects of your own," Mom asked Leslie, her gaze hopeful.

"No, but I do have a family announcement to make," Leslie said. "I just wish Jennifer was here to hear it too."

"You're pregnant!" Mom said, wriggling excitedly in her chair.

"No, God no. Mom, will you please stop with the baby talk." Leslie shuddered. "I didn't come to town just for a visit. I have an interview at Houston Methodist this week. If I get the job, I'm moving back to Texas."

"What?" Mom said. "But what about Boston General? It's one of the best hospitals in the entire country. I thought that's why you worked so hard to get your second residency there."

"Houston Methodist is the best in Texas," Leslie said.

"Which makes it the best in the world," Dad said reasonably.

"Obviously," Gabe agreed.

The two ladies from Kansas gave them odd looks while Leslie pled her case.

"I miss my friends. I miss my family. I miss Texas. And Houston isn't too far away from home. I'd get to see you all a lot more often."

"You can take the girl out of Texas," Dad said, "but not Texas out of the girl."

"Are you disappointed in me?" she asked Mom.

"Of course not!" Mom said quickly. "It's just . . . *Boston General*, Leslie. I would have given anything to have been in the position to work there at your age."

"But Daddy wouldn't have been happy in Massachusetts."

"And you aren't happy there," Daddy guessed.

Leslie lowered her eyes. "Everything is just so fast paced. And I'm not talking about the hospital. I can handle my work being crazy-stupid challenging, but when I have a moment, I'd like to be able to freaking breathe, you know?"

"And you think you'll find that in Houston?" Mom asked.

"She thinks she'll find that here," Gabe said. His roots were equally deep. He completely understood why she'd want to come home for good. "Good luck, sis. I hope you get the job." He reached over the table to pat Leslie's hand—her brain surgeon hand. How weird was that?

"I also have an interview at Seton," Leslie said quietly, almost as if she didn't want anyone to hear.

Mom gasped. "Don't throw your career away."

"Did you throw your career away by saving lives in your own community?" Leslie challenged. Mom had not only started her career at Seton, she still worked at that same hospital as the head of the cardiology department.

Gabe was suddenly glad he hadn't become a doctor. He knew his mother honestly wanted what was best for her children, but couldn't she see how she was making Leslie feel? Gabe knew exactly what his sister was feeling. And if he'd completed his PhD in physics as had been his original plan, he might have been having the exact same conversation with his physics professor father right now. At least Jennifer had been smart enough to major in mathematics. Though both his parents had opinions about her educational choices as well.

"Of course I don't think that," Mom said. "It's just . . . You're so brilliant, sweetheart. So talented. So special. And Seton? Seton is so *average*."

"Sometimes it's better to be a big fish in a little pond than a little fish in a big pond," Melanie said, glancing from future mother-in-law to future sister-in-law. "Am I right?"

Leslie gave Melanie a grateful smile, and Gabe loved his heart's choice a little more with every passing moment.

"I'm so intimidated right now," Nikki said. "Are you *all* doctors?" She glanced hopefully at Dad.

"Afraid so," Dad said with a wink. "But I don't save lives. I get my kicks by torturing college students."

Nikki swallowed.

"Did I say torturing?" Dad laughed. "I meant challenging. I get my kicks by *challenging* college students."

"He definitely meant torturing," Gabe said. "I've seen him laugh gleefully over failing grades more than once."

"Not everyone's got what it takes to pass physics," Dad said.

"I would be in that category," Melanie said, raising her hand sheepishly. "The lowest grade I ever got in my life was in physics."

"You never told me that," Gabe said. "Did you fail it?"

"I got a C," she said, grimacing. "C minus. I'm sure I could have done better with the right tutor." The heated look she gave Gabe made his palms go damp. He could definitely get behind tutoring Melanie Anderson.

Nikki laughed. "I doubt the two of you would have gotten any actual studying done."

Exactly.

"I'm not sure I can let my son marry a woman who earned a C minus in physics," Dad said. "Was it calculus-based physics at least?"

Melanie shook her head. "Nope. College physics," she said. "For non-majors."

Dad covered his chest with one hand. "Dr. Banner," he said to his wife. "I think you need to look at my heart. I might be dying."

"Oh, please," Mom said, rolling her eyes. "Stop that. She's going to think you're serious." She turned to Melanie and said, "I got a D in physics the first time I took it and decided to get some help the second go round. How do you think I met this guy?" She jabbed a thumb in Dad's direction.

"So Luke was your physics tutor in college?" Melanie asked.

Mom's grin was entirely too devious for Gabe's comfort, even though he already knew the story behind how his parents had met.

"No, love. He was the teacher."

"Ooo," Nikki said, wiggling her eyebrows. "Did he let you earn extra credit after class?"

"Hell no," Mom said. "He wouldn't even date me until after I graduated."

"It's inappropriate to date a student," Dad said. "No matter how much she throws herself at you."

Gabe laughed at his mother's outraged expression.

"I did *not* throw myself at you!"

"She wrote me love notes at the bottom of all her exams."

Mom licked her lips, refusing to meet anyone's eyes. "I was just thanking you for helping me understand the material."

"I felt thoroughly thanked, my love," he said. "And you have no idea how hard it was for me to maintain my professionalism."

"You weren't too professional," Mom claimed. "You still have copies of all my test papers."

"And I still take them out and read them from time to time."

And then his parents were kissing passionately. Gabe exchanged a disgusted look with his sister, who snorted and shook her head.

"We should get busy washing these dishes," Mom said, "so we can head home and leave these two alone with their houseguest."

Nikki beamed at being remembered.

Leslie smirked at her parents. "Get yourselves to bed early so you can relive your early years together, you mean."

When Mom stood and started to gather plates, Melanie jumped from her chair as if a rattlesnake had struck her in the ass. "No need," Melanie said. "I'll get the dishes."

"It's a standing rule in this family," Mom said. "The cook never washes the dishes." She gave Gabe a stern look, as if he'd broken that sacred rule.

"It's fine," Melanie said. "Really. I don't mind." She took the dishes from Mom's hands and carried them out of the dining room.

"Melanie, dear," Mom said, staring at Melanie's back. "I think your shirt is on wrong-side out. There's a tag . . ." Mom reached for the tag poking out through Melanie's hair at the nape of her neck, and Melanie scurried forward, her face redder than the tomato sauce on the plates she was carrying.

"I didn't realize," Melanie said. "Thanks. But I've got the dishes. Please sit down, Kathy."

Gabe didn't recall Melanie being particularly fond of washing dishes. Perhaps she was trying to impress his family—or escape their scrutiny. He felt bad for not pointing out her shirt was on wrong-side out earlier.

His mother followed Melanie, and after a moment of listening to them argue about who was going to do the dumb dishes, Gabe went to investigate.

"Please, Kathy, allow me," Melanie said.

She made a dive for the dishwasher when his mother moved to open it. And then Gabe realized why she was so insistent on doing the dishes. There were certain embarrassing items on the dishwasher's top rack.

"I should be the one to do the dishes," Gabe said. "You two go sit and visit. Maybe you can help Nikki come up with some ideas for the wedding."

Mom stopped trying to wrestle a spatula out of Melanie's grip and wrapped an arm around her shoulders. "Are you thinking a destination wedding? Or something a bit closer to home?"

"Actually," Melanie said, shooting Gabe a look of gratitude as she handed him the dirty spatula. "We were thinking of having the wedding here. In the woods around Gabe's house."

"Just as long as it doesn't involve riding those noisy ATVs of his," Mom said.

"What a great idea, Mom!" Gabe said, turning on the water in the sink. He decided it was probably best to sanitize the Sex Stallion skins on their own cycle rather than with the supper plates, but he couldn't very well just whip them out while his mom was watching him with her eyes narrowed.

"I'll pour sugar in your gas tanks if you even think about ruining your ceremony with those damned things," she threatened.

"We were actually thinking of something a little more sedate," Melanie said, directing Mom back to the dining room.

Thinking he was alone, Gabe opened the dishwasher just as his father hobbled into the room. Gabe slammed the door shut and smiled at Dad, hoping he didn't look too suspicious. The man was a teacher. He could spot a guilty conscience with practiced ease.

"You sure you're ready to settle down?" Dad asked quietly. He obviously didn't want to upset the wedding-planning women chatting excitedly in the dining room.

"With Melanie?" Gabe smiled. "One hundred percent sure."

"It's just a bit sudden is all. How long have you known her?"

"Long enough to know she's my one."

Dad smiled. "The physics of love. Completely unfathomable."

"Did you know right away with Mom?" Gabe asked.

"Yep. And it scared the hell out of me. You seem to be dealing well with the idea, however."

"Well, Melanie's not ten years younger than I am," Gabe said with a chuckle. "Or my student."

"That wasn't the scary part," Dad said. "The scary part was thinking I might have to live even a single day of my life without her."

There was no doubting which of his parents was the most romantic. He was pretty sure it was the same for himself and Melanie. When it came to love, Melanie was far more practical about her feelings than he was.

"I feel the same for Mel. And we're supposed to be men of science." Gabe snorted.

"The most important qualities for any scientist are a sense of wonder and being able to accept that there are things in this universe that we will never be able to explain."

I am my father's son, Gabe thought wryly.

Dad licked his lips and watched his fingers drum on the countertop. "Are you going to go back and finish your degree now that your band is over? I'm sure I could get you a late admission wavier for fall semester."

Gabe decided that asking that question was the real reason his father had cornered him in the kitchen.

"I've thought about it," Gabe said. "But I'm not ready to give up on my music just yet."

"You could always play drums as a hobby," Dad said.

"I could," Gabe said, "but I don't think I'd be satisfied. I will definitely let you know if I decide to go back to school. I'll play that nepotism card like a fiddle."

Dad slapped him on the back hard enough to sting. His smile lit up his entire face, even brightening his eyes. "Whatever makes you happy, son."

"Melanie makes me happy. Everything else good in my life is just gravy."

CHAPTER TWELVE

AFTER SAYING goodbye to Gabe's family and promising to have lunch with Leslie later in the week, Melanie collapsed on the sofa. Her body still hadn't fully recovered from her amazing ride on the Sex Stallion, but her mental exhaustion far surpassed her physical weariness.

"If I'm going to live here," Melanie said to Gabe, turning her head with more effort than she'd willingly admit to watch him approach, "you have to promise me one thing."

Gabe cringed. "I'm sorry they just showed up like that. I've told my parents at least a hundred times that they need to *call* before they stop in."

"That's not my concession." Though she could see how them showing up whenever they felt like it might be a problem.

"Name it," he said, sitting beside her on the sofa and wrapping an arm around her shoulders to draw her closer.

"We have to get a second dishwasher installed specifically for sex-gadget washing." She'd almost died of embarrassment when she thought her future mother-in-law would see those Sex Stallion skins hanging out on the top rack of the dishwasher. "Is it possible to install it in the sex-gadget room?"

Gabe laughed and gave her a tight squeeze. "That's a great idea. I'll start working on the plumbing tomorrow."

The tension drained out of Melanie's body, and she relaxed against him, her eyes drifting shut. They popped open again when a sound that reminded her of air compressors on carnival rides came from near Gabe's—and she supposed her—bedroom.

"Nikki, you'd better not be in there messing with my new toy," Melanie shouted.

Nikki emerged from the hallway holding Gabe's remote control. "You said you'd show me how it works."

"I'm too tired to move at the moment," Melanie said. "Let's just watch some TV or something."

"Gabe, are you too tired to show me?" Nikki asked.

Gabe perked up instantly. "Do you really want to know how it works?"

"I really want to ride it," Nikki said. "And I don't care if Mel got her cum all over it. I like Mel's cum."

Gabe stiffened, and Melanie slid a hand up his neck. "She doesn't know that from experience," Melanie assured him. "She thinks you'll find that sexy enough to let her get her way."

"I could know that from experience," Nikki said. "If you'd give me the chance to show you that I know my way around a pussy."

"Nikki, I'm not sure it's a good idea for you to get all worked up when you're trying to break your sex addiction," Gabe said.

"My doctor said it might help if I had a device to take the edge off. It could keep me from seeking another partner," Nikki said.

"Sounds like strange advice," Melanie said. "When you're fighting alcohol addiction, you don't drink wine to take the edge off."

"I'm just repeating what he said."

"I can give you a handheld vibrator," Gabe said. "I've made dozens of prototypes over the years."

Melanie snorted. "I can't believe you just offered to give my friend a vibrator."

"I wouldn't mind letting her give the Stallion a go," he whispered close to Melanie's ear, so Nikki wouldn't overhear. "See how another responds to it."

"I'm not sharing it with her," Melanie said. "It's mine." She already had a strange emotional attachment to the machine. Maybe because Gabe had invented it and put it together with such obvious care. Or maybe because it gave her amazing orgasms and her hormones had caused her to bond with the damned thing. Whatever the case, she did not want Nikki on it.

"I don't have to ride it," Nikki said in a sorrowful tone. "But you can still show me how it works, can't you, Gabe?"

"If Melanie doesn't mind."

"Melanie just wants to take a nap," Melanie said. "Show it to her, but you're not riding it, Nik."

Gabe kissed Melanie's temple and then shifted away,

allowing her to stretch out on the sofa. Not even the muffled sound of Gabe describing the functions of his machine, Nikki's responses, or the mechanical sounds coming from the small bedroom kept Melanie awake long enough to contemplate why she was okay with her fiancé showing her sex-addict of a best friend the innermost workings of his greatest achievement in sex toy inventions.

The next thing she knew, it was morning and she was sprawled naked across Gabe's—and she supposed now her—king-size bed. Groaning, with no recollection of how she'd gotten to bed or where her clothes had gone, she rubbed her face and concentrated on the noise that must have woken her. From the small bedroom next door came a high-pitched whirring, like one produced by a drill, only louder. Melanie sat up, found Gabe's side of the bed empty, and searched through a box of her clothes for something to cover her nakedness. She settled on an overlarge T-shirt since she couldn't locate her robe and made sure she put it on right-side out. How mortifying had it been that her future mother-in-law had caught her with her shirt wrong-side out? Melanie had planned to unpack her stuff last night, but apparently she'd been completely down for the count. So much for spending her first official romantic night in her new home with the love of her life. Thanks to her utter exhaustion, she didn't doubt that she'd even snored and drooled while she'd slept. All that noise coming from the small bedroom was probably Gabe building an escape hatch.

She walked extra slowly on sore and stiff legs as she went to investigate. She really did need to build up her strength, stamina, and flexibility. She found Gabe on his hands and knees drilling a hole through the floor in one corner of the room. Admiring his ass, Melanie crossed her arms and leaned against the doorframe.

"Isn't it a little early to be making all that noise?" she asked.

Gabe peeked at her over his shoulder. "Did I wake you?"

"I'm not sure. Probably."

"Sorry about that. And it's almost noon. Not exactly early."

"You're kidding!" She must have slept almost sixteen hours. Holy crap.

"I think maybe we should have started with one or two stimulators instead of all four at once. I made note of it."

"Where's Nikki? Did you have breakfast? What are your

plans for the day?"

"Nikki is snuggling with the dogs. I had some coffee. Need to go to town today and try to get in touch with Amanda since she never bothered to call me, and while I'm out, I think I'll purchase my lady's requested new dishwasher."

"Jacob's Amanda?" Melanie asked, trying to wrap her head around all the answers he'd volleyed at her.

"Yeah, I figured she might know what's going on in Jacob's head, because I sure as hell can't figure it out." Gabe cleared his throat. "Also need to stop by Lindsey's gynecologist to give my blood sample."

Melanie blew out a breath. "Sounds like we have a busy day," she said. "Assuming I'm invited to accompany you."

"Fair assumption," he said with a grin. "I've been twiddling my thumbs around here all morning waiting for you to find the strength to climb out of bed. I'd have harassed you about your laziness, but I feel sort of responsible."

He looked so cute when he brushed his hair back sheepishly that her heart fluttered.

"You are entirely responsible," she said with a laugh. "But I forgive you." She walked over and gave the Sex Stallion a pat. "I'll be seeing you later," she said. "Do we have time for me to take a shower?" she asked Gabe.

Gabe sniffed in her direction, and his nose crinkled in disgust. "Yes, we definitely have time for you to shower."

She swatted his ass before darting away and heading for the master bathroom. She'd forgotten how many shower heads the guy had installed. It took her a good twenty minutes to get the flow and temperature just right and then once she was in the soothing yet invigorating jets of water, she didn't want to get out.

"What's taking so long? Are you masturbating in there?" Gabe asked from somewhere beyond the steamed-up glass shower wall.

"No," she said. Well, maybe a little. But then no matter how she turned, she had jets aimed at her ass and both tits. What did he expect?

"Nikki's staying here with the dogs, so we have the entire day to ourselves." The shower door opened, and Gabe stepped inside. He was perfectly naked, and his cock was already standing at rigid attention.

"Does plumbing turn you on?" she asked with a grin, moving closer to press up against him.

"You turn me on," he said. "I've been in the other room thinking about you naked and alone in my shower for thirty minutes now."

"Our shower," she said, dropping a kiss on his collarbone.

"Yes," he whispered. "Ours."

By the time they'd gotten each other all messy and then clean again, it was well past lunchtime.

"Wear something nice," Gabe requested, standing behind her as she stared into the empty half of his walk-in closet. The half he'd so thoughtfully cleared out for her to use.

She'd hung up a few dresses, but most of her clothes were still in suitcases, bags, and boxes. And her winter wardrobe was back at her apartment in Kansas. She wondered if she'd ever need winter clothes in Texas.

"I'm taking you out to dinner after we run our errands."

"You don't have to wine and dine me, Mr. Banner. You already got into my pants."

"Prepared to be wined and dined for life."

He kissed her bare shoulder, and she shivered.

"Also prepare for me to be in your pants for life."

She laughed. "There is no way to prepare for that."

"I guess you'll just have to wing it, then."

He helped her pick out underwear—a sexy black lace set—and she chose a tight pair of black boxer briefs for him that made his ass look good enough to bite. She'd never had a man tell her what he wanted her to wear under her clothes. She wasn't sure why she found that simple request so sexy, so intimate. Her heart was literally throbbing as she watched him dress. She'd thought she'd been in love before, but it had never been like this.

"What are you grinning about?" he asked as he struggled to button his sleeves. She took over the task, still standing in her bra and panties, because who could think about putting on clothes when Gabe Banner was in the same room?

"I was thinking I was wrong about being in love."

The pained gasp he emitted made her heart twist.

"Not with you," she amended hurriedly. "I could never be wrong about you. I meant the men I dated in the past. I thought I loved them, but now . . ." She shook her head. "That wasn't love.

Affection maybe. Attraction, to some degree. But this? What I feel for you? This is what love is supposed to feel like."

"Mel," he whispered, and the next thing she knew, she was in his arms and being kissed until her knees went weak. When he drew away, he pressed her head against his chest, holding her there with one large hand. His breath came in ragged gasps, and his heart thudded to a powerful beat beneath her ear. "I am so in love with you, I can hardly breathe."

"I have an inhaler in my purse." When he said things like that, the emotions inside her swelled until she couldn't breathe either, so she had to joke or she'd die.

He laughed and lowered his hands to squeeze her ass. "Get dressed or we're never going to leave this room today."

"Promise?"

He groaned and pulled away from her, kissing her lightly. "I'll wait for you in the truck," he said.

"I'll try to hurry, but it takes me forever to do my hair," she said. But then she remembered Nikki was there. Nikki was amazingly proficient at calming Melanie's waist-length curls. Usually Melanie put her hair up in a sloppy bun or twist, but she knew Gabe liked it down—just not in the raccoon-nest fashion it ended up being when she styled it herself. "Could you send Nikki in here to help me?"

"After you put your clothes on," he said. "I see the way she looks at you."

"She didn't sleep with us last night, did she?" Melanie didn't know if she had or not. She didn't even remember going to bed and had slept half the day away.

"No. She fell asleep on the sofa as the filling in a Labrador sandwich."

Melanie chuckled, wishing she'd seen that. She reached for her go-to little black dress and slipped it over her head. "There," she said. "Though honestly, Gabe, it doesn't really matter. She's seen me naked a thousand times."

"Now that you're mine, no one gets to see you naked but me."

She rolled her eyes at his posturing, but didn't argue. She sort of liked when he was possessive of her. It gave her the right to be just as possessive of him.

Gabe left her to find her shoes. She was placing her most

expensive pairs of heels on her half of the shoe rack in the closet when Nikki came into the room, still in her pajamas, the two dogs trailing her.

"Gabe said you needed help," Nikki said, examining Melanie's elegant attire with one eyebrow raised. "Are you going somewhere fancy? I thought you were shopping for dishwashers or something equally boring."

"Gabe's taking me out to dinner after we run a few errands. I was going to wear my hair down, but you know I can't get it to look decent without your help."

"I'm on it," she said.

She found the bathroom box and searched for the various products and tools—hair dryer, curling brush—she'd need. Melanie slipped on a pair of black high heels and sat in front of the vanity mirror, applying her make-up while Nikki worked wonders with Melanie's stupid hair.

"I see you've made some new friends," Melanie said as Beau and Lady found comfortable spots on the bathroom rug to watch Nikki worshipfully.

"They're sweethearts," she said. "Both of them. If I ever run into the kid that hit Lady with his truck, I'll . . . I'll . . ." She gritted her teeth and brandished a hairbrush menacingly.

"He might still be out in the cornfield across the road looking for his keys."

"We're going to go bite him, aren't we, Beau?"

Beau barked, his tongue lolling to one side.

Nikki worked curl relaxer into Melanie's hair with both hands. "So will you and Gabe be out late?" she asked, her attention on Melanie's head.

"Probably. There should be some leftover lasagna in the fridge. You can heat it up for dinner." Melanie hoped Nikki didn't expect to accompany them. "Or we can bring you back something from the restaurant if you want."

"I'll be fine here with the dogs," Nikki said. "Gabe showed me how to massage Lady's shoulder so she doesn't get too stiff. It's not good to leave her alone so much. And she needs help off the porch so she doesn't have an accident in the house."

Melanie was glad that Nikki felt responsibility for the dog's well-being. She needed something to keep her occupied.

"Have you been massaging her shoulder this morning? I

think she's walking better today," Melanie said, pausing in applying her mascara to look at Nikki in the mirror.

Nikki grinned. "She loves it. And so does Beau. I can't leave him out."

"It's a good thing you're here to take care of them when Gabe and I have to be gone."

"Happy to be of assistance," Nikki said, dropping a little curtsy.

Melanie almost hated to ask her next question, but she was curious. "How were your nightmares last night?"

Nikki's smile widened, and she met Melanie's eyes in the mirror. "The only nightmare I had last night was when Beau passed lasagna gas in my face."

Melanie laughed and reached up to squeeze Nikki's hand. "That's fantastic. Well, not the doggie stink bombs, but that you didn't have nightmares."

Nikki licked her lips and lowered her gaze. "I feel . . . *safe* here."

Before Melanie could respond, Nikki switched on the hairdryer. That was all Melanie had ever wanted for Nikki, for her to feel safe. And useful. Needed and loved. She hoped Gabe was okay with their living situation becoming permanent, because Melanie wouldn't have the heart to send Nikki away.

When Nikki finally set the hairdryer aside, Melanie checked out her hair in the mirror. "You work miracles," Melanie said, turning her head this way and that.

"Thanks," Nikki said. She hugged Melanie's head to her belly. "For never turning your back on me. Never giving up on me. Just . . . Thanks."

"Don't make me cry," Melanie pleaded. "My mascara isn't waterproof."

Beau's snout was suddenly under Nikki's elbow, nudging her for attention.

"You want a hug too?" Nikki asked, releasing Melanie and dropping to her knees to hug the big black dog. He slobbered down the back of her shoulder as he panted happily, but Nikki didn't seem to mind.

"I have to say," Gabe said from the doorway, his eyes trained on his dog, "I'm a little jealous. You traitor."

"Oh," Nikki said. "Gabe needs a hug too."

Nikki jumped to her feet and leapt against Gabe's chest, both arms circling his neck. She squeezed him until he protested. "I can't breathe."

"Thanks for loving my Melanie the way she deserves to be loved," Nikki said.

Gabe met Melanie's eyes over Nikki's shoulder. "It's a privilege."

Nikki leaned away from Gabe, and his eyes widened. "Hey," he said. "Hands off the merchandise."

"I've always wanted to know if your ass feels as good as it looks," she said.

"Nikki!" Melanie bellowed.

"It does." She laughed and dashed out of the bathroom with Beau on her heels. Lady took a little longer to follow as she had to get her legs under her, but once she was standing, she trotted after her two exasperating friends.

"Can't blame her, I guess," Melanie said, rising from the bench in front of the vanity and squeezing Gabe's ass herself. "It is a nice ass."

"You look amazing," he said, nuzzling the side of her neck. "You do know we're just going shopping for a dishwasher, right?"

"I thought you were taking me out to dinner."

"You didn't have to go all out for the Taco Bell drive-through."

She poked him in the ribs, but played along. "I do love their quesadillas."

"If you're hungry for Mexican food, I'll take you to Fonda San Miguel. Their food is . . ." He rolled his eyes in bliss. "Or if you'd rather have a great view of Lake Travis, we can go to the Oasis. But decide quick; I'll need to make reservations for Fonda."

"A Mexican restaurant that requires a reservation?" Her stomach rumbled at the thought of food. "Sign me up. You're more gorgeous a view than I can handle as it is."

He actually blushed at her compliment and leaned in to steal a kiss. "I'll take you to the Oasis next time. Maybe Nikki would like to join us."

Melanie grabbed a banana to tide her over until dinner. Gabe followed her out of the house and down the driveway, wolf whistling and making suggestive comments as she concentrated on walking on gravel in heels. If any other man had been as obnoxiously obsessed with staring at her ass while she navigated the uneven terrain, she'd have told him to suck her banana, but when Gabe ogled her, it merely incited her to swing her hips a bit more.

He helped her up into the truck, his hands lingering on her waist longer than necessary.

"I should take you out more often," he said. "Show off my prize."

"For that," she said, tapping him on the shoulder with her yet unopened banana. "I'm going to eat this banana just for you." She massaged her lips with her teeth to plump them up and draw his attention to her mouth.

He released a long slow breath. "Then again, keeping you at home has certain advantages."

He shut her inside the truck and hurried around to the driver's side while she peeled the banana. Melanie took delicate nibbles from the tip of the sweet fruit, drawing bites into her mouth with overexaggerated licks and sucks.

"I can't watch," Gabe said, shaking his head and squeezing his eyes shut. "I'll never be able to drive if I do."

"I'll behave," she said. "In public. But the next time I get you alone in private, I'll be repaying you for inventing that Sex Stallion."

He chuckled and started the truck. "I'll be counting the seconds."

"You'll be getting more than seconds, Banner. I'm talking thirds and fourths here."

"I meant seconds of time, but I can go for thirds. Not sure about fourths."

He backed out of the driveway, and they were finally off to run their errands. Because they'd left late, they had to go to the OB/GYN clinic first so he could give his blood sample. Part of Melanie didn't want to know if he was about to become the father of some other woman's child, but she knew she'd need a couple of months to wrap her head around the idea and get her jealousy in check. She promised herself that if Gabe was to become a father, she'd be nothing but supportive and would never burden him with any hurt or negative feelings she continued to harbor. What had happened with Lindsey had occurred before they met, and while she didn't like the idea of him having had orgies with groupies, it wasn't her place to make him feel bad about it.

"Do you want to go inside or wait here?" Gabe said. "I'll leave the truck's AC running so you don't melt."

"I'll come with you."

"Are you sure?"

She nodded and opened the door, struggling not to face plant out of the huge truck as she tried to get her spiky heels safely to the ground without having her skirt fly up over her head. Gabe hurried around the truck to help her, and once they were walking toward the entrance, she noticed his hands were trembling as he clutched her fingers.

"Are you nervous?"

"I don't want this baby to be mine," he said quietly. "Happy, healthy and loved, but not mine."

She squeezed his hand because she felt exactly the same way, but said, "But if it is yours, I know it will be happy and loved." She leaned into his arm, her heart full to bursting as she imagined the children they'd have together in the future. She hoped he didn't make her wait too long to start a family. She couldn't think of anything grander than watching him hold their child for the first time.

At the reception desk, Gabe gave his name and informed the woman that he was supposed to give a sample for a paternity test. They sat among a room of women, a few obviously pregnant, while he waited to be called back. A few minutes later, Owen and Caitlyn emerged from the back of the office. Gabe was so busy staring at the floor that he didn't notice, so Melanie elbowed him and then called out, "Owen." She lifted her arm and waved.

Owen smiled and hurried over to meet them, towing Caitlyn behind him by one hand.

"Here for the paternity test?" Owen asked.

"Why else?" Gabe replied.

"You look queasy," he said to Gabe. "Lindsey had to give blood, but they just rubbed the inside of my cheek with a cotton swab."

"That's a relief," Gabe said, though he didn't look any less queasy. "Has everyone else already tested?"

"Tex was here earlier, and I'll let Kellen know later."

"Avoiding him is not going to solve your problem," Caitlyn said, giving Melanie a pointed look that she didn't understand.

Owen continued as if Caitlyn hadn't spoken. "I still can't get ahold of Jacob, and Adam's supposed to get his sample taken up in Dallas."

"How's your brother?" Gabe asked, and Melanie's heart twisted.

"Conscious," Owen said, but he didn't elaborate.

A nurse peeked out the door that led to the back of the office, and called Gabe's name. Melanie started to rise with him, but he pressed her back into the seat. "I'll be back in a few minutes."

Melanie watched Gabe follow the nurse, wondering why he didn't want her to go with him.

"Is there a bathroom around here?" Caitlyn asked.

Owen pointed toward the far corner of the room, and Caitlyn grabbed Melanie's wrist.

"Come with me," Caitlyn said. Girl code for *I need to talk to you without my man listening.*

Melanie excused herself and followed Caitlyn to the single unisex bathroom. Sharing it was not the least bit suspicious. Right . . .

Caitlyn switched on the light, and they both entered the fairly large bathroom. Melanie frowned at the exposed toilet while Caitlyn locked the door.

"I'm so glad I ran into you," Caitlyn said. "I don't have your number."

"What's this about?" Melanie asked. She scarcely knew Caitlyn and wasn't sure why Caitlyn wanted to talk to her.

"These men have made an absolute mess of their lives. Dawn and I are trying to figure out how to get them all back together. We were thinking of throwing a party, but don't think Jacob and Adam will come. What about Gabe? Is he as pissed off at them all as Owen is?"

Melanie scowled. "I don't think he's pissed at all. A bit lost and not sure what to do, but not angry. Well, maybe a little mad at Jacob, but we saw Adam yesterday and they got along just fine."

"You saw Adam?" Caitlyn sounded disbelieving, as if Melanie had said she'd met the pope.

"He's in Dallas with Madison. The poor woman is stuck in a plaster cast from her waist to her wrist. I guess that horse really messed up her shoulder."

"Has Adam made up with Jacob?"

Melanie snorted. "He said he'd talk to Jacob, but I honestly don't see that happening."

"The guys have to get this band back together. Or *we* have to get this band back together." Caitlyn waved one hand back and forth between them.

Melanie rather liked having Gabe all to herself and was in no rush to send him back on the road with all his fangirls trying to get a piece of her pie. She scratched her nose, trying to decide how best to explain her position to Caitlyn.

"Is that an engagement ring?" Caitlyn sputtered, grabbing Melanie's hand and staring down at her new rock.

"Oh. Yeah. Gabe proposed."

"That's it!" Caitlyn shouted, making Melanie's heart thump in surprise. "We'll throw an engagement party for you two. Kellen, Jacob, and Adam will have to come."

"Well, to be fair, you'd better throw one for Madison and Adam as well. He also popped the question."

Caitlyn's eyes went wide. "Shut up!"

Melanie pressed her lips together and drew her chin back. "Excuse me?"

"Here." Caitlyn handed her cellphone to Melanie. "We don't have time to sort this out right now. Give me your number. I'll hash out some details with Dawn and keep you in the loop."

"I'm not sure what you want from me." But Melanie obediently added her number to Caitlyn's contacts.

The door handle jiggled, and Caitlyn called out, "Occupied!" To Melanie, she said, "I'll explain better when we have more time to talk."

Still not sure what the woman was up to, Melanie returned Caitlyn's phone and followed her out of the bathroom. The woman waiting to use the facilities gave them an odd look but didn't say anything about the two of them hanging out in a unisex bathroom designed for one occupant.

Owen had taken a seat and was staring down at his phone, a

troubled crease in his brow.

Caitlyn sat in the chair beside him and took his hand. "Any news?"

"Chad will be stateside on Wednesday," he said.

"That soon? That has to be good news, doesn't it?" Caitlyn rubbed his back and nodded encouragingly.

Melanie was glad he had someone to depend on. The poor guy had been through a lot in the past week.

"I could sure use some good news," Owen said.

"Gabe has a little," Caitlyn said, pointing at Melanie's left hand with an ear-to-ear grin on her face.

Owen stared at Melanie's hand and then his eyes lifted to meet hers. "You're getting married?"

She grinned and nodded.

Owen jumped to his feet, hugging her as if she'd just told him he'd won the Publishers Clearing House sweepstakes. "That's fantastic," he said. "Does Gabe know?"

Melanie laughed. "Well, I hope so. He's the one I'm marrying."

Caitlyn winked repeatedly at Melanie as if she had something in her eye. "I was just telling Melanie that we should throw an engagement party for them. What do you think?"

"Will Kellen be there?" Owen asked, giving Caitlyn the evil eye, which stopped her spastic winking.

"We'd have to invite him, Owen. He's one of Gabe's best friends."

"Then I'm not coming."

Melanie tried to read Owen's and Caitlyn's minds, but she had no idea why Owen wouldn't want to see his best friend. Owen and Kellen were inseparable whenever she was around them. She didn't understand how that could have changed so quickly.

"Did Kellen . . . *do* something?" she asked, her curiosity sending politeness packing.

"Yeah," Owen said, his expression dark. "He kissed me. On the fucking lips." He pointed to his mouth as if Melanie would be able to see the evidence still there.

"Oh," Melanie said, and then she laughed. "I had a friend— a *female* friend—do that to me not long ago. It is rather upsetting."

"I'm assuming you told her to take a hike and to never speak to you again," Owen said, crossing his arms over his chest and nodding smugly at Caitlyn.

"Well, no." Melanie wasn't sure how much she should reveal about Nikki's psychological problems, so settled on telling her half of the truth. "She's currently living with me and Gabe. She was confused and knows she crossed a line. But people make mistakes. I'd hate to lose something as precious as a friendship over something as trivial as a little kiss."

"*Thank* you!" Caitlyn said emphatically, throwing her hands toward the ceiling.

"It wasn't trivial," Owen said between clenched teeth.

"Why?" Caitlyn said. "Because he made you *feel* something you aren't prepared to admit?"

People were starting to stare. Melanie touched Owen's arm to try to calm him—he was obviously very upset—but he pulled away. "I'm leaving," he said. "Tell Gabe I'll talk to him soon." And he stalked off.

"I'll call you," Caitlyn said quickly to Melanie and then hurried after Owen. "Don't walk away mad. Let's talk about this."

"I've already talked about it, but you don't seem to understand . . ."

Melanie didn't catch the end of his complaint as he exited through the first set of glass double doors that led outside.

Melanie smiled at the women staring at her—seeing as they could no longer stare at Owen and Caitlyn—then plopped down in the nearest chair and picked up a magazine. She was so glad Gabe's life wasn't in turmoil. He had a few problems, but nothing in comparison to Owen's—unless that baby ended up being Gabe's. She realized she was reading an article about breast pumps and dropped the magazine on the seat next to her.

Gabe came out a moment later, looking no less grim than he had when he'd gone back to give his DNA sample.

"Did Owen leave?" he asked. "I wanted to talk to him."

"He and Caitlyn were having a little argument," Melanie said with a shrug.

"Owen was arguing?" Gabe asked, turning toward the exit.

"Is that unusual for him?"

"Yeah." Gabe released a heavy sigh. "I guess I'm not the

only one whose life has fallen to pieces."

Melanie reached up and took his hand. "I don't think your life is going so bad," she said. "You are engaged to a pretty hot babe." She gave him the sexy come-hither look she sometimes practiced in the mirror.

"My one lifeboat in a sea of shit." He smiled, the light of happiness replacing his troubled gaze. "Let's go get your automatic dildo washer."

A nearby woman snorted, and then scrunched down in her chair, as if that would make her invisible.

"Okay," Melanie said with a scowl, "yeah, thanks for that. Let's tell the whole world I need one, why don't we?" But her Gabe was too wonderful to stay cross with for more than a millisecond.

CHAPTER THIRTEEN

GABE SIPPED his lime margarita and watched the light play with the highlights in Melanie's hair while she looked over the menu. Their new dishwasher was in the back of the truck, Amanda hadn't been home when they'd stopped by her house, and they'd made it to the restaurant just in time for their dinner reservation. After such a busy afternoon, it was nice to sit and enjoy Melanie's company. Hell, just looking at her was a splendid way to spend his evening. It almost allowed him to forget that his life really was a sea of shit at the moment.

"You never told me what Owen and Caitlyn were arguing about," Gabe said as Melanie debated between the Relleno de Picadillo and Cochinita Pibil. She couldn't go wrong with either. The food at this restaurant was always top-notch.

"Um . . . I'm not sure he wants you to know that," she said, flipping the menu over. "Maybe I should close my eyes and point at the menu. Order whatever I land on." She did just that and opened her eyes to read what her finger had selected. "Enchiladas de Pato. Duck? They have *duck* enchiladas. Can you believe it?"

"I'm sure they're delicious," he said. "Order a couple of things to try. We can always take leftovers home to Nikki." That comment sent her scouring the menu for dishes Nikki might like, but Gabe hadn't forgotten that she hadn't answered his question. "Does Owen and Caitlyn's disagreement have something to do with Kellen?" He was guessing, but obviously had done a good job, because Melanie went still.

"So you know why Owen's mad at Kellen?" she asked.

"Of course," Gabe lied, taking a sip of his margarita because he was a bad liar. "What do you think about their problem?"

"It's not that big a deal." Melanie shrugged. "A little unwanted kiss isn't the end of the world."

Gabe set his drink down. Hard. "One of them kissed you?"

Melanie's pretty brow screwed up. "What? No. I'm talking

about how Kellen kissed Owen and Owen completely freaked out over it."

Gabe blinked at her. "Kellen kissed Owen?"

Melanie's mouth dropped open. "You said you knew. You tricked me."

"On the mouth?" Gabe asked flatly.

"There are worse places he could have kissed him." Melanie giggled.

Gabe slapped his forehead. "No wonder Owen flipped the fuck out."

"Not a big deal."

"When a grown-ass man kisses you on the mouth, it's a very big fucking deal," Gabe said. "If he wanted him to, that's fine, but . . ." Gabe shook his head, having a hard time grasping that Kellen had the hots for Owen. That was what that kiss had been about, wasn't it? "What the fuck is happening to my friends? They've all lost their damned minds."

"Are you ready to order?" their server asked.

Of all the bad timing.

"Give us a minute," Gabe said, perhaps too harshly, because the young man darted away as if the kitchen were on fire.

"At least you're still sane," Melanie said, reaching for his hand.

He allowed her to hold it, but didn't turn his hand over to clasp hers in return. "That's funny, because I feel like I'm going crazy."

"Why?"

Probably because his usual release of aggression was to flail a pair of sticks against the skins of his drum kit, and he hadn't so much as held a drumstick in over a week. "I miss performing. I miss the road. I miss my band. I miss my life."

Melanie went perfectly still, her face transforming into an emotionless mask. He'd never seen her react that way and wasn't sure what to make of it. She released his hand and sat back in her chair.

"If that's what you want, I can go back to Kansas."

"What?" He shook his head. "That's not what I meant at all. I don't want those things to replace you. Don't you see? I want it all."

"And if you can't have it all, will I be enough?"

He blinked at her. Was she really asking him that? "Why shouldn't I be able to have it all?"

"You should," she said almost too quietly to hear over the din of the noisy restaurant. "But if your band never gets back together, am I enough to make you happy?"

That was a lot of burden to place on one person. It wasn't her job to make him happy. He was happy when he was with her, but he would always need more in his life. Everyone needed something to call their own. If it wasn't his band, at the very least Gabe would need a career he could be proud of.

"I'm unequivocally happy when I'm with you," he said. "But I'm not Nikki."

She cocked her head. "What's that supposed to mean?"

"That you're used to someone depending solely on you for their every happiness." Melanie liked Nikki's dependence on her. He'd seen the two of them together enough to recognize their dynamic.

"But I don't want that with you," she said.

"Are you sure? Because it sure seems that way to me."

Melanie's hand balled into a fist on the tabletop, and she lifted it to press it against her eye. "Why are we arguing about this?" She shook her head, then dropped her hand and lifted her gaze to meet his.

"I don't think you recognize what a difficult time I'm having, Mel. My whole world has been turned upside down."

"And mine hasn't? I left my family behind, my job, my apartment, and moved a thousand miles to be with you."

"And with Nikki."

"Fuck Nikki," she growled, tossing her hands in the air. "I'm here with you. Are you *that* jealous of her?"

"No." *Yes*, a part of him whispered back. "Do I have a reason to be jealous?"

"Why would you have a reason to be jealous?"

"Because . . . that kiss." Until that moment, he hadn't realized seeing Nikki kiss Melanie with more passion than he'd ever seen in his entire life had still been eating at him. He and Melanie had made amends over that incident immediately, but apparently he wasn't over it.

"That kiss meant nothing to me," Melanie said.

"But it meant something to her."

"Do you want me to send her away?"

He shook his head. "No. I want to find my big boy pants and put them on. I just can't seem to find them right now."

She smiled and then chuckled. "Sorry for laughing. I'm imagining you with red-striped pants pulled up to your pierced nipples."

"Yes," he said. "*Those* big boy pants. Have you seen them?"

"I threw them out. They clashed with your hair."

He laughed. "I do love you."

"And I love you. I'll try to be better at reading your mind so I know when you're more upset than you're letting on. I honestly didn't realize the breakup was bothering you so much or that you were dwelling on that stupid kiss."

"I'm an asshole," he said. "I shouldn't assume you know what's going on in my head."

She reached out for his hand. "You can tell me, you know. It's never going to change the way I feel about you. It might make me love you even more."

He lifted a brow. "To know I can't handle my personal shit? That will make you love me more."

"Yep," she said, squeezing his hand. "It makes me feel needed, and you know how obsessed I am with feeling needed." She winked at him, and he burst out laughing.

"I might not show it as well as Clinger—"

"Clinger?"

"AKA Nikki, but I do need you, Mel. Don't ever let something stupid I say drive you away. I never want that no matter how twisted my insides get sometimes."

"They wouldn't get so twisted if you'd just let it out," she said. "Now, can we order? I'm starving over here."

He pushed the complimentary chips and salsa in her direction and signaled the waiter that they were ready to place their order. Melanie decided on cheese enchiladas. Apparently her adventurous side had taken a hike sometime during their little spat. So Gabe ordered three entrees he'd never tried before—the three Melanie had originally been considering, because she had excellent taste and he was feeling a little reckless.

"Hungry?" Melanie asked when the waiter walked away.

"I am," he said, selecting a chip from their basket and dunking it into salsa.

"Are we going to try Amanda again before we head home?"

He crunched on his chip and asked, "Are you okay with that?"

"I should probably be worried that you're apparently stalking Jacob's ex-girlfriend, but I don't think you plan to kidnap her. At least not when I'm with you. So, yeah, we should stop by to see if she's home."

"I hope she knows why Jacob's acting so erratic. If we know the cause, maybe we can fix him."

"Someone needs to get him fixed. The jerk should not procreate."

Gabe snorted. "You only say that because you've never seen him with his daughter. That little girl is his entire universe."

"I don't understand how any guy who considers women his personal all-he-can-eat buffet can treat a daughter with respect."

"Woman who don't demand respect don't receive it."

"You're referring to Nikki, aren't you?"

"I'm referring to all the women who will do anything to bed him."

"And do you treat the women who want you with same disregard?"

He looked to his left and then to his right. "My line is a bit shorter than his. After all, I *am* just the drummer." A pang of longing twisted his gut. Or maybe it was the spicy salsa. "Or rather, I *was* just the drummer."

"You still are." She sipped at her margarita, her gorgeous hazel eyes never leaving his face.

"*Just* the drummer," he said, with a grin.

"You know you're important to the band," she said. "But if you want someone to fangirl all over you, you should whine to Nikki."

"I'm not whining."

"But you should whine. To Nikki. If you're feeling down, she'll lift your spirits to the clouds. I guarantee it."

"Is that the real reason you keep her around? As an ego fluffer?"

"Try it," Melanie said, brightening as the kitchen arrived with way too much food for their small table. "You'll like it."

As usual, the meal was fantastic and the company even better. Now that Melanie had met one of his sisters, he could share stories about their childhood and how he'd always felt like he was trying to live up to the images of his older siblings. His sisters had always been extremely competitive.

"One Father's Day they decided to get Dad ties. He has always dressed rather tame—being a physics professor and all—but on occasion he'll wear an over-the-top tie. So Jennifer got him a tie that lit up with bright LED stripes that periodically changed color and Leslie got him . . ." Gabe laughed as the memory sprang vividly to mind. ". . . a tie with a dog's ass. It had a tail that wagged in response to clapping. His students had a grand time with that one."

Melanie laughed. "Oh my God. I cannot imagine him wearing something like that."

"My sisters based their victory on how many times he wore each tie, so of course he had to wear them both regularly and equally. I wonder how hard it was on my parents to have such ultracompetitive children." He'd never thought about how their sibling rivalry might affect his parents. He'd always been caught up in the contest.

"So what kind of tie did you get him?" she asked.

"I'm the black sheep, so I didn't get him a tie at all." He winked at her. "I cheated and bought him a new fishing lure."

Melanie stole a triangle of his duck quesadilla and nibbled on one point. "Did he wear the lure around his neck when he taught class? He didn't leave you out, did he?"

"No. He took me fishing, and of course I insisted we go every time he wore a sister's tie that year, so win-win for me."

"You're such a rebel." She fed him a bite of her delicious creamy enchiladas, her gaze riveted to his mouth as he accepted her offering. "I guess I'm glad I was an only child. I got more parental attention than I could ever want."

"I'm sure that was tough at times too."

She shrugged. "Can't really complain. I never had to wonder if I was loved."

"I never wondered that either. I just never felt like I was the best."

"You'll always be their best son," she pointed out. "No matter what you do."

And he wasn't sure why that had never occurred to him. "That's why we need four kids, two boys and two girls. Let the sibling rivalry begin." He expected her to laugh, but she kept her gaze on her plate. He was starting to learn her cues, and this one said that something was bothering her. "I might be able to handle a couple more, but twenty-four is definitely the max."

"Twenty-four?" Her eyes went wide. "You'll have to knock up a couple dozen groupies if you want that many."

"But I want only you to have my babies," he said.

She relaxed her shoulders slightly. He guessed she was worried about the paternity test, and when she asked when he'd get the results about Lindsey's baby, he knew he was right.

"Three to five business days," he repeated what he'd been told at his appointment. "I can even look it up online."

"And it's accurate? The baby hasn't even been born yet."

"I guess some of the baby's DNA gets into the mother's bloodstream, and they have a way to separate baby DNA from mom DNA. That's why Lindsey had to give blood, not just a cheek-cell sample."

Melanie nodded and then invaded his dinner again to sample the delicious pork cooked in a banana leaf that he was glad he'd ordered.

"Help yourself," he said, capturing her fork with his.

She glanced up. "I'm sorry. Does it bother you to share food? I'll stop."

"I have no problem sharing my food," he said, capturing the bite she'd been after on his own fork. "But allow me."

He lifted the morsel to her mouth and carefully fed her the bite. She covered her mouth with her hand as she chewed. "Fantastic. I've never had such authentic Mexican food before. Everything is so flavorful and aromatic."

Gabe grinned.

"What are you grinning at?"

"I've never dated a woman who would use a word like *aromatic* in everyday conversation."

"That's why you aren't just dating me," she said. "You're marrying me."

"One of a million reasons why."

After dinner they headed across town to see if Amanda had returned home. Melanie was holding several to-go trays in a large plastic sack, the remnants of her meal. When they pulled into Amanda's drive, her lights were on and, for once, her car was there.

"I was starting to think she'd moved out of the country," Gabe said as he switched off the ignition.

A curtain near the front door moved, and then the lights inside immediately went off.

"I think she's avoiding you," Melanie said.

Even so, Amanda was in there, and he wouldn't leave until she talked to him or called the cops to have him removed from her property.

"Probably, but I'm not sure why she would," he said.

"Do you want me to come to the door with you? Maybe you'll look less threatening if I'm there."

He turned his head to stare at her in astonishment. "You think I'm threatening?"

"I don't, but if I didn't know you well and you showed up at my door after dark, I doubt I'd open it."

"Amanda knows me. I first met her at Jacob's wedding more than five years ago."

"Well, maybe she forgot who you are."

"Uh, I saw her backstage last week. She hasn't forgotten."

Melanie grinned at him. "You are pretty unforgettable. So should I go with you?"

"I'll try on my own. If I need you, I'll wave. I think she'd be less likely to talk in front of you, to be honest."

Melanie shrugged. "Whatever works for you. I'm easy."

"Just a little," he teased before kissing her. He slid out of the open truck door before she could slug him.

Cicadas chirruped loudly as he walked the path to Amanda's front door. He contemplated his options, trying to figure out how to get her to talk to him. He did know her, but they weren't exactly close, and she'd likely have to betray her own sister's trust to tell him what he needed to know. She might be okay with that, though. As much as he and his siblings squabbled, their rivalry came nowhere close to the discord between the Lange sisters.

When he knocked on the door and rang the doorbell, there was no answer. Not that he was surprised. On his second attempt a small cat came to sit in the windowsill near the front door and stared at him with large amber eyes.

"Amanda," Gabe called, knocking a third time. "I know you're in there. I saw you turn out the lights."

"Maybe they're on a timer," she said, followed by, "Shit!" After a few seconds she said, "What do you want, Gabe? I'm not up for company."

"Did you hear about the band breaking up?"

"And I suppose you think it's all my fault because I broke him."

He heard her sniff through the door.

"I didn't mean to break him."

So she had broken Jacob's heart. Jacob had hinted to as much when Gabe had seen him the afternoon before he'd declared the band split and abandoned the tour bus. But Jacob had been through heartache before. It wasn't likely that he'd destroy his career over any woman, no matter how much he loved her.

"So you broke up with him. Big deal." Gabe tried to play down Amanda's role in Jacob's undoing. "Why is he back with your sister? That's what I want to know."

"I said terrible things to him, Gabe. I even insulted his intelligence. You know how sensitive he is about his lack of education."

"Will you open the door?" Gabe said. "I can keep talking loud enough to wake your neighbors, but maybe you don't want them hearing this."

She didn't say anything for a long moment. A light switched on, and the curtain in the window near the door moved again. The curious cat was scooped off the sill by a feminine hand.

"I don't know anything," she said. "Just leave me to mourn in peace."

Gabe's heart skipped a beat. "What are you mourning? Did something happen to Julie?" That seed that Owen had planted about Julie's possible illness had apparently sprouted and taken root.

"I'm mourning the loss of the man I love—have loved for years. I can't believe he fucking went back to her," she shouted at the other side of the door.

"Wait. I thought *you* broke up with him."

"I did. Not because I wanted to."

He heard the door unlock, a chain slide in its track, and then the creak of the door hinges as she opened the heavy slab of wood about a foot. She had the cat securely in her grasp, but strangers apparently spooked the fur ball, and it struggled to be set down. As soon as its paws touched the floor, it sped off deep into the house.

"Are you okay?" he asked.

Amanda looked like hell. Her clothes were crumpled, her dirty-blond hair was actually dirty, and her eyes were bloodshot above tear-stained cheeks. What was worse was that she had the same misery in her eyes that Jacob had shown the last time Gabe had seen him.

She shrugged and hugged her arms around her body, rubbing her arms. "I didn't die," she said. "Just wish I had."

Gabe squeezed her shoulder. "If the two of you were meant to be together, you'll end up together."

"Tina won't let me see Julie," she blurted. "She says it's to keep me away from Jacob, but I offered to take my niece to the park, the way I do—*did*—almost every day since she was born and . . ." Her hands were shaking as she wiped away fresh tears. "If I had just kept loving him from afar as I had for all those years, then . . ."

Gabe's heart couldn't stand seeing a woman in tears. He had no choice but to pull her out onto the front step and into a comforting embrace. The truck door slammed behind him, and hurried footsteps came up the path. Amanda pulled away, using the hem of her rather grubby T-shirt to wipe her face.

"Hi, Amanda," Melanie said. "I'm not sure if you remember me."

Amanda nodded miserably. "Melanie, right?" At Melanie's nod, Amanda added, "Excuse me, but I need to go inside." She turned to look longingly into her cozy little cottage.

"Can we come in?" Gabe asked. He still didn't have the answers he wanted. Amanda said she hadn't wanted to break up with Jacob, and she was obviously as confused about Jacob returning to his ex as Gabe was, but there had to be some piece to this puzzle that Amanda knew and he didn't. Luckily for him, Amanda's ingrained Texan hospitality wouldn't let her turn them away.

Amanda opened the door all the way and said, "Yeah, come on in. Forgive the mess. Would you like some coffee? Tea? Tequila?" They followed her into the house, and she muttered, "Actually, no. I finished the tequila this morning. I might have some cheap wine around here somewhere."

Gabe had only been inside Amanda's house a few times. He found the short ceilings and small rooms a tad claustrophobic with their country-style furnishings, yet at the same time, each room was quaint and homey.

"Please," Amanda said. "Have a seat."

He and Melanie sat side by side on a loveseat while Amanda ventured further into the house. Her small calico cat peered out at them from beneath a chair in the corner.

"Here, kitty," Melanie said, extending her hand in the general direction of the cat. Her gesture of goodwill was completely ignored.

"Do you like cats?" Gabe was a dog person through and through. He preferred cats that were the outdoorsy type and kept rodents in check.

"I like all animals."

"Even spiders and lizards?"

Her nose crinkled. "Make that I like all mammals."

Amanda returned with three glasses of white wine. As she distributed them, he couldn't help but notice that her glass was over twice as full as theirs.

"Should I be concerned that you're on your way to alcoholism?" Gabe asked, nodding toward her glass.

"I've had a rough week," she said.

"I don't think you're allowed to feel this lousy when you're the one who did the breaking up." He was attempting to get more information out of her, but she didn't fall for his ploy.

"I'm allowed to feel as lousy I want."

"So you want to feel lousy?" Melanie asked, taking a small sip of wine.

"I deserve to feel lousy." Amanda tossed back her wine in several gulps and set her empty glass on the coffee table before leaning back in the armchair she was sitting in and covering her eyes with both palms. "My sister deserves to feel even lousier, and instead, she gets everything she wants."

A touch of bitterness there. Not that he blamed her. Tina did seem to get everything she wanted.

"Why does she even want Jacob back?" Gabe asked. "She hated him when they were married."

"She only hated that she couldn't control him. Now she

thinks that she can."

"And you don't?" Gabe asked. Because Gabe was pretty sure Jacob was not in control of the situation.

"Maybe. I don't know. He's different when he's with her."

"Yeah, he's miserable. That's what miserable Jacob looks like," Gabe said. "But last week, when he was with you, he seemed happy."

Amanda removed her hands from her face to look at him. "And I went and fucked that up."

"Why?" Melanie asked.

Amanda contemplated her guests for a long moment before closing her eyes again. "Because I'm a coward. At least this way he gets to be with Julie."

"Julie isn't sick, is she? She doesn't have cancer or some other horrible disease, does she?" Gabe needed to put that ugly thought to rest once and for all.

Amanda scowled at him. "No. Why would you ask that? Why would you even think that?"

"We're just trying to make sense of Jacob's actions," Gabe said. "Nothing he's done since last weekend makes a bit of sense."

"And what does Julie being sick have to do with Jacob's lack of sense?"

"It might explain why he's willing to go back with Tina. I honestly can't think of any reason but Julie that would make him consider her worth his time."

"I don't know why he went back to Tina. All I know is that she threatened to take Julie away from him if I didn't break up with him." Amanda covered her mouth with her hand and said in a muffled voice, "Damn wine."

"So that's why you broke up with him. Tina made you do it?"

"That's horrible," Melanie said.

"What's horrible is knowing how much I must have hurt him," Amanda said. Her eyes were glassy when she bit the side of her finger.

"Don't do that to yourself," Melanie said, leaning forward and placing a comforting hand on Amanda's knee. "Tina is definitely the horrible one for putting you in that position."

"But what can I do about it?" Amanda said. "If I try to talk to Jacob—even to tell him how sorry I am—I know Tina will use his feelings for Julie to keep him in check. To hurt him even more."

"Someone needs to tell him the truth," Gabe said, a plan finally forming in his previously blank mind. "What if I told him what a manipulative bitch he's currently living with?" Not that Jacob would be astonished by that revelation. He happened to know better than anyone on the planet what kind of person Tina was. "What if I told him that you haven't stopped caring about him? That Tina threatened you so you can't set things right, even though you want to."

Amanda's eyes widened. "You can't!"

"Why not?" Melanie asked. "At least he'll know what he's up against."

"You've never met my sister," Amanda pointed out, "and you already know what she's capable of. If she finds out—"

"Who's going to tell her?" Gabe asked. "Jacob?"

"She probably has him bugged."

Actually, Gabe would not put that past Tina, but surely she wouldn't go to that much trouble to keep Jacob under her thumb. Then again . . .

"You know the band can't go on without him," Gabe said. "You know that."

Amanda nodded solemnly. "And I'm truly sorry to have added to the strain that sent Jacob over the edge, but I don't think telling him I didn't really want to break up with him will change anything. It might even make things worse for him. At least this way he won't jeopardize his relationship with his daughter by contacting me."

"Aren't there laws against this kind of manipulation?" Melanie asked. She looked completely dumbfounded.

"Only if there are also laws against people being easily led."

"But she's using that little girl," Melanie said. "It's just . . . just wrong."

"I agree," Gabe said, and he wasn't going to stand by and let it continue to happen. "Sorry to drop in and run, Amanda, but it's getting late." He stood and patted Amanda's shoulder. "Hang in there. If you need anything, please call or text me. Don't make me show up on your doorstep unannounced."

She grinned. "You are obnoxiously persistent when you

have your mind set on something."

"I've noticed that too," Melanie said.

"I'll take that as a compliment," Gabe said, and after saying goodbye, he showed himself and Melanie to the door.

"You're going to let this go?" Melanie asked as they strolled toward the truck at the end of the driveway.

"Hell no. I hope you didn't have your heart set on making it home at a decent hour."

She snorted and shook her head. "We're going to Jacob's house, aren't we?"

"Naturally."

A LIGHT GLOWED in a room near the front of Jacob's house. It was well after nine o'clock, and Gabe would feel bad if he woke Julie, so he walked quietly to the front door and knocked rather than ringing the doorbell. He'd left Melanie to wait in the truck, figuring Jacob would be less likely to listen in front of a witness he didn't know well. Gabe's summons was answered after his second attempt, but Jacob didn't look overly happy to see him.

"A little late to drop by unannounced, don't you think?" Jacob asked, a heavy scowl crinkling his brow. "You're disturbing my family."

"I just came from Amanda's house," Gabe said.

A flicker of pain crossed over Jacob's face, but it was gone so quickly that Gabe thought maybe he imagined it.

"How nice for you," Jacob said, closing the door.

Gabe blocked the action with his foot, wincing as the door caught his toe.

"I thought you might want to know *why* she broke up with you."

"She told me why," Jacob said, his breath hitching with anguish. "I'm not smart enough for her. But you might be, Mr. Physics Major." Jacob pushed on the door, and Gabe lifted his forearm against it for added leverage.

"Amanda doesn't think that of you. Not at all." Gabe lowered his voice to a whisper in case someone was listening in. "Tina threatened to keep you from seeing Julie if Amanda didn't dump you."

Jacob's eyebrows drew together. "Is that so?"

"Who's at the door?" Tina's voice came from inside the house.

"Jehovah's Witness," Jacob called back.

"At this hour?" she questioned.

"You need to go," Jacob said to Gabe. "You'll ruin everything."

"*I'll* ruin everything?" Astonished, Gabe almost made the mistake of stepping back. "Did you hear what I said? Amanda still cares about you. You need to toss this ex of yours once and for all—"

"Since when is Gabe Banner a Jehovah's Witness?" Tina asked, coming around Jacob's broad body to stand next to him. She crossed her arms over her chest and tapped her toe as she glared at Jacob. "Well?"

"I was trying to get rid of him," Jacob said.

"Why?" Tina said. "You should invite him in. How do you ever expect to get Sole Regret back together if you don't patch things up with your bandmates?"

Gabe blinked, trying to register her words. She wanted Sole Regret to get back together? Wait—that didn't make sense.

"His girlfriend is waiting in the truck," Jacob said. "I'm sure he wants to get her home soon. He just stopped by to tell me something."

Gabe's head stopped reeling long enough for him to snap out of his confusion. "Uh, yeah. Remember what I told you, Jacob." He stared beseechingly into his eyes. "And act on it." Then again, maybe he should be trying to negotiate with Tina. Did her encouragement mean that it was *Jacob* who wanted the band to end? Gabe's tattered hope for reconciliation shredded further.

"Thanks for stopping by," Jacob said, closing the door in Gabe's face. Gabe leaned in close to the door to listen in on Tina's conversation with Jacob.

"What was that all about?" Tina asked, her voice muffled.

"Nothing important."

Nothing important?

Jacob said something else, but he was now too far from the door for Gabe to make out the words. Gabe released a frustrated breath and spun on his heel to return to the truck. The problem with bands was that they were made up of more than one person.

He was pretty sure he had Adam onboard with making amends, but now he wasn't sure that Jacob would even hear him out. Maybe the lot of them weren't worth Gabe's headache.

CHAPTER FOURTEEN

MELANIE WATCHED Gabe return to the truck where she waited for him in front of Jacob's lovely brick house. Though most of Gabe's face was concealed by shadows, she could tell by the firm line of his lips that things had not gone as planned. He climbed inside the truck and curled around the steering column, pressing his forehead against the wheel's upper curve.

"Fuck!" He took a swing at the dashboard, his knuckles hitting the plastic with a loud thud.

Melanie took his wrist and kissed his damaged knuckles. Her heart ached for him. She knew what it was like to have a friend who didn't make good decisions.

"Everything okay?" she asked, rubbing his firm-muscled back with one hand, clinging to his fingers with the other.

"He doesn't care that Amanda was basically blackmailed into dumping him. The knowledge wasn't even important to him."

"Poor Amanda," Melanie said. She could tell that the woman was hopelessly in love with Jacob Silverton, and though Melanie did not understand the man's appeal, she did understand heartache and wouldn't wish it on anyone.

Gabe shifted in his seat and leaned over the central console so he could wrap his arms loosely around her. Melanie wondered if he hated the piece of functional plastic between them as much as she did at that moment.

"You're the only thing sane in my life right now, Mel," he whispered, seeking her lips for a tender yet rousing kiss. "I don't know what I'd do without you."

"Well," she said, "you're not about to find out. I'm here for you. Always."

He held her a moment longer, his breath slowing and becoming more regular. "You better start needing me more," he said with a half-hearted chuckle. "I'm starting to feel like a leech."

"I need you," she said, kissing his jaw, his lips, his chin, and the tip of his nose. She wished there was more light in the truck than that coming in from a distant street lamp so that she could gaze into his gorgeous green eyes. "This feeling you give me? I can't do without it. Not ever."

"Is this what they call a codependent relationship?"

She shook her head slightly. "This is what they call a perfect match."

"Let's go home and be alone together. I need to feel you against me. All of you. Inside and out. All of you."

"All of you," she echoed, sliding a hand over his slightly scruffy jaw.

He drew away and started the truck, and after putting it in gear, reached over and took her hand. He kissed the backs of her fingers, her engagement ring, and the inside of her wrist.

"Maybe," he murmured against her rapidly thrumming pulse, "we should stay home. Never leave again." He lowered her hand to rest against his thigh, and she didn't need any encouragement to keep it there.

Becoming hermits sounded like a perfect plan to her, but she worried that such a life wouldn't be enough to satisfy him. He had a busy mind, an energetic body, and wicked creativity. Could she keep up with him? Make him happy? Inspire him to be all he was capable of being? She couldn't know for sure until she tried.

"We'll eventually run out of toilet paper," she joked. The weight of the responsibility to make such a complex man happy made her a tad uncomfortable.

"They do sell toilet paper online."

"But what if I want to try it before I buy it?"

He snorted. "I'd pay money to watch that."

He turned onto a now familiar road that led away from Austin and toward home.

"I promise you'll be okay, Gabe," she said, hoping those were the words he needed to hear. "Just let things happen."

"You make it sound so easy." He rolled his eyes, and she giggled, squeezing his thigh.

"Has anyone ever accused you of being a control freak?"

"Guilty as charged," he said. "And the next thing I plan to control is the frequency and duration of your orgasms."

She squirmed, her hand sliding up his thigh until her pinkie rested against his crotch. "Whatever makes you happy," she said, grinning to herself.

"Do you want to go to the lake tomorrow? Supposed to be a nice day. We'll take the dogs and Nikki. Unless, like you, she's afraid of bait. Then she stays home. I can only bait so many lines."

Melanie snorted, remembering their fishing trip to the lake last weekend and the squirmy pink larva he'd expected her to pierce with a hook. "I have no idea how she feels about fishing, but I'm still not touching maggots."

As soon as they pulled into the drive, the front door opened and Beau came bounding off the porch and across the yard to greet them. Lady and Nikki waited just outside the front door.

When they reached the bottom of the steps, Nikki asked, "Did you have a nice time? Any news about the band?"

"Yep," Gabe said, "and nope."

Melanie handed the bag of leftovers from the restaurant to Nikki. "Some delicious food in there, but I'm sure it's all cold by now."

"That's what microwaves are for."

"I'll worry about installing the dishwasher tomorrow," Gabe said, wrapping an arm around Melanie's back as soon as they entered the house. "I think it's time for bed." He kissed her neck and whispered, "Unless you'd rather ride the Stallion."

"You're the only stallion I want to ride tonight."

Nikki coughed and then headed through the great room and toward the kitchen. Melanie couldn't help but notice Nikki was walking a bit gingerly.

"Are you limping?" Melanie asked.

Nikki turned to look at her, her eyes wide and overly innocent. "Who, me? Or Lady?"

"You."

"Overdid my workout a bit." Nikki shrugged. "I'm fine. You two go on to bed. I'll just talk to the dogs some more."

She muttered something that Melanie couldn't quite make out, most likely about having to spend time alone. Nikki had never done well by herself.

"Want to go to the lake with me, Gabe, and the dogs tomorrow?"

Nikki closed the microwave door and spun around, her face brightening with an excited smile. "That sounds like fun."

"You'd better get to bed soon. We'll be rising early," Gabe said.

"Goodnight," Melanie said, tugging at the hem of Gabe's shirt. Lucky for her, he could take a hint.

Gabe steered Melanie toward the bedroom and soundly shut the door behind them. "Undress," he said, the command in his tone making her thighs quiver.

She presented her back to him and shifted her heavy curls over her shoulder. "Unzip me," she requested.

He bent to brush his lips against the sensitive skin just under her nape as he slowly lowered the zipper at her back. She was trembling with anticipation by the time her dress fell loose at her waist. She slid the straps from her shoulders and let the garment drop to her feet.

"I've been thinking about what you were wearing under that dress all evening," he murmured in her ear.

With Gabe's flick of the light switch, the lamps beside the bed came on, and she heard him blow out a slow breath. She stood perfectly still as he checked out her backside. She knew the lace that hung from the narrow strip of black satin circling her hips did more to show off her ass than to conceal it. And she did enjoy wearing sexy underwear, even when she didn't have a man to show it off to. She liked wearing it almost as much as she liked Gabe picking it out and then taking it off her.

"I was hoping you were wearing your belly chain." His finger slid beneath the slender chain that was attached to a piercing in her belly button. She only wore the chain when she was feeling particularly bold and sexy. Gabe made her feel both. "So glad you never disappoint."

His fingers pinched the back fastening of her bra and it sprang loose. He kissed her spine as he brushed the bra straps from her shoulders, and her bra hit the floor without him taking so much as a second glance at it. So he liked panties. She made a mental note to surprise him by going braless on occasion. He moved her hair to rest it against her bare back again, then gave her ass a swat that made her jump.

"Now walk away, baby," he whispered. "Real slow."

Smiling to herself, she stepped over the puddle of her black dress and crossed the large master bedroom toward the en suite bathroom, loving the way her high heels made her feel when she wore nothing else but a pair of panties, a belly chain, and a grin.

"Fuck me," he muttered.

"We'll get to that."

"You're exquisite," he said. "Those legs of yours . . . Dear God."

She had thousands of squats and lunges to thank for those legs. She was glad someone appreciated her hard work.

"Turn around," he said. "Slowly now, so you don't make my heart stop."

She laughed, delighted by his compliment, and started to turn.

"Okay, stop," he said, throwing up a hand when she hadn't managed even a quarter of a revolution. "I need to be naked for this."

God, she loved this man. Every fucking thing about him. She stopped in midturn and watched over her shoulder as his shirt, shoes, jeans, and underwear went flying. He even removed his Texas Rangers cap. She pressed her lips together around her tongue to hold in her amusement as he took a deep breath and planted his hands on both bare hips.

"Okay, continue," he said. "But slowly."

As she turned—slowly—she watched his already hard cock thicken even more and point upward at a sharp angle. Her hips tilted reflexively to accept all he had to offer.

"I can't decide if I like your back or front better," he said, his eyes searching her nearly nude body. "Or the top or the bottom."

"You don't have to pick. It's all yours."

His belly tightened, making his cock jerk. She didn't bother to squelch the shudder of desire that pulsed through her.

"Would you like me to take my panties off now?" she asked, shifting her shoulders back to lift her bare breasts.

He bit his lip, and then after a few seconds, gave a curt nod. She lowered her panties slowly, sliding the fabric over the curve of her hips, down her thighs, calves, and ankles, before stepping out of them. She lifted the sexy underwear and held them out in front of her. "I also have this design in red, in white, and in pink, if you'd like me to model them all."

"You'll have to show them to me some other time," he said, taking one step closer and then another.

Her heart rate kicked up. What was it about being stalked by the man she loved that was such a turn-on? When other men showed her the same attention, it might creep her out or frighten her or even make her angry. But when Gabe looked at her like he wanted to devour her whole, she handed him a fork.

She swallowed hard and licked her lips when he stopped moving to stand directly in front of her. The head of his cock was a fraction of an inch from her bare skin, and she didn't have the willpower to keep from swaying toward him so that it brushed her lower belly. Even though Melanie was in heels and almost five foot ten, Gabe was too tall to slide his cock between her thighs without certain adjustments.

"You can see that I want you," he said, shifting his hips slightly to rub his tip against her. "But do you want me as much?"

"You can't tell by looking at me?" Though the room was warm, her nipples were hard and swollen, and the flush on her skin had nothing to do with embarrassment.

He bent his knees and used his hand to slide his cock between her slightly parted thighs, rubbing against the hot, achy, slippery flesh between her legs. Her breath erupted in an excited huff.

"I think maybe you do want me," he said, staring into her eyes.

"*Maybe?*" She squirmed against him, hoping he might slip inside her. "There's no maybe. I want you. I always want you."

"But not as much as I want you."

"How can you possibly know that?"

"You're not moaning my name."

She straightened and pressed her hands against his hard chest, the barbell that pierced his nipple impossible to ignore. "And you're not moaning mine."

"Melanie," he moaned, sounding more like a ghost than an enthusiastic lover. "Melanieeeee."

Giggling, she slapped his chest. "How can anyone get into the mood with you joking around all the time?"

He turned his head and lifted one eyebrow. "You don't like to have fun in bed?"

"I love to have fun in bed."

"Then we'd better get in there and start having fun." He made suggestive eyes in the direction of the mattress.

Instead of making a wild leap for the bed, Melanie grabbed him firmly by the jaw and turned his face toward hers. His gorgeous green eyes blurred out of focus as she drew close enough to claim his mouth in a heated kiss. He groaned, his hands sliding to her ass to shift their bodies closer together.

She wasn't sure how she ended up on the bed, but the next thing she knew, she was sprawled on her back, and Gabe was kneeling on the floor between her legs, sucking and licking and rubbing his lips over her swollen clit until she was writhing in ecstasy.

"Oh God, I'm close," she said. "Don't stop. Don't—"

He didn't listen, damn him. Instead he rose to his feet and guided himself into her with one hand. Her few seconds of disappointment as her impending orgasm slipped away were entirely forgotten as he pounded into her, deep and hard, starting at a slow, grinding tempo and increasing his speed until she shattered in exquisite bliss. He didn't follow her over the edge but kept her suspended in shuddering aftershocks for eternal moments before slowing his tempo again. She quickly began to ride his next wave to the stars and pried opened her eyelids to watch him. His eyes were squeezed shut, and his brow was tight with intense concentration. He worked so hard to please her, and it always paid off. Sweat trickled down his hard chest and the sharp valley between his flexing abs as he worked his pelvis against her clit with every deep, churning stroke.

"Yes, Gabe, just like that," she encouraged as the first sparks of orgasm danced along her nerve endings. "Don't stop. So close. So cl—"

And he pulled out, dropping to his knees and sending her over the edge with his mouth. She clung to the covers, her back arching off the mattress, a shout of triumph escaping her lips. He leaned back to catch his breath and to allow her to tumble back down to earth. When she reached for him, he pressed a hand against her belly to keep her on her back and then returned to feasting on her overstimulated pussy. She doubted it was possible to reach orgasm again, but Gabe was relentless. Not wanting him to stop before she hit her peak this time, she didn't tell him when she was close, but something in the way her body was twitching must have provided sufficient evidence because just as she broke, he pulled his mouth away and stood again, finding her, claiming her orgasm with his cock. Her internal muscles gripped him hard, tugging at him, inviting him to follow her to nirvana.

"Fuck," he muttered and pulled out.

She felt the first pulse of his cum against her clit.

"Fuck," he said again, and pushed back inside her.

His thumb rubbed his cum into her tingling skin as he pumped his hips, and then he stiffened before shuddering against her. He collapsed forward, squashing her into the mattress, and she wrapped her arms and legs around him, pulling him closer. He could never be close enough, not even if they merged into one being.

"I love you," she whispered, and kissed his neck.

"Your pussy wrecked me," he murmured. "I wanted you to have more."

She grinned. Such a giving lover, even if his pillow talk was often less than romantic. "You wrecked my pussy," she said. "I couldn't take anymore."

"Give me an hour to recover and we'll see about that."

"*One* hour?" She kissed his neck again. "I'll probably need around eight, but you can try."

After a few minutes, she made him move to the bed so she could use the bathroom. When she returned, he was already asleep. She climbed in next to him, and he immediately spooned up against her, one hand cupping her breast, showing he wasn't quite asleep after all.

"I love you," he murmured. "I want to make sure I tell you that often."

"I love you," she returned, reaching behind her to get a hand on some bare skin.

"Wake me in an hour."

She might have if she hadn't been bone weary and completely satisfied. Neither of them stirred until sunlight streamed in from the triangular-shaped windows above the bed and a very excited black dog jumped on the bed to lick their faces.

"I thought we were leaving early," Nikki said from the foot of the bed.

Melanie lifted her head from the pillow, only to get pummeled in the face by a wagging tail. She lay back and lifted her hand to shield herself from the dog's enthusiastic assault.

"What time is it?" she asked.

"Beau," Gabe said sharply. "Down."

Beau got in a few extra licks and wags before he hopped off the bed and sat on his haunches next to Lady, who was staring at them from the floor beside the bed.

"Time to go to the lake," Nikki said.

"We'll be out in a while," Gabe said, drawing Melanie's body beneath him and settling between her hips.

She smiled up at him, wondering how a man so sleep tousled and with over a day's growth of beard could look so fucking sexy.

"How long is a while?" Nikki asked.

"Depends on how long it takes me to convince your friend here that she needs a morning quickie."

Melanie grinned up at him, her heart threatening to burst with overflowing love and happiness. "Not long then, Nikki," she said.

Nikki released an exasperated breath. "The newly in love are so annoying. All they want to do is fuck, fuck, fuck."

Beau barked as if in agreement.

"Twenty minutes," Gabe said, his hands sliding beneath the covers to prepare Melanie's body for the already hard dick that was poking her in the thigh. "Take the dogs out with you. They don't need to see this."

"*I* don't need to see this," Nikki said. She whistled at the dogs so they'd follow her out of the room.

Gabe peered over his shoulder at the shut door. "I figured she was the type who'd like to watch."

"More the type who'd like to participate," Melanie said.

"I'd never let her put her hands on you," he said. "You're mine."

"I am," she agreed. "And I'm not going to get my full twenty minutes if you don't stop talking."

"I just said that to get rid of her. It will be an hour at least." He leaned over her and opened the top drawer of the nightstand beside the bed. Within minutes, several of the toys he'd designed were laid out beside her like surgical instruments. "I'm in the mood to play this morning." He drew the flat of his tongue over one of her nipples, and she shuddered. "Are you game?"

"Hmm," she said, trying to make her face look serious. "Play with my gorgeous fiancé and his bangin' toys—both of which give me orgasm after orgasm—or sit on a hot boat and poke poor defenseless baby flies with fishing hooks? Decisions, decisions."

Gabe correctly presumed she preferred the first option. By the time they left the bedroom—thoroughly funned out, recently showered, and wearing matching smiles—it was near noon. Nikki had apparently given up on them hours ago and was sitting on the back deck with her laptop.

"We thought you'd be ready to go by now," Melanie teased as she peeked out the sliding door. Melanie had never explored the back yard of Gabe's house. They always sat on the front porch, so when she heard the sound of running water, she ventured out onto the deck to investigate. Nikki closed her laptop and hopped up to join Melanie at the deck railing.

"There's a creek down there," Nikki said, pointing Melanie's attention to its source. "And a little waterfall that feeds it."

"Oh wow!" Melanie said. "How did I miss this?"

"Probably because when you're with Gabe, you spend all your time on your back."

Melanie swatted at her, but Nikki dodged the playful slap.

"We should set up the wedding over there, under those trees," Nikki said, pointing out a small clearing next to the waterfall that wasn't exactly level but might hold a few dozen chairs.

"Yes, yes, yes! It's perfect." She gave Nikki an enthusiastic hug. "Is that what you've been working on all morning? Wedding plans?"

"Uh . . . sure," Nikki said. "Did you really not know this gorgeous area was back here?"

Melanie flushed. "Nope. Guess I have been spending too much time on my back."

Nikki laughed. "And who can blame you?"

"Are you ladies ready?" Gabe asked from the open patio door. "I got the boat hitched to the truck."

"You didn't tell me you had your own waterfall," Melanie accused, holding her hand out to him so he'd join her at the railing.

"That little thing," Gabe said. "It's hardly a trickle."

"It's magnificent." She pointed to the clearing Nikki had brought to her attention. "And I want to marry you right there."

"Right there, huh?" he said, drawing her against him and kissing her. "I could go for that. Or right here. Or anywhere you'll have me."

A pair of hands wedged between them and pushed them apart. "Don't you two start that again," Nikki said, "or we'll never make it to the lake, and I've been promising Beau all morning that he could go swimming."

"Are you sure Lady will be okay to go with us?" Melanie asked Gabe. "What if she gets her cast wet?"

"Good point. I'll have to bring her leash to keep her on the boat."

The five of them had a wonderful afternoon together. Nikki spent most of her time sunbathing and swimming with Beau. Poor Lady was stuck on the boat, but seemed happy to rest at Gabe's side while he baited his hook and Melanie's. They caught a few largemouth bass, which Gabe insisted they'd have for supper. Melanie was fine with eating their catch as long as she didn't have to clean them. In her opinion, fish guts were even less appealing than putting maggots on hooks.

The next few days passed in a blur, like they were on a carefree vacation. They hiked the woods around Gabe's house, visited with his parents, rode ATVs, tested several prototypes—including the New-And-Improved Sex Stallion—and had dinner out at the Oasis to enjoy the spectacular sunset over Lake Travis. Nikki often accompanied them, but she'd been spending quite a bit of time on her computer. When Melanie asked what she was up to, Nikki told her she was making plans. For the wedding, Melanie presumed, but Nikki wouldn't share any of them with her.

"A surprise," she said.

Melanie was so enjoying her new life with the man she loved, the friend she adored, and the two dogs who liked her almost as much as they adored Nikki that she had completely forgotten about Gabe's paternity test until one afternoon when they were sitting on the porch swing and his phone rang. As he read his phone's screen, he said, "Guess I'm about to find out if

I'm going to be a father."

And before Melanie could steel her nerves for the news to come, Gabe took a deep, steadying breath and accepted the call.

CHAPTER FIFTEEN

GABE HAD ALMOST CONVINCED himself that this trouble-free life with Melanie was his new reality. He'd intentionally unplugged from the outside world. He hadn't contacted Jacob or Adam again. He wasn't sure how Owen and his brother were faring. He didn't know if Kellen had made amends with his best friend—who he'd kissed on the mouth, for fuck's sake. And he hadn't given the prospect of fathering Lindsey's baby much thought. He had been thinking about knocking up Melanie, however. The more time they spent together, the more he realized that he *was* ready to start a family—with her, not with some girl from a one-night orgy—and that the only element lacking in his life was a stable career. But he did have money saved up—enough to get him through several years of expenses.

So when he accepted the call from the DNA testing service, he expected bad news. Expected it because life had been going so right for him for the past several days. Different from his norm, yes. But right.

"Yes, this is Gabriel Banner," he said to the woman on the phone.

He had a strange mind-disconnected-from-his-body feeling as he waited for her response. He clutched Melanie's hand, squeezing it far harder than he intended. Christ, his heart was about to beat itself through his ribs.

"The results show conclusively that you are not the paternal father of the subject's baby."

"Not?" he asked breathlessly, wanting to make sure he'd heard correctly.

"Not," she reiterated.

"Not," he repeated. Gabe melted back into the porch swing with relief. "Do the results say who the father is?"

"I cannot provide that information to anyone but the mother and the biological father," she said. "Do you have questions I *can* answer?"

Gabe shook his head, even though the woman couldn't see the motion. "Thanks for calling. You have a great day now." He hung up and drew Melanie into his arms.

"It's not yours?" she asked, her voice breathless.

"It's not mine."

"Oh, thank God." She twisted her body so she could cup his face between her hands and kiss him. "Not that you wouldn't make a terrific father." She kissed him again. "I just want you to make babies with me and no one else." He kissed her. "I'm sorry if that's selfish."

"It's not selfish. That's the way it should be," he said. "So let's go make one right now." Those were probably the most impulsive words to ever escape his lips.

"We do need more practice," she said with a giggle.

"I've had enough practice," he said. "I'm ready for the real deal."

"What?" Her eyes searched his. "I thought you wanted to wait."

"I don't want to wait anymore." He eased her away just far enough to see her face clearly. "Do you want to wait?"

She stared at him for a solid minute, her eyes still searching his. "No," she finally said.

Did that mean no, she didn't want a baby or no, she didn't want to wait? "No?"

"I want your baby inside me as soon as possible," she said, pushing away all vagueness.

He grinned and kissed her enthusiastically. Melanie Anderson wanted to be his wife and wanted to have his baby. Just a few weeks ago she'd been hesitant to give him a chance, and now they had a long and loving life before them. It was a good thing she'd given Sole Regret's tattooed, Mohawked drummer a try, or he might have never found true happiness.

"I'll have to stop taking my birth control," she said, nibbling his lip. "You're sure about this?"

"Yeah," he said, his heart brimming with joy. "Are you?"

Her smile was so brilliant, it almost blinded him. "Absolutely."

The front door opened, and Nikki came out onto the porch with Beau and Lady on her heels. She was carrying her laptop in one hand.

"Can I talk to you guys? It's kind of important."

"It can't be more important than the news Gabe just got," Melanie said.

Nikki brightened. "Is the band getting back together?"

Her eager gaze made Gabe feel more than a little guilty. He knew there were thousands of fans out there who, like Nikki, were waiting for news about the band making amends. Gabe hadn't given up on the idea, but it was pretty much out of his hands. Adam and Jacob were the ones who'd have to fix this mess. He, Owen, and Kellen would just have to wait until they came around. They could encourage a reconciliation, but they couldn't force one.

"No," Melanie said. "No news on that front yet. But he's not going to be a father."

Gabe's arms tightened around Melanie, and he squeezed her tightly. "Oh, yes, I am."

"We're going to try for a baby," Melanie said, wrapping her arms around his and pressing them even closer to her belly, "but Lindsey's baby isn't his."

"A baby! Really?" Nikki's happiness for them was genuine. "That's just . . ." She wiped at a tear with the back of her hand. "You're going to be the best mom, Mel. The absolute best."

Gabe wondered why he hadn't recognized Nikki's kindness from the start. Probably because it had been hard to see through the seductress mask she typically wore when she was around men. She didn't wear it around him, though. Wasn't he worth seducing? Naw, that couldn't be it. She just trusted him as a friend. He was pretty sure that was actually a big deal for her.

"And you're going to be the best auntie," Melanie told Nikki.

Gabe tensed slightly, but then relaxed. His dogs adored Nikki, and he absolutely trusted their judgment. Nikki wouldn't do anything to harm their child. She wouldn't be a bad influence. She might even babysit so Gabe could work on making baby number two with Melanie. But he was getting far ahead of himself.

"So what did you want to talk to us about?" Gabe asked. He actually hoped it was the wedding. Their relationship was moving forward rocket fast, but that wedding could not happen fast enough. He wanted this woman in his arms to be Mrs. Gabriel Banner as soon as possible. Nothing would make him happier.

Nikki cringed. "Don't be mad at me."

Melanie stiffened and sat up straighter on Gabe's lap. "Did you max out my credit card?"

Gabe didn't want money to be any consideration when it came to his wedding to Melanie. "If it's for the wedding—"

"It's not that," Nikki said. "I, uh, took a ride on the Sex Stallion on your date night last week."

"You didn't!" Melanie snarled.

"I know you told me not to, but something happened. I'm not sure how to tell you."

Gabe's eyes widened. "Did it hurt you?" Injuring someone was his greatest fear.

"Fuck no," Nikki said. "Best seven orgasms of my life. I filmed all of them for some guy I've been messaging on a fetish dating site."

"What?" Melanie sputtered.

"You have a fetish?" Gabe blurted. Not that he cared or wanted to know what it was. Okay, he couldn't lie, he *was* curious. Last time he checked, he was a guy.

"He published my video on a porn site. Eight hundred thousand views in three days."

Gabe's jaw dropped. That must be some video.

"Oh no, Nikki," Melanie said, scrambling off Gabe's lap and wrapping an arm around her friend's shoulders. "That's terrible. Are you okay?"

"Yeah, it's no big deal. You can't see my face. You can see everything else, but not my face."

Was it hot out here or was it just his fiancée and her best friend talking about a video centered around riding his masterpiece?

"Did you think we'd be mad because I told you to stay off of my Stallion?"

"You wouldn't have been able to resist it either, Mel."

"That's true. So then why would you think we'd be mad at *you*?" Melanie asked, holding Nikki by both shoulders to try to capture her gaze. Nikki still had her laptop clutched to her belly. "That guy shouldn't have posted that video without your permission."

"Actually . . ." Nikki squirmed and wouldn't meet Mel's eyes. "I told him he could."

"Then you must be worried because you're not supposed to be having sex right now. I don't think this actually counts, but if you need to talk to your therapist we'll take you back to Kansas."

Nikki shook her head. "The reason that video has so many views is not because of anything I did." Nikki grinned deviously. "Well, okay, I do look pretty sexy riding that thing, and I'm an excellent vocalizer."

Gabe suddenly needed a pillow. For his lap. And he needed to watch Melanie looking sexy riding the Sex Stallion and doing her own excellent vocalizing right now.

Melanie lifted her eyebrows and shook her head, waiting for Nikki to drop whatever bomb she was holding.

"Everyone wanted to know where to get one of those machines," Nikki said. "I figured they were all talk. I told them it was a prototype and there was only one in existence. Still, thousands of women and men all vying for an opportunity to own one or at least ride one. And then I got the idea to crowdfund and earn enough money to put the Sex Stallion into production. I set the price to participate super-high—a thousand dollars just to get on the waiting list. Of course, that thousand would count as a down payment and they'd be guaranteed a unit as soon as they were produced. I wasn't sure how much each machine would cost in the end. I estimated five thousand, and you will not believe how many people were willing to pay that."

"What are you saying, Nikki?" Gabe said, his heart racing. Cold sweat trickled down the middle of his back.

Melanie turned to stare at him, her face ashen, her mouth open wide.

"We've made two million dollars in that past three days."

"What?" Gabe bellowed.

"But now I sort of need you to make two thousand Stallions." Nikki smiled hugely, as if she'd given him the best news of his life.

"It took me ten years to build that one and perfect it," Gabe yelled.

Nikki flinched, but he couldn't help the rage boiling inside him. Was she crazy? Two *thousand* units! He was good at math, so he knew that at five thousand apiece he would gross ten million dollars, but still. How in the hell was he supposed to build two thousand of the damned things?

"But it is perfect," Nikki said. "It's time to share it with the world."

Melanie clutched her hands together. "Gabe, please tell me you filed a patent on it."

"Years ago," he said.

She released a long breath. "Good. Now, I know you don't know much about my past careers, but I used to be the office manager for a small manufacturing plant. And I know how to run the business end of things."

"And I can be the spokes—erm—the *moan* model," Nikki said, thrusting her hand in the air like an eager elementary school student.

"She's an excellent PR person, Gabe."

"That's what I went to college for," Nikki said.

"We'd need a larger team, of course," Melanie said. "Especially on the manufacturing end, and I don't know many people in Texas, but—" Her eyebrows drew together. "Doesn't Owen's girlfriend run her own alternate energy business in Houston?"

Gabe just stared at her as if she had seventeen nipples.

"Gabe?" Melanie said when he didn't respond.

"I guess," he said. "But what does Caitlyn's corporation have to do with sex toys?"

"Uh, everything," Melanie said. "It's not what you're making or selling but the structure of how to produce and distribute that most businesses have in common. I'll have to look into business laws in Texas. I'm sure they can't be that much different from those in Kansas."

"Isn't Texas notoriously business friendly?" Nikki said. "I'm sure this will be a piece of cake for you."

"You're forgetting something," Gabe said.

The pair of scheming women turned to look at him, questions in their eyes.

"It's my invention. What if I don't want to mass produce it? What if I want only Melanie to have one?"

Melanie laughed. "That's silly."

It didn't seem silly to him. It seemed special. A unique one-of-a-kind gift for his one and only true love.

Nikki popped open her laptop and showed Melanie her crowdsource funding page.

"Holy shit! There's a waiting list for the waiting list!" Melanie clapped her hands. "Baby," she said, turning to gaze adoringly at Gabe. "I'm so proud of your filthy, inventive mind right now."

Gabe had never seen her this excited about anything. Well, maybe when she was enjoying objects designed by his filthy, inventive mind. But definitely not about financial or business success.

"Gabe?" Nikki said, tilting her head to look at him. "Do you not want to give mind-blowing orgasms to all these people? They're counting on your Sex Stallion to bring them joy." She sat next to him on the porch swing and showed him the excited comments of people who'd slapped down a thousand dollars of their hard-earned money for a chance to be delighted by his invention.

After a few minutes of having his head filled with compliments about his brilliance, he closed his eyes, licked his lips, and swallowed his doubts. That future he'd been so uncertain about? This could be the answer. He'd never expected Nikki to be responsible for pushing him down a new path of success.

"Okay," he said. "Let's do this."

CHAPTER SIXTEEN

MELANIE PULLED into Gabe's driveway—she still had a hard time thinking of this gorgeous A-frame log home as hers—and shut off her engine. Nikki's car was gone, but Gabe's truck was in the drive, so she knew that he was home, even though the door didn't open and no dogs bounded excitedly off the porch to greet her. She tucked the little paper sack containing the pregnancy test she'd bought at the drugstore into her purse. She was only a few days late, so didn't want to get Gabe's hopes up, but hers were currently sky high.

The past few weeks had flown by like a whirlwind. It hadn't taken her long to file for a business license and organize the corporate structure of Bangin' Toys. After having been only a small part of a large accounting team for so long, she'd forgotten how much she enjoyed running a business and solving the little problems that always arose. They'd had to deal with some ordinances about the sexual nature of their products, so they'd settled on a location outside city limits. The first units were making their way through their small but highly skilled quality assurance department today. Of course she felt the need to be there to make sure everything was running smoothly. Gabe seemed keen to look the other way, however.

The typical little start-up hiccups weren't really an issue. The main delay to production was Gabe. He was insistent that they didn't mass produce a piece of junk. He wanted dedicated artisans creating each machine, not an assembly line of unskilled dildo-makers cranking out a subpar product. She'd tried to convince him that such a labor-intensive method of production would severely cut into their profits—showing him graphs and projections she'd generated to support her cause—but he refused to budge on that particular issue. And she respected him all the more because of it. But it had taken for-freaking-ever to find suitable employees, and they were still grossly understaffed.

Since Nikki was busy creating a PR maelstrom for the first shipments of the Sex Stallion, wedding plans had temporarily been set on the back burner. Caitlyn and Dawn were still throwing together an engagement party for both Gabe and Adam. Now that Madison was out of the hospital and staying with Adam in Austin, Melanie had run out of excuses to put it off any longer. The party was scheduled for tomorrow afternoon at Owen's house. The day had somehow crept up on Melanie while she'd been insanely busy getting Gabe's new corporation up and running.

Melanie opened her front door, trying to be quiet so she could sneak into the bathroom and pee on the test in her purse. She was immediately assaulted by a loud rhythmic thumping. The sound—heavy and hard—throbbed through her body with an intensity that only Gabe could create within her.

He was playing his drums.

She was pretty sure that he hadn't touched them since the night Jacob had walked off the tour bus almost a month before. Dancing to the beat—she couldn't help herself—she quietly shut the front door and tried to figure out where the sound was coming from. It filled the house from floor to rafters. Both dogs were sitting in the foyer staring up at the loft area over the kitchen. Oh. Right. The loft. She'd been up in the open spacious room a few times, but had never spent time there. The loft was Gabe's space, full of various drums, band paraphernalia, scientifically inclined nonfiction books, and the ugliest old recliner she'd ever seen. But drawn by the beat, she climbed the open wooden stairs and stood perched on the topmost step to stare.

Gabe was shirtless. His hair, which had grown out to almost completely cover his tattoos, had been shaved on the sides again. His Mohawk was at least four inches longer than when she'd met him and was fashioned into tall spikes. He wore studded leather cuffs on each wrist and an intense expression as he pounded away on the skins, his entire body—pumping legs, flailing arms— moving to the beat in his mind. A grimace of longing twisted his handsome features into an expression of elemental need.

Watching him—her rock star—play those drums as if a huge piece of him were missing without them made tears spring to Melanie's eyes. She swallowed the huge lump in her throat, but it did no good. Regret threatened to suffocate her.

What had she done? Barged into his life. Invited her friend to live in his house. Monopolized all his free time. Forced him to start a business he'd had no intention of starting. Turned his attention from making the music he loved to her.

She covered her mouth and said into her palm, "Oh God, I'm sorry." She'd been so focused on building their new life together that she'd completely steamrolled over the life he loved—the one he'd had before he'd met her.

The drumming stopped abruptly. Gabe slid his drumsticks under his snare as if ashamed that she'd caught him using them.

"I didn't realize you'd be home so soon," he said.

"Don't stop playing on my account," she said, rubbing wetness from her cheeks with her fingertips. "Please don't stop."

"Are you crying?"

She couldn't stay away. She rushed to his side and wrapped her arms around him, hugging the side of his head to her chest. "You haven't played since I moved in."

"It's noisy," he said. "I didn't want to disturb you."

She laughed, kissing the recently shaved side of his head. "It wouldn't disturb me. And if it did, I'd just go sit on the porch. You need this, Gabe. This drumming. It's part of you."

"Honestly, I haven't felt like playing. I figured it would just remind me of everything Jacob took from me when the selfish bastard dismembered the band." He twisted so he could look up into her eyes. "I'd forgotten how fun it is." He grinned, and her heart melted. "I don't know if Sole Regret will ever get back together or if I'll ever play drums professionally again, but I will play them for fun."

Melanie laughed because the man made her so damned happy, she couldn't help it. "I'm glad. And I want your band to get back together. I really do."

"Are you sure? You can tell me the truth. I won't be upset. I know you don't buy into the whole rock star gig." He rolled his eyes at her. "You're so not impressed."

But she was impressed. More than impressed. "Watching you play the drums is the most erotic experience I've ever had."

He snorted "More erotic than riding the Sex Stallion?"

"Way more erotic than any sex toy."

"Sounds like a challenge." He smirked and wiggled his

eyebrows at her. "That's one way to inspire my filthy, inventive mind."

"Play for me, Gabe," she said. But then she shook her head and added, "No, play for yourself. Lose yourself in your rhythm. That's what really turns me on."

His bass drum thudded, and she jumped. Within seconds his entire body was moving again. She couldn't look away. Not when her ears began to ache from the loudness. Not when her breathing quickened and her heart started to race. And certainly not when sweat began to trickle down his flexing pecs, abs, and back. As enticing as his lean, muscular body was, it was that look of intense concentration, of love—a look she recognized from their bedroom—as he played that drew her closer and closer until she was close enough to touch him.

Sole Regret needed to get back together. She wasn't sure why it hadn't seemed all that important to her until now. Maybe because she simply hadn't recognized how important it was to Gabe. And if the band was important to him, it was important to her.

Unable to keep her hands to herself another second, she reached out and touched his shoulder. His skin was damp with sweat and cool to the touch, but she could feel the heat just beneath the surface. His concentration shattered, he stumbled over a beat and then lowered his sticks, gathering them into one fist. He wrapped his free arm around the backs of her thighs.

"Are you sufficiently turned on?" he asked. "Or should I continue?"

"You should always continue," she said. "But this isn't about me at all. It's about you. I'm an idiot for not seeing it before. Can you forgive me?"

He cocked his head to one side, confusion written across every devastatingly gorgeous line of his face. "Forgive you? For what?"

"For not trying to help you get the band together."

"You went with me to talk to Adam, as well as to Jacob and even Amanda."

"But I didn't *do* anything."

"Baby, that's not your responsibility." He set his sticks down on his snare drum, freeing his hand to take hers. "Standing beside me while I sort this shit out, that's all I require of you." He lifted her hand to his lips. "And you've done a fine job of that. You've stood by me through it all."

"But I want to fix it."

He laughed softly and kissed her wrist. "You wouldn't be you if you didn't want to fix problems for someone you care about, but the ball is bouncing between Jacob and Adam now. We just have to be patient and hope we aren't eighty years old before they set their differences aside and stop being selfish jackasses."

She bit her lip, trying to think up a course of action. "There has to be something we can do. Are they both coming to the party tomorrow?"

Gabe shrugged, his gentle, seeking kisses along the inside of her wrist and palm wreaking havoc with her pulse as well as her ability to keep her hands from trembling.

"I know Adam will be there," he said. "It's his party too. Jacob was invited, and I was planning to ask him to be my best man if he comes, but I'm not sure if he'll show."

"He'd better come," she said, and it sounded like a threat. Because she knew if Jacob bailed on their engagement party, his indifference would hurt Gabe, even if Gabe somehow managed to hide his feelings.

"If he doesn't, I'll just ask one of the other guys to stand up with me. It's no big deal."

But it was a big deal. And she planned to make sure the right person was her groom's best man when Gabe pledged his forever to her. If that person was Jacob "Ego-Maniac" Silverton, so be it.

"So," she said, hoping that a subject change would wipe the melancholy from her lover's face. "Is there any way to make love while drumming?"

He bit his lip. "Make love?" He shook his head. "Doubtful. Fuck? Oh yeah. I can definitely fuck while drumming. Do you think you could handle the bass?"

"I don't know," she said. "What do I have to do?"

He shifted his stool back and stood, wrapping his fingers around her hips and arranging her in front of him facing the drum kit. He moved in close behind her, rubbing the hard bulge in his pants against her ass while his hands slid up her sides to cup her breasts.

"There are three pedals on the floor in front of you," he said. "Step on one."

Distracted by the feel of his body behind her and the exertion-intensified masculine scent of him—the man smelled like sex, and her hormones were raging in response—she wasn't sure where the floor was, much less the three pedals. When she didn't move, he nudged her side with his elbow.

"Go on now. I won't be able to drum, fuck, and hit the bass pedal. You have to help me out."

She liked being helpful. She looked down, and beyond the snare drum in front of her knees, she spotted the pedals he'd mentioned. "I don't think I can reach them. There's a drum in my way."

"Good point," he said. "And your pants are in my way."

She unfastened her pants and shimmied out of them, her flip-flops, and her underwear before kicking them all aside. "One problem solved."

His soft chuckle near her ear made her shiver with anticipation. One of his hands massaged her breast, the other moved down her belly to cup her sex. A finger slipped between her lips to tease her clit.

"I also can't drum with my hands full of glorious Melanie," he whispered.

"I guess this idea is a no-go then," she said, leaning back against him and opening her legs to give him better access. That was fine with her as long as he didn't stop touching her.

As usual, he was up for the challenge. She groaned in protest when he moved away and picked up the snare drum, shifting it to his right side. The space in front of her was now open.

"Step forward," he said when she expected him to haul her down the stairs to their bedroom. "We're going to try something."

Always up for one of his experiments, Melanie stepped forward.

"Can you reach the bass drum pedal now?"

She pressed her foot down on a hard pedal, and one of his bass drums thudded.

"Good," he said. "You control how fast we go."

She turned her head to look at him, but he pressed a hand in the center of her back and she leaned over the center drum. Was the drum under her elbows called a tom or was it just a bigger snare? She wasn't sure, but it was probably something the wife of a drummer should know. She heard his pants unzip and the sound of fabric rustling behind her. When the tip of his cock nudged her opening, she gasped and her extended leg tensed, lightly pressing the pedal and producing another soft thud.

"That's it," he said, working his way deeper, retreating slightly, going deeper still, until he was buried to the root within her. "Every time you push that pedal, I'm going to thrust."

"Oh," she said, a hot flush burning her cheeks. So that was how she was going to control the rhythm.

"I suggest you start out slow," he said. "Until I get the hang of this."

His drumstick tapped against the snare to his right, sounding like a typical rock intro, and she stomped the bass pedal. Holding her hip with his left hand and doing a rather impressive one-handed drum roll with his right, he pulled out and thrust into her before retreating slowly. Oh, but she wanted him deep, so she pressed the bass pedal and true to his word, he thrust forward. The motion was a bit awkward at first, because she had to lift her foot several inches before pressing down on the pedal, but it didn't take her long to use that motion to intensify his pleasure and her own. Soon she was thudding with a steady rhythm, twisting her hips slightly with each downbeat, and he was thrusting in time, filling the pauses with one-handed intricate stick work on the snare. Surprisingly, their drum duet even sounded good—strong and steady.

As her excitement built, so did the rate of her rhythm, until her leg cramped and she had to stop. Oh, but she wasn't ready for him to stop as he stilled behind her.

"You okay?" he asked, his hand sliding up and down her hip.

"Leg cramp!"

"Happens to the best of us," he said. "Here, hold my stick."

She giggled but took the drumstick he held out in front of her and sighed in bliss when his now-free hand began to massage her smarting thigh. "That's better," she said.

"You know what I do when I get a cramp in my leg?"

She had no clue, because it wasn't like he could stop playing in the middle of a song and employ a masseuse to give his leg a rub-down. "What?" she asked.

"Use the other leg."

"Great suggestion," she said.

"When in doubt, ask a professional."

She'd never been with a man who could make her laugh during sex. Well, that wasn't one hundred percent true. She'd been with one guy who'd made her crack up every time he climbed on top of her, but she'd been laughing at him, not with him. The dude wouldn't have been able to find an erogenous zone even if flashing neon arrows pointed the way. But Gabe made sex fun. Intimate too. And she couldn't imagine them ever getting bored inside the bedroom or out. She had a lifetime to look forward to with him.

"Okay," she said. "I can continue now."

She bent her arm back to hand him his drumstick, and he tapped out a rhythm on the rim of his snare.

"From the top now."

And she was giggling again, but she lifted her opposite foot and stopped on a different pedal. The thud it produced was slightly lower in pitch than the original drum. She began to experiment with all three pedals, switching between legs as necessary and working the hard, thrusting cock inside her until she shattered into a million pieces of pure satisfaction. She clung to the drum in front of her and rocked back into Gabe, encouraging him to pound into her as she cried out in bliss. He tossed the drumstick aside and grasped both of her hips, giving her the deep, hard thrusts she craved. Within seconds she pulled him over the edge with her as they moved together to find a few more seconds of ecstasy.

Her legs went all wobbly, and he had to draw her back solidly against his chest to keep her from toppling forward into the drum kit.

The only problem she could see with these adventuresome sexual encounters was that there was never a bed handy for her to collapse upon once they finished.

"So," Gabe said, kissing her shoulder, "it turns out Force can drum and fuck at the same time, but only with able assistance."

She laughed, loving him a little more with each passing

moment. "That was fun," she said, "but I really need to lie down. Is it possible to put a bed in every room of the house?"

"We could limit ourselves to the bedroom."

The sound of his low voice near her ear made her already tantalized nerve endings throb in delight.

"Why would we want to do that?"

He chuckled. "We wouldn't."

He pulled out and traces of their joining trickled down her thigh. She didn't mind until he directed her to his drummer's stool.

"Rest here for a minute."

"I'll get cum all over your seat," she protested.

"I honestly don't care," he said with an ornery smirk.

Looking up at him, she was reminded that he'd shaved his head and looked every inch the hardcore metal drummer. "I thought you were going to let your hair grow out," she said.

"Momentary lapse of judgment," he said, running a hand over the smooth skin tattooed with a wicked-looking dragon tribal design.

"For the record, you look sexy that way," she said, and licked her lips.

He knelt between her knees and stared up into her eyes. "Don't tell me you get the hots for rock stars now."

"Just you," she said, resting her arms on his shoulders and linking her hands behind his neck.

"Let's keep it that way."

The sound of the front door creaking open was followed by happy-dog whimpering and the excited scrape of dog nails across the floor.

"Honeys, I'm home," Nikki called into the house.

Melanie's eyes widened, and she dropped down off the stool, unsure if she was visible through the loft railing from the ground floor. She crawled toward her discarded underwear and lay flat on the floor to pull them on. Her first stop would be the bathroom as soon as she was decent enough to face her friend. She needed to clean up as well as take a whiz on a pregnancy test stick.

"Where are you guys?" Nikki's voice carried from down below. "Are you two going at it on the Sex Stallion again? Now is not the time to make more changes to the design, you know."

"No," Gabe called, his pants securely in place. He leaned up against the railing and peered down into the great room below. "We were up here playing drums."

"Oh, really?" Nikki said, her footsteps approaching the bottom of the wooden staircase. "Sorry I missed it."

"We were also fucking, so you weren't invited," Gabe said.

"Gabe!" Melanie hissed, squirming into her pants. Nikki hadn't had sex in almost a month, so they tried not to talk about it in front of her.

"Sorry I missed that too," Nikki said, her voice now even with the floor where Melanie was busy fastening her jeans.

Melanie rolled over and still lying on the floor, smiled at Nikki. "Did you find a dress for the party?"

"Heads are going to turn," Nikki said with a self-satisfied grin. "Wish you had come with me."

"Too much to do at the office today," Melanie said. The first units were being shipped out on Monday, and they needed everything to align without foreseeable problems.

"Like what?" Nikki teased. "Screwing your boss?"

"Business partner," Gabe corrected. "However, I do say she needs to leave a few business matters to the manager she hired so she'll have time to engage in more screwing with her partner."

"I'm just worried that something will go wrong with the first shipments," Melanie said.

"And if something does, you'll fix it. Fixing problems is what you do best," Gabe said.

Which reminded her of yet another problem she needed to fix.

"I need to go to the bathroom," she said. "What are we making for dinner?"

The three of them had gotten into a routine of cooking together. Melanie was glad Gabe's kitchen was large enough for them to spend that time together, though Gabe often manned the grill on the back deck while Nikki cut up fresh veggies and Melanie cooked side dishes on the six-burner gas stove she so adored.

"Grilled chicken," Nikki said.

Gabe headed toward the narrow loft stairs. "I'll start the grill."

"I'll be in to help soon," Melanie said as she followed Gabe down the steps. Her legs were still weak, so she clung to the railing as she descended. She grabbed her purse and cellphone before she headed for the master bathroom, locking the door behind her. She started by texting Caitlyn.

How are the party plans going? Need any help?

While she waited for a response, she stripped off her panties so she could wash up. The last thing she needed was a damned UTI. She needed to pee too, but had some instructions to read first.

Caitlyn responded with *All set* and the thumbs-up emoji.

Now that Melanie had her attention, she texted: *Do you happen to have Jacob Silverton's number?*

I don't think so. Why don't you get it from Gabe?

I don't want Gabe to know I'm contacting him.

Interesting. Caitlyn had punctuated that single word with a smirking emoji.

Melanie cringed, not wanting Caitlyn to know her reason for contacting Jacob, but better Caitlyn know than Gabe. An instant later, a second message from Caitlyn came through.

I'll ask Owen for Jacob's number. Just a minute.

Once Melanie had Jacob's number, she sat on the edge of the tub, took a deep breath, and dialed him. This plan had better work. Her pregnancy test would just have to wait.

CHAPTER SEVENTEEN

GABE DECIDED that waiting for *two* women to get ready for a party was an exercise in unlimited patience. Melanie's hair wasn't cooperating. Nikki didn't like the way her bra made her boobs look in her new red dress. Melanie decided her pink dress clashed with Nikki's outfit, so she changed to a black dress, which meant also changing shoes and accessories to match. They'd almost made it to the car when Melanie realized that she'd forgotten to switch to a different handbag. As far as Gabe was concerned, her little pink purse looked fine with her curve-hugging black dress. Not a soul on the planet would notice her purse when she was wearing that dress. But she insisted, so they waited.

By the time they reached the party, almost everyone had already arrived. Seeing as Owen's house wasn't all that large, most of the guests had congregated in the back yard. As Gabe, with a case of beer under one arm, followed the ladies—each carrying a dish to share with the crowd—he smiled to himself, no longer perturbed by their tardiness. They both looked smashingly gorgeous as they happily chatted about Nikki's new high heels poking into the sod. Of the pair of beauties, he happened to prefer the leggy brunette and her waist-length wavy hair, but he had a soft spot for her flirty best friend, who he now considered one of his best friends as well.

"Oh, bride and groom number two are finally here," Dawn shouted, clapping enthusiastically, which encouraged a round of cheers. The tall, elegant redhead waved them toward the back yard. Did that mean Kellen was there? Had he and Owen finally made up? Last he'd heard, they were still avoiding each other.

As Gabe rounded the corner, he popped up on his toes to scan the crowd. There were benefits to being the tallest man present. He spotted Kellen by the lanai, talking to Sally. Gabe wondered why their well-endowed stage manager was even talking to any of them. The band—or rather, *Jacob*—had unexpectedly put her and the rest of their regular touring crew out of a job. Maybe the crew could at least collect unemployment checks. He certainly hoped so. Gabe wasn't sure how that worked.

Other members of their road crew were present as well, and they seemed to be getting along fine with each other. They even greeted Gabe as he passed with the beer he intended to add to the huge tubs of ice on the patio. He was slapped on the back and congratulated more times than he could count. Melanie abandoned Nikki to a pack of anxious male admirers and stood at Gabe's side. He was filled with both pride and wonder that he'd managed to score such a prize. He spotted his parents and Leslie and sent them a friendly wave to gain their attention. But before he could cross the lawn to offer them a proper hello, Tex caught his arm. He hadn't seen the band's bus driver since the night Jacob had walked out on them. Speaking of Jacob . . . A quick scan of the crowd told Gabe he wasn't there. Or maybe he was in the house, because Owen was nowhere to be seen either. Nor was Adam in the yard, though Madison and her enormous cast were easy to spot on a lounge chair beneath a shade tree.

"How've you been?" Tex asked, drawing Gabe's attention back to himself. "Can't believe you managed to hook this little hottie."

Tex poked Melanie in the side, and she squeaked in protest.

"He has a very tempting hook," Melanie said with a smile. She squeezed Gabe's hand and leaned against his arm. "For the most part: maggot-less."

Gabe snorted, but based on the baffled stare Tex sent in her direction, he obviously didn't get her inside joke.

"Have you seen Lindsey?" Tex asked. "That girl is about to pop. Sure glad that kid ain't mine." Tex raised his eyebrows at Gabe, his question clear.

"I'm sure your wife is glad to hear that as well."

Tex glanced over his shoulder. Said wife was talking to their youngest roadie, Jordan, who kept looking around as if he needed an escape plan.

"She don't know nothing about that business," Tex said. "No reason to tell her."

Melanie frowned at him.

"So I'm guessing since she . . ." Tex jerked his head in

Melanie's direction. ". . . agreed to marry you, the kid ain't yours neither."

"I'd have married him regardless," Melanie said, standing up to her full height and squeezing Gabe's hand even harder.

"Is it yours?" Tex asked Gabe, no longer beating around the bush.

"It's not mine."

"Whose then?" he asked. "The DNA lady wouldn't tell me shit. Just my own results."

"Same here."

"But the guys must have told you."

Gabe shook his head. "No one has said anything to me," he said. "And I'm not rude enough to ask."

Gabe's intentional barb took a moment to sink through Tex's rather thick skull.

"I didn't mean to be rude or nothing." He slapped Gabe on the back hard enough to make him step forward. "Well, congratulations on your upcoming wedding. Couldn't have happened to a greater guy. She's a sweet-looking gal."

Melanie prickled, but managed to keep her thoughts to herself.

"Thanks, Tex," Gabe said, slapping the guy on the back twice as hard as he'd been slapped. The blow was sure to leave a mark. "We should be sending out invitations soon."

"Am I invited?"

"Of course. Any guy in the band knows better than to get on your bad side. You have too much blackmail material on all of us."

Tex guffawed. "You ain't lying. You've got plenty on me as well." He shook Gabe's hand. "I'll let you get back to your party." He lowered his voice to a whisper to say, "So glad you and me is off the hook with that brat."

Melanie drew in a breath, and Gabe knew she was about to give Tex an earful, so Gabe turned to face her, giving Tex a moment to move away. "He's a little rough, but he means well," Gabe said. "And you really should be glad Lindsey's baby isn't his."

Melanie blew out her breath and nodded. "I am definitely glad for that."

"I wonder where Adam and Owen are," he said, scanning

the crowd again. His parents were now talking to Adam's loser of a dad, a conversation Gabe didn't want to get in the middle of. He found a safer location to hang out near the lanai. "Let's go say hey to Kellen."

"Jacob isn't here?" Melanie asked as they crossed under a trellis supporting huge, fragrant yellow roses and stepped onto a large brick patio. Gabe knew that Owen had spent a lot of time fixing up the inside of his little cottage, but he'd done a spectacular job on the outside as well.

"I'm not surprised Jacob bailed," Gabe said, but in truth he was disappointed. He'd hoped to ask him to be his best man today, but if Jacob couldn't be bothered to show up for an engagement party, how could Gabe count on him to stand up for him at his wedding?

"Jerk," Melanie muttered, but she brightened when Kellen reached out to give her a hug.

"You look gorgeous," he said. "Must be all the happy radiating off of you."

Gabe slicked the non-existent hair off the side of his head. "I do look good, don't I?"

Melanie laughed, a sound that would forever bring a smile to Gabe's face.

"I think he was complimenting me," Melanie said.

Kellen took a step back. "Wow," he said, his gaze traveling the length of Melanie's figure. "You look even more radiant than he does."

Melanie laughed again and knuckled Kellen in his shoulder—which was bare since the guy seldom wore a shirt.

"Are you and Owen talking again?" Gabe asked.

Kellen lowered his gaze, the smile disappearing from his bronze-toned face. "No. He's been spending most of his time with his brother, which he should. I just wish he'd lean on me a little. He looks like he's about to fall over dead."

"Chad's home?"

Kellen nodded. "He refused to stay in the hospital, so Owen brought him home to take care of him. I don't think he knew what he was in for."

Curiosity seeped through Gabe's veins. He wanted to know everything that had happened to Chad, how severe his injuries were. Were they talking Owen changing Chad's adult diapers and feeding him with a spoon or driving him to appointments or what? Gabe didn't ask, though. It didn't seem his place.

"I saw Tex harassing you," Kellen said. "Did he ask you if you were the father of Lindsey's baby?"

"Good guess."

"And did you tell him?"

"Yeah. It isn't mine, so why wouldn't I?" Gabe shrugged, but again he was struck by curiosity. "Did you tell him your results?" That was a little less nosy than *tell me, tell me, tell me, Kellen. Is the baby yours? Huh, is it?*

Kellen took a draw off his beer and then brightened as a certain redhead crossed the patio in his direction. "No, I didn't tell him. It's none of his business."

But was it the business of a close personal friend and former band member? Gabe and Melanie both stared at Kellen in anticipation, but he wrapped an arm around Dawn and kissed her neck. "Isn't she stunning?" he asked no one in particular.

Dawn kissed· him gently. "Owen's in the kitchen," she whispered. "Take that salad from Melanie and bring it inside. It'll give you an excuse to talk to him."

"It won't work," Kellen said, but he held his hands out to accept the dish Melanie was still hauling around in her free hand. "But I'll try."

Dawn watched Kellen walk away, a look of concern on her pretty face. Was that look because Kellen had fucked up his most treasured friendship or because he was about to become a father?

"So how have you been?" Melanie asked, reaching out to give Dawn's wrist a friendly squeeze.

"Busy. Kellen and I just got back from Venice."

"Venice!" Melanie glanced quickly at Gabe and then back to Dawn.

"I'm working on a musical score with some Hollywood bigshots, and I thought it might cheer Kellen up to get away for a couple of weeks. Of course, Owen is using his absence as more ammunition against him. Poor guy. I was going to take him with me to Milan as well, but maybe he should stay here and try to smooth things over with Owen instead."

"Milan!" Melanie said, glancing at Gabe again and then back to Dawn. "How romantic. You should take Kellen for sure. Owen will get over it."

"I'm not so sure," Dawn said. "Owen's pissed off and jealous at the same time. Makes for a rather unreasonable individual."

"Have you ever been to Europe?" Gabe asked Melanie.

She shook her head. "I've never been farther than Texas. Well, Idaho once, for a convention, but I don't think that counts as being a world traveler." Both she and Dawn chuckled.

"Do you want to go?"

Melanie's breath caught, and the sparkle in her eyes made him glad that he'd been smart enough to ask. "Oh, Gabe, that would be so wonderful."

Gabe grinned. "I happen to have some time off. We should go. Assuming I can manage to drag you away from the business."

"Let's go for our honeymoon," Melanie said.

"Congratulations, by the way. I'm not sure if I told you that," Dawn said. "I'm sincerely happy for you both."

"Aw, thanks," Melanie said. The women shared a quick hug. "So tell me all about Venice and Milan, and where else have you been? Rome? Italy must be amazing. I want to see everything."

"Do go to Prague," Dawn said. "It's my favorite European city."

"Prague, really? What's so great about Prague?"

Feeling rather third-wheelish as the ladies twittered on and on about travel destinations, Gabe excused himself to say hi to his family. He was glad that Adam's father had wandered off to find someone else to annoy.

"I see your tattoos are showing again," Mom said before she placed a hand on his cheek and kissed him.

Gabe rolled his eyes at his sister, who sniggered. Leslie was back to being the best daughter ever since she'd listened to their mom and accepted the position in Houston—a far better opportunity—instead of the one in Austin. Gabe had a feeling, however, that it wouldn't be long before Leslie ended up as his mother's colleague at Seton.

"Where's your lovely bride?" Dad asked, leaning heavily on his cane as he glanced around Gabe's body only to find emptiness behind him.

"Talking with Little Miss Worldly Dawn O'Reilly about where to go on our honeymoon."

"Please say you're going to Bali and that you're taking your favorite sister," Leslie said.

"Not a chance," Gabe said, kissing her smooth cheek. "Jennifer is too busy to go on vacation with us."

Leslie pinched his arm. Hard.

"Besides," Gabe said, "she wants to go to Europe, not to Bali."

"Can you afford that, son?" Dad asked, a worried crease in his brow. "With the tour being canceled and all those lawsuits against the band springing up, I wouldn't want you to short yourself trying to impress your lady."

Gabe had tried not to think about the lawsuits. His band's business affairs had been structured separately from his individual money, so no one could touch his personal funds. He hoped. He'd still take a hit—a huge one—on future royalties, but the money he had already banked should be safe.

"I'm okay financially," he said. He hadn't told his parents about his new business venture. Wasn't sure how to broach the subject, actually. What would he say? *Yo, Mom and Dad, I'm making millions inventing and selling Bangin' Toys, high-end sexual aids. Don't worry about me.* At least not financially. Morally? Well, that was a different matter entirely.

A few minutes later, Melanie joined them. She hugged his parents and Leslie. Stars were dancing in her eyes, her head no doubt full of all the sights they'd see in Europe.

"My parents should be here soon," she said. "They got hung up in some road construction in Oklahoma this morning and are running late. I can't wait for them to meet you all. They'll be excited to find you don't all have Mohawks and tattoos on your scalps."

His family members stared at her with wide eyes. His dad blinked first and turned his gaze to Gabe.

"Are your future in-laws having a difficult time accepting your poor sense of style?" he asked.

Gabe snorted and wrapped an arm around Melanie's waist to draw her against his side. Even though the July heat was sweltering hot, he wanted her close.

"If Leslie or Jennifer brought home a guy who looked like me, wouldn't you be reluctant to accept him as the future father of your grandchildren?" When Dad opened his mouth to protest, Gabe lifted a finger at him. "Be honest."

"It might take me a while to get used to the idea," Dad said.

"They've already come around," Melanie said. "I didn't give them a choice. I love Gabe. I choose to love him and at the same time have no choice in the matter. So they both know love me, love my rock star."

His mom and sister practically melted on the spot, and Gabe doubted it had much to do with the brutal midsummer heat.

"You see why I have to marry her?" Gabe said, turning his head to brush his lips against her hair. "You just don't pass up a love like hers."

"So when's the big day?" Mom asked, her smile lighting up her eyes. "We keep hearing you're making plans, but haven't heard any concrete date."

"The last Saturday in August," Melanie said.

Mom's bottom lip quivered. "That's less than six weeks away."

"I couldn't stand to wait any longer than that," Melanie said, glancing up at Gabe and gifting him with her most dazzling smile. "We have an important reason to get married as soon as possible."

Because he was impatient. That was a very important reason.

A sudden hush fell over the mingling partygoers. Gabe turned, looking for the source of everyone's sudden attention. Owen was wheeling his older brother down the makeshift plywood ramp that had been built over the back steps of the house.

"I can do it," Chad grumbled testily, and Owen lifted his hands from the wheelchair grips. The chair zoomed down the ramp until Chad caught the wheels with both bandaged hands. In fact, there wasn't much of him that wasn't bandaged. Half of his dark blond hair had been shaved, and a large white bandage covered one side of his head all the way to the corner of his eye and the top of his ear. He had another bandage on his neck and probably more beneath his loose baby-blue T-shirt and gray running shorts. The most gut-wrenching bandage was the one that encased the stump of his right leg that now ended just above the knee.

Gabe swallowed the sudden knot in his throat, trying to process what this damaged war hero had gone through over the past few weeks and what he'd continue to go through for the rest of his life. Gabe was so utterly shocked that he couldn't help but stare, awash with sympathy.

Chad looked from one solemn face to the next. "I told Owen this was a mistake. Sorry to ruin your fun." He spun his chair around, but his path was blocked by Lindsey, who did indeed look like she was about to pop that baby out right there on the patio. Gabe knew she still had a good two months before she was due; what kind of giant newborn was she incubating? Lindsey leaned forward and touched Chad's cheek, whispering into his ear. He shook his head slightly, his gaze trained downward.

"Hey, Chad," Gabe shouted, not sure what had come over him. "Nice haircut. You don't mind if I steal that style as my own, do you?"

Half the crowd gasped. The other half gaped at Gabe as if he'd just challenged Chad to a one-legged ass-kicking contest. Chad's head whipped around, and Chad leveled Gabe with a challenging stare.

"Banner, you aren't cool enough to pull this off."

Gabe's feet were moving forward on their own, and he was tugging a reluctant Melanie along behind him. "That's a fact. Chad Mitchell has always been the coolest guy on this block."

"That's because only old ladies live on this block," Kellen quipped. "Oh, and Owen here." He clapped Owen on the back, and Owen immediately drew away, as if Kellen were wearing a leprosy-infected glove.

A few nervous laughs twittered through the crowd.

"I'm glad you made it home," Gabe said when he stopped in front of Chad's chair.

He hated that Chad had to crane his neck to look up at him, so he crouched down and took Chad's hand for a punishing handshake. Chad gripped Gabe's fingers so hard, Gabe would probably never play drums again, but he got it. Chad needed to feel strong, to feel whole. Gabe held his grip and urged Melanie forward with his free hand.

"This is Melanie. My fiancée."

Chad smiled up at her guardedly. "So this is the girl who stole Gabe Banner's heart."

"It's nice to meet you," Melanie said. "I now see why Owen

sent you off to fight the bad guys overseas. There's no way he'd ever get laid in the shadow of a hot-looking brother like you."

"Don't I know it," Owen said, and he actually grinned. His gaze shifted to his brother and his smile vanished before he ducked his head and glanced away.

"Eh, he might have a chance now," Chad said.

Melanie's smile faltered, but then she shook her head. "I doubt that. And thank you for fighting to keep us safe." She leaned in and kissed his cheek. "I know those words don't mean much—"

Chad released Gabe's hand and took Melanie's. "They mean more than you realize." He then released her hand to push his chair back several inches and said, "What does a guy have to do around here to get himself a cold beer?"

Owen practically tripped over his own feet trying to get to the nearest tub of ice.

"Thanks for coming, Chad," Gabe said. He left the *I know it wasn't easy* part unsaid.

"Thanks for having me. And congratulations. I'm glad you found someone who loves you."

The sadness in Chad's eyes stole Gabe's breath, but the display of his grief was gone in an instant as he claimed his beer from his brother and wheeled off to mingle.

Lindsey appeared at Gabe's elbow and squeezed his arm with both hands. "Thanks for making him feel normal."

How else should he make him feel?

But before Gabe could even open his mouth to comment, Lindsey hurried after Chad, barely acknowledging young Jordan, who was all smiles as he made his move to talk to her.

"I think Lindsey likes him," Melanie said quietly.

"Who? Jordan?" Gabe asked, watching Lindsey walk away from the young, blond-haired roadie without so much as a glance in his direction.

"Not in the slightest. I think she likes Chad."

"What's not to like?" Gabe shrugged.

Melanie suddenly squeaked with excitement and darted off toward the grassy area of the yard. She hugged her mom first and then her dad, who both looked road weary. Gabe headed in that direction, his thoughts turning to Jacob for some reason. Probably because Melanie's parents could drive ten hours to make it to the party, but Jacob couldn't even be bothered to drive across town.

"Thanks for coming," Gabe said. "How was the drive?"

"Summer road construction is utter hell," Melanie's dad grumbled.

"Oh, Mark. Just think of how nice the roads will be when they're finished," Linda said.

"The problem is they're never finished," Gabe said. "They just move to a different section."

"Truth!" Mark said. He shook Gabe's hand. "I hope you've been taking good care of my little girl."

"She does an excellent job taking care of herself," Gabe said, earning a bright smile from Melanie. "I just try to stay out of her way."

Mark chuckled. "She gets that from her mother."

Gabe glanced around for his parents and found them walking toward their small group. Dad was limping along slower than usual, which surprised Gabe. The warm weather was usually good for his joints. Sometimes it struck him that his parents were aging. There was no getting around that fact.

After introductions were made, Gabe attempted to break the ice. "So Melanie's got an appointment tomorrow to get her first tattoo. I do think my name in bold letters across her forehead will look amazing. So glad she thought of it."

Without missing a beat, Melanie said, "I just can't decide on a color. Do I go with fuchsia or neon green?" She tilted her head and tapped her cheek reflectively.

"Oh, honey," Mom said, a hand over her mouth.

"Over my dead body," Mark bellowed.

Dad and Linda exchanged eye rolls before trying to calm their respective mates.

"It's a joke, dear," Linda said, patting Mark consolingly.

"I don't think she's the type to get any tattoo," Dad said, smiling at Melanie.

"Actually," Melanie said, "I've been thinking of getting one on my back. But no names. Not even Gabe's. And definitely not one anywhere near my head."

Gabe felt awkwardly aroused by the idea of Melanie getting a tattoo on her back. It would be a bit of added scenery for him to admire during her continued drum lessons. But he had one condition.

"The only way I would ever let you get a tattoo—"

"*Let* me?" Melanie's eyebrows rose.

"—is if I get to watch," he finished.

She grinned. "You can even help me pick it out since you'll be seeing it a lot more than I will." She flushed and then turned wide eyes toward their parents. "I mean because I can't really see my back, can I?"

Especially not during those drum lessons.

Mealtime was announced by Caitlyn, and Melanie visibly relaxed. She'd totally backed herself into an embarrassing corner with that tattoo announcement.

"Does this mean you're completely over your aversion to tattoos?" Gabe asked her as they made their way to the end of the chow line. Their parents were walking and chatting directly in front of them. He was glad they all got along. It would make those huge holiday get-togethers less stressful.

"I love your tattoos," she said, and left it at that. He wouldn't push the envelope by getting some barbwire inked around his wrist. He knew it was her main trigger.

A breathless Nikki got into line behind them. She was talking animatedly to Adam.

"And so then I was like, I have got to try this thing. If it can make Melanie scream like that, it has to be pretty amazing."

She was blabbing about their business enterprise to Adam? Who'd be next, Gabe's mom?

"Uh, Nikki . . ." Gabe tried to catch her attention.

"Holy fuck, I came so hard I thought I was going to explode."

Adam chuckled at that and grabbed two plates—the second presumably for his injured fiancée.

"So," Nikki continued loudly, "after I caught my breath, and trust me it took a while, I went and got my camera phone and set it up to record—"

"Nikki!" Melanie shouted.

"Oh, hey, Mel," she said. "I was just telling Adam about how we all became millionaires thanks to your fiancé's dirty mind and my moment of genius."

"You're telling more than Adam," Gabe said, glancing ahead. Sure enough, two sets of curious parents were hanging on

Nikki's every word.

"Hi, Mr. and Mrs. Anderson," Nikki said, throwing them a cheerful wave. "When did you get here?"

"About half an hour ago," Mark said, his tone rather cold.

"That's nice." She turned back to Adam. "So anyway, I'm bucking around on Gabe's invention, getting off like you would not believe. Actually, I can show you the video if you're interested."

"I don't think Madison would approve," Adam said with a smirk.

"Right. I always forget about her." Nikki glanced toward the tree where they'd last seen Madison. "So my video went viral on this website and everyone wanted to—"

Melanie grabbed Nikki's arm. "Could you keep it down? There are respectable people here."

Nikki snorted and busted out laughing. "Where?" She looked around, and her gaze landed on the four real adults at the party. "Right. I guess I'll have to finish telling you about it later," she said to Adam. "If Madison will let you off your leash."

Adam stiffened slightly, but then his gaze found the woman who held his leash and he smiled. "I wouldn't count on it," he said.

Gabe grinned. Madison *was* trying to glare a hole through Nikki's narrow back.

"So," Dad said, falling back in line to stand beside Gabe, "what's this about an invention?"

Gabe could feel his ears burning with embarrassment. "It's nothing. Nikki's crazy, you know."

"I am not crazy," Nikki shouted. "I'm an addict. Like Adam."

Adam huffed. "Not like me, sweetheart." Then he shrugged. "Well, maybe a little like me."

"Exactly like you, except sex is my drug of choice."

Every man within earshot perked up at that news.

"And just like Adam, I'm rehabilitated."

The attentive male perkiness flattened, and people began to fill their plates again.

"Best not to draw attention to your addiction," Melanie advised quietly.

"Why not? How can I ever get better if I don't admit I have

a problem?"

"But you don't have to admit it to everyone," Melanie said.

Nikki looked to Adam for validation, and he nodded. "Yeah, it does work best that way. The worst thing she can do is hide her addiction. That makes it too easy to slip back into old habits."

Melanie straightened, and Gabe was pretty sure she was about to go off on yet another member of his former band.

"But you do need to be careful," Adam said. "Some people will use your problems against you, rather than trying to help you out."

Melanie smiled at Adam, but he was looking the other way. She lifted a hand and stroked the back of Nikki's head. "Whatever you need to do to heal, honey," she said. "I just worry about you. Adam's right. You have to be careful."

Nikki melted. "I know, Mel. And I know it's hard for you to understand what it's like for me because you've never had an addiction. But Adam understands. He gets it."

So that was why she always glommed onto Adam the second she saw him. Her trust in him was actually kind of sweet. One look at Madison told Gabe that his fiancée didn't think Nikki's budding friendship—or perhaps, *sponsorship*—was sweet in the slightest.

"Well, long story short, we're making sex toys now," Nikki said. "Melanie runs the business, Gabe invents the toys, and I do PR. Pretty neat, huh?"

"That's a lot to have accomplished in a few weeks," Adam said.

"I know, right?" Nikki beamed with pride. "And we're just getting started. You should see all the pervy stuff Gabe has invented."

Adam snorted. "I can only imagine."

Gabe very much wanted to get the hell out of the line. Especially since he was sure that not only had his parents heard Nikki's entire spiel, but so had his future in-laws.

After filling his plate, Gabe found a shady patch of grass and sat down. Melanie and both sets of their parents sat in a little circle facing him. Leslie was chatting with Caitlyn at the end of the buffet line. Nikki had gone off with Adam, which meant the subject of his new business venture might actually be dropped.

The six in their little group ate in terse silence for several long minutes.

"You know, son, they say you should never mix business and pleasure," Dad quipped. He set his plate down so he could release a deep belly laugh without dropping his food.

"Luke," Mom said, "this isn't funny. This is our only son's future."

"Are you having fun, son?" Dad asked.

"Inventing things?" Gabe intentionally left out what those things were and nodded. "Yeah, I'm having a ton of fun."

"And do you feel challenged by your work? Do you feel passionate about it?" Dad pressed. Though he'd recently retired, he was clearly wearing his college advisory professor hat at the moment.

"Absolutely."

"And do you honestly think this venture can financially support your new family?"

Gabe glanced at Melanie and smiled. "I do."

"Then I'm proud," Dad said.

Mom reached forward to pat Gabe's knee. "I'm proud too, but I'll crow about your success quietly to myself, if you don't mind."

Gabe laughed. "I don't mind."

"What exactly are you tangled up in, Melanie?" Mark asked his daughter.

"It's just a business, Dad. You know how much I've always wanted to run my own business. I just never had a product worth producing and selling. And well . . . Now I do."

"Kids these days," Mark said, shaking his head, but the subject shifted to the weather, and Gabe felt an immense sense of relief.

His parents claimed to be proud of him even though they knew all about—well, maybe not *all* about—his new business venture, and Mark hadn't hog-tied Melanie, thrown her in the trunk of his car, and hauled her back to Kansas, so all was right in his world. Well, almost everything was perfect. His band was still a mess, but if they never got back together, he could have a long and satisfying, truly happy and blessed life with Melanie at his side.

A tall figure moved into his peripheral vision, and Gabe

glanced up into a pair of mirrored sunglasses. Jacob crouched beside him.

"So a little birdy told me that you were in need of my services," Jacob said. He peered around Gabe and waved at Melanie. "Hello there, little birdy."

Gabe looked from Melanie, who was positively beaming, to Jacob.

"Your services?" Gabe asked.

"As your best man." Jacob lifted his hands. "If I heard wrong, I'll quietly back away and you can pretend this never happened."

"You're not getting off that easy," Gabe said, the kernel of hope that Sole Regret would reconcile bursting into full bloom. Jacob had come. He did still care. "Jacob, will you do me the honor of being my best man at my wedding?"

"Dude, that sounded like a marriage proposal."

Jacob shoved him, but Gabe was too damned happy to flash his man card and slip into caveman mode to save face. "Well? Will you?"

"How can I say no to you, Banner? I'll be there."

"Go grab some food," Melanie said. She scooted over to pat the grass between herself and Gabe. "I saved a spot for you."

"I can't stay. Tina doesn't know I'm here, but I did want to make an appearance. Congratulations, by the way. You'll have to send all the wedding info to my secret email account unless you want Tina as up in your business as she is in mine."

"Why don't you just get rid of her?" Gabe asked. Problem solved.

"I'll never get rid of her," Jacob said, "until she wants to get rid of me."

Gabe frowned. Apparently the guy was still off his rocker.

"I also heard that Adam is getting married," Jacob said. "True?"

"Yeah. I don't think they're in the same rush that me and Melanie are in though."

"Why are you in a rush?" Jacob asked. He leaned around Gabe to look at Melanie. "Did he go and knock you up already?"

Her cheeks went delightfully pink. "Well . . . this isn't exactly how I wanted to tell him . . ."

Gabe's heart skipped a beat and started thudding at a tempo

even the fastest drummer alive couldn't hope to match.

"Wait," he said, breathlessly. "Does that mean . . ."

Melanie nodded. "According to the little stick I peed on this morning, you're going to be a daddy."

He pulled her into his arms and kissed her with every shred of passion he possessed. His world had never been so thoroughly rocked, and he was one hundred percent ready to roll with his sweet Melanie forever, no matter what challenges life might bring their way.

ABOUT THE AUTHOR

Combining her love for romantic fiction and rock 'n roll, Olivia Cunning writes erotic romance centered around rock musicians. Raised on hard rock music from the cradle, she attended her first Styx concert at age six and fell instantly in love with live music. She's been known to travel over a thousand miles just to see a favorite band in concert. As a teen, she discovered her second love, romantic fiction—first, voraciously reading steamy romance novels and then penning her own. Growing up as the daughter of a career soldier, she's lived all over the United States and overseas. She currently lives in Illinois. To learn more about Olivia and her books, please visit www.oliviacunning.com.

Made in United States
Orlando, FL
18 March 2023

31160890R00228